CHAMPION OF SORROWS

KRISTEN M. LONG

A THIEF OF SORROWS NOVEL

II

Champion
of
Sorrows
A Thief of Sorrows Novel
II

First published in the United States of America in February 2024
By Kristen M. Long Books LLC
www.kristenmlong.com
PO Box 816 Jasper, TN 37347

Champion of Sorrows
Book 2 of the Thief of Sorrows Series

First Edition 0 123456789
Hardcover: ISBN: 979-8-9868360-3-4
Paperback: ISBN: 979-8-9868360-4-1

CONTENT WARNING:

Please be aware that this book does contain scenes that might be disturbing to some readers with scenes of emotional, physical, and sexual abuse, physical abuse of a child, human trafficking, suicidal ideation, depression, PTSD, sexual assault, and violence (including but not limited to scenes of torture and death).

HALCINARIA
WILDS OF THE NORTH
HELECDOL MOUNTAINS
ORONILMA MOUNTAINS
BRIARHOLE
HELECDOL MINES
ELENARTA
ADRIAM RIVER
THORNWOOD
WHISPER
FOXCLOVE
LENDA RIVER
SEA OF CALCA
HARROW HALL
BLACKWATER
AIRONMAR

PREVIOUSLY IN

THIEF OF SORROWS

Isolde Cotheran, heir to the territory of Thornwood, serves as the masked vigilante known throughout the kingdom of Arnoria as, the Hood—the Thief of Sorrows. She, along with her cadre of thieves and assassins—Malaki, Blyana, and Cillian—not only steal from the rich and corrupted, but they also kill them too. In the world of Arnoria, hierarchy is everything. Those at the top are their kind, the virya—beings blessed by the gods with deadly, unnatural powers. Their powers range from having the ability to transform into animals, to manipulating water, earth, and wind. When she and her cadre sneak into a neighboring territory, Foxclove, to rescue abused humans and half-bloods, Isolde kills their Lord, Dagan. When rummaging through his things, she finds a letter from the vicious king, Erebus Tenebriath, thanking him for his continued service and a piece of elithrium—a highly regulated element that is deadly to a virya.

Once the mission is complete, Isolde prepares for Lestahere, a three-day meeting between the seven territories of the kingdom at Briarhole. Isolde's uncle, Alaric Cotheran, sees this as the perfect opportunity for her to learn her role as heir to Thornwood. At the meeting, news of the Dagan's death sparks a desperate need to capture the Hood. Isolde presents the idea to hold a bounty for the capture of the Hood, with gold pledged from each of the territories. As they discuss where to keep the fortune, Gage, the Right Hand of the king and murderer of Isolde's first love, Kamden, arrives and announces his new role as Lord of Foxclove by order of King Tenebriath. With him is Liam, Isolde's secret lover who was shunned from Thornwood for willingly joining the King's army by being a participant in the Tournament of the Guard.

With a plan in place, Isolde, and her cadre sneak into Foxclove and steal the bounty from Gage. With his ego bruised, Gage ventures to Thornwood and asks Isolde for her hand in marriage. Which of course she adamantly refuses and Gage proceeds to kidnap all the children who attend story hour every week at Thornwood in order to force her hand. Reading for humans and half-bloods is a crime punishable by death in Arnoria, making Isolde's literary activities boarding on treasonous.

With the gold secured in their hideout in Blackford Forest, Isolde and the others set out to redistribute the stolen wealth. Territory by territory, they visit the Lords and Ladies of Arnoria. At Harrow Hall, Lord Milt, confesses that he too has received a piece of elithrium from King Tenebriath in return for sending his people to the capital. None of which have returned, and no word has reached him of what the king is using his people for. Lord Ferden of Dolinmere confesses to having received the same gift and demands. But when she ventures to Blackwater, Lady Yvaine transforms into a black vulture, standing nearly twenty-five tall. She, along with Blyana, nearly die trying to escape.

When they arrive back at Thornwood, they learn all the children of Thornwood, Foxclove, and a local town, Whisper, have been taken by the king's men. One of the children is the first student Isolde taught to read, Tanor, son of Thornwood's smithy, Tarvo. The next day, Gage arrives at Thornwood unannounced and asks for Isolde's hand in marriage yet again. When she refuses, he reveals he is the one who took the children and is more than willing to use them as a means of forcing her hand. After Gage leaves, Liam sneaks into Thornwood and informs Isolde that Gage has already issued orders to take the children of Briarhole and her good friend, Zibiah, wife of Volkran, Lord of Briarhole, to Elenarta as well.

Isolde becomes more desperate and reckless as she and her team devise a plan to rescue them before Gage can put his plan into action. The night before Zibiah and the children are to be taken, Isolde and her cadre, including her aunt and uncle, Galaena and Alaric, devise a plan to sneak into Briarhole. While Liam sets fire to the warehouses along the Briarhole Manor, Isolde, Malaki, Blyana, and Cillian sneak into the dungeons and escort small groups of slaves through the front gate and out to the river where Alaric and Galaena wait with boats. As Isolde and Zibiah are bringing out the last group, a lone soldier spots them. Forcing Zibiah to leave her behind, Isolde leads the guards through Briarhole and comes face to face with Gage, Volkran, and Liam.

A fight ensues, resulting in Volkran nearly beating Isolde to death before the ring on her hand—an heirloom from her mother— awakens a deeper level of power than she ever knew possible. As Isolde tightens a rope of air around Volkran's neck, Liam begs her to spare him, and despite her better judgement, she obliges. She doesn't have time to ponder this newfound ability before Gage attacks and delivers a fatal wound down the left side of Isolde's ribcage. Only through sheer skill is she able to land a blow that disarms and deforms Gage, giving her time to run. Malaki finds her bleeding out at the bottom of a stairwell. He carries her out the side door and just before they disappear into the forest, Isolde catches sight of Zibiah and part of the children they tried to rescue being thrown into cages, bound for Elenarta.

Malaki uses his healing ability to keep Isolde alive just long enough to get her back to their hideout in Blackford Forest. Days later, after excruciating healing, Isolde awakens to the memories of Briarhole. Racked with guilt, all she can do is wait. Alaric and Galaena arrive with youthful faces, confirming Isolde's fear that they had been forced to use their power once again. Cillian and Blyana deliver news that the ones they had managed to save made it to the next checkpoint in their journey to safety.

After a few weeks, a letter arrives for Isolde from King Tenebriath, commanding her presence at the Tournament of the Guard in Elenarta. With a way into the capital, Isolde begins to make a plan for retrieving what was stolen from her and exacting her revenge.

CHAPTER 1

"*L*ove *knows no depths, my minnow.*"

Not even the sound of her dead mother's voice could keep away the darkness or dull the torment.

Pain.

Agony.

Fear.

They were Zibiah's only companions—her only reality. Their presence was a constant assurance in her life. The only truths she could depend on. They lived with her in this world of darkness—in this well of cold despair.

Yet not a single thread of regret found its way to her, where she dwelt deep beneath the mountain. There was but a single thought keeping her sanity anchored.

She's safe...she's safe...Isolde is safe.

Zibiah would have heard if that wasn't the case. She would have known if Isolde had been captured. It wouldn't have surprised her if they had forced them to share the same cell. To take part in each other's misery. To share in the echoing screams filling the damp, stone walls which were now her whole world.

She's safe...she's safe. Her secret is safe.

The words chanted through Zibiah's mind. They filled her with a victorious hope nearly bringing a smile to her battered, maimed face. Not that the rest of her was better off. Not a single inch of her body was spared their wrath. Blood's unmistakable scent filled the chilled, dark air. They always left her in the dark. Blind, completely at their mercy.

If only they possessed such a thing.

The sound of keys jingling sent her body into tremors of terror. Zibiah ground her teeth at the response. The chains holding her in place rattled with each quiver of fear running through her frame. It was a learned behavior they had beaten and carved into her over and over again.

The healers had come, of course. Those bound to serve the crown always came after they had had their fun. Earth magic forced its way beneath her skin, seeping into her bones and flesh. Making her new and ready to start again.

"You cannot fall. You cannot give in, Zibiah."

Her father's words echoed in Zibiah's mind. His strong, loving voice filled her soul, soothing the dread threatening to overtake her.

"You are a daughter of the sea and are commanded by no one."

Even as the cell door swung open and her father's voice faded into the furthest depths of her heart, into a place no one and nothing could touch it, the fear remained. The terror for what was to come settled into her bones like a cold winter's chill. The sound of familiar footsteps filled the air, and all Zibiah could do was wait for the agony.

"Hello, Hood."

Eyes, bright and hard as polished sapphires, smiled down at her. His voice carried through the dark like a frozen hymn. A beautiful fatality. Cold, alluring, and deadly.

"Remind me," Gage said, his voice blending with the sound of a blade scraping against the stone above her head. "Where did we leave off?" Fear trickled down Zibiah's spine, but her lips remained sealed. Resolve settled into her newly mended bones as she braced for what was to come.

"No matter." A dark smile spread across his scarred face as the glint of the impossibly sharp dagger danced in his eyes. "We'll start from the beginning."

CHAPTER 2

"You really must be as stupid as you look," Isolde Cotheran said, tugging back on the bowstring.

Bits of fiber dug into the worn leather coating the tips of her callused fingers. The arrow's sharp, unforgiving elithrium edge rose to point at the soldier before her. His dark, cold eyes narrowed on the eerily green metal, knowing it meant death for someone like him, for someone like her.

A virya.

A blade, sharp and finely made, was clutched in his hand. Its own living metal pressed against the throat of a small boy he clutched to his steel-plated chest.

"How is this possible?" he demanded. His deep, baritone voice bounced off the walls of the small cottage. "We captured you at Briarhole!"

"Clearly not," Isolde said, her eyes trained on the blade kissing the boy's neck. "Your king is a coward and a moron. Pinning my crimes on an innocent civilian because he's too stupid to capture me, not very kingly of him."

"I'll cut your tongue out for that, Hood." A tear trickled down the boy's dirt encrusted face, leaving a trail of clean, shiny skin in its wake.

A small, humorless laugh lifted from Isolde's cloth-covered lips. "I'm shaking."

"On second thought." The soldier's hand, buried in the boy's sandy blonde hair twisted, forcing his head back. A wail of pain pierced the air and the boy's tears flowed like rivers of sorrow down his face. "I'll take this worthless, little shit's life instead."

A breath caught in Isolde's throat as the blade slid across the boy's neck in one fluid jerk. A strangled cry filled the air and she let the arrow fly. Its tip punctured the chest plate encasing the soldier's torso, sending him flying back over the small table occupying the center of the room.

Jerking a dagger free from its scabbard at her hip, Isolde kicked the table blocking her path out of the way. It collided with the far wall, shattering into bits of worn wood that rained down on the bodies littering the blood-stained floor.

"My men will find you," he said. The edge of his boots scraped against the floor, desperate to escape the fate he had just sentenced himself to. Labored breaths fell from his lips, causing blood to seep through the wound on his chest. "And when they do——"

"They'll die just as you will," she retorted. "Well, perhaps not quite as painfully." Isolde brought the dagger down on top of the man's foot, the blade puncturing leather, skin, and bone. Its sharp edge wedged itself into the floorboards, holding him in place.

A cry ripped from the soldier's mouth. It echoed along with a blade's cold, steely cry as Isolde pulled another free from her belt. Moving with a speed only her kind was capable of, her fingers shot out and gripped the man's bottom teeth. She forced his jaw wide at an unnatural, unbearable angle. He shook his head from side to side and dug the tips of his fingers into the lining of her black tunic.

"Hands to yourself."

Isolde swiped the blade through the air and the soldier's hands fell to the floor with a sickening, wet thud. He held up what remained of his arms and two bloody stumps stared back at him. A garbled, shocked gasp danced across her knuckles.

"You wanted a tongue," the Hood said, driving the back of his head into the floor. "Let me give you one."

His cries of pain died away with every piece of tongue Isolde carved free. The edges of the soldier's teeth dug into her fingers at the sight of the mutilated prize she held before him.

"There," she smiled. "I hope you're satisfied." With the flick of her wrist, the mass of now useless flesh disappeared into the forest of flames dwelling in the base of the fireplace.

"You hurt my people." Her voice filtered through the mask in a distorted whisper laced with cold rage. "Very, *very* foolish of you." Placing the palm of her hand under his chin, Isolde slammed the soldier's mouth shut and held.

Spurts of air leaked around his lips, but not enough to rid him of the bloody river pouring down his throat. The heel of Isolde's hand pressed into his jaw, forcing his lips to stay sealed. He fought against her hold, pushing the ends of his now handless arms against her chest. They slid against her leathers, soaking her tunic in blood. Isolde merely stared down at him, her gaze never deviating from his, never missing a second of his fear.

After a few moments, the rise and fall of his chest ceased and the desperate gasps of air quieted. Only when Isolde saw his power's presence fade from his unseeing eyes, did she finally release him.

Death left nothing but dark quietness in its wake. Save for the small snaps of kindling burning in the meager fireplace. Isolde tried her best to ignore them. To ignore the memories of scorching pain that sound brought forth. Forcing away the past, she ripped the blade and arrow from the dead soldier's flesh. A black pool of chilling blood circled his maimed body. But the Hood didn't look to him, did not give him a second thought.

Uncaring of where she treaded, Isolde made her way to the small boy, and knelt at his side. Bits of curly, sandy blonde hair kissed his closed, sunken eyelids. A look of peace covered his face. One that gave Isolde the false hope he could be sleeping. How desperately she wanted that to be true. But the horrible slash running from one side of his neck to the other, like an angry, taunting smile, spoke of that impossibility.

He can't be older than six…

"I'm sorry," she said, gently brushing the soft tendrils of hair from his face. "I'm so sorry, little one." Tiny freckles decorated his pale cheeks and the bridge of his button nose. He reminded her of Tanor at that age. Tanor…the boy she had failed. The one now facing the horrors of the capital…

Because she taught him to read.

Because she held story hour.

All because of her.

A bit of light caught Isolde's eye and bile rose in her throat. The emblem of Erebus Tenebriath stared up at her from the golden coins decorating the cottage floor. Its snake eye was set in a perfect triangle and speckled with blood.

Isolde's power prowled forth once more. The king of Arnoria's face flashed in her mind, drawing the monster's sharp, unforgiving claws across the bars of her self-control. It whispered to her, demanded one thing.

Kill him.

Every bone groaned as that rage, that unshakable fury began to grow. To consume her every thought, to seize her every desire, and make it its own. The ring on Isolde's right hand, the one that had belonged to her mother so long ago, warmed beneath the leather glove's lining. The pad of her thumb stroked the feather band and the diamond it held in its gilded embrace.

Ever since she had awoken that seemingly endless well of power at Briarhole, Isolde had felt the pull of the ring. Tempting her, demanding her to use that power, to let the monster within out. But she knew her limits. If she gave into the call, there would be no stopping what lurked beneath her skin. She would become what she feared most, the one thing she could never let see the light of day again.

"Isolde?"

Malaki's voice, the one thing that could pull her back from the abyss, echoed through the air behind her. The pressure of his familiar, assuring hand gripped her shoulder. The faintest hint of smoky sandalwood and the lingering drifts of a storm penetrated her mask.

"We were too late."

She couldn't bring herself to look away from the boy. To see the bodies of his parents splayed across the floor. They would all join the countless faces of others she had failed during her nearly thirty years as the Hood of Arnoria. Faces of those she had failed at Foxclove...at Thornwood...at Briarhole. The souls who visited her at night, the ones who haunted her in the day, and never seemed to leave.

"I'm sorry," Isolde said again, touching the boy's cheek. Taking a deep breath, she willed herself to stand, her leathers glistening with blood and stiff with sweat.

"They were farmers," Malaki said. While the mask covering his face distorted his deep, rich voice, every word was laced with undeniable anger. "People who never hurt anyone."

Isolde's hands began to shake around the hilts of her daggers. The sharp blades, as much a part of her as the bow she carried, had laid waste to nearly every soldier scattered around the room. Their bodies were now nothing but heaps of ruined flesh and armor.

"They came to collect the new taxes Erebus implemented," Malaki continued. Her second-in-command squeezed the handle of the massive axe at his side, the wood groaning in protest. "They couldn't pay. Erebus knew they wouldn't be able to."

"Of course, he knew," Isolde said. They had come to give what they could to the humans and half-bloods who needed it most. To those who would fall under the weight of the heavy taxes Erebus had placed on them.

"This is my doing," Isolde said, shoving the daggers back into the scabbards at her sides. "Erebus wouldn't have raised the taxes if I hadn't suggested the bounty at Foxclove. I never should have put the idea in their heads."

"This would have happened regardless, and you know it," Malaki said, taking a step forward, his hand outstretched as if to grab onto her shoulder. But she stepped away, not wanting his comfort.

It had been her plan to stage as the bait at Foxclove. Her plan to place a bounty on her own head that had driven the taxes beyond reach. The Hood felt the family's blood on her. Soaking and staining yet another part of her soul. She was responsible...She was to blame.

Forcing what air she could down her throat, Isolde shoved the thoughts away. She would deal with it at a later time. When only darkness and solitude held her company, would she face it all.

"Are there more?" she asked, trying to hide the note of irritated pain in her voice. The scar at her side throbbed, making the task of sliding the bloody arrows into the quiver at her back less than enjoyable. Malaki shifted his feet from side to side. His unease was palpable and his lips infuriatingly silent. "Spit it out, Malaki."

"There was another battalion," he said at last, tone coated with patience. "Heading to the eastern side of the city. As far as I know, they haven't harmed anyone."

"*Yet.*" The word felt like a curse on Isolde's tongue. "It's a matter of when, not if."

"We need to leave, Isolde." The words left his lips like a plea. "You aren't fully healed yet—"

"Since when does that particular fact matter?"

"It matters," he said, through gritted teeth. "You are no good to anyone injured or dead!"

"And what excuse is that to those who are suffering?" Her voice was low but filled with fire. "Do you think a parent wants to hear I did nothing because I wasn't feeling well? Or that I chose to not act because I wasn't feeling up to it?" Isolde shook her head. "If the people we care about don't hate me already, they most certainly will after that."

She turned to look up at him, at the man who had been her closest friend for decades. The only one she trusted completely and irrevocably. He wore the same evergreen hood he always did. A faint light shone in the depths of his hazel eyes. They held years of memory. 265 years, to be exact.

"You know good and well they wouldn't think that of you," Malaki said. "Stop trying to take the blame for something that isn't your fault. It isn't attractive and I know how important that is to you."

Isolde's eyebrow cocked beneath the lining of her hood that was black as the darkest night. "Everything is attractive on me, Malaki," she said, her chin lifting. "Even righteous self-blame. You'd think after being at my side for over half a century you'd know that by now."

Without waiting for a response, Isolde dropped to one knee and began collecting the gold coins scattered across the floor. The last thing she wanted was for Erebus to get his hands on them again.

"Not one of your finer qualities," Malaki mumbled, bending down to join her. They worked in silence until the sound of footsteps filled the air. Cillian and Blyana, the other members of her beloved cadre, stepped into the blood-soaked cottage.

"I see things aren't any better on this side of the village," Cillian said.

Without having to be asked, they started to retrieve the soiled coins from the massacre before them. The scar on Isolde's side burned with pain but she ignored it. Refused to acknowledge the twinging spasms running down her back and side. While the wound had healed over, she wasn't immune to the occasional lash of pain if she turned the wrong way.

"It might take longer," Malaki had said. Every night he had tried to heal what damage Gage's blade had left behind. The gentle touches of his earth wielding magic had eased the pain and knitted the torn flesh together once more. "With your unnaturally rapid healing abilities, it'll heal fully in time." That had been weeks ago, and Isolde was growing impatient. They left for Elenarta in two days. She needed to be ready.

When all the coins had been collected, Isolde looked to the small family one final time. "They'll pay," she said, allowing the edge of sorrow and shame to drive deeper, burn hotter. "I swear it."

Blyana stepped forward. Her pale, blue eyes shone with fury. "Yes, they will."

Vengeance and bloodlust filled every word. Cloaked in a violet hood now stained with blood and ash, Blyana looked like a living nightmare. Speckles of red decorated what little bit of her pale face shown beneath her hood. A light filled her eyes, giving a brief glimpse at the ferocious, spotted leopard lurking beneath.

"We finished depositing the rest of the coin to the southern and western sides of the city," Cillian said. "They should have plenty to cover whatever ridiculous taxes Erebus wishes to throw their way."

"Were any of them harmed?" Isolde asked, shoving up from the ground to stow the small bag of coins into her pocket. The price of a life, of several, felt heavy at her side.

Cillian's lean shoulders shrugged as a heavy sigh filtered through his dark, brown mask. "They all were. In one way or another." Flickers of power danced in his obsidian gaze, like the tail end of a shooting star across a moonless night.

Isolde raked her eyes down his form, unsurprised to find he too was covered in blood. There wasn't a chance in hell Cillian or Blyana would have let that go unpunished. She turned to Malaki, her brow cocked in challenge. "Do you think we should intervene now?"

Before he could answer, a cry cleaved through the night. Isolde froze, her eyes darting to the door. Another cry followed. Then another…and another.

Fear and adrenaline poured into Isolde's veins, giving her little choice. She sprinted out the door and into the night, leaving a wake of death and her cadre behind.

Hints of fog drifted through the small cottages running along the deserted street. Windows stared back like cold, dead eyes. Not a soul came forward, not a single face shone through the dark. The cool, night air kissed what part of her face was left exposed as she raced down alley after alley.

She could feel Malaki at her back. His silent, sure steps were a constant assurance. They took a sharp right, heading north, to the town square. Isolde's power hummed in her veins when the sound of voices reached her. The street corner loomed up ahead and Isolde slowed her pace. The feeling of the bow's handle covered her with a small sense of security as she withdrew it from her back. Keeping within the confines of the shadows, the Hood peered around the side of the building, and her heart sank.

A ring of soldiers, clad in polished armor, stood around what remained of the villagers. Blood made its presence known on nearly every single one of them. Soldiers shoved against those who fought to reach the children and elders being held off to the side. Their blades glistened in the light of the torches placed around the perimeter.

"You know the price for not paying your taxes," a soldier snarled, his massive hand shoving a woman to the ground. The back of her head struck the cobblestones, spilling her long, ebony hair around her shoulders like ink. "And yet despite our good king's mercy, you still refuse to pay! But if you want someone to blame," the soldier said, his lip curling into a sneer, "you can blame the Hood."

Self-hatred burned through Isolde's chest and spread to her hand that rose to pluck an arrow from the quiver. The others stirred at her back, the grips on their weapons tightening.

"The Hood is the only one who has ever fought for us!" one of the men in the crowd roared. "He is for the people, Tenebriath is for himself! A spineless coward who murders children!"

The soldier turned to the man who dared speak and dragged the length of the elithrium sword from the scabbard at his side, with a slow, deliberate tug. The shriek of metal filled the chilled late-night air, stoking the fear lingering in its midst.

"You dare say a word against the rightful king of Arnoria?"

"He is no king of mine." The withered lines of the old man's face, peppered with grey stubble, grew into a content smile as he looked to the stars. In a final act of defiance, the man pressed the middle and pointer finger of his right hand to his lips. And as he placed them directly over his heart, his voice rose over the crowd like the first rays of dawn. Powerful and unforgettable. "Enyalmen damor!"

The sound of the old viryian language was like a shot through Isolde's heart. It sent a muted echo of pain through her soul, touching every dark part of her past like an unwanted caress.

The soldier's smile faded, and the sword clutched in his grasp rose overhead. "You'll regret that, old man."

Instinct seized control as Isolde notched the arrow into place and let it fly. The feathered tail shot past her cheek, leaving behind the wind's tender, familiar kiss. The sound of metal shredding iron and flesh seemed to still time itself.

The soldier's hands tightened around the sword hanging in the air. But after a moment, the sharp blade fell from his grip and clattered to the street. His knees followed, crashing to the ground beside his weapon, his armor groaning under the impact. Surprise filled the old man's eyes as he took in the soldier at his feet. With one final gasp, the soldier fell, leaving the shaft of the Hood's arrow that had been buried in the back of his head, pointing towards the dying night sky.

Moving like the nightmare she was, Isolde unleashed the Hood's wrath. Arrow after arrow flew through the air. Their lethal tips disappeared into the eyes and necks of the soldiers they met. Fresh blood ran between the cobblestones, painting the square red.

Malaki moved past her and began cutting his way through the small group emerging from the depths of a tavern to the left. His axe glistened in the light of the torches while Secrettaker remained tucked in its sheath at his side. It was a weapon not generally used in battle, but one reserved for those unfortunate enough to be taken alive.

"It's the Hood!" one of the soldiers roared. "Kill them! Kill them all!"

Cries from the humans and half-bloods trapped within the chaos shook Isolde to the core, forcing her to look back. The soldiers' blades slashed through the air, cutting down the humans and half-bloods who still drew breath. Isolde's hands were slick as she tried and failed to pull an arrow from the quiver.

"Please!"

Her attention darted to the right, to a woman cowering beneath the shadow of a soldier. Her arms were draped around her children, forcing them behind her. "Please don't—" Her words died away as a sword disappeared through the center of her chest. The cries of her children hammered against Isolde's skull, and something deep within her began to unwind.

Blinding rage broke through the final barrier keeping the power within at bay. Her emotions had been too raw, too unchecked leaving a crack in her defenses. The monster's furious will came forth, shattering the wall she had placed around it. Every bone in Isolde's body began to shift, bend, and break.

Her mother's ring warmed beneath the leather of her glove as bar after bar of her control was ripped away. Isolde fought to regain it, to shove that murderous creature back into the cage she had built. But the harder she fought, the stronger its desire became. A desire that was dark, powerful, and god-like.

"Hood!" Malaki's terrified voice brushed the edges of her mind. But it was too late.

The creature dominated every fragment, every facet of who she was; coating her humanity with a violent, savage will that was not her own. Pain crashed through Isolde like waves upon a shore. It pommeled her like the winds that rolled across the Wilds of the North.

Only one thought remained when the last bit of her skin and humanity were ripped apart.

Blood will flow.

Chapter 3

"Hood!"

Malaki froze, his heart racing with panic at the sight of the stark white feathers erupting from Isolde's form, at the colossal falcon that stood in her place.

A cry of pure fury belted from her throat. It pierced through all who remained in the courtyard like a bolt of fear. Her bright, murderous gaze swept the square. It was the look of a virya who was on the verge of losing reality, of losing themselves to their most basic nature. Rational thought fought for dominance in her emerald eyes. Their depths brimming with rivers of pure silver were ignited by light that was not her own. A power that was cold and unforgiving.

Malaki turned back to the soldiers infecting the square. To the men pressing elithrium blades to the throats of the people Isolde had sworn to protect, the ones who had sealed their fates. A small part of him felt smug at the sight of the bravery draining from their faces and undiluted terror flaring to life in their eyes. He could have sworn the hint of urine now hung in the air.

Isolde's head turned, following his gaze like the predator she was. Reality slammed into Malaki's gut like a blow. He knew there was no stopping the massacre that was about to take place. There would be no possibility, no hope of stopping the twenty-five-foot monster from painting a village red.

Again.

With a thrust of her wings, Isolde shot into the sky and took a sharp turn back to the ground. The tips of her merciless talons wracked through the sea of armor, ensnaring soldier after soldier in their grasp. Wails of pain filled the night. Their obnoxiously fine armor crumbled beneath Isolde's grip. Torn limbs fell to the ground, some striking the heads of those who remained. Drops of blood fell like rain on the brim of his hood. But Isolde gave no reprieve. She continued to swoop down again and again, hoisting soldiers into the air. Her beak snapped left and right, shredding flesh from bone.

"What do we do?" Cillian asked, pulling Blyana to his side, ensuring he was in front of her. "We can't say her name and we don't stand a chance of stopping her. Not here anyway."

Malaki's teeth clenched beneath the mask. Humans cowered together at the far end of the square. A few tried to run down the alleyways, but many stood frozen, shackled by terror as they watched the one who loved them more than her own life, become a living nightmare.

So far, Isolde had only targeted those she saw as a threat. But that would only last so long. Eventually they would all look the same, they would all be her enemy—even him.

Just like the day Kamden died.

She hadn't meant to hurt them—not the villagers anyway. But they were no match for her heartbroken fury or the creature she had kept hidden for so very long. That night still haunted Isolde, still burned in the depths of her soul—an ember of agony refusing to die. Malaki saw it. Every time the mention of her power surfaced, that painful remembrance was there.

Flesh maimed with bite marks, bodies mutilated beyond recognition, and a river of blood that had to be washed from the cobblestone streets, were all that remained in the wake of Isolde's shattered heart. All had fallen victim to her wrath, both innocent and guilty. An entire village paid the price for a crime that could never be undone.

A screech jarred Malaki from the past and thrust him back into reality. They had to eliminate the threat Isolde saw first. Not a single soldier could be left standing in the village. Otherwise, there would be no hope of pulling her away. No hope in denying history a chance to repeat itself.

"Kill the soldiers," Malaki ordered, his distorted voice ringing with the authority of a general in battle.

"All of them?" Blyana asked. A hint of glee hung in her voice, a longing for violence ringing in her tone.

Malaki nodded, and her small hands encircled the hilts of the daggers at her side. The elegant, deadly blades were made from the very elithrium that had once been used to imprison her so many years ago. "Leave none alive."

The corners of Blyana's eyes crinkled, hinting at the vicious smile lurking behind her mask. Her small voice carried like a purr through the night. "With pleasure."

Malaki launched into the fray after her, Cillian close on his heels. He targeted the soldiers off to the right, careful to stay well out of Isolde's destructive path. The blade of his axe disappeared in the chest of one of the soldiers standing guard over the group of children. Only the gurgled sound of death escaped his lips as Malaki wrenched the blade free, sending him crumbling to the ground. Terror filled the children's eyes. Eyes that were far too young, far too innocent to have seen such things.

"Run home," Malaki said, mindful of his tone. "Don't look back."

They scampered away before the final word left his tongue. Their bare feet clapped against the ground as they ran to their parents who met them in the dark alleyways.

Breaths left Malaki's chest in rapid pants, causing the stubble-covered skin beneath his mask to become hot and sticky. Wisps of blood and smoke penetrated the fabric, bringing forth memories of battles long forgotten.

Isolde landed next to a statue erected in the center of the square. The crown of her head hovered at least another five feet over it, making her look enormous. Not a single feather was spared from the savagery she had exacted upon Erebus's men. Her chest heaved, and the light in her eyes dimmed. The falcon's head shook from side to side, her beak snapping.

"She's fighting it," Blyana said. Her shoulders, which barely came to Malaki's elbows, shook with exhaustion.

"But not fast enough," said Cillian, a look of doubt etching into his gaze.

"We need to get her out of the village." Fear's icy fingers gripped Malaki's heart. "Into the forest with Alaric and Gal." A dark realization settled into the pit of his stomach. There was only one way they were getting Isolde out of here. And none of them were going to like it.

Steeling his nerve, Malaki threw a hand forward, his fingers aimed at Isolde. Power trickled through his veins, power stemming from the earth itself. Vines erupted between the cobblestones, their bodies thick and covered in leaves. They latched onto Isolde with an unbreakable grip.

She shrieked and fought against their hold. The tip of her deadly beak bit at the vines constricting around her torso and legs. Where she severed one, two more sprouted up to takes its place.

"That won't hold her," Cillian said.

"It's not meant to," grunted Malaki, his gaze trained only on the massive falcon in front of him. She thrashed in the hold of his power. The vines caging her wings were weak and frail. Their shafts snapping like threads of silk.

"Then what is your brilliant plan?" Blyana asked. "I know you're more powerful than that, Malaki. Unless you really are *that* tired."

"You know what I'm capable of, Bly," he said, as a low, deadly growl rumbled up his throat. "We can't risk her changing back here or losing herself completely to her power."

"What is it you want then?" Cillian asked, his feet shifting uncomfortably when Isolde tore through another batch of vines.

"To make her angry."

As if hearing his words, Isolde's eyes swiveled to him and narrowed. Even after being at her side all her life, Malaki still trembled at the might of that gaze. Light shone from their depths as a cry broke through her beak. It pierced the night air, forcing them to clap their hands over their ears.

"I think you succeeded," Cillian said, taking a step away. His fingers snagged Blyana's hand, pulling her along. "I know annoying her is usually my job and normally I would commend you for your efforts, but you've out done yourself."

"We need to lure her away," Malaki said, sending another wave of vines crashing over her. "We need her angry enough to chase us and leave the village behind. So, work that annoying charm of yours, Cill, and help me!"

"You think I'm charming?" Cillian asked, placing a hand over his heart. "I knew you loved me, old man."

"Don't call me that," growled Malaki, forcing himself to stay focused. Small groups of humans still remained in the square and already tiny fragments of his self-control were beginning to fray. "Bly, make sure all the humans are out of the area."

Cillian's jaw flexed, his dark eyes sweeping the square. "I'll go," he said, his fingers gripping Blyana's, refusing to let her go. "You stay with Malaki."

"Don't take this the wrong way," Blyana said, "but between the two of us, you're the scarier monster. The last thing we need are them too petrified to run."

"That's debatable," Cillian said, his fingers still locked around hers.

"I'll be fine, Cill," she said. "You worry about keeping Papa Bear safe. Gods know he's going to need all the help he can get when she finally breaks free."

Blyana shot him a wink before working her hand from Cillian's grip and dashing around the square. Cillian watched her go, his eyes ignited with worry. Worry only a mate could possess.

"She'll be fine," Malaki said, with dash of annoyance. "Quit coddling her."

A rumble echoed through Cillian's teeth as he sent a wave of solid air across the square. It slammed into Isolde's chest, pushing her off-kilter just enough for Malaki to ensnare a wing in a thicket of vines.

"Don't tell me how to treat her, Malaki," Cillian said, those cold, hard eyes narrowing. "She is mine to protect, not yours. You have your hands full as it is."

Isolde's shriek of fury rang in Malaki's ears. Diving deeper into his power, past the limits he had set a long time ago, he forced the ground beneath her talons to crack and vibrate. Her wings fought against the vines' hold, attempting to steady herself.

"That's not what I'm trying to do," he gritted. "With a head like that it's impossible to make you listen. I'm thinking of Bly. I tried the same thing with Isolde, and you know where that got me?" One of Isolde's wings broke through the snare and stretched towards the sky.

"A seriously pissed off Isolde?"

"A nearly dead one."

Cillian paused. His hands stretched out before him, and the hint of the wind played at his fingertips. The power died away into the night, died at the sight of the haunted look filling his half-covered face.

Briarhole had changed Cillian. Malaki wasn't sure what had initiated it. Was it the close call they had experienced on the river…or Isolde's nearly dying that made Cillian far more protective of Blyana, of his mate? Either way, the hovering was going to get both, if not all of them, killed if he didn't stop.

"The harder you push, the tighter you hold on, the more she will grow to resent you." Malaki's power pulsated around him, and a sheen of sweat covered his brow. "I know you love her, Cill. But you've never tried to stop her before. Don't start now out of fear."

Malaki saw Cillian's gaze move to where Blyana was herding a group of humans out of the square. Even through the mask, he could see a small tick in Cillian's jaw. Briarhole hadn't been the only event to leave its mark on him. Blackwater still hung fresh in his friend's mind. Blyana had nearly died that night…and Cillian had never forgotten.

"I hate it when your old ass is right," Cillian grumbled, throwing a gust of solid air at Isolde, forcing her down once more.

"It must be terrible to feel that way all the time then," he said with a smirk, covering Isolde in a bed of stone. Out of the corner of his eye, Malaki spotted Blyana pushing the last group of humans down the small alleyway heading west. She sent him a nod, causing a flicker of light to dance across her reflective, grey eyes.

"That's everyone," Malaki said, forcing more of his power into the earth that encased Isolde, holding her in place. A bead of sweat trickled down his temple and disappeared into the fabric of his mask, his arms quaking with effort. While he was an earth wielder, manipulating the earth itself was a facet of his power he had never mastered.

Blyana returned to their sides. The dagger glistened in her hands, wet with fresh blood. "Now the fun begins," Malaki said, his voice straining.

"*Fun*," Cillian scoffed. His hands spread wide to form a blanket of solid air. It pressed down on top of the layer of earth covering Isolde's back, causing a shriek to erupt from her beak. "You have a very twisted view of fun, Malaki. Is this something we need to discuss later?"

"You were the one who said I don't know how to have fun."

"He didn't mean the kind that will send Isolde into a savage rage, trying to kill us all," said Blyana.

With one last burst of anger, Isolde broke free, shattering their power's hold. Blades of red tinged wings pierced the remaining vines and stretched towards the sky, covering the square in dirt and foliage. Her eyes raked across the grounds until they landed on them.

"Time to run?" Cillian asked.

Malaki tucked the axe into the holder on his back. "I'd say so."

Without thinking twice, he turned on his heel and sprinted down the deserted street. Cillian and Blyana's feet pounded into the puddles of blood covering the ground. Houses, quiet and dark, sped by in a blur of faceless, blackened windows. Much to Malaki's relief, not a single person crossed their paths.

Reaching into his pocket, he snagged the bag of coins they had collected at the farmer's house. As they ran, he scattered the coins along the eastern side of the village, leaving behind a golden trail of bloodied wealth and security. The outskirts of the village came into view with the tips of the trees occupying Blackford Forest peeking out over the rooftops. They rounded the final corner leading to freedom, their steps chased by a massive, hovering shadow.

Malaki pushed harder, willing his power into every step he took. The first brush of exhaustion caressed his mind like briars upon bare skin. He could feel the swells of power around him, in the creatures it dwelt within. But he didn't dare reach out. If he attempted to take from them now, his reach could travel to the others, and steal away their life by mistake. No, he would have to wait.

The shadows of Blackford passed overhead, concealing them in darkness. Only then did Malaki dare turn his sights to the sky. Through the canopy, he found nothing but the stars staring back at him. The stars that, according to legend, served as the gods' individual realms. Malaki couldn't have cared less. The gods had never been of much use to him in the past and unlike Galaena, he didn't look for guidance from them now.

Breaking right, Malaki stopped just off the beaten path. Each breath felt like a lick of a flame down his throat. He braced the palms of his hands on his hips and took deep breaths in through his nose and out through his mouth. Cillian and Blyana halted beside him, their chests heaving.

"Where are Alaric and Gal?" Cillian asked, his voice ragged.

"They'll be by the river," Malaki said, forcing the words around the burning lump in his throat. While he was a virya, running had never been his forte. His power lay in his strength and fighting, not long-distance running.

"They better be," Blyana said, turning her eyes to the canopy above. "We're going to need them." Isolde could be anywhere. While she was untrained in this particular form, hunting had always been a skill her monstrous form loved to indulge in.

"Let's keep moving," Malaki said, veering south, leading them further into Blackford.

Cillian groaned. "Surely, we're getting close," he huffed, his hand clutching at his side.

"Don't tell me you're tired already, Cill," Malaki said, unable to hide the exhaustion in his own voice. "Surely you aren't going to let an old man out run you."

"That's rich coming from someone who couldn't catch me the last time we—"

"Cillian!" Blyana's cry pierced the night a second before Isolde's body broke through a small opening in the canopy. Blyana pulled him to the ground, the tip of a talon narrowly missing his face. Malaki's power blazed through his veins, sending a branch into Isolde's path. It caught the falcon square in the chest, slamming her to the ground.

Malaki's power, the dark force lingering beneath the surface, roared to life in an instant. Its unstoppable might rammed into his immovable will, releasing an echo of power through his soul. Fissures, fine as shattered glass, snaked their way up the walls of his mind as he watched the falcon slowly rise.

And as Isolde turned to face him, Malaki saw no other way around it. He gave into the call of his power, gave into the curse the gods had placed him under. It ripped through his skin like a knife through softened butter.

The newly formed scar running along his back burned as it too was destroyed. Massive paws replaced his hands and feet. Claws, sharp as daggers, dug into the earth as the bear took form. Already its savage will fought against his own. Anger blazed within his mind, drawing him to the threat, to Isolde. He turned to the one who held his heart and life in her hands. To the one he would do anything for.

She shrieked and fanned out her massive wings in an attempt to look bigger. But Malaki knew it was futile. He would be the one walking away from this fight. There was no alternative, no second option apart from her death. The monster smiled at the thought, his tongue already salivating for the taste of the falcon's blood.

No! Malaki told himself, ripping the chains of control away. *Not her…never her.* Malaki's paws dug into the forest floor, his teeth bared as he took a step forward. The soft snap of a twig brought him up short and his attention turned.

From the depths of the forest, a wall of golden fur shimmered in the shadows. Familiar grey eyes, ones he'd known nearly all his life, stared at the creature before them.

Galaena.

The mountain lion's lip pulled back as a deep, menacing growl rumbled through her throat to dance across the tops of the trees. Her sharp claws punctured the bed of decaying leaves littering the ground. They crinkled as she stalked forward, the ridges of her shoulder blades shifting left to right as she took her place at his side.

Malaki fought the urge to growl in warning, forcing himself to focus on Isolde instead. She looked between the two of them. For just a moment, he thought he saw understanding. For a moment, he thought he saw Isolde in the depths of those emerald eyes.

More movement drew Malaki's eye as Alaric broke through the tree line. His eyes, filled with centuries of memory and pain, scanned the clearing. Cillian shifted to his left, taking a portion of the burden he carried. A large net of chain-linked mail laced with elithrium was clutched between them. Blyana held a bow—Isolde's bow. An arrow was notched and ready. It looked absurdly large in her small yet deadly hands.

Isolde let out a cry of desperate anger as she tried to take flight. Before she could breech the first branches of the forest, Galaena sprang forward and collided with her midair.

Their colossal bodies slammed into the dirt, shaking the ground beneath Malaki's paws. His lips pulled back as Galaena pinned the falcon to the ground and pressed her fangs against Isolde's throat. She fought against the hold, trying to turn her head enough to latch onto the mountain lion's neck. Galaena only pressed her teeth further, tightening her hold as a menacing growl rumbled through her chest.

Alaric sprinted forward as much as his maimed leg would allow. The chainmail dragged behind him, tearing bits of grass from the forest floor. With a grunt, he and Cillian cast the blanket of tainted metal out, draping it over his wife and niece.

Malaki turned all his attention inward, forcing himself to stay rooted to the spot. The beast inside racked against the confines of his mind, demanding blood, demanding death. He looked to Isolde, needing something to draw him back from the endless abyss. To anchor him to his humanity.

Her features began to shrink, drawing out a sigh of relief that ghosted over his jagged teeth. She looked so small beneath the massive cat's paw that was spread across the length of her shoulders, holding her to the ground.

Malaki's growl ripped through the air, his teeth bared at Galaena, drawing Alaric's attention.

"Easy now, brother," the Lord of Thornwood said, taking a tentative step forward. His hand, free of the cane, was held out before him. "You know Gal won't hurt her."

Malaki felt his will shudder beneath the might of his power, as if his strength had finally given way. But still he looked to Isolde. To the person who was fighting to remember who she truly was...just like him.

CHAPTER 4

Tendrils of power, small but still tangible, slowly began to disappear into the cage Isolde had painstakingly crafted in her mind. The blanket of elithrium chain mail leeched the power from within, draining it of its hold.

Carefully, the stones of control she used to keep the monster at bay formed the wall in her mind once more. Each piece was torturous to place. It always was.

A weakened snarl ripped from her lips as she forced her bones to break again and again until all the pieces were firmly in their rightful place. At last she felt the soft, dry forest floor beneath her skin. Galaena's chest was splayed across Isolde's, still holding her in place.

"Hope I wasn't interrupting anything too important," Isolde said, letting her head fall back.

Galaena sighed, her words coated in dark humor. "Nothing but preparing to invade the capital and commit treason."

"Nothing out of the ordinary then."

Ripples of laughter hung in the air as Galaena rested her forehead on Isolde's shoulder.

"Not for us," she agreed. "Care to take this off, darling?"

Alaric was at her side in an instant, peeling back the chain mail. With a grunt, Galaena pushed herself up, her arms shaking with exhaustion. Despite having transformed multiple times since Briarhole, it still took a toll on her. Alaric even more so. Every time the crocodile made an appearance, an ache lingered in the tissues of his maimed leg.

Isolde looked around to see Malaki kneeling a few paces away. Cillian stood by, the heavy, elithrium chain-linked mail once covering them, was now clutched in his hands.

"Malaki?"

A growl was his only answer, his teeth gritting in effort. Hands that had slowly shrunk were balled into fists and braced against the ground.

"Breathe, Malaki," Isolde said, her voice a calm, gentle whisper.

A ripple cascaded down his form. "I believe that's my line to you."

"I figured I'd borrow it," she said. "Especially, after you tried to smother me with vines and dirt."

"Well, when you throw a tantrum," Cillian said, tossing the chain mail away as a cocky grin spread across his face. "You get put in time out."

Isolde let a gesture fly from her hand, her eyes narrowing.

"Isolde!" Alaric, chided. "That is not becoming."

"Yeah Isolde," Cillian said. "That's very unladylike."

"That's rich coming from you," Blyana said, stuffing the arrow back into the quiver.

"I'm a gentleman," Cillian said, his hand pressing against his chest, his face shining with mocking offense. "I'm always polite, gracious, considerate, compassionate, understanding—"

"Please don't harm yourself by using such big words, Cill," Isolde said, rising to dust her back side off. "I can smell the smoke from here."

Blyana chuckled, and Cillian shot Isolde a vulgar gesture of his own.

"Are you alright?" she asked, turning her attention back to Malaki.

"Fine," he said. His hazel eyes still held a hint of light but nothing beyond his control. "Just took me by surprise is all."

"You aren't the only one." Alaric's piercing, grey eyes zeroed in on her. "What the hell happened?"

"It was nothing," Isolde said, suddenly finding the tips of her boots rather interesting. She couldn't stand the look in his eyes. The shadow of anger and the glint of disappointment.

"Clearly not," her uncle said, tone biting.

"Alaric…" Galaena began, but her words died in the wake of her husband's heated stare.

"What happened, Isolde?" Alaric demanded.

Isolde tried to make sense of it, tried to recall the very thoughts that had run through her mind moments before she lost control. But all she could remember was undiluted rage. Rage for the deaths of so many who were guilty of nothing more than being different, who were pawns being played between a vigilante and a tyrant.

And her mother's ring. The golden, feathered band felt cool beneath her glove, its power now quiet, but never fully asleep.

Isolde shook her head, causing strings of sweaty, dark brown hair, now littered with bits of earth and tree limbs, to tumble into her face. "I don't know," she said, her tongue grazing over her cracked lips. "I just... lost control."

"That much is apparent," said Alaric, his words laced with the same tone she'd hated as a child. Petulant, irritated, and disappointed.

"You make it sound as if I chose it. That I did it on purpose, Alaric," Isolde snapped. "Turning into a savage monster isn't my idea of a pleasant time. It won't happen again."

"It can't happen again!" Alaric said, his voice rising. "Need I remind you where we are headed? Who and what awaits us?"

"Yes," Isolde said, knotting her arms over her chest. "Clearly, I've forgotten, so please, tell me what awaits us. Erebus…Gage…the children I failed to save hanging from the walls of Elenarta. Zibiah's head on a spike to welcome us to the capital." Her words carried over the clearing. They hung in the air like a dark omen. Only the sound of Fane's wings broke the silence as he flew down from the trees to land on Isolde's shoulder.

The hawk's soft, velvet feathers brushed her cheek, and his small, lithe body scooted in close to nuzzle into her hair. Isolde nearly smiled at the touch of comfort her dear friend was offering. But not even Fane could distract her from what was to come.

"Whatever you tell me, Alaric," Isolde said. "I've already imagined something far worse. There isn't a scenario I haven't already thought of."

Malaki took a step forward. "It wasn't her fault, Alaric. If you had just seen—"

"I have seen," Alaric said, his lips pulling back over a row of sharp teeth. Hints of scales erupted along his jaw line. "That and then some. So, have you. Don't downplay this as a simple loss of control, Malaki." Her uncle's eyes turned back to her. "You know this cannot happen, Isolde. You cannot lose control!"

"I'm terribly sorry I don't measure up to your level of expected perfection, Alaric," said Isolde, dropping into a mocking bow, sweeping the back of her hand across the forest floor. Galaena shifted behind Alaric, her body tensing and eyes dropping to the ground. Alaric lowered his gaze, their depths filled with a shame that Isolde ignored.

"It wasn't intentional," Isolde said, straightening. A tired sigh broke through her lips. "It's…it's getting harder to control and I don't understand why."

The monster within growled inwardly at the taste of the fear Isolde had worked so hard to fight. But it was true; she knew it was. This wasn't an enemy she could conquer head-on. There was no blood to be spilled in this case...save her own.

"It's something we can work on," Galaena said, her voice easing the guilt burning in Isolde's chest. "We can get it under control." Galaena ran a hand up Alaric's arm, and the grip on his cane eased. "It's a good thing this happened when it did. We leave in a few days anyway. I think we all needed to let out that energy."

She had a point. Isolde now felt the confines of her power were sturdy and solid. Satiated and satisfied. But it wouldn't stay silent for long. The hammering fury of the beast was non-stop. A relentless demand that never fully ceased, never stopped trying to find a way out.

Something had changed in her at Briarhole. A shift in her very being she couldn't explain. Isolde pulled the glove free and looked down at her mother's ring. The metal warmed against her skin and the diamond shone in the moonlight. A slight breeze drifted through the trees, causing her hair to sway in its current and wrap around Fane's feathers. The power called to her. It fit into her own like a key to a lock.

Something has changed.

Alaric's voice ripped her from the depths of her mind. "If she weren't off playing Hood again this wouldn't have happened."

A growl echoed through Malaki's chest, and Blyana's eyes hardened. Even Cillian's tensed, his jaw ticking as he looked at Alaric with a coldness that rarely crossed her friend's handsome, sun-kissed face. An uneasy silence filled the clearing, one that left Isolde feeling the sting of her uncle's words like the edge of a blade to her heart.

A heavy sigh fell from his lips at the look of shock and hurt etched into her face. "I didn't mean that, Isolde," he said, taking a seat on the trunk of a fallen tree sprawled along the edge of the clearing. "I'm just ...worried."

"And you don't think I am?" she asked. "You think I don't care about the consequences of what my actions have brought? About the price others are paying for what I have done?" Her throat bobbed with the emotions she refused to acknowledge.

"I'm deserving of my own fair share of guilt, Alaric. But the last thing I need is for you to ram that truth down my throat. I am so sorry I do not measure up to everything you expected me to be."

"You do, Isolde," Alaric said, tapping the ground with the end of his cane. "You are far more than I could have ever hoped you would be." His voice was much kinder, far gentler than she had been expecting. It caught her off guard and made her feel like a child again. She almost wanted his anger instead. "You just…You cannot lose control like that again," Alaric said again, as if the fact hadn't already been beating itself into her mind like a smithy upon an anvil.

"I don't need you to repeat yourself, Alaric," Isolde said, biting against the anger lapping at her resolve. "I couldn't just leave them. I couldn't do nothing!" Bolts of white-hot pain shot through her side as her hand swiped through the air, back to the village she left in bloody shambles. A stifled grunt broke through her lips, drawing Malaki's unwanted attention.

"I'm fine," she said instantly, refusing to meet his concerned gaze.

"Good to know." Without warning, he spun her around and pulled her to the stump to the right of Alaric. "Sit."

Malaki's tone rang with authority, one that she had no interest or energy to fight against. With a sigh of irritation, Isolde plopped down and began pulling her leathers and tunic free.

Galaena's nose wrinkled as bits of blood and gore fell to the forest floor. "We need to teach you how to fight without getting so dirty." Her gloved forefinger and thumb pinched the hem of her discarded cloak and held it up, nose wrinkling. "You'll spend the entire Thornwood fortune on clothes alone."

"I have a reputation to uphold, Gal," Isolde said, pulling the tunic up and over her head, forcing Fane to take flight. Gooseflesh erupted across her exposed skin, save for the small elastic band used to keep her breasts flattened and in place. "I'd hate to disappoint the people."

"Yes," Cillian said, tucking Blyana into his side. "We'd hate for them to be let down with the lack of bloodshed. Either way it doesn't matter, we all know I'm their favorite anyway."

The familiar sensation of Malaki's power pressed into her side. His warm, callused palm glided over the hideous reminder left by Gage. She flinched at his touch, but Malaki simply waited patiently for her to relax into his hand once more.

"Shifting seems to make it worse," he said. Isolde could feel the tendrils of his magic working along the scar, searching and mending what damage had been done. Hints of sandalwood, smoke, and the trace of a storm lingered in the air around him.

"The scar has healed over, but there's still some damage to the tissue not even my power can heal fully. That's something your unnatural healing abilities will have to take care of with rest," Malaki said, his eyes cutting to her. The hint of a tattoo peaked beneath the lining of his tunic as he shifted his stance. A name, encased in a bedding of ebony thorns and vines, glistened against his copper skin. "Not that you're unaware of that already."

Isolde reached up to clasp Malaki's hand resting on her shoulder. His pinky wrapped around her own, holding her in place. Her skin felt tight with the cooled, crinkled blood painting her hands.

"We are heading into the belly of the beast," Cillian said, cutting through the tension. "Let's hope another visit from your other self isn't in our near future."

"It's been years since we were at the capital," Galaena said, her grey eyes hardening with memory. "There's no telling what kind of changes Erebus has made."

"I'm sure he's done far more than redecorate," said Isolde. She twisted around to pluck her tunic from the ground, and a bolt of pain shot through her side. A gasp fell from her lips before she could stop it.

"That's it," Malaki said, turning her to face him, his finger raised. "No more training."

"You don't get to make that call, Malaki!" said Isolde. "It was just a spasm. There isn't even any blood."

"I'm bigger and older than you," Malaki said with a smirk that grated her nerves. "Just because you say you're fine, doesn't make it true." His hazel eyes scanned her blood-covered form. "And if that wound is still hurting, it means you need rest." She opened her mouth to argue but Malaki beat her to it. "We aren't going out again. We've covered all the villages we can. The lords and ladies of Arnoria are going to have to do their jobs and actually look after their own. Taking care of yourself is but an extension of you taking care of them."

Isolde bit her tongue. She hated to admit it, but he was right. This wasn't a normal mission. A trickle of fear chilled her blood at the thought. "Fine," she said with a heavy, defeated sigh.

"Let's get back home," Blyana said. "We don't want to keep Nan up any longer than we already have."

"It is getting late," Cillian agreed, his lips pressing into the top of her head. His mischievous eyes slid to Malaki. "Wouldn't want to have Malaki out past his bedtime. We know how grumpy old people get when they miss out on sleep."

Without warning, Malaki launched across the clearing. His colossal arms locked around Cillian's waist as he slammed him into the ground. Blyana dodged to the right, narrowly avoiding being taken down herself. The two virya wrestled across the small clearing. Snarls and fits of laughter filled the night as Cillian managed to slip from Malaki's grip over and over again.

"Children." Blyana chuckled, walking over to Isolde who gingerly rose from the stump.

"He's *your* mate," Isolde said, a tired smile tugging at the corners of her lips.

But before she could take a step forward, Alaric came to stand before her. His eyes, normally so serious and piercing, were soft and beseeching. Tenderly, he took her right hand in his. Her mother's ring rested on her ring finger, where it had remained since the day Galaena had gifted it to her years ago. The perfect, untarnished diamond glistened in ribbons of moonlight streaking through the canopy above. Alaric stared down at it, his jaw clenching.

"Please don't do that again, Isolde." The words were strangled and hoarse, as if it took every ounce of effort for him to get them out.

"I can't promise I won't be the Hood again," Isolde said, trying to pull her hand free. "Or that I won't lose control again. You know I can't do that!"

"That's not what I'm asking," he said, refusing to relinquish his hold. Her uncle squeezed his eyes shut before lifting his face to her. A line of silver ringed his deep, grey eyes. "Please...do not ever bow to me again."

Agony painted ridges in his perfect, beautiful face. A face that had unwillingly been made young again. Isolde could see the ghosts that haunted him, the shame and regret he bore. A remembrance of a time that had been turned into ash and scattered to the winds so very long ago. "Even in jest, I beg you. Please...*don't.*"

Isolde's mouth became a desert as the weight of his words fell upon her. The look in his eyes cut her to the core, dousing any anger still lingering within. Words hung at the back of her throat, itching, demanding to be released, but the pain in her heart, in her very soul kept them at bay. All she could do was cling to them harder and nod her head in agreement.

A shaky sigh broke from Alaric's lips as his arms, warm and familiar, wrapped around her. Isolde froze, her arms held out to the side. "The blood, Alaric," she murmured, afraid to stain his clothes with the death that covered her. Even through the tunic, blood still found a way to paint her skin.

Isolde felt so dirty, so completely unworthy of the love he offered in that moment. But he only drew her closer, held her tighter. "I don't care," he said, pressing his fingers into her skin. "My hands are just as bloody as yours. If not more so."

A shuddery breath racked through Isolde's chest, and she wrapped her arms around him. The scent, Alaric's scent—fresh parchment and crisp lemon—drifted through the air as she buried her face in his shoulder. His hands held her in place, cradling her head like a child.

And as she clung to him, Isolde felt another pair of arms wrap around her. Galaena's scent mingled with Alaric's. Honey, earth, and iron wrapped around her in a wave of familiarity.

"We are not worthy of such a gesture," Galaena whispered, her fingers gently grazing through Isolde's soiled hair. "Not from you, Isolde."

CHAPTER 5

The day of their departure came far too soon for the heir of Thornwood.

Isolde lingered by the fireplace in the library. Not even a hint of ash dusted the lining of its inner walls or the pristine grate resting on the stone floor. Years ago, she had taken to storing books within its cold, cavernous confines. Books just for herself that would be considered inappropriate in certain circles.

Early morning light poured through the stained-glass windows of the eastern wall of Thornwood's library. It spilled across the spines of the books lining the bookshelves. Stories, thousands of them, Isolde had lived and helped others live as well.

The air was too thin. Far too quiet for her liking. She hadn't set foot in here since Malaki deemed her well enough to leave their hideout. Two weeks. That was how long he had forced her to stay hidden in their cave in the heart of Blackford Forest. Two weeks to sit and stew over their disastrous, bloody failure at Briarhole. Her fingertips absently traced the scar at her side through the lining of her travel dress.

"Fucking Gage," she growled. The pain was still fresh in her mind. The roaring inferno that burned her alive every time Nan applied the antidote was etched into her mind, scorching into her memory like a brand.

Gage hadn't been the only one to leave a scar that night. She had granted him one of his own. Two, in fact. One for each side of his despicable, infuriatingly handsome face. The mark she left on all who crossed her, the mark of the Hood of Arnoria. Isolde smiled at the memory of his cries, of his blood soaking into his tunic and britches.

"Can't hide those, you bastard."

The sound of pecking came from the far window, drawing Isolde from her dark satisfaction. A flash of light danced across a bed of feathers.

"You're so impatient," Isolde mumbled, pulling the window open, the iron hinges creaking. A breeze of fresh morning air drifted in, as Fane shot into the room. He landed on her shoulder and nibbled at a wave of hair running down her shoulder, his knowing eyes narrowing.

"Sensitive this morning, are we?" she asked, reaching up to stroke his chest. The hawk, who had been her companion for longer than she could remember, huffed and snipped at the fringes of her travel dress. But as she ran the back of her fingers down his chest, Fane melted into her touch. His intelligent gaze softened, and a soft chirp sang from his beak.

"I knew you loved me," Isolde whispered, stroking the top of his head. With a sigh, Isolde locked the window and turned back to the painfully vacant room. Without reason, she began walking down the rows of shelves, her eyes scanning the various stories housed within each one. Lives…loves…deaths…

The echoed memory of story hour played out before her. Empty chairs sat at the empty tables occupying the space. A cold, terrifying thought fell on her heart at the sight, like the last warm breeze of summer before fall seized control.

Was it over?

Finality dug its sharp, piercing claws in deep at the possibility. The empty tables...the empty chairs...the lifeless fireplace were all that remained.

Is story hour gone?

Isolde looked around again and took in every detail she could. What books sat where...the way streams of light from the stained-glass windows danced across the polished floor...the little chairs that looked up to hers. She let every detail settle in, as if it were the last time she would see it. She branded it into her mind, into her very being to have and cherish always.

It felt as if death, the maker of change himself, hovered at her side. Waiting...wanting...demanding. He was a greedy companion—always taking, never giving. Isolde's teeth ground and her stubborn will cut off the tendrils of fear threatening to take root.

That would not be her future.

"We are coming," Isolde said, her voice a harsh whisper. "I promise." She scanned the stack of books she had set aside for story hour months ago. Ones she had hoped they would enjoy. "We are coming."

Fane brushed his cheek against hers and a soft coo lifted from his chest. Isolde could have sworn he felt and shared in her agony, in the guilt pummeling through her without mercy.

The enormity of what they were facing settled into Isolde's bones like lead. It felt like a weight had been dropped into her very soul and threatened to drown her in it.

Elenarta...the capital of Arnoria. A fortress, once beautiful and breathtaking to behold, now was a den of savage monsters. Creatures dressed in finery who hid behind the law of a false, ruthless imposter. One who ruled without mercy and preyed on the weak.

And for the first time, Isolde felt afraid. She looked to the east, to Blackford Forest and the dawn caressing the tops of the trees that filled it. She felt him in that moment. Felt him as if he were standing there at her side.

"Kamden."

Pain and joy ripped through Isolde like a tidal wave, mercilessly battering her soul while she stood in awe of it. His voice came to her like a gentle reminder from the past.

"*You do not bow to fear, Isolde Cotheran.*"

Kamden had said it so many times. But one stood out from the rest. The night she had planned to deliver the news of forsaking her power and position to become human. To live and die with him.

She had been petrified of Alaric. Sick with worry over what he would think…how he would react to her making that kind of decision. But Kamden had been there. He had always been there when she needed him.

"This is ours," she had told him, her head falling into the crook of his arm as they lay together. "Our kingdom."

His chest rumbled with a chuckle. "Of course," he had said, bringing her fingers to his lips. "Whatever you want it to be."

"I want a place for us." Her eyes had scanned the canopy above and ran along the boundaries of the meadow. Hints of dark clouds crawled by, casting them in shadow. "A place away from responsibility, from Thornwood. A place where we can be free…where we can have peace."

"You are my peace, Isolde," Kamden had said, brushing his lips across her brow. "My light, my dream, my heart. As long as you are with me, I will always have peace."

Happiness, far more than Isolde could have thought possible, blossomed in her heart. "Alaric will understand," Kamden had said, planting a kiss on her brow. "So, will Malaki. Go on. The sooner you tell them, the sooner we can finish our story." She left him there, a book in his hand and a smile on his face. "I'll be here when you get back."

But when she returned, all Isolde found was a future that never would come to pass. A world that was shattered. Kamden had been tortured, beaten, and mutilated beyond recognition. His blood painted the forest floor that now held his grave. It was his resting place. His final home.

"Do you bow to fear?" Kamden's voice echoed through her mind.

"No," Isolde said in return, a bit of her resolve coming back.

"Who does it bow to?"

"To me."

A tear escaped before Isolde could stop it. It landed by her foot, leaving behind a tiny puddle on the clean stone floor. Squaring her shoulders, she looked once more to Blackford, to the one who kept her heart safe in his grave.

She had spent the night at Kamden's grave. There was nowhere else she would rather spend her final night at Thornwood—nestled beneath the sweeping limbs of the andacovie tree, wrapped in his memory. She told him of her plan, of what lay ahead in Elenarta. And as she had drifted off to sleep, with the scent of fresh roses and pine in the air, his presence hung around her like a warm remembrance. It gave her the peace he had promised so many years ago.

Isolde closed her eyes and took a deep breath, basking in his memory one final time. "I miss you," she said. "Always, I miss you."

With a final sweep of her safe haven, Isolde shoved the smothering heartache down and reached under the lip of the unused fireplace. She snagged the bag of sweets she hid from Cillian and popped one into her mouth. A small, satisfied smile tugged at the corners of her mouth as the sugar melted across her tongue, leaving behind hints of orange and honey. When the library door clicked closed, Isolde told herself over and over again. "This is not the end…This is not the end."

The halls of Thornwood felt dark, as if a shadow had fallen upon it. Even the company occupying the courtyard seemed to be holding their breath. Malaki waited on his gelding, with Versa's reins resting securely in his hands.

"I do hope you plan on sharing those," he said, looking pointedly at the bag clutched to her chest.

"Finders keepers," Isolde said, pulling herself up into the saddle before tossing another sweet into her mouth.

"Is that so?"

Malaki reached around to the side pocket of his saddle and pulled out a small sack of his own. Isolde could smell them instantly, the sweets in her hand long forgotten.

"Give me one," she demanded, swiping a hand through the air. Keeping the bag well out of reach, Malaki let a cocky grin pull at his lips as he lifted a single cookie from the bag. Raspberry jam sprinkled with extra powdered sugar, coated his fingers.

"Finders keepers," Malaki said, his hazel eyes shining. "Your rules, not mine." Before she could stop him, Malaki shoved the cookie and all of its sugary deliciousness into his mouth. A mocking moan of satisfaction rumbled through his chest, causing her teeth to grind. "They're so good," he said, licking the frosting from his fingertips.

"Give me a cookie!" Isolde growled, her temper flaring.

Malaki grinned. "Fine."

Isolde boiled with rage as he plucked another from the bag and proceeded to lick away every scrap of icing. When only a naked cookie remained, Malaki, with a mouth smeared in pink, raspberry sugar, extended it to her. "There you are."

Isolde curled her lip at the offering. "I'm not a savage."

"Your loss then." The cookie disappeared into his mouth in one bite.

"Are you digging into yours already?" Cillian asked, pulling up beside them. A dusting of white power decorated the top of a bag tied to the horn of his saddle. "Nan told you to make those last."

Malaki simply shrugged and devoured another while never looking away from Isolde's infuriated gaze.

"He couldn't resist seeing her face." Blyana chuckled, pulling Felix to a stop on Isolde's left. A bag of her own dangled from her belt loop.

Isolde looked between them. "Where's my damn bag?"

"She ran out," Cillian said, his smile growing. "But Nan said you would understand."

"Like hell," Isolde said, twisting around, her eyes scouring the company for Nan.

"Calm down," said Malaki. He pulled a pack from his satchel, this one noticeably larger than the other three. "Serves you right though. You never share."

Isolde snagged the bag from his grasp and tugged at the strings refusing to open up. "When have you ever known me to share food, Malaki?" she asked before shoving a cookie into her mouth. "It's an endearing trait of mine."

"It most certainly is a trait," Malaki muttered. "Not sure about the endearing part."

Vulgarity danced on Isolde's tongue alongside the cookie crumbles and jam when Alaric rode forward. He glanced down at the bag of sweets in her hand and the sugar coating her lips, his head shaking. "Did your aunt teach you nothing of manners?"

"She gave it her best effort," Isolde said around a mouthful of sugar and dough. Alaric simply rolled his eyes again and moved back toward the front of the company where Galaena waited. She pressed a hand to his shoulder, drawing a soft, loving smile from his far too serious face.

Just beyond her aunt's shoulder, another figure at the front of the company snagged her attention. Light from the early sun cut across the waves of his ebony hair brushing the tops of his shoulders.

"Liam!"

Black leather, the uniform of a Captain of the Guard, stretched across the impressive swell of muscle lining his chest and thighs. His black stallion looked massive, like a wall of shadow beneath him. His dark eyes were forward, and a look of coldness hung about his face. A coldness that did not fit him at all.

"He arrived this morning," Malaki said. His tone, once filled with jesting, now held nothing but contempt. "Along with a battalion of soldiers. Apparently, Erebus believes Thornwood needs a royal escort to Elenarta."

"How thorough of him," Isolde said. A smile crept onto her face when Liam turned his eyes her way. Light and relief ignited in their depths at the sight of her. A hidden smile tugged on the corners of his stubble-covered jaw. He sent her a wink before turning back to the front. A brush of disappointment covered her heart.

"He's here on business," Cillian said. A smile, one that was gentle and understanding, played at the corners of his lips. "I'm sure he has many captain-related things to attend to. He'll see you soon."

Of all her beloved cadre, Cillian was the one who supported her relationship with Liam the most. He seemed to understand, or at least accept, the choice she made. And Isolde loved him all the more for it.

"I hope so."

The company, led by Liam and a procession of soldiers loyal to Thornwood, stepped through the open gates. Tendrils of morning dew drifted between Versa's long legs like ribbons of smoke. The air was quiet, as if the world itself had taken a pause. Not a single bird graced them with their morning melodies. Even Fane sat quietly on Isolde's shoulder. Just before passing through, she pulled back on the reins, willing Versa to halt. She turned and looked back at the manor.

The open courtyard she played in as a child was deserted, save for a few servants and workers who stayed behind. Their eyes were swimming with a hope that felt like lead in Isolde's stomach.

Tarvo, Tanor's father and Thornwood's trusted smithy, and Asha, a seamstress from Whisper, were among them.

"Bring him home," Tarvo had said the night before. His head bowed over Isolde's hands he held in his callused grip. "Please, Lady Isolde. Bring Tanor home."

Tanor was Tarvo's only son and the last surviving member of his family—an heir to nothing but his father's love. Tanor had been the first student Isolde had ever taught to read. He was a favorite of hers who had been stolen, along with Asha's daughter, Insil, and taken to the capital. Taken as punishment for refusing Gage's hand in marriage. And while there was no written law against reading to humans and half-bloods, Isolde felt quite certain Erebus Tenebriath would see it differently.

"I promise," Isolde had said, gripping Tarvo's hands before throwing her arms around his soot-covered shoulders. "I promise, Tarvo. I will bring Tanor home."

Something deep within told Isolde to wait one moment longer. To gaze up at the windows looking out into the forest. To the trees leading to Blackford and their hideout beyond. A den of thieves and assassins that had become a home…that had become her family.

Isolde recalled all the memories they had shared. Both good and bad. A tremor of fearful sorrow pierced her heart at the thought of never walking the halls of Thornwood again, of never seeing Kamden's grave again. She wished now she had gone to see it this morning. Just one more time…

Versa stilled beneath Isolde. The long trails of her mane fell over her eyes in a sheet of night. Her feet were unnaturally still as Isolde kept her eyes on the sun cresting over the fine shingled roof, cascading

Thornwood in a bed of warm, golden light.

Words did not come for her. There were none. Not for this. With a heavy sigh, Isolde led Versa back onto the road where her family waited. And for once, she prayed to the gods she cursed, that it would not be the last time she saw the place that had become her home.

It was a solemn trek, one that soured Isolde's mood over the days that never seemed to end. A sense of restlessness plagued every waking moment, like an itch she could not scratch. Even the creature within was anxious. The beast lurked night and day at the walls of her mind. It prowled, always searching for a way out, always looking for a weak spot in her control.

Isolde looked down at her right hand gently holding the reins in its grasp. Beneath the fine leather glove sat her mother's ring. The diamond had grown brighter, clearer since the night at Briarhole.

A stir of wind blew through the company and the echo of that raw power thrummed in her blood. It was wild and terrifyingly intoxicating. She had considered using it again on more than one occasion. Just to see what would happen.

But every time the thought entered her mind, it became too much to bear. The need to unleash, to conquer…to dominate…It nearly consumed her, body, mind, and soul. Reluctantly, she kept that part of herself locked away. Hidden from the others and the rest of the world.

They couldn't know. Especially Malaki.

He would only worry, she thought every time indecision pressed into her mind. The last thing Malaki needed was another reason to be concerned. Or to think she needed to be watched more closely.

A part of her wanted that power; craved it so desperately it was next to impossible to resist. But every time she thought of it, every time it drew her to the edge, Isolde sensed what she would become. It would turn her into something she had worked so hard to avoid.

A true monster.

"This is taking an eternity," Isolde grumbled, stretching her arms towards the canopy; forcing herself to think of anything else. "We've been traveling endlessly, and I still can't see Oronilma."

Malaki cast a glance over his shoulder. "It's not like we're traveling to Briarhole, Isolde. And I believe you remember what caused our long journey then."

"I don't expect someone whose attire consists of training britches and a tunic to understand," she said, her legs aching and stiff. "Leave my wardrobe out of this. Gal packed just as many dresses as I did. If not more!"

"Yes," Galaena said, from atop her horse, a few paces ahead. "But I am the Lady of Thornwood. It is expected."

"And an heir is not?"

"I'm sure not even the king himself has the wardrobe you do, Isolde," Blyana laughed.

Cillian's chuckle carried along behind his mate's. "A wardrobe fit for royalty."

The main path weaved its way along the forest floor. Liam rode among those who took position at the front. He occasionally looked back, his eyes warming every time they found her.

She sent a small nod, hoping that would pacify him. But as she adjusted herself in the saddle, his eyes traveled to the planes of her travel dress. Heat ignited in his gaze and subdued longing drew his mouth into a tight, impatient line. A wicked, taunting smile tugged onto Isolde's lips. It had been so long since she had been touched. Since she had felt his hands on her bare skin.

The very same thought seemed to cross Liam's mind as well.

Heated darkness filled his gaze, and the grip on his reins tightened. She bit her bottom lip to hide a look of amusement as a soldier tapped Liam's shoulder, drawing his attention away.

Clearing her thoughts, she squirmed in the saddle, and the amusement instantly morphed into a groan. The thin scar tissue tugged beneath the snug corset. It wasn't painful anymore. Not really. Now it served as an occasional annoyance.

"Do we need to stop?" Malaki asked, eyes lit with worry. "It's been a couple days since I healed you—"

"No stopping," Isolde said, cutting him off. Through sheer will, her hand constricted around the pommel of the saddle, and the tips of her nails dug into the leather lining of her gloves. "We aren't wasting anymore time. Besides, it's much better actually."

The ageless russet skin bunched as a frown pulled at the corners of Malaki's lips. "You always say that."

"Because it's true."

"Yeah," he said, tone filled with mocking humor. "I'm sure it is."

Isolde rolled her eyes, her temper flaring. "I'm not something that constantly needs to be fixed, Malaki. Or watched over."

"There is nothing about you that needs fixing, Isolde," Malaki said, his fingers weaving their way through the reins. "You are not capable of being broken. I never meant to insinuate you were." Silence fell between them. But when he spoke again, his eyes remained forward. "I'm terribly sorry if my concern for you is such a nuisance. But I will always look after you. Even your foolishness and hard headedness can't stop that."

The hint of a smile ghosted the edge of Isolde's mouth. "Stubborn ass," she grumbled.

A mischievous grin spread across his own, making years disappear from his already youthful face. The world seemed far brighter and brimmed with hope when he wore a smile. He forced his gelding's flank into Versa's side, nudging her off the path. The mare's ears flattened against her skull before snapping at the gelding's flank in return, forcing him to retreat.

"A little hypocritical don't you…" Malaki's voice faded away into the sound of pounding hooves filling the dense, forest air. It ricocheted off the trunks of the trees lining the road.

Isolde had but a split second to shift her gaze to the left, to where the two roads converged into one. At the exact spot Alaric had paused to look back.

"Isolde—" Alaric's words died on his lips as a mass of bodies broke through the tree line. They came like a storm cloud, descending from the northwest. Body after body bled through the trees like ink. A massive black wave that crashed forward, severing the company of Thornwood in two.

Alaric's stallion reared on its hind legs. His hooves punched into the sky as a cry ripped through his mouth. Alaric's hold on the reins slipped and his back collided with the unforgiving forest floor. His crimson cloak, the one Asha had worked tirelessly on to match his mate's, was now smeared with mud and leaves. Alaric's mouth gapped open, and the tips of his fingers clung to his chest, desperate for air.

"Alaric!" Isolde cried, forcing Versa forward. The mare snorted as she worked her way through the crowd of soldiers lining the road. "Move!" she ordered, her voice ringing with authority that none dared challenge. She leapt from the saddle to Alaric's side. His breathes were uneven and labored, face pale and eyes wide. Gently, Isolde forced a small stream of air over her uncle's lips, allowing his lungs time to adjust.

Galaena threw herself off her horse to land at his other side. "Alaric!"

"I'm alright," he said, his voice hoarse and shallow. "Just knocked the breath out of me." Together, Isolde and Galaena, grabbed his shoulders and hoisted him up. A grimace, one he tried and failed to hide, flickered across his face. His maimed leg refused to take any weight, forcing Galaena to hold him up.

A large silver panther snarled in the center of the black and purple banners surrounding Thornwood. The symbol of Volkran's house, stared down at them, its fangs on full display.

"A man wouldn't have fallen off his horse, Cotheran," a deep voice sneered. "At least, not a real one." The Lord of Briarhole and Zibiah's husband, Volkran, smiled down from his massive black stallion.

Galaena straightened to her fullest height at her husband's side, her eyes burning with hatred. A low growl rumbled through her chest as her lips pulled into a snarl.

"Do you really think you're one to give advice on how to be a man, Lord Volkran?" Isolde asked. "In my experience, the mark of a real man isn't finding it necessary to claim to be one." She gave him an unimpressed glance. "Doesn't seem to be the case for you."

Hatred swelled in Volkran's face. A blush of red painted the tan skin stretching across his cheeks.

"And let's not forget," Isolde said, pressing forward. "You were the one who was shown mercy by the Hood. A human sympathizer. Doesn't really speak well for your manhood if someone like that can put you on your ass."

Volkran's dark eyes narrowed. "A human sympathizer who will be dealt with. And if you don't want to meet the same fate, you little whore, mind how you speak to me." A cruel smile stretched across his face as he thrust a gloved finger her way. "Or I will teach you the same lesson I taught my traitorous wife, Zibiah."

Isolde felt the blood drain from her face.

"That is the second time you have called Lady Isolde a whore in my presence, Volkran," Malaki growled, shoving the black stallion back and placing himself between them. "There will not be a third."

"Brave words from a disgraced warrior of old," Volkran said, his piercing eyes probing Malaki. "We'll see how well they hold up in the capital."

A retort danced on the tip of Isolde's tongue, but her words fell silent. To the right, far off the beaten path, the distinct sound of footsteps filled the air. Many…many footsteps.

Malaki stilled at her side, his eyes scanning the trees. The feeling of his power brushed her skin, its touch light but unquestionably powerful. His hands balled into fists, causing the leather lining of his gloves to groan in protest.

"To the right," Isolde whispered. Her hands disappeared into the lining of her dress to grip the pommel of the blades hidden within. For just a moment, her eyes flew to the cargo behind the caravan. To the luggage that housed her bow. The phantom touch of an arrow brushed her fingers as the sound of more footsteps penetrated the air.

"Wishing Alaric had let you carry the bow now?" Malaki murmured, his voice far too low for Volkran's ears.

"Damn propriety," she said, squeezing the pommel of her dagger. "Whatever moron decided a woman possessing a weapon was unseemly had clearly lost to one in the past. Men and their fragile egos."

"Alaric," Galaena said, her eyes glowing. Her hand traveled to the dagger at her side. Lines of worry chiseled onto her face, disturbing the ageless perfection.

"I hear them." Alaric's grey eyes swept the tree line. The chestnut stallion at his side drove his hooves into the worn path.

Liam rode to stand beside Alaric, his eyes trained on the forest. A hand rested on his sword. "Nomads?" he asked, not breaking focus. "Local villagers, maybe?"

"It's possible," Alaric said, resting his hand on Turgon, the golden sword of the House of Cotheran, hanging at his side. "Either way, I think it'd be wise to move out of Blackford."

"This is nonsense," Volkran sneered. "Cowards afraid of ghosts in the woods." But a hint of uncertainty filled his voice. Even Lauram, who had remained silent at his benefactor's side, held a look of apprehension in his glossy, reddened eyes. The scent of whisky hung in the air about him like a vapor.

The sound of the first arrow piercing the air didn't register with Isolde until it found its mark in the heart of one of Volkran's soldiers. The impact threw him backwards to land face down on the warm earth. A stream of blood crept through the blades of grass lining his body. For a moment, time halted. Only stunned silence remained between the companies of Briarhole and Thornwood.

Then, like drops of black ink, elithrium-laced arrows rained down from the trees above. Isolde had just enough time to hear the whisper of their blades slicing through the air as she sent a gust of wind across the path before them. It pushed the arrows off course and into the trunks directly above their heads. Shadows hopped from one limb to another, their faces covered and blades glistening.

"Raiders!" Malaki roared, ripping the axe from the sheath running across his shoulder blades.

"Rat bastards," Volkran growled, descending from his stallion. The shriek of metal, one Isolde remembered, filled the air as he yanked his sword from the scabbard at his side. A twinge of anger and apprehension saturated her blood at the sight of it. "Get off that damn horse and fight!" he snarled over his shoulder to Lauram who remained frozen in the saddle. A look of drunken terror filled his eyes at the swarm of raiders surrounding them.

"Cover the back," Malaki growled, as he swung the axe in a wide arch.

Forcing herself to focus, Isolde yanked on Versa's reins. She threw herself into the saddle and kicked at her sides. Versa's hooves dug into the ground as she raced to the back of the caravan, raining dirt on all those she left behind.

Rays penetrating the canopy shone on the unforgiving edge of Isolde's blade as it sliced through the neck of the first raider to cross her path. Blood sprayed over Versa's flank in a splash of red and the raider fell to the ground behind them.

Bodies draped in strips of clothes that clung to their forms continued to fall from above. Cillian and Blyana had taken the left side of the carriage. Cillian's hands were outstretched, each wielding a blade that was an extension of himself. Their deadly points sailed through the air, carried by the power he wielded, only to disappear into the flesh of a raider and return once again to his outstretched palm.

Blyana was a force of beautiful terror. Flickers of light danced across the bloodied blades she wielded like musical instruments to sing a ballad of death. They found flesh with ease, leaving a trail of blood in its wake. Like an artist, she painted the forest crimson.

Isolde turned back to the caravan and her eyes widened. A beast of a man, one covered in filthy strips of cloth, had broken through and ripped the door to the carriage open. It slammed into the frame, causing a crack to run down its finely painted surface. From within, Isolde could see Nan and the look of terror on her face. It shone from the depths of her blue eyes…from Kamden's eyes.

"Nan!" Isolde's voice cut through the air and the blade in her hand followed.

A second later, a satisfying, wet thud penetrated the chaos, and the man fell to the ground, his foot resting on the top step. Isolde leapt from Versa's saddle and yanked the blade free from the back of his neck. Streaks of red stood stark against the pale blue hue of her fine travel dress as another attacker stepped forward.

A long, curved blade was clutched in his hands. The pungent stench of body odor filled Isolde's nose, causing bile to rise in her throat. He swung wide, oblivious to the danger he now faced. Ducking the blow, Isolde stooped low and drove the tip of her dagger just above the buckle of his belt. She felt his body tense beneath her touch, and a shuddered breath cleaved from his chest.

Jerking to the side, Isolde wrenched the blade free in a wide, unforgiven arch. The contents of his abdomen spilled out onto the ground, sloshing against the side of her boots with a wet slap.

"You could have spared the boots," Isolde grumbled in annoyance to the hollowed-out man at her feet.

Leaning into the carriage, she took in the drops of blood disappearing into the wrinkles of Nan's face. "Are you—"

"I'm alright, my rose," Nan said, her voice strained and shaking. Guilt and regret hammered against Isolde's skull at the sight. "It's not mine. I'm fine, I promise."

Isolde's eyes snagged on something small and sharp clutched in Nan's withered hands. "Good thing I was hungry." A small carving knife glistened in her grasp. Juice from the apple, now covered in dirt and blood, dripped from the edge.

"I think you had things under control," Isolde said, nodding to the blade. A roar of pain ripped through the air. The very sound piercing her heart like an arrow.

Through a break in the carnage unfolding, Isolde spotted a familiar figure sink to his knees. A bloom of red stretched across his right hip and spread down the length of his britches and up into his sweat-soaked tunic. An axe sat just out of reach, its blade glistening in a bed of trampled grass.

Another loomed above him. Their lithe frame was covered in strips of cloth and leather. Horror filled Isolde as the tip of the curved blade they carried rose to hover over his heart.

"Malaki!"

CHAPTER 6

Fear, cold and all-consuming, spread through Isolde. It filled her with every impossibility reality was threatening to make true. A vision of the blade piercing Malaki's chest shot through her mind and pierced her heart. She couldn't survive it. Couldn't endure to live in a world where Malaki…simply didn't.

"No…no…no!"

But the blade didn't move.

The slender fingers of the raider shook around the pommel. Their eyes bored into Malaki, wide and terrified. Even from where Isolde stood frozen, petrified with fear, she could see the hesitation.

Malaki, the last person Isolde expected to hesitate in the face of death, was still. Not a single shred of his attention was gifted to anyone or anything else…but the creature before him. Strips of cloth swept across the mask, shrouding the lower half of their face.

His lips pulled into a sneer she knew well. The raider's eyes widened, and the mask moved ever so slightly, hinting at a smile beneath. Their head tilted to the side as if in thoughtful curiosity. A sliver of deeply tanned skin peaked out from beneath.

The blade fell to rest at their side and the foot pressing into Malaki's chest, keeping him down, pulled away. They stared at one another, neither wanting to be the first to break away. With a heavy sigh, Malaki's head fell back to the ground, breaking their connection. The sound of a whistle, dulled by the mask covering the raider's face, pierced the air.

Isolde hardly noticed the remaining raiders as they disappear into the woods. A few remained behind. Either already dead or well on their way to following them into the afterlife. The clothed ghost lingering over Malaki cast him one final glance before turning on their heel and sprinting through the trees.

Fear and rage melted into one, propelling Isolde through the fray. Raider after raider stepped into her path, either to attack or escape. All fell dead at her feet, either by the touch of her blade or a whip of air snapping their necks.

She came to a stop at Malaki's side, her head shaking. "Oh, my gods." A wound ran down the side of Malaki's hip and across his right thigh. It was deep and held the same iridescent glow hers had possessed. Isolde's blood went cold.

"Malaki!" His name fell in a gasp of horror. Her knees gave out, driving her to the bloodied ground at his side, saturating her dress. Immediately, her hands pressed into his warm, mutilated flesh, willing the pieces to close. He roared in pain and the sound cleaved her heart in two.

"Nan!" She screamed, tears stinging her eyes. "Nan! I need the antidote now!"

"Tell me that isn't yours," he said, eyes darting to the blood covering Isolde's dress. His voice was a hollowed rasp, sharpened with pain.

"Most of it's going to be yours if you don't keep still," she said, pressing harder against the steady stream of blood beneath her palms. A cry lifted from Malaki's lips and Isolde felt a tear titter on the brink of falling. A glimmer of stark white bone glistened from around a wall of muscle at the edge of her hand. Her fingers shook over his far too pale skin.

Not him. She thought. *Please, not him!*

"Isolde!" Liam's voice pierced the fog of desperation suffocating her breath by breath.

She twisted to see him drive the tip of his blade through the heart of raider at her back. One she hadn't even noticed.

"Help him!" she gasped. Tears of fear and desperate anger hung at the edges of her eyes. "Please…please help him!"

Shoving the dead man away, Liam dropped to her side. The heavy pants leaving his chest stilled and his eyes widened. "Oh, shit!"

"Help him!" Isolde cried, taking his hands in her own. She forced them to Malaki's body, pushing them together to make the torn pieces of flesh whole again. "Please, Liam!"

Liam's gaze swept to Malaki, unsure if his former friend would welcome his help, even at the brink of death. But Malaki's eyes were squeezed shut, his teeth bared against the waves of agony that were undoubtedly burning through his body. Needing no further confirmation, Liam licked his lips and turned his attention back to the task at hand.

"Helurtu," Malaki said, through pants. "It was Helurtu." He raised a finger slick with blood to the trees on his right.

Isolde scanned the forest until she caught a glimpse of a retreating figure. They were nothing but a speck of light in the forest, there one moment and gone the next. Without thinking, Isolde reached forward and snagged Malaki's axe from where it lay at his side. The blood-covered blade winked back at her, its edge smiling with a vengeful promise.

"Where are you going?" Liam asked. The blood flow had begun to cease but not entirely. With the elithrium present, there was only one thing that would help him now. Out of the corner of her eye, Isolde saw Nan approaching, her hands filled with the ingredients needed for the antidote.

"To stab that bitch in the face," Isolde growled.

"Don't even think about it," Liam said, his teeth gritting, war raging in his gaze.

"I never do." The weight of the axe settled into her grip. "And don't boss me around."

"Isolde," Liam growled, raising a hand to reach for her. But a cry of pain slipped past Malaki's lips, forcing Liam's attention back down on the gaping wound beneath his palms. A fresh stream of blood seeped through Liam's fingers, soaking Malaki's further.

"Don't you dare leave him, Liam!" Isolde said, her voice cold and filled with the promise of death.

"Isolde, no!" Malaki moaned, trying and failing to sit up. The tips of his fingers grazed the back of her hand as she slipped just beyond his reach. Streaks of his blood painted her skin, stoking that furious anger even more.

"Keep pressure, Liam," Nan said, as she dropped to Malaki's side, her hands already busy working on the antidote.

"I forbid you to die," Isolde said before taking off into the shadow of the forest, leaving behind the sound of Malaki's panic and pain.

Isolde sprinted through Blackford. Bloodlust encased her mind, consuming every sense, every part of her sanity. Malaki's blood, hot and wet, coated her hands. It drove a wedge of fear into her heart, a fear so potent she could almost taste it on her tongue. The axe, which normally felt cumbersome and heavy, was light in her grip, as if it too wanted revenge.

The trees seemed to move on their own as she pushed forward. Branches that once stood in her path drifted to the side, giving her a wide berth.

The unmistakable scent of Malaki's blood filled the air. Every step her prey took was another bread crumb left behind. Pieces of blood-soaked clothes caressed everything they passed. The bushes, the trees, the air itself guided Isolde forward. Before long, the sound of retreating footsteps reached her ears. The beast within smiled, its fangs bared.

A snarl ripped through Isolde's teeth, and she veered south. A few seconds later, she caught sight of them. Rays of sunlight danced over the hooded figure darting between the bellies of oaks and maple trees.

They were fast but...not fast enough.

As they cleared the tree line, entering a small glen, Isolde thrust her right hand forward. Her mother's ring hummed with power, and a gust of wind shot out.

It collided with Helurtu's back, sending them sprawling face-first into the dirt. Isolde broke through the trees and brought the axe overhead. A savage glee filled her veins as her muscles tensed. Helurtu turned just in time to see the axe's unforgiving edge and rolled to the side, narrowly avoiding a blow that would have severed them in two.

The impact split the earth with a thud, sending waves of painful vibrations up Isolde's hands and arms. The heel of Helurtu's boot slammed into her ribcage on the right, forcing a breath of air from Isolde's lungs. Agony erupted along her side, ripping a grunt of irritation through her clenched teeth.

Bitch.

A growl rolled over Isolde's tongue as she wrenched the axe free, the worn wood groaning. Drawing her shoulders back, Isolde took in the hooded raider before her.

The top of their head, covered in strips of cloth both new and old, ended where Isolde's shoulders began. Pits of blackest night filled their piercing, hate-filled eyes. But the skin around them held a beautiful, deep tan hue. A look only someone who was kissed by the sun itself would possess. The mask covering their face was made of worn, brown leather stressed from overuse, with small deposits of salt sprinkling its surface.

"Helurtu, I presume," Isolde greeted with a sarcastic wave of her hand. "It's a relief to put a face with the name…or a partial face I suppose."

Only the slightest narrowing of those obsidian eyes answered back. Isolde wasn't sure if it was out of fear…or if they were simply waiting to strike. She had a suspicion it was the latter.

"Tell me," Isolde said, a cocky grin pulling at her lips. "Where might I find such a cloak? I've never seen garments such as these."

Truly, Isolde found the coat to be rather odd. Odd but unique. It was constructed of many strands of various kinds of leather and cloth forming one singular piece ending at the waist. A pair of worn britches disappeared into a pair of knee-high leather boots, the likes of which had seen better days.

"I must know before I kill you." Isolde's voice was sweet but sharp as a blade. "Would be a shame to take such a secret to your very early, very shallow grave."

"Do you always talk this much?" Soft undertones coated their words, along with a flair of annoyance Isolde could only smile at. One that only a woman could possess.

"It does speak," Isolde said. "Or she speaks, I should say. And yes, I do." A smug, vicious smile pulled at her lips. "Providing riveting conversation is one of my finer qualities."

"What are your others?" Helurtu asked, her fingers flexing around the hilt of the long, curved blade at her side. "Playing the part of a pretty little doll, hosting parties, and living off the backs of others?"

"Well, I don't know about being a doll, but I am known to be rather beautiful," Isolde said, waving a hand about her face in a flourish while the other clung to Malaki's axe, her anger burning brighter. "And I do throw one hell of a party. But taking from others, I believe that's your job."

"I only take from those who take from the less fortunate. From rich pricks like you and that asshole uncle of yours who force people into servitude."

Cold malice flashed in Isolde's eyes. "The Lord of Thornwood has never stolen anything," she said, her tone laced with a bite. "Nor does our house force anyone to stay who does not wish to be there. We are not the same. Don't you dare paint us as such."

"Strike a nerve, did I?" A humorless chuckle bled through Helurtu's mask. "You're all the same. Spoiled, selfish parasites living off the lives of humans and half-bloods. You are no different than the bastard who sits on the throne and calls himself king."

"And by attacking caravans of innocent people," Isolde said, taking a step to the right, "how are you any different than they are?"

Helurtu matched her step for step. The strange yet beautiful blade glistened in her hands. Dark, ruby stains of blood coated its edge, muting the elithrium's glow. Helurtu's grip was relaxed, casual even, as if there weren't a true threat present at all.

Isolde's eyes narrowed at her ease. *Cocky bitch.*

"I'm not," Helurtu said, raising the sword in front of her. The curved tip stared back at Isolde, the sun dancing across the sharp edge. "I'm merely leveling the playing field."

"Well, don't let me keep you," Isolde said, spreading her arms wide. "Get on with it then."

Helurtu shot forward, and their blades met midair. The shock of the blow forced Isolde back a pace. Sharp pain radiated down her left side as she shoved back, driving Helurtu towards the tree line.

They danced around each other. Step matched for step, blow

matched for blow. Blades of grass crunched beneath their feet. Tiny rivers of blood snaked their way through the layers of cloth covering Helurtu's arms with every kiss of Malaki's axe. Overstepping a strike, Isolde felt the fresh sting of a cut as the tip of the curved blade kissed the back of her thigh.

Before long, Isolde's arms began to grow tired. Her power clawed at her control, demanding to be released. But she shoved the thought away, causing her to lose focus for just a moment.

But a moment was more than enough.

Isolde's grip loosened, sending a bolt of panic through her chest. One well-placed strike by Helurtu sent Malaki's beloved weapon, flying into the trees, where it embedded into the body of an oak.

Isolde didn't hesitate. She yanked the blade at her hip free from the sheath, sending a faint whine echoing through the clearing like a death bell.

"That's cute," Helurtu said, her voice dripping in disdain. "But I suppose it was too much for you to stick to one weapon. Not that I expected any less from someone like you."

"Someone like me?"

"Yes," Helurtu sneered. "Someone who always gets what they want. Someone who always has the means to win. No matter the cost."

"Come now," Isolde said, her chest heaving, side burning. "We both know you're not a beacon of fairness or one who plays by the rules. It's one of the things we have in common. But by all means, don't start holding back on my account."

The edges of Helurtu's eyes crinkled, the hint of a smile peeking out from beneath the mask. "As you wish, *my lady*."

Isolde moved like the wind itself. She dodged every blow Helurtu threw her way, scooting away each time she came near. The edge of her blade tried and failed with each jab to touch Isolde's skin again. But one thrust had the tip of the sword disappearing into the lining of

Isolde's gown.

Helurtu ripped the blade free, taking the fabric along with it. The kiss of a breeze touched the scar at Isolde's side and caressed the ones lingering on her back, filling her with furious panic. Her anger only grew at the small gasp echoing around them. Helurtu's eyes burned into her maimed skin, her dark gaze flickering to Isolde's flushed face and back down again. No pity filled her eyes, only morbid curiosity.

"Impressive," she said, with a shrug of indifference. "Not an accessory I would expect from a wealthy bitch like you."

"Don't go soft on me now," Isolde said, striding forward, fighting the disgust and shame snaking its way across her skin. "Mercy does not become you."

Sweat glistened at the corner of Helurtu's mask, and heavy breaths came from beneath with every strike she landed against Isolde's dagger. And as she turned, Helurtu's eyes squinting into the rays of the sun that had managed to break through the canopy, Isolde saw her opening. Throwing all her weight and fury into the blow, Isolde drove her elbow into Helurtu's stomach.

A cruel smile spread across her face at the sound of the breathless gasp of pain escaping the leather mask's confinement. Helurtu doubled over, clutching her abdomen.

"This dress was a favorite of mine," Isolde said, driving her fist clutching the blade into the bridge of Helurtu's nose. The unmistakable sound of shattering bone drew a smile to Isolde's face.

Streams of tears flooded her hooded eyes, making it impossible for Helurtu to see Isolde drop to the ground and sweep her leg out over the forest floor. A second later, Helurtu's back slammed into the ground, leaving her gasping for air.

Isolde wasted no time in kicking the blade free from her grip, snapping the bones of her wrist for good measure. A cry, barely contained through Helurtu's gritted teeth filled the air.

"That mask looks awfully stifling," said Isolde, straddling Helurtu's hips to hold her in place. "Allow me."

Her merciless fingers gripped the mask and hood on Helurtu's head and ripped it free. A mess of startling white braids and long whips of hair spilled around them. A bed of snow cushioned her head against the vibrant green, luscious grass. A touch of winter in the heart of spring.

A ping of jealousy at the girl's beauty nestled into Isolde's chest. At the flawless skin and eyes pure as night. Even covered in blood and nose shattered, it was impossible to deny Helurtu's beauty. A thin layer of frost began to form over Helurtu's skin and Isolde pressed the blade to her throat.

"An ice wielder?" Isolde murmured. "You're just full of surprises, aren't you? Why didn't you use your powers?"

"I won't use magic to kill you," she said with a sneer. Bits of frost crept up her neck and onto Isolde's blade. Tiny crystals, beautiful and shimmering, worked their way up the dagger. "I want to kill you with my bare hands."

"Well, you seem to be doing a fine job so far. For someone who claims to be the Hood, you're quite the disappointment."

Helurtu thrashed against Isolde's hold. Her hands broke free of their cage and rose to lock around Isolde's throat. A well of power rushed forward and drew out every bit of air lingering in Helurtu's chest.

Panicked and gasping for air, Helurtu fell back to the ground, her fingers prying at her throat, mouth gaping open. After a moment, Isolde released her hold, granting her only enough air to keep from fainting.

"How does it feel?" Isolde asked, pressing the blade further, her fury burning.

"How...how does what f-feel?" Helurtu gasped.

A cold, wicked smile pulled onto Isolde's lips. "Knowing that my face will be the last thing you see before you die. What a sight."

For the briefest of seconds, Helurtu saw her death and looked terrified. But the fear soon vanished as quickly as it came, giving way to the anger dwelling within. Anger and resignation.

The first layer of skin split, sending a drop of blood spilling across Helurtu's throat. The sight froze Isolde in place. A shadow, like the soft caress of a summer night, brushed the corners of her mind. It softened the bloodlust, the insatiable need for vengeance burning through her veins.

The blade remained unmoving yet unwilling to spill another drop of blood, as if the very thought of Helurtu's death would cause a pain she could not bear. And not just her…but someone else as well.

A thought, one that Isolde couldn't entirely claim as her own, entered her mind.

"You don't kill the humans," she said. "Or the half-bloods. Tell me why."

"They're innocent," Helurtu answered in a wheezy gasp.

A sense or feeling seemed to take control, one Isolde couldn't explain—one she didn't understand. She looked down at Helurtu. At the woman who, given the right circumstances, could have been Isolde herself.

She was a monster, a killer, that much was certain.

But so am I.

Isolde looked into her eyes and saw nothing but the truth staring back. A mirror image of the same ferocity living within herself.

"Indeed, they are," said Isolde, grip on the blade still firm. "But so are a lot of people you've killed."

"Guilty by association."

"If we lived by those rules, we would all be dead." Isolde released the grip on her power, allowing more air to flow into Helurtu's lungs.

"But I understand your anger."

"You're the heir to Thornwood," Helurtu spat. "A spoiled bitch who was born with so much silver cutlery up her ass, I'd wager you glistened in the sun. What could you know of such things?"

"More than you think," said Isolde. "And it was gold, not silver."

Off in the distance, the sound of footsteps echoed through the trees. Helurtu followed Isolde's gaze, jaw clenching tight. The blade still pressed to her throat bobbed as she swallowed against its edge.

"What are you waiting for?" Helurtu asked, her teeth bared. "Kill me!"

Malaki filled Isolde's mind. The sight of the wound burned in her head like wildfire. She felt the bloodlust return, the desire to slit Helurtu's throat from side to side roared back to life.

Yet as she pressed the blade to Helurtu's skin once more, that same shadow returned. It felt unworldly, like a presence that did and did not belong. It cradled her mind like dark tendrils of night slipping between the trees of the forest. A darkness lingering on the brink of absolution and destruction. The faintest pressure ghosted across her hand clutching the dagger, holding it in place. Two words filled her head, soothing away the need for death that was burning through her veins.

Spare her.

It was a request, a plea for mercy that held such weight it was one Isolde could not ignore even if she wanted to.

"My conscience is already burdened enough as it is." A shaky breath fell from Isolde's lips. "I don't need your death adding to the weight. You spared him when you could have chosen differently. I owe you a life." She couldn't tell Helurtu the truth. Isolde wasn't even sure what the truth was other than what she felt deep within her heart.

Helurtu had to live.

Forcing her knees to straighten, Isolde rose and took a few steps back. Slowly, she reined in the power, allowing Helurtu to sit up and breathe freely.

Her dark eyes softened. They held a hint of confusion Isolde couldn't even begin to understand herself. Nor did she have the time to even attempt it. "We are not enemies, Helurtu," Isolde continued. "I believe in what you're doing. But your methods leave much to be desired."

"And who are you to lecture me?" she demanded, rising to her feet. "A little princess who has had everything given to her. No hardships, no troubles apart from spilling a bit of tea on your fine dress. What could you possibly know?"

"Isolde!" Liam's voice cut through the air like a clap of thunder.

"I know you want justice," Isolde said, her eyes darting to the tree line "We're on the same side of the board in that regard. We just find ourselves playing from a different set of rules. But we both want the same thing."

Helurtu looked down her bloody, misshapen nose. "And what's that?"

"A better world."

Wisps of snowy white hair danced before Helurtu's eyes that had lost a facet of their hardness. Their gaze, once harboring such hostility, now seemed softer...curious, even.

"A better world?"

Isolde nodded. "A world where the dream of peace doesn't remain a dream, and hope isn't a fairytale parents whisper to their children at night."

Liam's footsteps echoed through the clearing. It wouldn't be long before he burst through the trees and there would be no stopping him then.

"Go," Isolde ordered. Blatant disbelief and distrust painted Helurtu's face as she took a tentative step back.

"I still don't understand!" Helurtu demanded. "I nearly killed one of your men," her feet shifted uncomfortably. "I might have." A flicker of worry danced across her face. It was there one moment, then gone the next.

"You didn't," Isolde said, with a smug grin. "It'll take far more than the likes of you to kill him."

Helurtu's eyes narrowed at the insult. "Still...he's one of yours. I would not have shown you such a mercy."

"Like I said. You had the opportunity to kill someone I care about. Someone I love. Instead, you showed him mercy. This is me returning the favor," said Isolde. "Besides, I'd wager living with the knowledge that a pampered, cake eating bitch with a golden asshole bested you, would be a far worse fate."

Heat filled Helurtu's gaze as a wild, savage grin spread across her face. "This isn't over."

Isolde saw she meant it, saw the slight sparkle of challenge in her eyes. A smile of violent excitement crept onto Isolde's face. "I would be disappointed to have it any other way." Helurtu turned to leave, the ends of her braids and loose strands brushing the small of her back. "What of your dead?" Helurtu paused and a look of sadness found its way to her face. "We can bury them with our own if you—"

"Leave them." Her voice low and chiseled from stone. "There are no rituals, no burials for us. All that remains is an empty shell. Not who we really are."

"I'll make sure they are treated with respect," Isolde promised.

Helurtu nodded and the hint of a smile tugged at her lips. "Next time, I won't take it easy on you. Next time, you die, bitch." Without another word, Helurtu disappeared into the shadows of Blackford Forest with the promise of death hanging in the air.

"Looking forward to it," Isolde said a moment before Liam burst through the tree line and the last flicker of white, silvery hair disappeared into a sea of green.

"Isolde!" Liam's hands slid up the sides of her neck to cradle her face. "Are you alright?" Dried blood, Malaki's blood, covered his palms and wrists. His eyes, bright and burning panic, roved over every inch of her.

"Of course, I am," Isolde said, wrapping her fingers around his wrists, holding him in place. "You honestly think a fake Hood could defeat me?"

She felt the sigh of relief swell in his chest, slowing the rapid heartbeat beneath. "Never," he breathed, planting a kiss in her hair. The tips of her fingers dug into his back, and her head pressed into the crook of his shoulder. Warmth spread through her as the adrenaline coursing through her veins began to slowly die away.

"Is Malaki alright?"

"He'll live," Liam said, his voice rough. "After Nan applied the antidote, I was able to seal off the wound. But just barely. He's a far better healer than I could ever dream of being. But he'll need time to heal. He's on mandatory bedrest until Nan says otherwise. Along with several other men. Nan and Galaena are already making arrangements to set up camp for the next few days at least."

"I'm sure he's thrilled with that." She needed to see him. To see with her own eyes that he was indeed alive before she could release the ball of anxiety pressing into her chest. "Let's head back."

"Wait," Liam said, his eyes fixed on the gaping hole at her side. "Your dress is torn."

She felt the brush of Liam's fingers at her side, their path running along the skin so close to the scar ravaging her flesh. The same panic as before roared to life.

"Stop, Liam," Isolde said, her chest tightening. "I told you, I'm fine!" But it was too late. Liam's hand froze, his throat bobbing. The pad of his hand rested over the newly formed scar. The delicate tissue stung slightly at the breath of his touch.

The dark eyes she knew so well grew wide, their gaze fixed and filled with horrified disbelief. "Isolde…" His fingers trailed along the ridges of the jagged crevasse. "What…what—?"

Isolde shoved his hand away and pulled the edge of the dress tightly around her. "A little parting present from Gage that night at Briarhole."

Liam remained frozen before her. "Gage, did *this*?" Light, bright and churning with rage, filled his eyes that couldn't seem to break away from her side.

"Yes. I got distracted and…paid the price for it."

"I've never known you to get distracted, especially while fighting," said Liam. "How?"

Isolde couldn't bring herself to look at him. "I heard the children crying, screaming for help. I…I looked away for just a moment and…"

She felt his eyes on her face, felt their touch like a brand. Still, she couldn't meet his gaze, could not stand the look of pity that was undoubtedly there.

The tips of Liam's fingers grazed the back of her hand clutched to her side. "Isolde—" She flinched from his touch, her fingers tightening on the ruined fabric. "Isolde." Her name fell from his lips in a growl. A sound both furious and horrified.

"Just go!" she said, shoving his hand away. Isolde turned to the tree line, her eyes swimming as she tugged the garment around her tighter. Off in the distance, she heard a pair of footsteps coming their way. Ones she would know anywhere, and the last thing she needed was for them to see her like this.

"Please." The softness of Liam's voice penetrated her defenses, allowing every ounce of disgust and pain she felt for herself to leak through.

"I said go!" Authority and anger laced every word. "They need you back at the camp. Far more than I do right now."

A stinging silence hung between them. It felt thick as iron and just as cold. Without another word, Liam dropped his outstretched hand and disappeared into the forest. Isolde forced a shaky sigh through her lips, willing the tears away.

How could he possibly desire you now? The same terrible voice filled Isolde's mind as she fought to keep it at bay. *Hideous ... deformed ... scarred ... monster.*

Blyana and Cillian raced into the clearing, yanking Isolde free from the well of despair. Forcing the lump in her throat down, Isolde plastered a smug, convincing smile onto her face despite the war of emotions raging in her heart.

"Now we know for sure who is the most beautiful," Isolde said, pointing to the cut streaking down Cillian's right eye, severing his brow in half. A faint sheen glistened around its edges and a trail of blood trickled down his cheek.

"Thank you, Lady Isolde." A grin, unrestrained and handsome, filled Cillian's bloody face. "I'm so glad you've come to terms with that fact. It's difficult being the best looking in Thornwood, but it is a burden I am willing to bear." Scars were of little consequence to him. Something Isolde appreciated in him.

The first time he had laid eyes on the scars decorating Isolde's body, Cillian had simply nodded and removed his shirt to reveal the marred flesh lying beneath. Anger-filled tears had threatened to spill across Isolde's cheeks at the sight.

"Give me a name." It was a demand, one Isolde wished he had obeyed. "Tell me who hurt you, Cillian."

"Don't waste tears or fill your heart with anger for something that cannot be undone, Isolde," Cillian had said, his eyes falling to the reminders of his past. "They can't hurt me anymore. Now, they serve as a reminder of what I never want to be."

Blyana's sharp gaze lingered on the point in the tree line Helurtu had disappeared through. "Was it truly him?" she asked, pulling Isolde back to the present. "Was it Helurtu?"

"Well, he is a *she*," Isolde corrected, walking over to retrieve Malaki's axe from where it rested in the belly of the oak. "And yes, it was."

"She?" Cillian said, his gaze following Blyana's.

"Don't sound so surprised," Isolde said, playfully nudging him with her shoulder as she passed.

"What is it with you women and your insatiable need to wear a mask and cause mayhem?" Cillian mumbled.

"You like it when we cause mayhem," Blyana said with a smile. "Don't lie."

Cillian opened his mouth to retort but stopped dead in his tracks. His gaze was locked onto Helurtu's blade where it rested in the grass at his feet. He stared as if he couldn't pull himself away, like it had captured him. Mind…body…and soul. A tremor worked its way up his hand and into his arm until Cillian's whole frame was shaking. Carefully, he wrapped his fingers around the pommel and held it before him.

"Cill?" Isolde said.

Cillian continued to stare at the wide face of the blood-encrusted blade. It was decorated in a strange language Isolde had never seen before. He had the look of a man struck with horror, a man who was experiencing a nightmare coming true before his very eyes.

Blyana was at his side in an instant. "Cillian," she said, her voice like a breath of wind, a soft, gentle caress. Cautiously, she laid a hand over her mate's cheek.

After a moment, Cillian cleared his throat. "It's nothing," he said at last shaking himself free. The lean cords of muscle running up the length of his arm, disappearing beneath his sleeves, flexed as his grip on the blade tightened.

"Don't do that," Blyana said. "I don't hide from you; don't hide from me." He looked away from the blade to stare at her, his throat bobbing.

"You've seen this kind of blade before haven't you, Cill?" Isolde asked.

He turned his gaze to Isolde. "Yes," Cillian said, his voice a hollow whisper.

"Where?" she asked.

Isolde had never pressed Cillian about his past, had never asked for more than what he was willing to give. He had been a poor, desperate man the day he snuck into Thornwood manor. It had been clear to Isolde, even then, that Cillian was running from something. A force had driven him into Blackford Forest in the dead of winter, barefoot and covered in nothing but scraps of clothes and scars.

"From my homeland," he said at last, a muscle feathering in his jaw. A crease formed on his brow, causing a bead of blood to fall from the cut that was now a permanent addition to his face.

A fire burned within Cillian's gaze as the words fell like a curse. "The Forgotten Lands…from Endurmure."

CHAPTER 7

The pain in Malaki's side hadn't registered at all as he gazed into orbs of purest night. An eternity lay in their depths—fierce and terrifyingly beautiful.

The mutinous strands of hair, white as purest snow, drifted over her hooded eyes in the afternoon breeze. Sunlight brimmed the hood concealing her face. It framed her figure in the most alluring…infuriating way possible. It had only been a week or so since the attack and still she infected his mind.

Helurtu was his enemy, his adversary in every way. But even as the blade in her hand hovered over his heart, Malaki felt something stir. A part of him, the very essence of who he was, reached out. A piece of himself that had never awoken before suddenly turned its head and stilled in her presence.

"Do it," he had said, his voice laced with fury, pain rippling through his body. "Do it, you coward!"

Helurtu had remained still, her eyes unnervingly focused and enchanting. "Why are you so eager for death?" she had asked. Even her voice filled his spirit, shattering through barrier after barrier. Leaving him bare and raw.

"Why are you so unwilling to give it?" he shot back, the fringes of his vision blurring. "You were more than happy to earlier."

The hint of a smile peeked from beneath the makeshift mask up into the corners of her eyes that had burned their way into his soul. "Perhaps, I like to play with my food a little more before I eat them."

Pain ripped through Malaki's side as Nan applied another dose of the antidote to the wound, yanking him back into the present. A good amount of elithrium had come out easily, leaving behind only a trace of black residue in its wake.

A growl rumbled through his lips.

I'm going to kill that bitch.

"Come now, Malaki," Nan said, her warm, stern voice carrying over the steady noise of the surrounding camp. The echoes of moans and piercing cries of agony filled the air around him. "Even Isolde didn't make this much fuss."

"Isolde was blissfully unconscious for most of it," he said. His words worked their way through gritted teeth. The tips of his fingers inched toward the wound, needing to do something, anything to relieve the pain.

"Yes, and she was beaten to a pulp with far worse wounds than yours," said Nan, smacking his hand away. "Stop fidgeting!"

"That hurts!" he said, his voice louder than he had intended.

"Stop being such a baby," Isolde said from where she lounged in the corner of the tent. "You're supposed to be my second-in-command. I do have a reputation to maintain."

"Your reputation is the least of my concerns at the moment," Malaki said, shoving the roaring beast that lingered at the edges of his mind back into its cage.

Cillian's laugh came from the opposite side of the tent, the one housing the wine. "Yes, he has far more pressing matters to concern himself with at the moment. Like the rumors of him being bested by a vigilante…a female vigilante no less."

"I feel quite certain you would have fared no better," Blyana said, her eyes hard on her mate, who only cast her a grin over the rim of his glass. "And you certainly would make more of a fuss than Malaki. We both know your pain tolerance is laughable." Her gaze, full of concern, landed on the hideous wound grinning up at her from his thigh and hip.

"I'm fine, Bly," Malaki said, forcing a smile onto his face. A smile he hoped would pacify her. She had been to his tent every day, fussing just as much as Nan and Isolde like an annoying sister he loved deeply. But the bead of sweat rolling down his face didn't go unnoticed, and her gaze narrowed.

"Liar," she growled back.

"Never claimed to not be one," Malaki said. He braced for the pain that followed as Nan placed a clean bandage over the wound.

"I can't believe you let her live," Cillian said, his eyes shifting to Isolde. "How very un-Hood of you."

Isolde's gaze snapped to Malaki. She had explained her reasoning earlier, before the others had arrived. "She spared you," she had said. "I owed her a life."

A life was spared; a life was given. It was one of the things he loved about Isolde. Her ability to show mercy, even in the darkest of times. Still, as the wound sang with agony, Malaki wished she had left something a little more permanent than wounded pride.

"I can't be predictable all the time, Cill. Where's the fun in that?" She crossed her legs and leaned back into the chair. "Just like I can't be seen striding into Elenarta with a second-in-command in your state." Her attention shifted back to Malaki. A freshly baked, pastry lingered on the edges of her fingertips. Yet it remained whole. A telltale sign, Malaki knew, Isolde was worried. If food didn't cross her lips, something was wrong.

"Funny, I don't recall treating you in such a way. Seems I have a far better bedside manner than you."

Isolde's brow quirked. "Since when have you ever known me to be gentle…or comforting?"

Malaki huffed a reply as Nan removed the last bit of the black-tinged, pink mess away. "There," she said, depositing the soiled cloth into the basin on the floor. "It shouldn't be much longer. Now, you just need to rest."

Malaki's mouth set with a grimace as he took in the freshly cleaned wound. "It's only been a week, Malaki. It'll take time," she said, reading the look of irritation on his face. Despite the wound appearing just as hideous as it did before, he supposed he was lucky. If Nan, gods forbid Liam, hadn't been there…

"Let Liam help," said Isolde, as if reading his mind. "He can at least heal it enough to close it."

Malaki's head jerked around to face her, forcing a wince of pain from his usually stoic expression. It wasn't the first time they had had this argument. Nor would it be the last. "No."

"You're such an ass." Isolde's lips pulled into a thin, stubborn line. Her eyes, eyes he had known for decades, glowed back in irritation.

"Takes one to know one, *Lady Isolde*," he shot back. Fire burned through his side as he turned back to rest on the pillow.

Isolde's voice flittered through the air, her tone filled with mocking sweetness. "I could command you."

It was an empty threat. One Isolde always gave when she didn't get her way with something.

"I'm quivering with fear," he muttered back, eyes rolling. Nan stood and made to drape a blanket over his lower half. The pressure of the thin, cotton sheet drifted over the cut, forcing a hiss from his lips.

"Please, Malaki." There was no jesting, no hint of mockery left in Isolde's voice. Now only concern remained. He could feel her eyes on him, sensing the worry that came with it. "Liam can—"

"I said no, Isolde!" His voice rang through the tent with an air of finality. Nan's hands went still, the water dripping from her fingertips. "All I need is to rest, and so do you. I will hear no more of this!"

Isolde was quiet for a moment, her eyes lingering on the tips of her boots. It wouldn't last. He knew it wouldn't. Tossing the uneaten pastry back onto the tray, Isolde rose to her feet, her eyes brimming with fury and hurt. "I'm perfectly well," she said, her voice laced with steel as she rose to her feet. "Which is more than I can say for you."

She ripped the tent's flap aside and disappeared into the setting sun. Her scent lingered in the air, roses, the forest, and just the hint of ember. Cillian and Blyana followed behind without a word. Malaki shook his head, his thumb and forefinger pinching the bridge of his nose.

"Be patient," Nan said, still posed on the edge of the stool at his side. "She joshes, but she was terrified for you. We all were."

"I know she's worried, Nan," said Malaki. "But I wish she wouldn't be. I am not worthy of that kind of devotion or love. She had no business going after Helurtu—placing herself in danger needlessly." He shook his head, causing strands of sweat-slick hair to fall across his brow. "She does that enough already."

"Why would you think that, Malaki?" Nan asked, her eyes shining with concern that had his heart twisting.

"Because I failed her." It was a fact, a cold, hard truth to his reality. The pain of that failure scorched through him like fire. "And for her to risk her life by going after that bitch for my sake—"

"Watch your mouth," said Nan, her eyes hard as sapphires.

"Forgive me," he said, a blushing painting his cheeks. "But she shouldn't have done that. Her life is far more valuable than mine."

Nan's warm, withered fingers gripped Malaki's hand with a fierceness that startled him. The other came to cup his stubble-peppered chin, forcing him to look up. "You listen to me very closely, Malaki." Her eyes were so serious, so piercingly focused he felt like a child beneath their gaze.

"You did not fail Isolde. What happened all those years ago..." Nan's hand shook, and her eyes swam with memory and sorrow. "It wasn't your fault. You never were and never will be a failure. Not to me, not to anyone else, and especially not to Isolde. Your life is precious. *You* are precious." Nan's grip tightened as she leaned in close. "Do not torture yourself with guilt that doesn't belong to you."

Her words sent fissures snaking their way up the walls of defense he'd placed around his heart. The very walls he had worked so hard to protect. The ones safeguarding every single fault Malaki had placed on himself. Every trespass, every failure. It crumbled beneath her kind words, beneath her warm, loving smile. Or was it someone else who had struck a blow and caused the first crack?

"I just wish she would reserve some of that same worry for herself sometimes. She needs a dose of self-preservation."

"I'm not arguing that fact," said Nan, her hand patting his cheek. "But Isolde is not someone who tends to be too concerned about herself."

Malaki looked to the small slit in the tent's opening to the stream of light cutting through the darkness. "She needs to." He looked back at her, to the eyes that matched the ones of the boy Isolde had loved so long ago. Loved with such a fierceness he marveled at her strength to endure what his death had done to her. Malaki remembered him too. And the memory was like agony.

Teaching Kamden to fight was one of the fondest memories he had. How small he was at the time. The top of his head barely reaching

Malaki's hip when he first held a training sword. The way he looked at Isolde even as a boy, was something he had only seen a handful of times before. It was the way he had looked at Aurora.

Nan nodded. "Perhaps Liam—"

Malaki couldn't fight the growl slipping through his teeth. "I want him nowhere near me…or her."

"Well, he is," said Nan, her mouth suddenly pulling into a tight line, her tone firm and unyielding. "Whether you like it or not, Liam is in Isolde's life. Because she chooses it. Because she wants him there, Malaki."

"You weren't at Briarhole. There was an entire battalion of soldiers he failed to mention. He is the reason we lost Zibiah. Liam is why Isolde bears another scar!"

Nan took a deep breath before dropping her hands into her lap and turning to face him head on. "Be honest with me, and yourself." A look of pity softened her face as she interlaced her fingers on her knees. "Do you truly believe that, Malaki?" A breath caught in his throat, the words refusing to move. "You really believe in your heart that Liam, your friend—"

He opened his mouth to argue but Nan held up her hand to stop him.

"Liam is your friend. He had a horrible choice to make, and he made it for more than just himself. He left Isolde behind because he thought it was the right thing to do for Thornwood, for you, and for Alaric. You remember what happens in those trials. The death, the blood, not knowing if you are going to live from one day to the next. The rules changing on the whim of a man whose heart is cold as ice. Liam endured that for all of us. So, don't tell me he is not your friend. And don't forget," Nan said, her lips quivering and eyes shining, "Kamden loved him too. You trained them together, taught them to fight side by side like brothers. He might as well be my son too."

Malaki kept his mouth clamped shut, his teeth grinding. The weight of Nan's words fell on him like blows, each one weighted down with the truth they possessed. The Tournament of the Guard was nothing short of a bloodbath. One meant to entertain the nobles and keep the territories in line. He shuddered at the memory.

"But aside from that," Nan said, picking up the cloth draped across the side of the bowl. "Do you honestly believe he would betray Isolde and purposefully put her in harm's way?"

Malaki's gaze drifted to the world beyond. Isolde's laughter carried with the warm, evening breeze drifting through the camp. The very sound tempered his anger, easing the war raging in his chest. Every part of him wanted to say yes, that Liam would do anything to make Isolde see reason—*his* reason.

But memories of Liam and Kamden training together at Thornwood flooded back. Liam was a few years younger than Kamden. A quiet, shy child who had not been wanted. A boy left to the mercies of a world that did not tolerate weakness. Kamden immediately took him under his wing, offering him a place in his and Isolde's world. After a few weeks, the three were inseparable.

The pride Malaki felt when Liam disarmed him for the first time…the way he made a smile blossom on Isolde's face…But it all fell into shadow in the wake of another memory that came forward. One of Liam standing before him and Alaric, no longer a boy, but a man who had chosen a side.

Liam stood at the footsteps of Thornwood, and a soldier's uniform took the place of the humble tunic and trousers he normally wore. The colors of Tenebriath stood in stark contrast to the lovely, pale blue dress Isolde wore that day. The day he left to volunteer as Alaric's champion in the tournament.

"I can never forgive him for joining that bastard," said Malaki. Isolde's laugh echoed through the caravan again. The sound made

Malaki's heart so light, the hint of a smile bloomed at the corners of his mouth. But the smile faded as Liam's trailed along behind it. It was a haunting remembrance of what could have been, a harsh reminder of what once was. "But no, Nan. I don't believe he would intentionally harm her."

The night of Briarhole returned to him. The sight of the second battalion swarming the riverbank as he pushed the humans on, forcing them to paddle harder, his panic rising. Arrow after arrow launched into the air. Galaena had used a tidal wave of water to knock most of them out of the way, but some found their mark. He could still hear the cries when the arrows' heads disappeared into the flesh of those onboard. The haunting warmth of their blood lingered on his skin. Body after body fell into the river, never to be seen again.

"Hood!" Nyla's small, terrified voice had filled the night. The sound buried itself into Malaki's heart as he ran his axe down the back of a virya. His eyes had shot to the tallest tower in Briarhole. The very one he and the others had scaled just months before. He remembered plummeting into a well of blackened fear, of unshakable terror as spears and arrows slammed into the rock as Isolde climbed. And there was nothing he could do to help.

Out of the corner of his eye, Malaki had spotted a small figure push past the humans and virya onboard. Her small face bruised and deformed was focused on Isolde. "Nyla!" he had roared, shoving the dead body away. "Nyla, stop!"

But it was too late. She had plunged into the river headfirst. Without hesitation, Malaki launched into the water after her. As his head sank beneath the surface, the furious hiss of a crocodile and the menacing growl of a mountain lion rippled across the water. His eyes swept the depths of the Lenda River. But only blackened nothingness stared back.

Malaki shook himself free of his nightmares that followed. Of the memories of Isolde's broken, bloody body. Of the feeling of her fleeting heartbeat beneath his palms. He shifted on the cot, sending a wave of pain radiating up his hip and across the broad planes of his thigh.

"Liam might not have meant to cause the damage he did. But that doesn't mean he isn't responsible or that I forgive him, Nan."

Melancholy crept into Nan's face, deepening the worry in her eyes. He hated that look, especially from her. Even as a 256-year-old bastard charity case, he felt Nan was the closest thing to a mother he had ever possessed. The last thing he wanted was to cause her pain.

"There is no exception where Isolde is concerned," Malaki continued. "No boundary that can or will go uncrossed. She's far too important."

"I know she is." Nan's hands absently smoothed out the edges of her dress. "But so are you."

"She needs to see that," he said, pressing forward, completely ignoring her words where he was concerned. His voice dropped so low he thought Nan might not be able to hear. "The Hood cannot continue."

Malaki had never been on board with Isolde's decision to masquerade as the Hood. It went against every oath he had ever made. But he saw the day she had declared her intentions, there was no stopping it. At the time, he thought leaving was his only option. His only way to not see her meet the same fate as so many others he had loved. The night he intended to leave, to disappear into the dark, he had found her in the library. She had been fast asleep with a pair of his favorite boots nestled to her chest. It was the same trick she had used as a child when it was time for him to leave on another mission.

"You can't leave without your boots," she had said, her wide, serious eyes staring up at him. Ringlets of dark brown curls embedded with flames of ruby red framed her face. She couldn't have been older than five at the time. "Your feet will get cold, Malaki."

Her little voice had worked on him then, just as her spirited self-sacrifice did now. She loved her people, that much was certain. It was that small facet of reality keeping him at her side. That and the fact that he loved her.

Loved her just as fiercely as any father loved his daughter…as any brother loved his annoying, little sister…as any friend loved his most trusted companion. There was no option of leaving Isolde's side. There never was, and there never would be.

"She can't keep doing this," he said, pulling himself from the past. "It's going to get her killed."

"There will come a time when Isolde will put down the mask. There will be a day when she will understand, when she will accept the truth." Nan licked her lips, her gaze moving to the flap dancing in the breeze and the world beyond.

"Isolde's time will come. I know it will." A small knowing smile played on Nan's face, deepening the lines framing her mouth and eyes. "Perhaps, it will take my bones being in the ground before that day arrives, but it will. Until then, this is all she can give, and we all need to accept that."

"I know it's all she can give, Nan." Malaki's gaze fell to the names sprawled across his chest. A final resting place inked upon his skin in blackened repentance. A grave of sorts for those who had nothing left, souls without bodies left to bury. "And it is enough. But what will she do when the past cannot be escaped?"

Liam walked through the rows of tents lining the path snaking through Blackford Forest. His mind was scattered, brimming with worry and rage. All he could see was the scar. The horrible mark that both infuriated and terrified him.

She should never have gone. Liam's thoughts raced as he headed in the direction of Isolde's tent. *I should have done more. I should have stopped it!* He could still feel it on his fingers, branding itself into his flesh as if it were his own.

He'd been surprised when she sought him out. Even more so for her reasoning. "I need you to try and heal, Malaki."

A humorless laugh instantly fell from his lips. "I'm not welcome there, Isolde. You know this." He couldn't stop his eyes as they traveled down to her side, to the hideous reminder of that night lingering beneath her tunic.

"I'm not giving him a choice in the matter." Her impossibly beautiful eyes dropped, and her arms knitted across her chest. "He didn't give me one at Briarhole. I'm not giving him one now."

"So, you're placing me at the forefront of his wrath?" Liam asked, matching her stance.

A knowing smirk played out on her lips. Lips, he wanted nothing more than to taste…to devour…to devour him. "It's not like he can catch you right now."

"No," Liam said, the hint of a smile tugging on his mouth. "But I doubt that will stop him."

Isolde's tongue ran over her lips, forcing him to stop a groan from bubbling to the surface. "Please, Liam," she said. "Do this, for me."

It was the sound in her voice, the desperate plea that had him knocking on the tent's frame. "Come in!" The sound of Nan's voice filled him with a sense of peace he had cherished as a boy.

The moonlight cut through the darkness as he pulled the flap back and stepped inside. Hints of fresh linen and charred oak filled the air.

"What are you doing here?"

Malaki's tone, once filling him with such hope and security, now only grew apprehension and reproach in the pit of his stomach. Liam searched until he found his former friend spread across a fur-lined lounger near the small fire in the far corner. A white bandage, tinged with pink and black ran across his right hip and down his leg.

"Isolde asked me to come," Liam said, squaring his shoulders.

"That's very considerate of you," Nan said, coming to stand before him. Shadows filled the wrinkles that ran across her face in rivets of time. "He can use all the help he can get."

"Not from him," Malaki spat, trying to push himself up. Beads of sweat formed on his brow from the effort, and he fell back with a grunt.

"I just got it to stop bleeding," Nan said over her shoulder, her tone hard. "If you break it open, I won't save you from Isolde—or Bly."

Malaki merely rolled his eyes, but Liam caught the slight twinge of pain flittering across his face.

"Thank you," Nan whispered, her hand cupping his cheek.

"Of course, Nan," Liam said with a small smile.

"I'll leave you to it then." Throwing Malaki one last stern look of warning, Nan shuffled out of the tent, throwing them into a moment of soft light only to leave them in awkward, silent darkness.

"Get on with it then," Malaki said, with the wave of his hand.

Liam fought the urge to roll his eyes and plucked a chair from the nearby table. The legs scraped against the floor as he positioned it next to Malaki and took a seat. His eyes immediately fell to the wound, and a twinge of anger flared in his chest. Fury at the reminder of what lay on Isolde's side and the bastard who put it there.

"I take it you've seen Isolde." It jerked him from his thoughts like the crack of a whip. "I can't imagine that pissed off look on your face is for my sake."

"I did," Liam said, shifting in the seat. "Although, despite what you might think of me. Seeing you hurt doesn't bring any pleasure." Taking a deep breath, Liam dug into the shallow well of his power housing his healing ability. He could feel it around him, the essence of life he could use to help him heal. But his lack of experience gave him pause.

The last thing he wanted was some poor soul dropping dead outside their door. Keeping his focus on the plants just outside the tent, Liam began to pull that power to him. It was slow work, methodical and tedious. While their stores were minimal, there was plenty to pull from in the forest.

The palms of his hands hovered over the wound. He could feel it pulsating. The disruption of muscle and skin felt foreign and odd. Concentrating, Liam slowly brought his power forward.

Malaki bit his bottom lip, his hazel eyes hard as topaz. "You are aware she nearly died, right?" Liam felt the blood drain from his face. "With the amount of blood she lost, Isolde should be in a grave now."

"Why isn't she?" he asked, doing his best to concentrate.

"I don't know," said Malaki, his tone flat. "She's always been…different when it comes to healing. Then again, you would have known that if you had come to see her. How many times did you come to see her, Liam?"

Liam's teeth dug into the side of his cheek. "She asked for you," Malaki continued. "So many times, she asked where you were…if you were safe. And still you didn't come."

I couldn't come, he wanted to say. *I was doing everything I could to ensure Zibiah and those children survived the trip to Elenarta.* But his excuse would mean nothing. So his lips remained sealed.

"One of them, Volkran, I believe, beat her so badly he broke nearly every bone in her face," Malaki said, uncaring of the effort Liam was expelling. "He shattered her sternum…cracked all the ribs on the left side of her body. And your Right Hand," Malaki's lip turning up in disgust, "Nearly gutted her."

Liam's mouth ran dry. "I…I didn't know." His eyes flickered up to meet Malaki's.

"You wouldn't, would you? Too busy following orders. Playing the obedient lap dog for your master." Malaki's lips twisted into a sneer. "Must be exhausting."

"I didn't have a choice," Liam snapped. "I couldn't leave! I…I couldn't get away." A bead of sweat trickled down the back of Liam's neck. Wave after wave of hurt coated anger battered against the confines of his mind. "I had to follow orders. If I'd abandoned my post, that would have put her and everyone else at risk."

"Always an excuse," Malaki mused, a cold, sarcastic smile forming onto his face. "Don't worry, she doesn't blame you for not coming. But do enlighten me. Why didn't you tell us about the extra soldiers waiting along the riverbank?"

"As I said before," Liam said, keeping his eyes down, "I didn't know they were going to be there! I told you everything I knew at the time."

Suspicion filled Malaki's eyes. "Awfully convenient to have soldiers in the one place, the person you claim to care so much about won't be." Accusation shone in the depths of his gaze. Years of hatred and betrayal echoed in his words.

"I didn't betray her, Malaki," said Liam. "I would never betray Isolde."

"No, I'm sure you wouldn't betray *Isolde*."

Liam scoffed, his hands dropping to the bend of his hips. There was no convincing him. Liam would never stand a chance of regaining Malaki's trust.

"Why are you even here?" Malaki asked. "It can't be just because you're under orders."

"I am your royal escort to Elenarta. I'm here to make sure Isolde and the House of Cotheran arrive unscathed," Liam said, shoving his shoulders back putting on the full weight of his position as Captain of the Guard. "And yes, I can be here because I was ordered to by King Tenebriath."

"We don't need or want you here," Malaki sneered, his eyes glowing. "We can handle getting to Elenarta without our hand being held by the king's errand boy."

"It doesn't matter what you need or want, Malaki," said Liam, his tone ringing with authority. "It's the king's demand."

"Well, we wouldn't want to disappoint *him*, now would we?"

"I would watch what I say," Liam warned, his teeth grating. "This isn't the same Elenarta you remember. He isn't the king you served under. Running your mouth will get you killed."

Anger flared in Malaki's gaze. "I don't need or desire the advice of a traitor."

"Clearly you do." Liam leaned forward, invading as much of Malaki's space as he dared. "I don't give a damn if you get yourself killed. My only concern is Isolde and the pain it will cause her if you're executed because of your inability to keep your mouth shut."

The faintest light echoed in the depths of Malaki's eyes and the corners of his mouth tugged into a tight, unforgiving line. "You'll never deserve her."

Anger and hurt wove their way around Liam's heart. A knife would have been preferable. Yet years of training, not only with the man before him, but as a soldier in Erebus's army, kept his temper in check.

"Get some rest. We leave at first light." Liam rose from the chair, covering Malaki in his shadow. "I'm here if you need an extra hand for healing. But do not make the mistake of believing it's for your benefit."

As he pushed through the flap and stepped out into the dead of night, Liam felt a shift in his heart. Plates of iron and stone fell into place, as if a part of him, a hope he had been carrying for so long, had been laid to rest. And he couldn't help but feel sad at the loss.

CHAPTER 8

Blyana had never seen anything so grand.

Apart from Cillian, Elenarta—or what she could see of it anyway—was the most glorious sight she had ever laid eyes upon. It was beauty beyond words or thought. She wondered how such a thing could possibly exist.

Three stars, visible even in the light of the noon day, hung over the three tallest peaks of the Oronilma Mountains.

"They represent the gods and the powers they saw fit to bless us with," Blyana's mother had told her. "Water, wind, and earth."

"What of Nar?" Blyana was but a child at the time. She looked down at the stars her sister, Phontine, had scribbled on a piece of parchment. A beautiful picture, one she had created from their mother's words alone. "Where is the god of fire's star?" At the time, Blyana had felt pity for the god. For the one who was left alone, who stood apart from the rest, and was known only for destruction and death.

"Some believe," her mother had said, "Nar kept the light for himself. Much like he did his power. So he remains here. Bound to our world until he gives up what he holds most dear—his power."

The shimmering remnants of the gods of old guided the company out of the forest and onto the final stretch of their journey. Blyana looked back to Blackford, to the forest that had been her home for so long, and an ache filled her chest.

"We'll see it again, love," Cillian said at her side. His dimpled smile covered her heart with a blanket of ease. Towering hills, glorious and vast, stretched out before them. Houses of varying size and status lined their path. Not a single being dared step out to meet them. No kind welcome greeted the company of Thornwood.

Much to Blyana and the others' relief, Malaki had returned to the saddle. A grimace was set on the corners of his mouth from where he rode at Isolde's side, the only hint to the pain Blyana knew was still burning through his side.

It had been a week since the attack. A week since that bitch had nearly taken someone she cared about. Irritation loomed in Blyana's chest. She still didn't understand why Isolde hadn't gutted her.

"She spared him, Bly," Isolde had said, her emerald, silver gaze refusing to meet hers. "Besides, that's not my revenge to take."

"Never stopped you before," Blyana had argued. "You are the Hood of Arnoria, the Thief of Sorrows. Revenge is what you're known for."

"I hope that's not all I'm remembered for," she had said, a small, sad smile creeping on to her face. "Besides, I'd hate to deprive Malaki of the satisfaction of dealing with her himself."

Blyana rolled her eyes at Isolde's back. She hadn't pressed the issue. Not with Malaki on the mend and the task at hand looming over their heads like a blade.

Liam rode to Isolde's right. It was impossible to stop the wave of anger at the sight. The faintest of growls rumbled through her chest, causing Liam's head to turn. His gaze met her own for only the briefest of moments before his eyes returned forward. A look of sadness hung in their depths.

Blyana didn't care. Her hatred went beyond apologies. Beyond whatever regret Liam claimed to harbor. "He is why Vara still lives," she had told Cillian when he finally demanded to know where her hatred for him came from. "She killed my family after Isolde paid the debt against me and he refused to stand aside when I came for her. Refused to grant me justice for my family. That's why I hate him, Cillian. Why I will always hate him."

Swallowing the lump of malice and sorrow, Blyana forced herself from the past and looked to the road ahead. To her surprise, the wide expanse of land was pristine and beautiful. As if painstakingly kept in near perfect condition. Everything, even the flowers growing along the path, were without blemish, untarnished, and unspoiled.

Nearing the end of the quaint village, a small squadron of soldiers came into view. Blinding light reflected off the plates of armor covering their chests and heads. Liam rode ahead, leaving Isolde and the others in his wake.

"Must be the first check point," Cillian said, his fingers absently grazing the pommel of the dagger at his hip.

"It's early in the trip, Cill," Blyana said, resting a bare hand on his thigh. "Let's not kill anyone just yet."

"You're asking an awful lot of me, love."

"Well," said a voice from her right. "You must be the company plaything." Blyana's gaze whipped around to land on a soldier loitering off to the side. His eyes were fixed on her bare hand splayed across Cillian's thigh. On the serpent tattoo that stood in glaring contrast to her pale skin. "I'll bet Madame Vara fetched a pretty coin for letting them take you so far away."

The same paralyzing fear Vara's name stirred inside Blyana's heart awakened. Memories of the past flooded her mind. Every pain, every unwanted touch came rushing back in an instant.

"I wonder if Cotheran will let you play with us for a while," he said, taking a step closer. The same lustful, disgusting gaze so many had cast her way shone from his dark eyes. She could practically feel it on her flesh like fingers.

Without thinking, Blyana's fingers constrict around the handle of the blade at her side. "My mate gets jealous," she said, pressing her fingers into Cillian's thigh, willing him to stay calm. Cillian remained unmoving, his muscles locked. But Blyana could feel the rage in every tremor rippling beneath her palm.

The man shot Cillian a passing glance, his shoulder shrugging with indifference. "He can learn to share. With someone like you, he'd have to get accustomed to the idea of used goods."

Fury, red and blinding, filled Blyana's gaze. Moving at a speed only a virya could manage, she yanked the dagger free from its scabbard. Light flickered across the blade as its edge sliced through the air. The soldier's helmet tumbled to the ground, the leather strap under his chin severed.

"If your intention is to fuck me, sir," Blyana said, pressing the blade against the soldier's chin, forcing him to look up, "insulting me, isn't the way to go about it. Damaged goods or not."

"Drop your weapon!"

Blyana's head snapped up to find a sea of eyes staring at her. Pride swelled in Malaki and Isolde's gazes, their hands already constricting around the weapons gleaming at their sides. Another soldier, one who's armor held intricate carvings in the metal's surface, stormed through the company.

"As captain of this platoon, I command you drop the weapon this instant, you whore—" The male's words died away as Alaric's knuckles slammed into the side of his helmet. He staggered back and pressed a chain mail glove to the side of his head.

"How dare you speak to someone of my house in such a manner!" Alaric snarled, his eyes glowing in fury. "Blyana is my niece's companion, a member of my house, my family!" Alaric stepped closer, his eyes cold and teeth bared. "Be grateful I don't kill him and you for the insult."

Crumbled metal covered the right side of the soldier's face. It pressed against his lips, garbling every word that fell from his mouth. "Apologies, Lord Cotheran," he said. "I will see to it he is dealt with immediately."

"Allow me," Cillian said. His movements were a blur as his hand slashed through the air in a wide arch. A wail of pain, one filled with anger and surprise, exploded from the soldier Blyana held in her grip.

Blood oozed from between his fingers as he fell to the ground at Felix's feet. "You bastard!" A horrendous crater, cleaving his eye in two, screamed down the left side of his face. "My eye…you cut my eye!"

"To help you remember" A soft, dangerous smile tugging on Cillian's lips. He forced his steed between Blyana and the soldier crying at her feet. "Shall we, love?"

They left the small horde of Erebus's men to tend to the wounded. Blyana reached into her satchel and shoved on the pair of gloves she always kept on hand, needing to hide the reminder of what she was.

A breath caught in her chest as the fine suede brushed across her stained skin. It sent a wave of insignificance crashing over her, suffocating the peace she once had. Memories of her past shuffled through Blyana's mind like flour through a sieve. Each grain was laid bare. Every imperfection cast into the light of self-judgment and blame.

Blyana's eyes glanced nervously to Isolde. Her back straight and head held high—the very symbol of what it meant to be strong.

Someone untarnished, someone worthy of dwelling in such a beautiful place.

She belongs here.

The thought cast a shadow over Blyana's heart. It gave light to their differences, their statuses in life. Not that Isolde ever made her feel such a way—far from, it in fact. In all the years Blyana had lived at Thornwood, Isolde had done everything in her power to make her feel at home and her equal in every way. But as the first of the shadows of Oronilma crossed over Felix's head, a coldness swept through Blyana's limbs.

Dirty...spoiled...ruined.

Her gloved forefinger scrapped against the tattoo at her left thumb. She could still feel the elithrium needle driving into her skin, the horrible burn of the ink used to permanently mark Madame Vara's claim on her. It felt like the sun itself was shining from her hand, highlighting who and what she was.

When she looked up again, a startled gasp slipped through her lips. Isolde was looking back at her. Those strange eyes were focused on her hand, on the finger that refused to stop digging. A slight frown was etched onto Isolde's face, her brow furrowing. Self-consciousness spread through Blyana, and she quickly dropped Isolde's gaze.

She's ashamed to have me here.

The thought scorched through her like a flame. Blyana knew it wasn't true. She knew Isolde would never feel that way about her. But still the thought lingered. And as a wave of familiar despair threatened to pull her under, a strong hand engulfed hers in its grip.

"My love," Cillian whispered. His voice was so soft, so reassuring, she couldn't help but smile at the sound. It was the one thing that would always pull her from the darkness. Already he was fighting away the shadows, the unshakable dread festering in her heart.

"I'm alright," Blyana said, working her fingers to lock with his. The bond hummed between them, a warm presence neither could live without. Cillian pulled her hand to him and began to gently pull the glove free. Blyana yanked her hand back instantly. The faintest hint of green disappeared beneath the cuff as she secured the glove back into place.

Cillian frowned. "What is it?"

"It's nothing."

She worked her fingers through the reins, needing something, anything to anchor to besides the chains of self-doubt wrapping around her throat. Wind kissed the tears lining Blyana's eyes. How badly she wanted to be rid of it. To forget what had happened. But the horrors of the past were as marked into her very soul as the tattoo on her skin.

"Bly, it's not nothing." Cillian's voice was low but still held the same gentleness it always did. "I can tell it's not. I can *feel* that it's not."

It wasn't a normal occurrence for a mated pair. Most only possessed a bond, a tether from one heart to the other. But what she and Cillian had was special. They could pass emotions, feelings from one mate to the other.

"It is rare," Galaena had told her and Isolde when Blyana had first felt it. "Not even Alaric and I have such a gift. Cherish it, Bly."

It had been an adjustment in the beginning, feeling Cillian's emotions. Having access to something so precious and beautifully foreign. Now it was a comfort, a way to easily communicate. But it also left her open and exposed. There was nowhere for her to hide. No way to mask the pain. Disgust slid across her skin like oil. It was all laid bare for Cillian to see, to feel.

"What am I doing here, Cill?" Blyana shook her head, causing tendrils of pale golden hair to fall between them. "I'm not fit to be in a place as beautiful as this. This is no place for someone like me."

Cillian's shock reverberated through her chest, like an iron hammer striking an anvil. It hovered between them for a moment, suspended between the bond. Then sorrow, laced with fury took its place. "Why would you say that?"

Blyana refused to look back at him. Refused to meet his worried stare.

A heavy sigh left his chest when she remained silent. "You claim to be unworthy of this place. But love, it's this place and these *people* who dwell here." His lip turned up into a sneer. "They are the ones who are unworthy."

Blyana wanted to believe him. Wanted desperately for his words to hold even an ounce of the truth they seemed so desperate to convey. But Vara's words sank their fangs into her mind, her voice so venomous, so intoxicating.

"Your worth is here," Vara had said, pointing to the massive four poster bed. Black silk lined the mattress. It had been the night of her auction, the night her life shattered and became anything but her own. "And this is all your pathetic life will ever amount to. A few moments of pleasure and a handful of coins. Never forget that."

"You are not there," Cillian said, tucking a piece of hair behind her ear. "You're with me, Isolde, and Malaki. No one will hurt you. You're safe, Blyana. You…are…*safe*."

The familiar sting of tears rose, and as Blyana's eyes lifted to where Isolde rode ahead. Cillian's sharp, knowing eyes didn't miss it. "You think Isolde believes you're not worthy?"

Blyana couldn't bring herself to look at him.

"I can assure you," Cillian said, his fingers cupping her cheek, "she is the last person who would ever think that of you. Apart from me, of course."

"I know," Blyana said, allowing herself to fall into his touch. A shaky breath lifted from her lips. "I know, it's just…old habits and old thoughts are hard to kill sometimes."

Cillian leaned forward, and a cocky, loving smile spread across his face. "Let me help." The feel of his lips grazed the corner of her mouth and lingered. Heat flooded Blyana's cheeks, and she turned into the kiss, sealing her mouth to his. Love swelled in Blyana's heart as Cillian's fingers twined in her hair, holding her to him.

A soft caress brushed Blyana's heart. It was so pure and light it filled her to the brim. She answered in kind. Her heart swelled with emotion, with love that sang down the bond to rest in Cillian's chest.

Far too soon, Cillian broke away. But his hand remained. The pools of starry darkness she loved more than life itself held her in their infinite embrace. "Your past does not define you. No one does." The pad of his thumb brushed her bottom lip, sending a quiver of delicate desire down Blyana's spine. "Don't let the opinions of those who do not matter steal your joy, Bly."

"You are my joy, Cill," she said. A shuddered breath ghosted across Blyana's lips as she pressed her forehead to his. "As long as I have you, there is nothing they can truly do to me."

Alaric and Galaena passed beneath the first gate heading into the city of Elenarta. Galaena's lips were pulled into a thin line, her shoulders squared and chin held high. A tremor seemed to roll through her form, a shudder that was impossible to hide. Isolde leaned forward, her fingers reaching for her aunt who rode a few paces ahead. But at the last moment, they curled into a fist and fell back to her side.

Blyana knew there was history in Elenarta for Lord and Lady Cotheran. That they had once stood with the Viributhians and had paid the price for their loyalty. It had been a small mercy Erebus had let them live. A mercy not made out of kindness but of cruelty. They, along with Malaki, were made examples of. A constant reminder to the people of what revolution or insurrection would bring.

"It was our home," Malaki had told her. "A place we all hoped to start a family in. Raise children. Help Arnoria grow." Malaki had simply shaken his head as decades of pain filled his eyes. "Now it's a graveyard for dreams and hopes that were never answered."

Alaric's back remained straight as a sheet of steel, and his eyes were forward. The mask of the Lord of Thornwood had been firmly put in place once again. Malaki, despite the pain undoubtedly burning through his side, kept every muscle locked. Blyana didn't miss the stark white grip he kept on Secrettaker as the shadow of the first gate brushed over their heads.

Malice, cold and merciless, filled Cillian's eyes. They burned with a hatred Blyana had never seen before. His lips, surrounded by a layer of dark stubble, were pulled into a grim line, making his features far more angular, more aggressive and savage. A ghost of the past lingered in his gaze. An old anger seemed to burn through him like an inferno, vicious and all consuming. One he kept well-hidden and far away from their bond.

"Cill?" Her hand gripped his shoulder, pulling him back to her once more.

After a moment, the anger disappeared, and a familiar smile pulled at his lips. "Don't mind me, love," Cillian said, his head nodding to where Malaki rode. "I can't let Malaki be the only brooding male in the company."

"I might be hurt, but I can still kick your ass," Malaki said, fighting through the pain to twist around in the saddle to shoot Cillian a hateful look.

A playful smirk danced at the corner of Cillian's expressive lips. "Just like you did to Helurtu?" A rumble echoed through Malaki's gritted teeth. "I'll leave the humiliating defeats to you, old man."

A whisper of Malaki's power leaked into his eyes, and they blazed with life. He turned and a wince of pain lashed across his face. The palm of his hand flew to his hip, drawing a grunt to the edge of his lips.

"Don't poke fun at the injured," Isolde snapped, shooting Cillian a warning look. "Do control your mate, Bly." Her tone was light, and a smile danced on her face.

Blyana's heart lifted a little at the sight. "You ask the impossible."

The outer most ring of the capital continued for miles. Its pristine, colossal wall wound itself along the base of the mountain range. "The walls were created centuries ago," Malaki had explained. "Forged by the kingdom's most powerful earth wielders. The far edges are welded to the rock face, making it nearly impossible to penetrate. In all the years they've existed, nothing and no one has ever breached them."

Before long, the well-manicured ground gave way to impeccably kept streets. One main lane wound its way through the middle ring, breaking off into smaller streets containing residences and shops.

Navigating their way through the various cobblestone pathways was anything but easy. Unlike the outskirts of Elenarta, the streets of the city were flooded with virya of every class. Venders of every kind littered the walkway with tables and stands. Homemade goods decorated every surface. From weapons to fine silk gowns to delicious looking pastries, everything was at their fingertips. Blyana's mouth watered at the sight of the various chocolate dishes one stand offered. She made a mental note to return once they left for Thornwood.

Men and women hovered around the corners, their outfits leaving little to the imagination. A woman, beautiful and voluptuous, boldly stepped out onto the street beside Liam as he passed, her hand grazing up his thigh.

"Would the brave soldier care for some company?"

A cold light filled Isolde's eyes as a growl of warning ripped through her teeth.

"As you can see I am spoken for," Liam said, lifting the woman's hand away.

Pouting, the woman moved on to the next male in line, the same seductive smile returning. The back of Isolde's crimson dress tugged against her squared shoulders as she shifted in the saddle, her jaw clenching. Liam hid a chuckle behind a gloved hand as a blush of red spread across his cheeks.

Blyana stifled a growl at the sight. While she would never forgive Liam, Blyana knew what he meant to Isolde. Knew that he had pulled her back from a darkness not unlike her own. And for that reason alone, she forced herself to keep the peace, willing herself to tolerate his presence.

Flowers of every kind littered the cobblestone streets as they moved into the residential portion of the capital. Every step was a lovely patchwork of floral decay. Their scents filled the air with a sweet, warm fragrance.

Despite the beauty, Blyana felt their every move being watched. The blood-red serpent's eye of the House of Tenebriath hung from every doorway and atop every roof they passed. Its slit pupil bore down on them. Ever present, ever watchful.

Isolde looked to the streets, a warm smile forming on her face. Off to the right, a child stood amongst the crowd. How Isolde had spotted her, Blyana couldn't begin to guess. She was so small—not even six years old—the crowd seemed to swallow her whole.

Her face, while dirty and unkempt, was filled with hope as she offered up flower after flower to those who crossed her path. None looked her way. Not a soul paid any mind to the little girl and all she had to offer.

A softness fell across Isolde's face as she mumbled something to Malaki, and he immediately raised a fist, signaling for the company to halt. Dismounting, Isolde passed her reins to Liam who took them with a knowing smile. Blyana followed suit, tossing her own to Cillian.

"Couldn't resist, could you?" Blyana asked, reaching Isolde's side.

A smile filled her face. "I never can."

They made their way to the tiny flower barrier. The ends of their dresses grazed over the broken petals at their feet. Poverty hung in the air like a vapor. Every mouth was begging for one thing or another. Food, drink, company, healing...Even here, in the crowning jewel of Arnoria, the virya were poor.

"Lady Isolde!" The little girl cried in delight when Isolde stopped before her. Her hair was matted and dirty but still held a beautiful hue of chestnut brown. "You're really here!"

How Isolde's name had made its way to the capital, let alone into this girl's ears was beyond her. Unease crept into Blyana's limbs. The tips of her fingers grazed the dagger at her side, her cautious eyes roving the crowd.

Isolde merely smiled. "I am indeed. You seem to know my name, but I have not had the pleasure of yours."

"Camalora," the girl said sheepishly. She took in the finery covering Isolde from head to toe. Her little hand pressed into her hair, attempting to smooth away the curls and knots embedded throughout. A look of shame found its way into her wide, dark blue eyes.

"A beautiful name for a little girl whose own beauty puts the flowers to shame," Isolde said, kneeling down to sit on her heels. A shy smile spread across Camalora's face, her cheeks warming at Isolde's kind words. "This is my good friend, Blyana." Isolde waved a hand behind her, urging Blyana to squat down beside her.

Blyana gave the child a smile of her own as she kneeled. "You have such beautiful flowers, Camalora."

"Would you like one?" She extended a purple wildflower to each of them. Blyana's heart ached at the generosity.

"Thank you," Isolde said, placing it behind her ear. "How do I look?" Blyana followed suit and tucked a flower into the folds of her hair.

Camalora giggled. "Like the princess Mama used to tell me about. The one who lived here before. Mama said she used to wear flowers in her hair too."

"What a very pretty princess she must have been," Isolde said. "And for you…" Reaching around to the back of her neck, Isolde unfastened the necklace that held a single diamond. She slipped the thin, golden chain over Camalora's head to place it on her thin, dirt-covered neck. Blyana's eyes snapped to the crowd, watchful of anyone who might harm the girl for what could easily feed a family for a month. But none were watching. All had turned their eyes to where Alaric and Galaena were passing out coins.

Isolde tilted her head with an appraising eye. "Now you look like the sun."

"I cannot take such a thing," Camalora said. Her eyes said it all. The thankfulness and the unworthiness she felt were clear and bright.

"Of course, you can!" Isolde said. "It looks better on you anyway."

"Camalora!" a voice cried, from somewhere within the crowd. The girl quickly stuffed the jewel beneath the lining of her baggy, worn dress.

"What are you doing?" A woman, who Blyana assumed was the girl's mother, demanded. She gripped Camalora by the arm and tore her worry filled eyes away to Isolde. A look of shock etched across her face. But a snarl soon followed.

"I apologize for keeping, Camalora," Isolde said as she rose. "I was just—"

The woman shoved Camalora behind her, creating a barrier. "Stay away from my child," she growled through clenched teeth; her nose was just a breath away from touching Isolde's. A look of hatred and years of hard labor marred her features. Anger swelled in Blyana's chest, driving her to step forward. Her fingers gripped the pommel of the dagger hidden at her side.

"Haven't your *good deeds* killed enough children already?"

The sneer was so low Blyana wasn't sure she had heard correctly. But the look of painful shock shining from Isolde's face said she had. Without another word, the woman turned and shoved her way through the crowd, towing Camalora behind her.

Pain filled Isolde's flawless face and her eyes dropped to the ground where the rest of Camalora's flowers now lay. Blyana turned back to the crowd, searching for the woman, her anger burning. But the feeling of Isolde's fingers on her arm kept her in place.

"Leave her, Bly," Isolde said. "She didn't say anything that wasn't true."

"You can't believe that," Blyana said, her teeth set. "It's not your fault, Isolde!"

Swallowing hard, Isolde forced a look of indifference onto her face. A look Blyana knew was a mask, as real as the one she hid behind as the Hood. "Apparently it is."

Without another word, Isolde made her way back through the crowd and leapt onto Versa's back. Blyana cast one final look back into the crowd. *How wrong they are.*

Blyana regained her seat on top of Felix, and they continued on. Isolde was quiet for a while. Not even the beauty of the Adriam River and its crystal-clear water could draw the look of pain from her face. It snaked through the capital like a giant, sleeping serpent and disappeared into the mountains, heading for the Sea of Calca.

The palace loomed over them. A kaleidoscopic collection of massive towers peered down at them through glassless eyes. Their peaks rose from the mountain's stony flesh and stretched towards the sky.

Soldiers stood shoulder to shoulder along the entire length of the final wall standing thirty feet tall. An elithrium spear, the metal shining with an eerie green, was clutched in each gloved hand. A sword of the finest quality, rested at their sides. All along the wall, archers were poised and ready, with an arrow notched into the finest bows she had ever seen.

"I think it's safe to say these are not Foxclove guards." Blyana's eyes skittered across them like a stone on a pond. "Not even Briarhole."

"Brutal, proficient killers," Cillian said. "I would expect nothing less from Erebus."

A set of doors, fifty feet in height and made of solid, white stone, rose before them. "At least they left the doors unscathed." Galaena's voice, cold and edged, carried on a breath of wind running through the cadre.

"They were created by earth wielders who specialize in working with stone," Alaric said. "Nothing in all of creation could shatter them. They would be fools to even try."

Carvings of the gods covered their surface. Nar, god of fire, and Vae, goddess of air, stood to the right. Their gazes were fixed on Ceto, the goddess of water, and Kian, the god of earth, who resided on the left. Blyana gave little interest for any of them.

They were adored by her parents. Revered and worshipped by her sisters. But never by her. And despite the devotion they received, they had done nothing to help those she loved. Cillian too held a look of disdain. Clearly, the gods had done little to earn his favor either.

One final wall stood between them and the halls of Elenarta. Thirty feet of pure white stone ran the length of the courtyard. It's perfectly polished surface glinted in the light of the afternoon sun. The soldiers manning the boundaries stood as shadows against its surface.

A grate, made of elithrium-laced iron, rose in an archway upon their approach, beckoning them to enter. From the center of the rafters that lined the arch's ceiling, bits of cloth danced around the small bundles swinging in the wind. Fear chilled in Blyana's gut. Fear and horror. But it wasn't until they drew closer that Isolde's sharp gasp pierced the silence.

A head of ruby hair, set in spirals of dried blood, danced in the light breeze. The freckles upon her cheeks looked far darker than Blyana remembered.

"Mary!" Anger and sorrow filled the name as it fell from Isolde's trembling lips. The leather of the reins gripped in her hands groaned. Ragged breaths escaped between her teeth.

"Isolde," Malaki said. "Breathe!"

But she didn't hear him or pretended not to. All she did was stare at the dead girl above them. At the girl Tanor, Isolde's beloved student, had convinced her to teach to read. Light shone from Isolde's eyes as a snarl played on the edge of her lips.

"You have to calm down," Liam said, through his teeth. His hand gripped her at the elbow, but she shook him off. The snarl only grew louder, her chest heaving. "Isolde, control yourself!" His fingers latched on again, gripping tighter. "Please, Isolde!"

Blyana's gaze locked on Liam's fingers pressing into the fabric of Isolde's dress. Her own beast roared in anger, the sound echoing in her mind like a thunder. Memories of hands seizing her, bruising her flesh, stoked that hatred even more. She drove Felix forward, knocking Liam's horse away from Versa.

"You do not order her," Blyana seethed. Her voice, even to her, was as cold and sharp as the blade at her side. "And if you value your hand, or your life for that matter, do not ever grab her like that again."

Liam's eyes darkened at the threat before him. His power stirred as shock gave way to agitation. "I would never hurt her, Blyana," he said. "I didn't mean to—"

"You don't mean to do a lot of things, Liam," Blyana said, cutting him off. "But my promise still stands—never again."

"She can't lose control here," Liam said. "He will kill her and all of us!"

"We understand, Liam," said Cillian, coming to stand beside her, blocking Liam from her view. His jaw was set, and a sharpness lingered in his gaze, giving Liam pause. "Thank you for your help."

Isolde continued to stare at Mary. Cuts ran down the lengths of her arms to her fingerless hands. Blood, black and dry, coated her skin like paint. A deep gash had been made across her throat and two trails of blood cascaded down her cheeks from empty eye sockets. A sign hung from her neck.

The human who dared to read

"Isolde."

The sound of Malaki's voice seemed to jar her from her thoughts and Isolde turned to see the same look of tortured anger in his eyes. The faintest hint of light shone from the depths of his eyes. Anger practically rolled off his colossal shoulders in waves—off both of them.

Up ahead, Alaric and Galaena waited.

Galaena's hands were shaking with rage as she steered her horse onward, Alaric at her back. Isolde followed behind, tearing herself away from the girl whose death Blyana knew would haunt her friend forever.

"Monsters," Cillian said. He cast Mary one final look before he bowed his head and pressed on.

"I'm so sorry, Mary."

Blyana's small voice, only the hint of a whisper, felt like thunder in her ears. She steered Felix away and entered the beautiful hell of Elenarta.

CHAPTER 9

Isolde's cold stare crawled up the colossal doors. The gods in their mocking, infinite might stare down at her in what she could only assume was contempt. Contempt for her failures, for her hatred of them, for a choice made so very long ago. She couldn't help but look back at the archway.

I'm sorry, Isolde said to the girl who couldn't hear her. To the girl she had sentenced to die by teaching her to read. *So, so sorry.* They hadn't even been in Elenarta for a day and already she was failing. Terror, sharp but blazing hot, scorched through her like a bolt of lightning.

Were the others dead as well?

Forcing away the paralyzing thought, Isolde took in the perimeter. Soldier after soldier lined the towering wall that created the final impenetrable barrier to the palace. Their eyes, pits of hollowed darkness, stared straight ahead in unwavering focus. As if their sole reason for existing was to stand at post. To guard, to protect…to kill if necessary. Cords of muscle rippled beneath what little skin their black-plated armor left exposed—which wasn't much to speak of.

A heartlessness lived within their eyes. One unbreakable as the massive set of fifty-foot doors before them. Unease clawed at Isolde's throat at the sight, forcing her attention back to the caravan. Deep within the confines of the carriage, Nan's withered hands gripped the windowsill, her swollen knuckles pale and trembling. There wasn't a doubt in Isolde's mind that Nan had seen what had been done to Mary and her heart ached.

"Bly," Isolde murmured, glancing over her shoulder. "Do me a favor and ask Nan to meet us in our chambers. We'll say she is not feeling well if anyone asks of her whereabouts."

"Of course," she said, offering a shallow nod before turning Felix back to the carriage. Isolde cast a brief glance at Cillian, his face chiseled from stone. Malaki shifted at her side and a small grunt slipped past his lips.

"Malaki—"

"As you are so fond of saying," he said, his gaze sweeping across the elithrium weapons clutched in the soldiers' hands. "I'm fine."

"Imitation is the highest form of flattery." Her mask of indifference fit into place to hide the raging sorrow burning in her heart.

"I don't think the world could handle more than one of you, Isolde. It has a hard enough time dealing with the one it's got."

"She has to keep things interesting, Malaki," said Cillian, as Blyana returned to his side. "Especially when it comes to you. Spontaneity is the spice of life. Wouldn't want you getting dull before your time, now would we?"

Malaki's growl of irritation, one he reserved only for Cillian, was masked by the sound of tiny, scurrying feet. A male whose features, while youthful, reminded Isolde of a rat, scampered down the fine, polished steps. His eyes were bead-like and held nothing but contempt and mistrust. The creature's little nose was turned up and yellow teeth peeked from beneath his curling lip.

"And who chooses to arrive so late the evening before the tournament?" he demanded. His hand disappeared into the depths of the black cloak draped around his small frame to retrieve a soiled handkerchief.

"House Cotheran," Alaric said. His voice carried through the courtyard with the authority of a lord. "We're here by His Majesty's direct invitation." Stepping forward, his cane clicking on the fine polished steps, Alaric offered by the invitation Isolde had read countless times.

Snatching it from Alaric's hand, the little rodent looked over Erebus's words with a scrutinizing eye. After a moment, he glanced up and swept his gaze along the company. Isolde felt a shudder of revulsion as his unsettling focus landed on her. "And I suppose you are Lady Isolde?" A twisted grin formed on his pock-ridden, narrow face.

"In the flesh," Isolde said with the wave of her hand, her voice laden with sarcasm. She forced her mouth into a grin, willing every ounce of civility she could manage into the smile. "You have the expressed pleasure in knowing who I am," she said, her brow cocking. "But I believe I am at loss for who you are."

"Forgive me, my lady," the creature said, his arm sweeping forward with an air of mockery. "I am Zego. Personal servant to King Tenebriath."

Isolde forced the smile to remain, her eyes narrowing. "Charmed."

"His Majesty, greets you," Zego continued, drawing himself up to his fullest height—which wasn't saying much. "Although, he was expecting you much sooner."

"Not according to his letter," Isolde said, pointing to the envelope now clutched to his chest. "If His Majesty had wished me here sooner, he should have chosen his words more carefully."

A hush descended over the courtyard. Even the soldiers who lined the walls seemed to give pause. Zego balked, his mouth dropping at her blatant disrespect for the king, at his doorstep, nonetheless.

Not that Isolde cared.

"Do carry on, Zego," she said, plastering on a grin, her voice layered with sugary falseness. "It's been a long journey."

Liam stifled a sigh to her side, but Isolde ignored him. He should have known the people of Elenarta wouldn't be spared her tongue. No matter who they claimed to be. Silence continued to fill the air save for the occasional snap of a flag lining the lip of the walls above them. While the cocky smile remained, Isolde's eyes grew cold and full of challenge as she thrust the full weight of her gaze upon him.

"This way, my lady," Zego said at last, extending an arm up the stairs, his shoulders drooping into a submissive bow.

They left their horses in the care of the royal stable hands. "You'll regret it if you don't give her a few extra sugar cubes," Isolde warned them with a devilish smile. Two stable boys looked up at Versa, their faces full of uncertainty.

"Yes, my lady," the older of the two said, reluctantly taking the reins.

"She's really a big softy," Isolde whispered, passing a bag of peppermints to the smaller of the two. "Don't let her push you around." Versa followed easily enough as they whispered promises of sweets in her ear.

Another ensured Isolde's excessive amount of luggage would be looked after and that Nan would be placed in one of the available servants' quarters.

"Absolutely not," Isolde said, stopping the servant dead in his tracks. "She is of my house, and she will stay in our quarters."

"But...but Lady Isolde," he stammered, his confused, nervous gaze flickering to Zego who waited at the foot of the stairs. "It's not appropriate for a human to share quarters with—"

"Is that a refusal I'm hearing?" Isolde asked, her eyes flashing. The mask of Isolde Cotheran, heir to Thornwood, fell into place like it was second skin. It was a weapon like any other. One she had no problem wielding to ensure she wouldn't be separated from Nan. "Are you denying a personal guest of King Tenebriath? I can't imagine he would be pleased to hear that I was treated in such a manner. Rumors of his leniency are not well known in Thornwood."

The man bowed deeply, his eyes wide with fear. "Very well, my lady. It will be as you wish."

Isolde offered him a stiff nod and continued forward after pressing a few gold coins into his palm. She trailed behind Alaric and Galaena, who kept pace with Zego just a few steps ahead. Malaki and Liam hovered at her sides. Cillian and Blyana took up the back, their steps sure and light. Isolde felt the presence of her cadre encase her like a suit of armor, making the vice gripping her chest a little more bearable. As they reached the landing, the set of thick, white doors swung open with a groan, allowing light to spill into the towering entryway within.

Memories swept across her mind like breaths of wind across the grassy plains of Dolinmere. Their touch was feather-light and filled with such warmth she wasn't sure how to contain it all. Others laid waste to her heart and the walls she had built around it.

A breath caught in Isolde's throat at the sight of the familiar cavernous walls. They stretched up to disappear into the blinding light filtering in from the invisible ceiling above. It was a glorious creation carved from the mountain itself, willed into reality by the virya of old. Their earth wielding abilities were etched into every inch of the palace beneath the stars.

Openings, strategically placed and shaped, decorated the stone above, allowing streams of light to guide their way. The golden fringe Insil's mother, Asha, had painstakingly embroidered into Alaric's and

Galaena's coats, glistened as they walked. A small beacon of light in a well of darkness.

Faces turned at the sound of their approach. Murmurs soon followed. Whispers of the past Isolde knew they too recalled. "You mustn't react," Alaric had said the night before they left. They all stood together in one of the sitting rooms. A fire, mercifully small, burned in the mouth of the fireplace. "Cotheran is a traitor's name now. One you bear and will be targeted for."

"You ask a lot from me, Alaric," Isolde said, swirling a goblet of wine. "Holding my tongue has never been my forte."

"That's an understatement," Malaki had said. She shot him a gesture from her hand and continued on.

"Surely, you don't expect—"

"I—We," Alaric said, with a nod to Galaena. "Expect you to behave. And that goes for all of you." He took his time in looking each member of the cadre, of his family, in the eye. "I don't care what they say or do. No fighting." His gaze came to land on her, and he held it for another beat. "No fighting…no fighting…" he said to each of them, making sure they understood. "They're just words. They hold all the meaning and power you allow them to. Keep them powerless."

Isolde hardly spared a glance at those who had stopped to gawk. Fine carvings, intricate and beautiful, ran along the arches lining their path. Arches gave way to balconies jutting into the open air, giving them a breathing-taking glimpse of what truly lay beneath the surface.

"No matter how much time has passed," Alaric said, "the beauty of this place never ceases to amaze me."

It was miraculous in its complexity, in the incomparable might of what the virya could create out of greed. Of just how high their power could climb. Every archway was beautifully, painstakingly carved with one element or another…save one. Marble waves ran along the base of the walls to meet the carved gusts of wind sweeping down from the ceiling. And vines, much like the ones decorating Malaki's skin, clung to the archways and doorframes as if they were alive. Yet not a single pillar or stone-covered wall showcased the god of fire. Not a single flame left its mark.

Even deep within the depths of the mountain, sunlight filled the corridors. But not a single ray left a comforting touch upon Isolde's skin. Not an ounce of warmth filled her soul in this place—not anymore.

Minutes passed as the company of Thornwood followed Zego. The stone floor beneath Isolde's feet glistened. It had been impeccably kept. Bridges of stone were suspended over endless glistening caverns beneath their feet. Caverns that had been pillaged and foraged across the centuries for the priceless metals and jewels lying deep in the heart of the mountain.

"One of the kings of old was a lover of such beautiful things," Galaena had told her as a child. "It was his desire to forge the most stunning pieces of jewelry ever created. King Thasius Viributhian, the most talented earth wielder in living memory, had an affinity for manipulating precious metals. An affinity that drove him into madness. A madness that forced him to order his fellow earth wielders to dig deeper into Oronilma."

Isolde could remember the sadness in her aunt's face. "Gold and silver were harvested from the mountain's flesh. Jewels of every kind imaginable were brought before him every day. Eventually, King Thasius became obsessed with treasure, sick with jealousy and greed."

"Is that what killed him?" Isolde had asked one day as she peered over the edges of one of the many bridges dwelling within the palace. Her eyes scanned the vast emptiness below. A darkness, cold and vast, stared back.

"No," Galaena had said, her fingers tightening around her small hand. "His son, Illias, believed the wealth, the beauty of his father's own creation had poisoned his mind. He became jealous, protective over what he had ripped from Oronilma. Illias reported the last time he saw his father was when he descended into the mines, taking all of the precious pieces he had helped create with him. Supposedly, a vault lies at the bottom of those caverns that can only be found by a Viributhian and be opened by their blood alone."

Isolde had looked over the edge once again, pulling on Galaena's hand. A chill had run up her spine at the thought of someone being down there. Trapped in the dark, alone forever.

Galaena sighed and tugged Isolde to her side. "Oronilma took back what had been stolen."

"Breathe." Blyana's voice echoed from behind, drawing Isolde's attention. Cillian hovered at the edge of the first stone bridge crossing their path; his face paled with terror.

"At me," Blyana said, working her small hand into his. "Look only at me." Cillian's eyes flicked to her but immediately returned to the chasms below, his frame shaking.

"Look at Bly," Malaki said. His warm, deep voice filled the air and ricocheted into the depths below. "Only at her, Cill."

Gulping down a breath of strangled air, Cillian forced himself to meet his mate's patient, loving gaze. A shuddering breath left his chest, and he took one tentative step onto the bridge.

"That's it," Blyana said. "At me…only at me." Together, step by step, they slowly made their way across. Isolde stayed close. Fringes of air lingered on her fingertips, ready to act on her command. Pity that she didn't dare let reach her face filled Isolde's chest for her dear friend. There had to be a way to help him….

But as Cillian took the final step off the first of many, many bridge crossings to come, she knew this wasn't something she could help with. This particular scar ran deep. Yet as a smile, one unrestrained and filled with pride spread across Cillian's face, Isolde felt a twinge of hope.

His eyes glistened as he pulled Blyana to his side and placed a kiss on her brow. "Thank you, love." Isolde couldn't help him. But perhaps, his mate could.

Before long, they came to a final corridor. Massive archways, made of the same glimmering marble stood thirty feet overhead on either side. Isolde marveled at the grandeur, at the extravagance King Illias, son of Thasius, had wished to bestow upon his wife. One that would help hide the scars his father had placed on their beloved home.

A palace that would be without rival—that was what Illias had promised.

Isolde cringed at another dark fragment of their viryian history. At the knowledge that so many earth wielding virya died for this place to exist. They had been worked night and day, driven beyond their limits to create the wonder before her. Nearly all had fallen. Their sacrifice painted the walls in blood and power. The few who survived never touched their power again, forsaking the gift of the gods, and died long ago.

"Just through here," Zego said, nodding to a pair of ornate doors set in pearl and pale gold. They opened upon their approach.

Light spilled through the skylight, consuming the central part of the ceiling towering a hundred feet over their heads. Isolde's gaze swept the room, taking note of everyone present. Soldiers and virya, ones she assumed were there to take court, lined the walls. Finery cascaded from them in yards of silk and velvet. Jewels shone from their throats and fingers like colorful stars. Their eyes were fixed and pointed.

Isolde ignored them, her brow arched with indifference.

Towering arches lined the walls of the throne room, giving a glimpse of the mountains that lay beyond. Waterfalls, large and small, running down the length of the rock faces of the surrounding mountains, glistened in the light of the afternoon sun. Beautiful marble covered every surface, save for the yards of gossamer curtains swaying in the gentle breeze.

But Isolde paid no attention to any of it. She turned her focus forward, and a lump lodged itself in the back of her throat. There was nothing that could have prepared her for the unstoppable wave of malice filling her heart. For the hatred crashing down on her will and self-control.

No, her eyes, her anger were focused solely on the dais. A single throne resided where two had once stood so many years ago.

"Your Majesty," Zego said, his body bending into a bow. "May I present Lady Isolde of House Cotheran, and Lord and Lady Cotheran."

Swallowing bile, Isolde forced herself into a curtsy. The crimson red fabric of her dress swelled around her feet like a pool of blood against the pristine white marble floor. The others followed suit, and it churned her anger all the more.

"What a pleasure it is to have the House of Cotheran in my home once again." His voice was as deep and sensual as she remembered. "Rise."

Isolde rose to meet a pair of steel-grey eyes. They held a coldness that hinted along the edge of savagery. An echo of light ringed his irises, giving her a glimpse at the power lingering just beneath the surface. A crown of obsidian black steel rested upon a bed of thick silver hair.

Erebus Tenebriath.

His long, pale fingers traced the thigh of a beautiful blonde female sprawled across his lap. She grinned in exaggerated pleasure, her lips full and sickeningly red. A gasp escaped Blyana who stood at Isolde's side. She turned to see her friend's eyes grow wide with disbelief.

"Phontine?" Tears and confusion swelled in Blyana's gaze as she took a step forward.

The female draped across the king's lap froze. Her eyes widened for only a fraction of a second before they hardened into something else entirely. Pure hatred.

"Bly?" Cillian said, resting a hand on her arm. "What—"

"My sister," she said, her voice hardly that of a whisper.

"Sister?" Looking closer, Isolde could see the resemblance was impossible to deny. Their eyes held the same stunning shade of blue and the look of stubbornness now etched onto Phontine's face was wholly Blyana's.

Cillian shook his head. "I thought Vara—"

"She killed my family. Or at least…I thought she did." Blyana's pale blue eyes never left Phontine, who had taken to ignoring them entirely. Her fingers played with the ends of Erebus's hair and her lips curled into a smile that didn't come close to reaching her eyes.

"Thank you for your gracious invitation, Your Majesty," Alaric said, his rich, melodic voice severing their conversation. "We are honored to be in the capital once more."

"And you, Lady Isolde?" The hint of smile danced behind a golden goblet hovering at the edge of Erebus's lips. "Are you…*honored* to be back in the capital once more?"

"So, happy I could just burst, Your Majesty," Isolde said, her smile sarcastic and wide.

"Such spirit," Erebus said, as the tips of his fingers grazed the bare, pale skin of Phontine's upper thigh. "We could use a little more fire in this court. Wouldn't you agree, Phontine?"

"Yes, my king," Phontine said, her voice airy and filled with lust that nearly had Isolde convinced. But she knew it was a practiced sound, a learned response. The hint of growl seeped through Blyana's clenched teeth at Isolde's back.

Cillian shifted beside her, his tone darkening. "Easy, love."

"It's been sometime since you've graced these halls, Alaric" Erebus said. "Tell me, how do things fare in my favorite little territory?"

Alaric cleared his throat and placed his hands behind his back. "Crops have more than doubled this year, Your Grace. Crime has dropped dramatically, and the people are in good standing. I am delighted to report all is well."

"All is well," Erebus mused. "And what of the Hood? Would you say his existence is a reflection of…*all is well?*"

"Of course not, Your Majesty," Alaric said, with an awkward bow, his leg refusing to cooperate. "I was under the impression the Hood had been captured."

"The culprit has indeed been apprehended," said Erebus with a nod. "But not his co-conspirators. Surely, you don't believe this *thief* acted alone. Have you any news of their whereabouts, perhaps?"

"No, Your Grace," Alaric said, his hands balling into fists behind his back. "I'm afraid no news has reached Thornwood regarding the Hood's companions."

"What a shame," Erebus said, his fingers playing with the locks of silken, golden hair falling down Phontine's shoulder. "I suppose that means taxes in Thornwood will be raised ten percent until you can provide me with information or the outlaws themselves. Perhaps that will encourage your territory to work harder in bringing these cowards to justice."

A growl reverberated through Isolde's chest. She opened her mouth to argue, fingers curling into claws at her side. Galaena's hand flew out to grab her, stopping the dangerous words before they had a chance to fall. "As you wish, Your Grace," her aunt said with a stiff bow.

Erebus's gaze fell to Galaena's hand locked around at Isolde's wrist. A look of intrigue blossomed across his handsome face. "It has come to my attention, Lady Isolde, that you have not yet presented your power to my court. Nor is there any public record of you having done so in Thornwood." Isolde could feel the tremor roll through her company, and Galaena's grip tightened. "I'm sure you're well aware it is a matter of law. All virya are to make their abilities public. Your companions have done so, like the good citizens they are…but not you. Which leads me to wonder why, the heir of Thornwood, has kept herself locked way for so long."

She had only returned to Elenarta once before. Even then, she had hidden beneath the mask and cloak, never daring to step foot back into the palace—not that she wanted to. She and Malaki had stayed on the outskirts of the capital and only emerged during Liam's trials. She would never abandon him to face that fate alone.

"My duties as heir have kept me rather busy. I do apologize for any distress my absence might have inflicted," Isolde said, her voice strained with forced civility. "My power is a falcon, Your Majesty, and an air wielder."

"Falcon *and* an air wielder," Erebus said. "That is most interesting to hear." A cold smile pulled at the edges of his lips. "I would like a demonstration."

Alaric stepped forward. "Your Grace, it has been a very long journey, and my niece is—"

"Silence!" Erebus roared, his hands swiping through the air like a blade. A burst of jagged ice exploded at Alaric's feet, their sharp points caging him in place. "I think your niece is capable of one transformation. I find it hard to believe someone under your guidance possesses such lack of control that this simple request is too much for her handle." His gazed shifted to her, a brow quirking in expectation. "Lady Isolde?"

Isolde fought against the terror saturating her blood like a drop of ink in a vat of water. But what choice did she have? Swallowing against the lump of dread threatening to suffocate her, Isolde squared her shoulders and forced her lips into a smile. "As you wish."

The soldiers and virya lining the walls stirred as she made her way to the center of the throne room. The grips on their elithrium weapons tightened slightly, eyes glowing with the deadly threat she was about to become.

Isolde's eyes fell on Malaki who gave one encouraging nod. His lips formed a single word as she passed. *Breathe.*

Turning back to the dais, Isolde did as he instructed. Slowly …carefully, the hold on her control gave way. The full brunt of her power slammed against the restraints in her mind. She gritted and searched for the power she sought, refusing to let the true force of what dwelt within loose.

Focus! She told herself, refusing to acknowledge anything else other than the power she sought.

At last, the familiar current came forward on rapid wings. It wrapped her in its feathered embrace, cascading through to her very core. In an instant, Isolde's body grew, and her skin gave way to a plume of brilliant white feathers. A beak had replaced her face, and talons stood where her feet had once been. Their sharp tips pierced the stone, sending fissures scurrying through the floor and up the foundation of the dais. Her vision was frighteningly sharp, hearing unbearably clear.

Gasps and cries of shock from the onlookers who stood off to the side filled the air. Her cadre took a step back, their eyes guarded and on edge. A small part of Isolde marveled at how small they appeared. Ten feet, if not more, stood between the top of their heads and her own.

The distinct sound of clapping drew her attention back to the dais. Erebus was smiling, his hands having left Phontine's skin to clap around her waist. His rhythm was slow but incredibly loud and piercing.

"Impressive." A look of beguilement filled his eyes, bringing a slight shine to his predatory gaze. "Most impressive."

The words slid over Isolde like oil. Malice burned through her, feeding the beast that had locked its chains of control around her mind. A furious cry burst from the monster's beak, her eyes zeroing in on the king of Arnoria. Her wings snapped out, taking up nearly half of the massive walkway leading to the dais.

Dust and bits of crushed floor erupted into a cloud as she rose. The soldiers lining the walls stepped forward in unison. They moved as if a single mind was shared between them. Bows fit with elithrium arrows rose to meet her. Spears holding the same wicked glint were trained on her heart. Light pouring in from the glassless windows kissed her wings as she shot into the air.

"The first man to attack is the first man to die," Erebus growled, his voice laced with the promise of death. "Detain only!"

Frightened virya sprinted for the exit as Isolde dove forward. Their goblets tumbled to the floor and spilled wine across the marble like puddles of blood. Isolde didn't care. Her attention was on one thing and one thing alone. Erebus grinned from where he sat on the throne, his elbow braced on the cushioned armrest. Isolde snapped her wings through the air, forcing her body to go faster. Her talons lashed out, their tips aimed at Erebus's heart.

A dark, melodic chuckle broke through the fog of fury clouding Isolde's mind, along with the snap of Erebus's fingers. Without warning, the weight of an elithrium-laced chain mail slammed into her from above. She crashed into the floor, the impact cushioned by a small pillow of air encasing her body.

Gods bless, Cillian.

Panic and anger battled in Isolde's mind. Pain echoed through her back and travelled up into the shoulder that had met the ground. Little by little, her power receded, bowing to the hold of the elithrium.

"Isolde!" Malaki said, taking a step forward, his hand outstretched. His voice filled her mind, forcing that horrible power to retreat.

"Breathe, Isolde. One piece at a time."

Wrenching the reins of control from her power's grip, Isolde slowly, carefully replaced each and every stone. One by one, the wall began to form in her mind. The monster, the power she kept in the dark bared its teeth at the cage— at the prison she formed around it. At last, as she slammed the final piece into place, Isolde felt the kiss of the afternoon breeze on her chilled, clammy skin. The chain mail's cold, unforgiving touch was unbearable. Her chest squeezed with panic.

"Get it off me, Malaki," Isolde said, trying to hide the desperation in her voice. But the pleading…the fear…the anger bled through like water through a piece of cloth. "Alaric, get it off!"

"Remove this *now*!" Alaric growled. The soldiers ignored him and instead turned their eyes to Erebus. Isolde felt the weight of his stare like the blanket holding her down. It pressed her to the floor, holding her in place. She felt trapped…exposed…powerless beneath it. After a long moment, Erebus finally nodded.

The soldiers stepped forward and pried the impossibly heavy blanket of tainted metal from Isolde's body. With shaky arms, she pressed her palms to the floor and tried to rise. A soldier stepped to her side and his fingers grazed the sleeve of her dress.

"Whatever part of you touches her," Malaki snarled, "you lose." His fingers worked their way around Secrettaker—his voice laced with the promise of death. The soldier's hand dropped back to his side, and he took a cautious step back. Isolde slipped her hand into Malaki's and she rose on unsteady legs.

"Quite a display, Lady Isolde," Erebus said, leaning forward on his elbows. Blyana's sister was nowhere to be found, having vanished in the midst of her demonstration. "A little *untamed* perhaps…but that's a matter easily resolved with time."

Isolde stared up at him in unrestrained hatred. She was exhausted and her self-control was waning rapidly. Erebus seemed completely at ease by Isolde's attempt to murder him. As if he never saw her as a serious threat to begin with. The thought stoked her anger further.

Foolish bastard.

Erebus's lips pulled into a smile. But that was where the humor ended. His eyes hardened into pools of calculated steel. A chilling calm fell about the most powerful man in Arnoria. A calm that hung on the cusp of desolation...of visceral violence.

"Something you wish to say, Lady Isolde?" He asked. "Don't hold that wicked tongue of yours on my account."

"I wouldn't dare dream of using my tongue on any part of you, Your Grace," Isolde said, forcing a soft, seductive smile into place. "You're not worthy of such treatment." A flash of light ignited in the depths of Erebus's eyes. It hinted to the incredible power lurking just beneath the surface.

"Well, I shall pray for those who find themselves at your mercy," Erebus said, his gaze lingering on Isolde's lips. "I can't imagine being in your clutches is something one recovers from easily."

Isolde forced her smile to remain frozen, to hide the sneer that so eagerly wanted to shine.

"I suppose you all need time to get settled before the festivities tonight," Erebus said, leaning back into the throne, a look of amusement still etched onto his face. "Zego will show you to your quarters."

Isolde slid into a bow, leaning on Malaki for support, before following the rodent to another set of doors to the left. An odd expression painted Erebus's face as she passed the dais. One she couldn't place—one that set her teeth on edge. Instead of going deeper into the mountain, they were led to a set of luxurious rooms running along the mountain's face.

Cillian walked in front. His arm was draped securely, protectively around Blyana's thin waist. She hadn't said a word since the throne room. "There has to be an explanation," Cillian said, his lips brushing her crown of her head. "We'll figure it out."

Still she remained silent. Blyana's shoulders droop lower, curling in on herself.

"Bly?" Worry spread through Isolde when a shudder cascaded down Blyana's back, bringing her to a halt.

"How?" She asked, her voice hollow, eyes brimming with tears. "How can this be, Isolde?"

Isolde looked to Cillian, whose mouth was pulled into a tight line. "I don't know," Isolde said. "But we'll get to the bottom of it."

"She looked at me like," Blyana's words softened. A single tear broke free and slid down her cheek. "Like she hated me."

"That can't be it," Malaki said. "More than likely she was just surprised. I can't imagine she has the luxury of speaking her mind or having thoughts of her own, not with that bastard around."

"Keep your voice down!" Liam said, his teeth clenched. "You've been here before Malaki. You of all people should know this is not the place for this kind of talk!" He glanced back to where Zego had led them past a set of intricately carved wooden doors. The little cretin's eyes were forward, but it was clear he had heard every ounce of the conversation from the small, sickly smile formed on his face.

"I was in this palace centuries before you were born, boy," Malaki snarled, his eye glowing. "I do not take orders from you."

"Malaki!" Isolde said, stepping between them.

"If you want to stay alive you will," said Liam over Isolde's head. "You are the Bastard Prince. You will be a target here. It's a miracle the king let you"—Liam's gaze slid to where Galaena and Alaric waited down the hall—"or those two live after the fall. Do not give Erebus a reason to regret his decision."

"You must enjoy wasting air, Liam," said Malaki. "Because that is all you have done...is wasted your breath."

"And you must enjoy giving Zego a show," Isolde said. "Let's not provide him with anymore free entertainment tonight."

A deadly calm Isolde knew well descended over Malaki's face as he took a step closer. "Do not ever call me that again. Or I will kill you."

"Enough!" Isolde growled, pressing her palms to their chests.

"You might have trained me, Malaki. Taught me all I know about combat and how to be a good man. But this is not Thornwood." Liam's eyes blazed with power, with challenge. "You are nothing here. And there is only so much I can protect you from. Protect all of you from." His dark eyes moved from one face to the next. They landed on Isolde, and a facet of the coldness melted away.

"For her sake," he said, drawing his gaze back Malaki, "try to keep the death threats you throw at a captain in the King's Guard to a minimum."

Malaki's gaze flickered to Isolde before his mouth pulled into a tight line. "Never call me that again," he said. "That name died long ago."

Liam's shoulders relaxed, and a look of relief seemed to hang about the hard angles of his face. "I understand. It won't happen again." The tips of his gloved fingers brushed the back of Isolde's hand as he turned his attention to her. "The ball starts at dusk. I'll be the one dressed in black."

"Aren't you always?" She asked, her eyes rolling.

Isolde wanted nothing more than for him to stay. But instead, Liam let his hand fall away with the hint of a smile playing at the corners of his lips. Without looking back, her Captain of the Guard turned on his heel and walked back down the corridor. His boots echoed off the marble floor in practiced, measured steps.

CHAPTER 10

Hints of blackberry danced across Isolde's tongue as the last of the wine slid down her throat. "I'll give him one thing," she said, offering the servant who hurried forward to refill her goblet a grateful smile. "Erebus might be a bastard, but he does have delicious wine."

"You can thank Ferden for that," Alaric said, from where he lounged across the elegantly decorated table. "The vintage came from his vineyards. His earth wielders are the ones responsible for helping grow the grapes for the wine."

"Of course, they are," Isolde said, eying the lord of Dolinmere. He sat at a table all to himself, as far from the party as possible. Isolde had a feeling he preferred it that way, judging by the look of disgusted indifference on his youthful, handsome face. No one approached him, yet several virya cast curious glances his way.

"Had I known this is what Ferden was offering every time I snuck into his mansion," Isolde said, her voice dropping into a whisper, one only her cadre could hear, "I can't say I wouldn't have unmasked myself for a taste." The stem of the golden goblet twisted between her thumb and forefinger, catching the light of the extravagant chandeliers above. It matched the golden dress hugging her curves. Silk and hand-sewn beads cascaded down her form in rivers of gilded extravagance. It clung to her arms and ran across the span of her maimed back, hiding her behind a shield of gold.

"You and me both," Cillian said, already draining his second cupful.

"I thought you were more of a spirits man, Cill," Malaki said, taking a swig of the amber liquid lingering in the dregs of his own glass. The color matched the brass buttons sewn into the dark green fabric of a new tunic. It spread across his chest and hugged the hills of the muscles running along his arms.

Isolde fought the embers of ancient joy itching to spread and catch fire in her chest. He looked so much like the Malaki she remembered from long ago. The one who had called this place home.

"I don't discriminate," Cillian said. "Especially when it comes to alcohol."

"Or my sweets for that matter," Isolde said, her voice rumbling into her goblet, her eyes locking on her weapons expert. "Care to explain why I found my candy stores nearly empty, Cill?"

"I cannot speak on such matters," he said, a mischievous grin darkening his face. "Sounds like you need to keep a closer watch on your stores."

"I've killed for less," Isolde warned.

Cillian's smile grew with challenge. "Innocent until proven guilty, Lady Isolde."

"Tell us about the tournament, Malaki," Blyana said. "Anything to keep these two from killing each other over candy."

"It was worth dying for," Cillian said. "You know peppermint chocolates are my favorite."

"We'll see if you still feel that way." A smile, one laced with the promise of revenge, spread across Isolde's face, her teeth flashing.

"There are seven champions, one from each of the territories," Malaki began, twirling the whisky in his massive, callused hand. "They can be selected by lottery, appointed the task, or serve on a volunteer basis."

Isolde felt the air chill, felt the unspoken words linger about them like a horrible reminder of Liam's choice.

"The tournament consists of a series of trials," Malaki continued, ignoring the haze of awkwardness. "The number of which is determined by Erebus and the Master of Games who is selected before each tournament. Usually, this individual is a high-ranking officer or advisor to the crown. Someone prone to violence and who is…*creative* in their methods."

Isolde cringed inwardly. Liam's tournament had been a particularly violent one. She could still see the pools of blood covering the arena floor. Its coppery stench hung in the hot summer air, coating her nose and painting her tongue with the taste of death.

"But every trial has a purpose. A means of testing the limits of those unlucky enough to participate," Malaki said after draining the last of his drink. A servant appeared at his side a moment later, filling it once more. He offered her an awkward smile.

"I can't imagine these tasks are easy," Blyana said, the tips of her gloved fingers toying with the golden stem of the goblet. Rays of light from the priceless surface shimmered across the dress running down her tiny, lethal body in a waterfall of grey silk. Isolde's brow bunched at the sight of the gloves covering her friend's hands once again. While they made a lovely addition to the ensemble, Isolde knew it was out of the ordinary.

"No," Alaric said, drawing Isolde's attention. "They're designed to push the champions. To break them down, force them into using their most basic instincts. The ones they will need to survive, to serve in

Erebus's forces."

"That's not all they do," Galaena said, her face set in regretful sadness. "These trials force the champions to prove their loyalty. To prove they will do as ordered….no matter what. Just like Liam's tournament."

A painful lump lodged in Isolde's throat. Liam's second to last trial came to mind, along with the look of horror that had shone on his face as he took in the family of humans at his feet. There are five in all—a mother, father, and three children. His task was to decide who lived…who died…the manner in which they died…and the person who delivered their death to them.

Isolde swallowed a mouthful of wine that now tasted like ash and sorrow. "That Master of Games was a real sadistic bastard."

Alaric nodded. "Codrus's pleasure lay in the emotional pain he caused, not just the physical. His joy came from breaking spirits."

Isolde couldn't help but wonder if that day had broken Liam in some way, shattering a part of the man she cared so much for. The haunted look in his eyes as he drove the blade into the only human left standing, a young girl just on the cusp of womanhood, told her it must have. Liam had tried to cling to the hope at least one would survive, that one would be saved. But all that came…was heartache. Isolde's thoughts drifted to Codrus and cold, vicious glee formed in her mind.

"Please," he had begged her that night, blood trickling from the slit in his lip. "I am the Master of Games. I can make you rich…I can give you whatever you desire!" He crawled backwards out of the latrine, desperate to escape the crimson stained blades in her hands. Slow and steady she followed. "Whatever you want!"

"Can you give me life?" Isolde had asked. "Can you mend a shattered heart, Codrus?"

His face had paled in the wake of her question. Never had she wanted to maim someone so badly, to leave behind the Hood's mark for all to see. But she wasn't the Hood in that moment. She was simply a woman whose heart ached for the pain of another.

She had peeled the mask free from her face, and Codrus's eyes grew wide with recognition. "No, I don't believe you can." She had left him bleeding and writhing in pain on the bathroom floor. He would be found early the next morning, drained of every drop of blood and with a look of shock on his untouched face.

"The final event is always hand to hand combat," Malaki said, jarring Isolde from the bloody memory. "No weapons, only the powers and skills they possess. It ends when only one champion is left standing. Leaving no room for rebuke, no room for rematches. You either win… or die. There are no second chances."

"There is one stipulation," Alaric said. "If a champion is in danger of being eliminated and the lord or lady of a territory is willing to pay, Erebus has the power to keep them in the tournament." His grey gaze flickered to Galaena. "Of course, that particular wish has only been granted a handful of times."

"Pay or die," Isolde said, her lips curling in disgust. "Greed makes monsters of us all."

"Can the rules change?" Cillian asked, blotting away a rogue drop of dark, maroon liquid racing down his chin.

"Erebus started the tournament," Malaki said, his voice hard and unforgiving as stone, "as a means of reminding the people that they are at his mercy. That they are powerless." Ire shone in his gaze as the sound of trumpets rang through the air. "He can do as he wishes."

Wine sloshed over the side of Isolde's glass as she stood with the others, ruining the carpet at her feet. With an air of annoyance, she drove her heel into the stain and twisted her foot from side to side.

All eyes turned to the set of golden doors at the eastern end of the ballroom. Erebus descended like a storm upon land. A smirk, subtle but powerful, played at the edge of his mouth. The crowd parted without question, creating a walkway to the dais residing near the arched windows. Tendrils of pale, silver hair fell down his back and spread across broad shoulders like rays of moonlight. A crown, set with seven obsidian spikes, was nestled upon his brow.

"Good taste in wine and he knows how to dress," Isolde said. "Quite a shame he's a sadistic piece of shit."

Dressed in a pair of ash gray pants and tunic of the finest caliber, Erebus Tenebriath looked every bit the king he pretended to be. His house symbol, a golden triangle encasing a ruby snake eye, dangled from his neck. Fine black leather boots ending at his kneecaps clacked against the marble steps of the dais. A ruby red cloak clinging to his back splayed like a splash of blood across the throne as he took his seat.

"Awfully dramatic, don't you think?" Cillian murmured.

"You were expecting anything less?" Malaki answered with a humorless laugh.

When the trumpets ended their salute, the crowd moved as one, bowing deeply. Isolde bit down on the lining of her cheek and followed suit. Malaki sighed and placed a hand on her back, forcing her bow deeper. A growl of annoyance rumbled at the base of her throat.

"Rise," Erebus ordered with the flick of his wrist, and the masses obeyed. His eyes, piercing and luminous, roamed the ballroom, taking note of everyone in attendance.

Isolde cringed when their frigid gaze fell on her. The familiar look of intrigue that had been there earlier today slowly came to life. A part of her wanted to look away, to hide from the attention. But she refused to be the one to break first. Her brow cocked, and a soft, taunting smile kissed the edge of her freshly painted lips.

Amusement crossed Erebus face at the sight. One that only stoked Isolde's anger. He waved a casual hand through the air. "Carry on."

Cheers filled the ballroom, and the orchestra resumed their piece as if they hadn't been interrupted at all. Virya wove their way past each other like streams of water along a riverbed. Faces wearing false smiles occupied every direction Isolde looked, along with a frightening number of soldiers. Taking a sip of wine, her brow furrowed.

"What's that look for?" Malaki asked.

"Erebus hasn't left much of an opportunity for me to slip away," Isolde said, nodding to the soldiers around the room. "His defenses aren't as complacent as I hoped they would be."

A muscle ticked in Malaki's jaw as he followed her line of sight. "Not tonight they aren't." She knew what he meant, the underlying message his words hid. *Tonight is not the night.*

"We need to get to them, Malaki," Isolde said, her words brushing over the rim of her glass. "Before they end up like Mary. The longer we wait—"

"I know," Malaki said, his warm, tired eyes finding hers. "Believe me, I know." His hand rested across her bare knuckles, easily encasing her hand in his own. "But we need to be smart about this. We need to be patient. There can't be any connection to you or Thornwood."

The edge of Isolde's teeth bit into her cheek until she could taste blood. Malaki was right, she knew he was. Still, impatience stirred in her chest, causing her foot to tap beneath the table.

"We'll find a way," Malaki said. A promise hung in his words—a vow in and of itself.

"Would you care to dance, Lady Isolde?" She turned to find Liam behind her, his hand hovering between them. Just like he promised, he was dressed in black. "Before you tap a hole in the floor."

Malaki stiffened as he withdrew his hand to curl around his glass. "Is a soldier permitted to dance with a lady, *Captain*?"

A shadow fell across Liam's face as his eyes turned to Malaki. "Why of course he is," Isolde said, before another word could be spoken. After tossing back the last of her drink, Isolde deposited her goblet and slid her hand into Liam's awaiting palm.

Partygoers filled the dance floor, forcing Isolde into Liam's space. A tendril of happiness pulled at her heart as she breathed in his scent and allowed the music to fill her to the brim. He moved with such grace, such ease, like currents of wind snaking their way through the forest.

The dance was one Isolde knew well. It involved the shuffling of partners until the original couples were united once more. Isolde fell into step as easily as a bird took to flight. The music carried her, cradled her in its embrace just as much as Liam did.

"How are you?" His deep voice was a whisper at her ear.

"Better now," Isolde said. The tips of her fingers caressed the nape of his neck. Cords of muscle flexed beneath her touch.

Liam sighed and his cheek brushed the crown of her head. "As am I."

With a gentle squeeze of his hand, he sent a wave of warm, calming magic through her body before spinning to the outer ring of the dance floor. His fingers stayed clear of the scar at her side. She wasn't sure if it was out of respect or disgust. Either way, she was relieved.

"Have you heard anything about Helurtu?" she asked.

"Nothing since that day in Blackford." Liam shook his head. "They disappeared without a trace after the attack."

"Have you told anyone?"

"I can't," he said. "Not without causing an uproar."

"But if you report them," Isolde pressed, "wouldn't that give Zibiah hope? Would Erebus think the Hood is still on the loose?"

"Erebus has already been informed that a small group of raiders attacked Thornwood and Briarhole. He thinks all of them were killed, their bodies burned. There would be no reason for him to suspect the Hood was involved. Besides, Volkran and Gage are not the only ones who will face the king's wrath if that information is brought to light." A flicker of fear flashed in his eyes as they darted to the dais.

"He…he would punish you too?"

Liam nodded, causing strands of blackened curls to fall across his brow. "I'm under Gage's command. I would be held responsible just as much as him—along with the rest of the men."

Isolde didn't give a damn about the other men. They could rot for all she cared. But she would never put Liam in harm's way. Even for the sake of revenge, of saving those who had been stolen from her. No, she wouldn't do it.

"I won't say anything." The muscles of his shoulders eased beneath her palm. Fragments of golden light from her dress reflected off his chest like broken pieces of sunlight. Like stars in a bed of night. Her anger began to build the closer they moved to the dais. As they swept past, Isolde purposefully kept her eyes averted from the makeshift throne and the monster who sat upon it, not bothering to spare him a single glance. Notes of violin and piano blended together the closer they moved to the orchestra.

"Do you know where Zib is?" She asked, her voice hardly a whisper. "Or the children?"

Liam tensed beneath her touch. "Don't even think about it, Isolde." His voice was laced with warning.

"I'm not one of your soldiers you can command, Liam. Don't tell me what to think or not to think," Isolde said, her defenses rising. "Surely, you didn't think I would leave her to that fate. That I wouldn't at least try—"

"I thought you were smarter than this," Liam said, his jaw flexing. "I thought you understood there is no saving them. Not from this…not from *him*."

Isolde's blood chilled at Liam's words. "Are they dead, Liam?"

A war ragged in his eyes. Eyes of darkest brown that had seen just as much carnage as she had. It seemed to tear him in two, but still he kept up the dance, his feet never missing a step. Just as Nan had taught him.

"No," Liam said at last, his voice soft and reassuring. "They're not dead. But that doesn't mean they can be saved, Isolde. It's impossible."

Relief flooded Isolde's heart, causing a lump to form in her throat. She forced it down, forced herself to keep moving, to keep the mask in place. As long as their hearts still beat, she would try.

"Well," Isolde said, working the word around the lump in her throat, "impossibility is a specialty of mine. And you know how I love to prove people wrong."

Before Liam could respond, it was time to switch. Isolde slipped from his grip and into the arms of another. She tried to keep up polite conversation, but it was no use. Their words of flattery were of little interest to her. Liam's words rolled through her mind and broke against the confidence she once felt.

He's just worried, she thought to herself, refusing to bow to the weight of her uncertainty. *Just worried.*

The feeling of a new pair of arms slipping around her waist, pulling her from the depths of her thoughts. Isolde looked up into the eyes of her new partner and every muscle stiffened. Her power, raw and savage, roared to the surface in one mighty wave of burning hatred.

"How I've missed you, Lady Isolde." Fresh scars, deep and hideous, stretched against Gage's otherwise perfect golden skin. "I see you took the king up on his invitation," he purred. "Seeing as you were so adamant to refuse mine, I'm rather surprised."

"I would hardly call his letter an invitation," Isolde spat, not even attempting to hide the disgust in her tone. "A command is more appropriate. I'm sure I can find you a dictionary or a scholar perhaps who can help you learn the difference if you're having difficulty." She tried pulling away, revulsion coating her skin at his touch. But Gage simply yanked her into the throng of dancers.

"Come now," he whispered against the shell of her ear. "Be the well-bred lady I know is in there somewhere." His hold gave her no choice but to follow. Locks of his chestnut hair were pulled back into a neat ponytail at the nape of his neck. They shimmered against the smoky grey tunic stretched over the planes of his chest. It traveled down to a pair of charcoal britches that disappeared into a pair of knee-high black boots.

"There," he said, a charming smile forming on his ruined face. "Is that so hard?" His hand moved to her lower back, forcing the beads of her dress to press through the fabric and into her scarred flesh.

"You've changed since the last time I saw you, Gage," Isolde said, her lips curling into a mocking smile. "Do tell me who did that to your face. I must give them a reward for their efforts."

Fire flashed in Gage's eyes, and his hand constricted until the bones of her fingers popped. "What a very unkind thing to say," he said, his voice smooth as velvet but laced with violence.

"I was merely complimenting you on the improvements," Isolde said. "If I'm not mistaken, those are the marks of the Hood. I suppose he is good for something after all."

A cruel smile broke out onto Gage's face, making his scars all the more gruesome. "She."

A breath caught in Isolde's throat. "What?"

"I believe you mean *she*."

Isolde remained silent, keeping the mask of confusion firmly in place.

"Oh, I suppose you haven't heard the news," he said pulling her closer. Isolde pressed a hand to his chest, doing what she could to keep some distance between them. "We captured the Hood at Briarhole. It was your dear friend, Lady Zibiah."

Isolde froze in Gage's arms as a gasp ripped from her throat. She knew it was coming, to hear her friend formally accused of the crimes that painted her hands red.

"I can see this is rather shocking," Gage said. A row of perfect, white teeth raked over his bottom lip and released it with a smack. "How terribly upsetting it must be to discover your friend is a traitor to the crown."

"You lie!"

I would never," Gage said, false charm leaking into his voice. "Especially not to a lady."

"What have you done with her?" Isolde demanded, her teeth set on edge.

"Oh, nothing that would be proper for your ears," he cooed, releasing the unrelenting pressure on her hand to spin her out once more. "She isn't dead, if that's your concern—not yet anyway. The king doesn't want the Hood's death to be anything less than spectacular."

"Like any true savage," Isolde said, her lip curling. "You both are truly despicable."

"I would watch what you say, Isolde," Gage said, his gaze sharpening in warning. "Especially to your future husband."

"You still think I am going to marry you?" Isolde said, her voice ringing with the hilarity. "You're insane if you believe that. Or delusional. Let's be honest, it could be either one."

"Oh, I guarantee you will," Gage said, his eyes on her lips. "Because that traitorous bitch is not the only thing I brought back with me from Briarhole." Countless faces flashed in Isolde's mind, causing her to miss a step in the dance. Gage's grip on her waist tightened, holding her up right.

"I see that little detail found its way to you," said Gage. "I was worried you might need a little reminder of exactly where we stand. Like the little gift I left you at the gate."

Dread spilled into Isolde's blood. It hammered in her ears as something dark filled Gage's eyes. Shadows, or the very essence of them, lingered along the edges of the pools of crystal blue. Isolde trembled at the sight. At whatever power lurked beneath Gage's skin. She became utterly aware of his hands, unforgiving and probing.

"Get your hands off me, Gage," Isolde said, shoving against him. But his fingers only dug deeper, forcing the beads further into her skin. "Let go of me now!" Isolde growled, her power surging forward.

Amusement spread across his face, the scars highlighting the wickedness within. Still he refused to let go as he pushed her around the dance floor. "How long will you deny me? The Right Hand of the king and the heir of Thornwood—my, what a pair we would make."

Her lip pulled back into a snarl, and a fraction of her power bled through the walls of her control. "My threat still stands. Or have you forgotten what happened the last time you visited Thornwood?"

Gage pushed closer until every plane of his body was flushed against her own. Music and laughter filled the air, and Isolde felt her chest tighten. "I don't believe you're armed, at least not in this dress." His thumb ran along the laced sleeve at her wrist. "No place for a blade in here."

"You made the same mistake last time. And it almost cost you what little you have down there."

"You really do like to try my patience, don't you?" Without warning, Gage's fingers hooked around Isolde's wrist and twisted back at a cruel angle. She fought against the whimper but could do nothing for the shining, angry tears of pain glistening in her eyes. Still she continued to dance, denying him the satisfaction of seeing her break.

"There they are," Gage said, exhaling. "I do love your eyes when you're angry, Isolde." A chuckle rumbled over his lips that had pulled into a cruel, sadistic smile. It bled through his chest and into hers. "But I think I like them far better this way." A fraction of his hold released as he spun her towards the center of the dance floor.

He reeled her in, and Isolde's knee shot forward, the tip of her kneecap aiming for his crotch. But Gage was ready. His massive thigh moved to block the blow. "I can make you feel good, Isolde," Gage murmured. "I guarantee it."

"I highly doubt that," Isolde said. "If the rumors can be believed, I can't imagine you could make a woman feel anything but disappointment."

Gage's hand twisted again, forcing a small cry to bleed through Isolde's lips. The bones of her hand ached and throbbed as if they were on the brink of shattering. "Those rumors are false," he growled, light burning the depths of his eyes. "Or do I have to prove that to you as well? Let you experience what being with a real male feels like?"

"I've already been with a real male," Isolde said with a vicious smile, her eyes stinging with pain. "And *he* certainly did not disappoint."

"Liam, I assume?" Gage growled, his teeth bared. "Don't you think your legs would be better spread for the Right Hand of the king than a guard from the gutter?"

"Mind if I cut in?"

The sound of Malaki's voice sliced through the fog of fury and pain spreading through Isolde's mind. He stood with a subdued grin on the corner of his mouth. While his skin was pale and gleaming with sweat, Malaki still held the presence of a warrior. Of a man who walked side by side with death.

Gage's grip slackened, and Isolde ripped her hand free.

"Absolutely," she said, taking Malaki's hand. He began moving with the rest of the crowd, his grip secure but not painful. The rhythm of his steps stopped when Gage's voice cut through the air.

"We were in the middle of a private conversation, *bastard!*" Gage said, yanking Isolde free from Malaki's grip. "Your services are not required at the moment. So, why don't you go mingle with the rest of the peasants."

"Didn't really sound like polite conversation," Malaki said, bringing Gage to a halt. "Or at least not a conversation fit for a lady."

A look of disgust spread across Gage's face. "I don't believe it's any concern of yours what I discuss with my fiancée."

"Once again," Isolde said, fighting the urge to grab the blade buried in the folds of her dress and plunge it into Gage's neck, "you're deranged if you think I'm going to marry you." Gage's grip on her wrist grew, a hint of his temper showing beneath the fracture of his charming facade.

"Can you blame her?" Malaki asked, an amused grin forming on his face. "The only thing worse than being married to a male who isn't equipped to satisfy his wife is being married to a maimed one who can't satisfy her. Wouldn't want her to be the laughingstock of court, now would you?"

"You dare insult the king's Right Hand?" Spittle flew from Gage's lips as he threw Isolde's hand to the side and ripped the sword from his scabbard. The metal shrieked, sending a chill down Isolde's spine. It was a beautiful weapon, one adorned in rubies and streaked with elithrium. The scar at her side ached in remembrance.

Stunned silence filled the ballroom as the two massive virya stared in hatred across Isolde's head. "Insult implies dishonesty," Malaki said, his eyes glowing. "And I highly doubt so many would lie about your lack of…*substance*, Gage." He reached around to the back of his tunic, to where Secrettaker rested in the lining of his britches.

"Malaki, stop!" Isolde said. Her voice rang with panic, causing her second in command to pause.

"So, Viributhian's Bastard Prince still takes orders from a female," Gage snarled. "I see that particular habit hasn't changed at all. No wonder they're all dead."

A roar of fury ripped through a row of sharpened teeth glistening behind Malaki's curled lip. Isolde ignored the lash of anguish slicing through her heart as she stepped to block his path to Gage. "Malaki," she said, her voice harboring a note of gentleness. "Please, stop. They're just words."

Malaki's muscles locked and his eyes flickered to her for just a moment, not daring to look away from Gage for too long. Isolde could see the anger receded as he rose from his stance, not fully letting down his defenses.

"Such weakness," Gage sneered. "Not that I expected any less from the Bastard Prince."

Red painted Isolde's vision, her anger flaring to life like a flame. She turned back to Gage, her mouth open and tongue armed like a quiver of arrows. But her voice died away in the wake of another. "What is this commotion?"

Erebus materialized out of nowhere. His very presence seemed to take up the entire space, sapping the air itself.

"This filthy, traitorous rat insulted me, Your Majesty," Gage said, his sword still pointed at Malaki's heart.

"How weak you must be if mere words wound you so, Gage," Malaki said, his lips quirking in hatred.

Erebus's penetrating gaze turned to Malaki who stilled. Isolde's pulse hammered against her skull, saturating her blood with fear.

"Malaki," Erebus said, his eyes looking him up and down. "The Right Hand and General of Queen and King Viributhian…the Bastard Prince of Arnoria…has come home at last."

Malaki's eyes were glued to the floor, his hands balling into fists at his side. Isolde's teeth ground together, as she willed herself to stay calm. Erebus extended a single finger and lifted Malaki's chin.

"It is still considered rude to not look your king in the eye. Or have you forgotten?" Malaki quivered with rage at Erebus's touch.

Cautiously, Isolde stepped forward and placed a hand on Malaki's forearm. He trembled beneath her touch but kept his emotions in check. Reluctantly, he brought his gazed up to meet Erebus's. "I've forgotten nothing." His words were hard as stone and filled with such meaning Isolde's heart ached. Erebus kept his finger in place, his brow cocked. "King Erebus." The words grated through Malaki's teeth like steel upon stone.

"Good," Erebus said, flicking his finger away. "I'm thrilled to see you haven't lost all of your decorum, Malaki. But it seems there is still an issue that needs attending to. It is true you insulted my Right Hand?"

"His manners leave much to be desired."

"I can do with my future wife as I please!" Gage snarled.

"I wasn't aware I had accepted your proposal, Gage," Isolde said. "And with a face like yours, I don't intend to either."

Snickers echoed behind the hands and goblets of those littered around the ballroom. Whispers of the rumors Isolde had helped bring to light at Foxclove filled the air.

"Little bitch!" Gage took a step forward, his hand drawn back ready to strike her. Malaki immediately darted into his path, a feral growl rumbling through his chest. He stood a good three inches higher than Gage. But even with that advantage, it would be no contest. Malaki was injured and Gage's skill with a blade was nothing to scoff at. The scar at her side was proof of that.

Erebus raised his hand in warning, forcing Malaki to halt. Isolde felt the weight of his steely gaze, a gaze that almost seemed amused. She felt naked beneath it, exposed in a way she couldn't quite grasp.

"Well, I see no reason to make this a complicated matter. Let's say this." A calm look passed over Erebus's face, one Isolde assumed he wore as king when the time called for it. "If Lady Isolde agrees to let the matter drop," he said, sweeping a hand to her second-in-command who was still staring daggers at Gage, "Malaki, will not be punished for insulting the integrity of a member of my court. I believe that's more than fair. Wouldn't you agree?"

Anger burned through Isolde's marrow like wildfire. Off to the right, among the horde of Briarhole, Volkran chuckled into his glass.

His dark eyes brimmed with sickening delight. Lauram stood at his side, swaying from one foot to the other, his auburn hair tussled and unkempt.

Swallowing her pride and anger, knowing that any other answer would result in Malaki's death, Isolde forced herself into a curtsey. "That is generous of you, Your Majesty." Her tongue felt like lead as the words fell over here lips with such reluctance she was surprised they came out at all. "Thank you."

"I'm thrilled you think so, Lady Isolde. I'll consider the matter closed then," Erebus said, the same smile clinging to his face. "Everyone back to the party."

Gage sheathed his sword and cast a final look of promised retribution before disappearing into the crowd. Alaric and Galaena were working their way to the dance floor, but she sent them a subtle shake of her head.

"Isolde," Malaki said, his gentle fingers resting on her wrists that would undoubtedly harbor fresh bruises by the end of the night. Pink imprints of Gage's fingers lingered on her skin like a sore, haunting reminder.

"I'm fine," She swallowed, not allowing herself to think about what just happened. "They'll heal by tomorrow."

Liam appeared at her side, his eyes brimming with worry. "Isolde, I'm so sorry. Are you alright?"

"It's not your fau—"

"You have a lot to be sorry for," Malaki said, cutting her off. "Where were you while that monster had his hands all over the woman you claim to love so much?"

Shock gave way to fury, causing Liam's cheeks to burn.

"I hate to interrupt," Erebus said, arriving just in time to stop whatever words dangled on the tip of Liam's tongue. "Might I have a word with Lady Isolde for a moment, gentlemen?"

CHAPTER 11

"If it's not too much trouble, of course," Erebus said, the corner of his mouth curling, knowing she couldn't refuse. *What can he possibly want?*

Malaki stiffened at Isolde's side. His fingers, which rested on her elbow, tightened instantly.

Liam's head bowed and the face of an obedient soldier fell back into place with ease. "Of course, Your Majesty." His eyes rose to meet hers. *Please*, they seemed to say, *be smart in what you say.*

Malaki pried his fingers away and took a step back with what would hardly be considered a bow of his own. A heated look filled his gaze as he turned and made his way back through the crowd. The rest of her cadre stood waiting, their eyes heavy with worry.

"He doesn't care for me too much, does he," Erebus asked, following Malaki's retreat. "I suppose I can't blame him. I did kill his family, after all."

Isolde stilled, her mind racing with a mirage of thoughts pummeling against her control. Thoughts of a quiver full of her arrows puncturing every inch of his body— his blood painting the walls of Elenarta. But still, the mask of a lady waiting to do her king's bidding remained firmly in place.

"Walk with me," Erebus said, offering up his arm. Fighting her repulsion, Isolde lightly placed her hand on the luxurious fabric. It was incredibly soft, expensive, and finely tailored. Casually, Erebus patted her hand as he sighed, forcing her to feel the hard muscle beneath. The tip of his finger tugged back the sleeve of her dress, imbedding a chill beneath her skin.

Erebus's eyes narrowed ever so slightly at the sight of the marks Gage's grip left behind. "I do apologize for that unpleasantness," he said, leading them to the balcony overlooking the exquisite gardens below. A darkness filled his gaze, one that held history and memory. It turned the beautiful orbs of silver into pits of steel.

"Perhaps teaching your men some manners would be beneficial," Isolde said, her voice clipped, teetering on the border of incivility. "I can't imagine a king who allows his men to get away with such behavior is one who holds much respect with his subjects."

The cords of muscles running beneath Isolde's palm hardened. "You disagree with how I handled the situation, Lady Isolde?"

Isolde merely shrugged. "It's not my place to say, Your Grace."

"But clearly you have no issue with voicing your opinions," Erebus said. "No matter how they might affect the ones you claim to care so much about."

Isolde flinched beneath his chilled grip, her heart racing. "It was not my intention to—"

"Insult your king?" Erebus demanded, his voice hardening. "I never took you for a fool, Lady Isolde. I suggest you extend me the same curtesy. We both know the power words possess. How they can be wielded just as thoroughly, just as lethally as a blade." Erebus's voice held an allure of quiet power. An intoxicating sound that put Isolde on guard. "Your healer, Malaki, made a grave error tonight. He humiliated and questioned the authority of a soldier. My Right Hand, nonetheless. A crime punishable by death."

Isolde felt the blood drain from her face, and panic swelled in the pit of her stomach. Erebus continued to lead her further down the balcony, away from the light of the party. The night air whipped around her, driving the cold deeper. "He was just trying to protect me, Your Majesty."

"Does your honor possess more value than the authority of my men?" Erebus asked. "I showed him, and therein you, mercy. I can imagine his death, as justified as it might be, would only cause you pain. You should be thanking me for my leniency…not lecturing me on what I should or should not do with my position. You will find that I do not take kindly to ungratefulness in my court."

Isolde fell silent. Every ounce of her will power was focused on containing the well of rage festering in her mind. After a moment, she swallowed the pride threatening to choke her. "I do apologize, Your Majesty. It was not my intention to slight you or your rule."

A chuckle, cold as a winter's breeze, filtered through the night air. "I don't believe that for a moment. But I do accept your apology, no matter how not heartfelt it might be."

"Truly, Your Grace," Isolde said, through a brittle smile. "It was not my intention. Gage's advances are not something I want or care to be on the receiving end of. A fact I have made abundantly clear on multiple occasions."

Erebus's gaze shifted to the mountain range stretched out before them. Stars filled the night sky, their light twinkling in and out of existence. "The liberties Gage seems so willing to take with someone who is not his will be a matter dealt with, I can assure you." Isolde caught the faintest flicker of his eyes landing on the marks decorating her wrist once more. A burst of light, cold and powerful, breached the corner of his eyes.

Surprise, unwanted and foreign, swelled in Isolde's chest. "Thank you." The last thing she needed was to be in the clutches of a debt to Erebus Tenebriath.

"Speaking of Lord Gage," Erebus continued, releasing her from his frigid grasp, "I have heard some rather disturbing rumors, Lady Isolde."

"Do elaborate, Your Majesty, so that I might set the record straight."

"Well, I'm not sure how you can, not when so many have come forward to confirm what you are accused of." Under the heavy gaze of the king, a gaze that leveled people with a single touch, Isolde felt her mouth go dry. "Is it or is it not true you hold a weekly gathering at your manor for children? A *story hour*, I believe is what you call it. For both virya and human and whatever *spawn* lies between?"

"I wasn't aware reading was a crime." Her heart raced beneath the words that sounded so calm as they fell from her mouth.

"It is," Erebus said, his eyes narrowing, "to those who are not worthy of such things. Reading to the humans and half-bloods is a very grave, very dangerous crime, Lady Isolde."

"Why?"

"Why?' Erebus scoffed, resting his hands on the ornate railing. The fragile, cool light of the moon blended with the light from the party dancing on the tips of his crown. "Reading is a freedom that gives birth to ideas. Ideas lead to hope. Hope…leads to revolution. If you educate them, you arm them." He turned to her once more, his eyes lit with power. "We are the superior race, Lady Isolde. And I intend to keep it that way."

Isolde licked her lips as words that would end in death clung to the back of her throat. "They're children." She hated the frail, pleading tone in her voice. "What harm can a child do?"

"Yes," Erebus said, pushing away from the railing. "And what do children become?"

Her eyes fell to the railing at her side, unable to give an answer that wouldn't result in her head on a spike.

"You have committed a great act against me, Lady Isolde. And the kingdom for that matter." He placed an ice-cold finger beneath her chin, forcing her to look up at him. Light shone in his eyes, the same light she had seen in the throne room earlier that day. A dangerous, intriguing glow she couldn't look away from. "What do you suppose I should do about that?"

Pulling on the one thing she knew best with men like him, Isolde's eyebrow cocked, and a soft, seductive smile pulled at the edges of her lips. The tips of her fingers trailed along the edge of his hand holding her face. The light in his eyes grew at her touch. "Oh, I'm sure you've thought of something already, Your Majesty."

"Admittedly, killing you and your whole family was my first choice. Then I thought better of it." Erebus's lip quirked, and his finger dropped, releasing her from its frigid hold. "Killing you would only spark hatred in an already divided kingdom and I have no interest or need in making you a martyr. But joining me—"

"Never."

The word spilled from Isolde's mouth before she could stop it. It lifted from her lips in a single breath. The appeal of death only grew as the thought festered, infecting her mind.

A strange sensation ran over the surface of Isolde's lips a moment later. A tingling, painful chill spread and welded her mouth shut. Her fingers probed at the layer of frost covering her mouth, panic swelling in her chest.

"Do let me finish a sentence," Erebus chided. "It's bad manners to interrupt a king." Isolde forced a deep breath through her nose, willing her heart to calm. She fought back a growl with gritted teeth, her hands placed firmly at her side. "A lady of your breeding should know better."

Isolde's teeth ground, her face numbing to Erebus's power. The monster buried deep within snarled. *Not now… not now…*

"As I was saying," Erebus continued, "there are many in the kingdom who hold you in very high esteem. Who look to you for strength. Your allegiance, as the beloved maiden of Thornwood, will solidify my hold in this kingdom. You will join the tournament tomorrow as Thornwood's champion. And when you win,"—a dark smile spread across his face that seemed to glow in the moonlight—"you will serve in my court, at my side. Willingly…and permanently."

Isolde felt the effects of Erebus's magic fade, allowing her to speak. "Me? Join the tournament?" A small laugh escaped her frost-covered lips, her head shaking in disbelief.

"This is not a joke, my dear," Erebus said, his tone just as cold as the ice swimming through his veins. "I suggest you not treat it as such."

Isolde's mind was reeling. "I don't know the first thing about fighting."

"Lord Volkran has already informed me of the little band of raiders you met in Blackford." Her mouth snapped shut. *Fucking Volkran.* "He spoke most highly of your skill with a blade. Even your bravery in daring to chase after one of them on your own. I believe you're more than qualified."

Isolde shook her head. "How can I join?" she asked. "Bane is Thornwood's champion."

"It would seem your dear Bane, has agreed to relinquish the honor to you," Erebus said, the corner of his mouth turning up into a smirk.

Isolde's heart thundered so loud in her chest, she knew Erebus could hear it. "And why is that?"

Erebus shrugged. "He thought better of it."

"Did you kill him?" Isolde asked, already preparing for the answer. Bane was a quiet, kind man. One who loved Thornwood and her family.

A humorless and melodic laugh danced across his lips. "I am many things, but wasteful is not one of them. Especially, when it comes to spilling viryian blood. He is better served elsewhere."

Isolde breathed a sigh with relief, her heart marginally lighter. "And if I refuse?"

"Oh, I have my ways of persuading you." Erebus casually waved his hand behind him and a lone soldier, one she had not been aware of, stepped from the shadows clinging to the palace walls. A sharp whistle pierced the air, the sound carrying over the edge of the rail.

"Come have a look," Erebus said, gesturing to the garden below.

Slowly, Isolde forced one foot in front of the other, her heart hammering in her chest. A cry that nearly broke free slammed into the back of her teeth as she clamped them shut. There, huddled in the mass of lilies and roses, were the children taken from Briarhole, Foxclove, and Whisper.

"Here she is, children," Erebus called. "Just as I promised." Tear-stained eyes turned up to where she stood. Their familiar, terrified gazes burned into hers.

"Lady Isolde?" A small gasp broke through her defense at the sound of that voice. "Lady Isolde, is that you?" Tanor stepped forward. Moonlight caught the golden curls clinging to his brow as a soldier latched onto his arm, keeping him in place.

"Tanor," Isolde said, her voice weak and trembling. "Tanor, it's…it's alright." Her words sounded hollow, even to her.

"That one's important to you, it seems. Very interesting." Erebus mused.

Isolde had to brace her hands against the railing to keep from losing her grip on reality. Her head fell between her shoulders, stretching the scars on her back and side. Insil was pressed into Tanor's side. The half-moon scar streaking across her cheek stood in stark contrast with her porcelain skin. Her eyes were so wide, so full of fear.

"You're a very intelligent woman, Lady Isolde. But I'll make this simple. If you do not compete, they will die," Erebus said, his voice soft as a lover's caress. He came to stand behind her and placed his hands on the railing next to her own, caging her in. A polished ruby, bright and pure, glistened from his left pinky finger. So pure, it had to have come from the depths of Oronilma itself.

"If you fail in this tournament," he whispered into the shell of her ear, causing her to shiver, "I will make sure you bear witness to the last breath each one of them takes. You will hear every plea that falls from their lips. Every drop of their blood will be spilled before your eyes."

"Punish me," she said, her voice a strangled rasp. "Publicly. Make me an example."

"As I've told you before, I am many things, but wasteful is not one of them. And I don't intend on wasting any part of you if I can help it," Erebus murmured. She felt the bridge of Erebus' nose travel along the length of her neck, breathing in her scent, sending a shiver of disgust down her spine. "This is your punishment, my dear. Win the tournament, serve me, and they live. Refuse or fail, and they die, my little falcon." He waved his hand through the air and the soldiers began pulling the children away.

"Lady Isolde!" Tanor cried, shoving against the guard's unforgiving grip. "Please, Lady Isolde!"

"He seems to be quite fond of you too," Erebus said. "Another one of your students, perhaps?"

Isolde remained quiet, her lips firmly pressed together.

"You saw upon your arrival I'm not above killing children," he said, pushing away from the railing to move back to the door. "They're a weakness, Lady Isolde. Your pressure point. One I can press at any time of my choosing."

"And what of your weaknesses?" Isolde asked, her voice low and full of lethal promise.

Erebus paused mid-step. The only sounds remaining were the cries of those below and the faint snap of the flags as they tossed in the evening wind. Erebus tilted his chin back to her, his eyes cold and hard as ice.

"My weaknesses..." He turned his full gaze upon her now, and a tremor of cold cascaded down her spine. The look in his eyes was haunting and filled with a torturous melancholy. "There is no weakness left in me. I killed it years ago." Sorrow, frigid and brutal, stared back at Isolde. It was a gaze filled with desolate despair, but one that also held acceptance in its midst.

Erebus turned to leave once more, but a question shot from Isolde's mouth before she could stop it. "And what of the Lady of Briarhole?" She asked. "What of Zibiah?"

"I take it you've heard?" Isolde's lips pressed into a thin line as she turned to face him fully. Allowing her silence to answer for her.

"You care for the Hood?" Erebus asked, a look of disgust crossing his face. Isolde remained quiet, her face impassive. "I can't say I'm surprised given your love of the humans and half-bloods. But rest assured she is alive—for now."

"I request to see her," Isolde said in a rush.

A thoughtful look softened the harsh lines of the king's face. "My father was cruel man," Erebus said, his tone cold and matter of fact. "Cruel but brilliant. He was a sadistic creature who held power above all else. But he had a saying for those who faced the consequences of the choices they had made. "When the darkness of the past has been lifted, those who stand in its light will burn beneath it."

Erebus turned his unforgiving gaze to her. "No, Lady Isolde." It was an answer, a tone that rang with authority. "Zibiah is paying for her crimes. It would be in your best interest to forget her."

A retort rose on her tongue, but Isolde was unable to produce it.

For in the next breath, Erebus's smooth voice filled the air. "And one more thing." He turned on his heel and strode to stand before her, dwarfing her in shadow. "There seems to have been a slight miscommunication on one point."

"And what point might that be, Your Majesty?" The next words to fall from Erebus' mouth rippled over Isolde's skin like claps of thunder, a death toll to her very soul.

"You will marry Gage." Shock stilled Isolde's heart, and her mouth parted in a sigh of horror. "By the end of the tournament."

Disbelief gave way to unrelenting fury. "I wasn't aware I had accepted Gage's proposal," Isolde said, her voice broadening on the edge of a snarl.

"And I wasn't aware your opinion or desire mattered in this situation," Erebus retorted, his brow rising. "You sealed that particular fate for yourself tonight when you publicly humiliated and undermined my Right Hand. An offense I will show no leniency for. You will marry him. And you will both serve at my side. Otherwise…"

Erebus's gaze flickered beyond the balcony. Isolde could still hear the children as they were being escorted back to whatever hellhole they were being held in. "I'm sure you understand. I can't have my Right Hand fighting with another member of my court, now can I?"

CHAPTER 12

"Worse fates have been dealt to those who are guilty of far less," Erebus said, as Isolde's world crumbled at his feet. "Be grateful for the one you've been granted." He strode back to the ballroom with his head held high and a look of smug serenity painted on his face.

It felt as if the hand of fate had wrapped its cruel fingers around Isolde's throat and tightened. Squeezing...crushing, leaving her breathless and hollow. Despite the well of power humming through her blood, not a single breath of air filled her chest. Isolde's heartbeat became too fast as she strode across the balcony and back into the party. Far, far too fast. She shoved her way through the crowd filling the ballroom, faces passing in a blur. Words and voices jumbled in her head in a mess of noise and chaos. They meshed and blended with the children's pleas and Erebus's damning declaration.

Fighting her way through the crowd, Isolde felt the pressure build. The walls seemed to move in, forcing her to move faster. The gilded doorway passed overhead, her fingers clutching at her chest.

"Lady Isolde," Lauram said, shoving away from the wall on her left. He teetered to the side, his eyes bloodshot and unfocused. Wine's unmistakable scent hung in the air around him. "Ssssoo good to…to see you again. I'm still wa..waiting for that dance—"

Lauram's words died as Isolde's fist collided with the side of his face. The heir to Briarhole fell to the ground at her feet in drunken heap. A trickle of blood seeped from his lips, staining the white marble floor.

"Keep waiting," Isolde said, without breaking stride, her knuckles barking in pain. Moans followed in her wake, but she ignored them. Air…she needed air.

Before long, she entered a stretch of hallways, each one housing a series of archways cut into the walls themselves. The peaks of the mountain range glistened in the light of the full moon, its beams highlighting the path before her.

Panic and anger slashed through Isolde's heart the further she walked. Her breaths left her chest in rapid pants. But as hope gave way to despair, a sound brought her to a halt.

"Move it, you little shits!"

A whip's crack echoed through the night, and a wail of pain followed behind. Leaning over the railing of an archway, Isolde gazed down one of the narrow cobblestone streets beyond the inner wall surrounding the palace. At the far end of an alley, its walls lined with shadows and empty windows, she caught sight of a small body hitting the ground. A faint cry carried through the night. A cry so soft and frail Isolde knew it was a child. One she had heard before.

"Nyla!"

The soldier stalked forward to stand over her tiny frame and she curled into herself, withering beneath his shadow. Even from that distance, Isolde could see how small she was. How starved and broken she had become in such a short time. Isolde's lips pulled back over her teeth and the tips of her fingers dug into the ancient stone beneath her palms.

"On your feet," he snarled, gripping a chunk of her blonde hair, and yanking her to her feet. "Unless you want another one." He shoved her forward into the group of children half hidden in shadow, her small cry echoing through the night sky.

Isolde's resolve burned into cinders. She threw legs over the edge, ripping the seam of her beautiful, golden gown. The open air covered her like a second skin as she leapt. The wind kissed the bare flesh of her upper thighs as she fell. The street, which resided fifty feet below, rose to meet her. Throwing her hands out, pulling on the well of power that dwelt within, Isolde sent a blast of wind shooting to the ground beneath, cushioning the blow.

She struck the unforgiving stone, snapping the heels of her overly priced shoes instantly on impact. Rivers of cracked stone shot out around her like webs of fractured glass. Her mother's ring hummed with power. It burned with a ferocity Isolde welcomed with open arms. Without a second thought, she took off across the open courtyard, keeping to the shadows. The soldiers manning the inner wall kept their eyes forward. Their attention wasn't wasted on those trying to break out of Elenarta but was reserved for those trying to break in.

The monster within prowled at the corners of Isolde's mind. It sank its fangs deeper into her will with every step she took, filling her head with a bloodlust she could not and did not want to forsake. The blade she kept strapped at her thigh winked in the light of the torches lining the streets as she yanked it from the sheath.

The neck of the first soldier who dared enter her path lay open at its touch. He fell to the ground without a word, filling the rivets of cobblestone with blood. Still she didn't stop. Another came forward, his sword drawn, eyes glowing with power.

"Stop!" he cried, raising the blade to meet her own. "Stop in the name of King—" Isolde skirted the edge of his sword and drove the dagger into the back of his head. Only silence followed, save for the clinking of his armor as he fell to the ground.

She rounded a corner and came face to face with a pair of glowing, terror-filled eyes. "Lady Isolde," the soldier said, his eyes wide and full of uncertainty. She wasn't sure how he recognized her, nor did she care. "Please stop, Lady Iso-" Her blade slashed across his bare throat, silencing his pleas for mercy. Blood cascaded down his, disappearing beneath the plate of shining armor. Blinded by rage, she shoved him into a deserted alleyway.

Isolde could still hear the small group. Their cries bounced between the walls lining the street, filling her head like chimes of torture. But any sign of them, any hint as to where they had gone…was lost. A cry of fury exploded from her lips as her eyes snapped to her reflection in a shop window on her left. Blood splattered the golden dress and painted her skin. She was a nightmare, a vision of beauty painted in death.

Where are they? The same panic began to rise in her chest, her attention returning to the deserted streets. *Where are they?* But every way she turned, every street she searched, was empty. At last, Isolde turned the final corner leading out of the residential district and stopped short. A massive grate, one that would put Briarhole's to shame, stood in her way. In the depths of the shadows, Isolde caught sight of the last few children being shoved into the darkness of the dungeons.

"Close the gate!" A soldier called, his voice filling the air.

Slowly, like the mouth of a giant, the teeth of the grate lowered. Panic swelled in her chest, driving her forward. But as she took a step, nearly stepping out from the shadow's secure embrace, a battalion of soldiers came into view. Shoulder to shoulder, they formed a single impenetrable line along the front of the dungeon's entrance. A thud boomed through the air as the grate slammed closed. Another followed behind, one that came from deeper within. Then another…and another.

"Shit!" Isolde hissed. Adrenaline and anger burned through her veins like molten lead. *I need to get to them.* Her mind raced with plans, each one falling into ash. *I need to get to them now!*

"Isolde!" She turned to the sound of her name. The unmistakable shadow who had been at her side for so long shuffled down the alley, Secrettaker's clutched in his hand.

"Malaki," she said, pointing a finger back to the dungeon. "I saw them." Her voice was a rasp, a terrible sound bouncing off the immaculate stone walls. Cillian and Blyana broke through the darkness of the alleyway, each clutching a bloody blade in their grasp.

Malaki stopped before her, his brow glistening with sweat. A patch of wet fabric clung to his side, to the wound that had undoubtedly reopened. Worry shone from his gaze at the sight of the blood that was not her own. "Isolde…"

"I saw them!" She said, her voice rising. "Malaki, I saw them!"

"The children?" Blyana asked, her eyes darting to the dungeons at Isolde's back.

Isolde nodded. "They're alive but they're… they're…" Tears of anger and grief swelled in her eyes and the back of her hand pressed to her lips. "I have to get to them," she said turning on her heel, not even noticing her feet were now bare.

Malaki's strong yet gentle hands landed on her shoulders, bringing her to a halt. She fought against his hold, desperate to keep moving. But he merely held her tighter and turned her around to face him.

"Breathe," Malaki said, bringing the palms of his hands to cup her face, forcing her to look only at him. "With me." She fought against his grip, her fingers digging into the flesh of his wrists. Secrettaker's pommel brushed the side of her face, its surface warm and smooth. But Malaki didn't budge. "Breathe, Isolde," he repeated, "with me."

Bits of his power, what little he could spare, seeped into her skin. Its soft touch forced her heart to slow, forced the unstoppable storm in her chest to calm. "Don't you dare try to calm me!" she snarled, trying to yank away from his hold.

But Malaki only held her tighter. "With me."

Defeated, Isolde closed her eyes and pulled all of her focus into matching Malaki's every breath. Air pushed in and out of her lungs, clearing her head. But as the clouds of panic gave way, reality drove its unrelenting claws deeper. Isolde's teeth ground as the weight of it all crashed down in one mighty blow.

"Malaki…"

"We'll get them," Malaki said. "I promise. We just need time to plan. During the tournament, we can—"

"He's making me join," Isolde said, her jaw feathering beneath his palm.

A breath caught in Malaki chest. "What?"

"The tournament," she said. "Erebus is forcing me to join the tournament as Thornwood's champion."

A beat of silent disbelief hung between all. It was severed as curse after curse fell from Cillian's lips. "Fucking prick, king asshole, bastard!" he growled, gripping the back of his head. Blyana didn't move; she was frozen at his side.

Realization ignited in Malaki's eyes. Furious horror filled his gaze as a slight tremor racked through his arms, causing him to cling tighter. Reaching up, Isolde gripped Malaki's forearms, anchoring her to him and said, "Stay with me." Her voice was hard as steel. "I need you here. I need you with me, Malaki."

"Isolde," Malaki said, his voice a gravely whisper, his eyes filling with light. "This tournament it's…it's—"

"I know," Isolde said, her fingers pressing into his forearms. "I know."

"Why?" Cillian demanded. "Why is Erebus doing this?"

Isolde forced Malaki's hands from her cheeks. "Because of story hour and my involvement with the humans and half-bloods. He knows I taught them how to read, or at the very least he suspects it. Winning the right to *serve* him is my punishment."

Malaki's eyes squeezed shut, his jaw feathering. She could see the regret, the blame etched onto his face. "We should never have come here," he said. "We could have found another way…" He was at a loss for words. There were none that could change the path fate had shoved them down.

"That's not all," Isolde said, swallowing the lump in her throat.

"What else could there possibly be?" Anger laced Cillian's words. Anger that burned not at her…but for her.

Isolde licked her lips, bracing for the bit of truth that would hurt them the most. "Apparently, there will be a wedding in my future after all."

Blyana's voice filled with the promise of death. "To whom?"

"Oh, I'm sure you can guess who my betrothed is."

Shock radiated from Malaki. Murderous fury lined his face as he shook beneath Isolde's palms. "Like hell you are," he growled.

"That bastard will die before we let that happen," Blyana growled. The pad of her finger brushed against the knuckle of her left thumb. A soft, deadly rumble echoed from her chest.

"Erebus left me no choice, Bly," Isolde said. "Not that an order from that bastard would ever stop me." The creature lurking beneath her skin bared its teeth. Sharp claws racked down her self-control, demanding so much bloodshed Isolde trembled. "You all know how well I do with ultimatums."

"Yes, we do," Malaki said with the shake of his head. "It never works out well for the one trying to force it on you."

"He'd have better luck forcing the sun to set in the east and rise in the west," Isolde said, shoving the dagger back into the scabbard at her thigh. "But Gage isn't what's important right now. Getting the children and Zibiah out is our priority. As far as the tournament goes…we'll take it one trial at a time. I can handle it."

"You shouldn't have to handle it," Malaki said. "Or any of it. This shouldn't be your burden to bear!" Pain ravaged his face as he began pacing back and forth, Secrettaker tapping against his hip.

Isolde stepped into his path and wrapped her arms around his waist. Careful of the wound at his side, she willed every ounce of love she had to give into him. "It's not your burden either, Malaki. We'll get through this." How desperately she wanted to believe her own words. To believe there still was hope in this new reality they had been thrown into.

His arms came to wrap around her, encasing her in his scent and warmth. It was impossible to miss the small tremor rolling through his frame. "I can't lose you," Malaki said. "Not now, not here."

"You will never lose me," Isolde said, her grip tightening on the ridiculous tunic he had worn just for her. She felt so small in his arms…so safe…so secure. "I'm here. No matter what happens, I'm here."

"We won't let him hurt you, Isolde." Cillian's voice carried on the warm night air. "He can't have you." Each word was plated with a promise. A wonderful, violent promise.

"Gage's time will come," Blyana said, and the thought filled Isolde with savage glee. She reached forward and took Blyana's small hand in one of her own. The warmth from her callused skin seeped through the blood-stained gloves covering Blyana's hands. Threads of air created by Cillian's power wove their way around their wrists, holding them together. Making them one.

"Yes, he will," Isolde said, her grip tightening. "But not now." She pulled back to look at Malaki. "You know why I came here. What I intend to do. You need to understand. You all do." She looked each of them in the eye. "There is no line I won't cross, no risk I won't take to get Zibiah and those children out. I need you to understand that."

Malaki's hazel gaze didn't flinch away from the truth in her words. "I understand."

"Which means no second guessing me," Isolde pressed. "No telling me something is too dangerous. I need you on my side."

"We're with you, Isolde. All of us," Malaki said. "Alaric…Gal… Nan. You aren't alone in this fight. We're with you."

Blyana's grip tightened on Isolde's fingers. "Always."

Cillian nodded. "No matter what fate you choose. No matter what path you take. Our place is by your side."

Isolde felt Cillian's words solidify themselves into her very being. A ferocious strength grew within her heart. A terrifying beast, born of ice and fire, prowled in her soul. And in that moment, as they stood together, covered in blood, surrounded by the beauty of Elenarta and all the despair it harbored, Isolde felt more at peace than she had in so many years.

"There is one positive thing we have going for us," Malaki said.

"What's that?" Isolde asked.

Malaki pulled back but kept his hands firmly planted on her shoulders. "They think they have the Hood. They think they're safe from her wrath."

A vicious grin spread across Isolde's blood-speckled face. "How wrong they are."

Isolde drew her legs up and placed her chin on the silk nightgown covering her knees where she sat on the balcony ledge. A soft, tired sigh pushed its way through her lips. Drifts of night air caressed her cheeks and brushed tendrils of her hair across her bare shoulders.

She had waited until they were all asleep before daring to venture outside. With the tournament starting in the morning, Isolde needed a moment of peace. A moment of quiet to herself. To think…to plan. The sound of Nan's soft, deep breaths drew a smile to her lips. It had taken a long time for the tears to stop, to calm her down enough to rest.

"It'll be alright," Isolde had said as Nan clung to her. "Trust me, Nan. I've been through worse scraps than this."

"No," Nan had said, her blue eyes sparkling with tears. "No, you haven't, my rose. You know what this tournament is…what its purpose is."

Isolde shut her eyes to the reality. She knew all too well what this tournament was created for. Her mind drifted to Liam. To the look of crushing horror in his eyes the night he was crowned victor of his own tournament. She had sat with him the whole night. How she had longed to touch him, to hold him in her arms. But every time she tried, he would flinch away.

"I'm a monster," he had said. Blood of the champion he had slaughtered, the one he had beaten until every breath of air had left his body, still stained his hands…his arms…his face. "How can you stand to touch me?" His dark eyes were filled with such guilt Isolde's heart broke. "How could you possibly want me now?"

Isolde sighed at the memory of her words. At the truth, they still held even now as she was facing the same horrors he had defeated. "Because I know your heart, Liam," Isolde had said. "I know the light that dwells within it. A light no amount of darkness will ever destroy." Her fingers gently, carefully rested on his cheek, pulling his face to her. "Because you're a good man who was forced to do something terrible for the sake of sparing another from having to endure the same fate. You are *good*, Liam!"

Isolde sighed as her gaze traveled across the capital to the easternmost part of the city. It snagged on something half hidden behind the swell on the mountain's base. Flags, ones bearing Erebus's symbol, lined the rim of the arena walls. A sense of dread fell into Isolde's gut like a chunk of ice.

Liam wasn't the same after coming back from the tournament. She had a feeling, one running so deep she knew it had to be true, that her fate would be no different than his. Isolde had never shied from death, whether she was the one escorting it or nearly receiving it. But another fact made her fingers grip her legs, pulling them tighter to her chest.

Gage knew her weaknesses. He held so many of them in his heartless grasp. As did Erebus, which for no reason Isolde could understand seemed far worse. And as she stared out at the arena bathed in light from the new sun brushing across the snowcapped peaks of Oronilma, Isolde thought of Kamden. Of what he would make of all this…of what he would make of her. It seemed like only yesterday they were running through the palace hallways, Nan's worrisome voice echoing behind as they raced across the stone bridges.

And as Isolde looked out onto the place she once called home, she allowed Kamden's memory to fill her entirely. His face…his laugh…his smile. He had been her happiness. A place of solitude and peace where nothing could harm her. A beacon of light in a world of darkness. She clung to the sound of his voice and the words filling it. The ones that had kept her alive so far.

"I do not bow to fear," Isolde whispered, as dawn broke over the mountain peaks. "It bows to me."

CHAPTER 13

The air felt thick in Liam's chest, suffocating and hot. Perhaps it was the girl who walked at his side that made him feel this way, as if she had stolen the very breath from his lungs with her presence alone. Isolde always had that effect on him, even as a boy. His body, his mind refused to work in her presence. Refused to acknowledge anything but her.

Reluctantly, Liam's eyes flickered to Isolde's ribcage. The haunted memory of the ruined flesh still lingered beneath his fingertips. Her once smooth skin was now left with a mark of horrifying remembrance. A mark he hadn't stopped, one he had failed to protect her from. Liam's hand flexed at his side. Rage at Gage for having been the one responsible for putting it there filled his chest.

"How are you?" he asked, as they stepped into the sunlight coating the streets of Elenarta. He needed to say something, anything to end the silence between them.

"As well as can be expected," Isolde said, her mouth twisting into a grimace. "I'm being forced into a competition where my prizes are an unwanted brute of a husband, children enslaved, and a role in serving the false king of Arnoria. Apart from that, what could I possibly have to complain about?"

Heat flooded Liam's cheeks as he pressed on, his boots clicking against the cobblestones. He knew what Erebus had demanded of her. It was all Gage had talked about the night before.

"That little bitch," Gage had said, polishing off another goblet of mead. The girl on his lap winced as his fingers mercilessly, possessively dug into her hips. "Isolde will be my wife. She has no say in the matter now. And the first thing I'm doing as soon as it's done is kill that cripple and his bitch warrior wife."

He pulled the girl against his crotch, his hands squeezing. "And as for the Bastard Prince," Gage's face twisted into a cruel smile, "he can serve as her personal healer and be the one to patch up the mess when she doesn't behave. My wedding present to Isolde. She'll learn to hold her tongue, one way or another."

Liam had kept his fists hidden under the table as rage, blinding and all-consuming, turned his vision red. He had grown accustomed to hiding his feelings from Gage. But now, he found it nearly impossible.

"We'll figure something out," Liam said at last.

"I already have," she said, her eyes flickering to him. "But I need your help."

"My stance has not changed since we last spoke." He could practically feel her penetrating gaze sweep over him like the kiss of a flame. "You know how I feel about this."

"I am doing this with or without you," Isolde said, drawing her shoulders back. A fiery indignation flared to life in those strange emerald and silver depths. He couldn't help but slow ever so slightly and let his eyes drift to her backside, his favorite part of her. A part he wanted more than anything to touch right then. "I will not leave them to that fate. Nor will I leave Zib in whatever hell hole Erebus has her in. Please help me!"

Her words pulled him back into reality, forcing him to adjust his belt to hide the evidence of where his thoughts had gone. Her temper had always evoked something in him, awakened a part of himself he would give only to her. They passed a lone door leading to a small alcove…hidden… well out of the way.

No one would be there now…Flickers of their time in Blackford Forest and the library at Briarhole slammed into him, making his desire all the more apparent. Cheers from the arena began to echo down the street, causing Isolde's steps to falter before picking up again with new determination.

Shame coated Liam's desire, dousing it thoroughly. *She's about to go into the arena, you asshole!* The thoughts echoed through his mind on a wave of bitter resentment. *To play a part in something she has no choice but to participate in. Get your mind where it belongs!*

"Isolde," Liam said, his teeth on edge, the worry building in his chest. He knew what horrors lurked within the mines of the Oronilma Mountains. What nightmares were bred from within the dungeons of Elenarta. Nightmares Zibiah was facing as they spoke. A chill of sorrow and dread draped over his shoulders at the thought.

I'm so sorry, Zib.

"Do you intended to resurrect the Hood?" Liam asked, willing himself to not think of her. They had reached a tunnel leading to the underbelly of the massive arena. Echoes of cries and cheers vibrated through the bedrock. Their demand for blood, for death permeated the air like an early morning fog. The look in her eyes told him all he needed to know.

"Do you really need to ask?"

They stepped through a side door and into a nearly deserted hallway. Its path disappeared down a path curving to the left and right. Two soldiers stood a short distance away, heavy elithrium blades hung at their sides. Neither held the same quality as the one he possessed, but the same eerie glow shone in the light of the torches along the wall. He had seen them before but only in passing. There was no point in learning who they were. They were nameless faces in a sea of armor and blades.

Liam rested his hands on Isolde's shoulders, bringing her to a halt. The muscles beneath tensed then relaxed at his touch, making other thoughts reenter his mind. "Please tell me you are not going to resurrect the Hood." Despite every ounce of effort, he was not able to keep the begging from his voice. The pleading to save herself, to fight another day. To live with him…for him.

Isolde's lips pulled up into a sarcastic smile that was all Hood and Liam's heart sank. "She never died." Her voice was a silken, fiery caress that stirred his blood and turned his hope into ash.

"Please, Isolde, don't do this."

"Sir?" The word echoed through the corridor, ripping his attention away. "The king has a schedule to keep," one of the soldiers said. His scrutinizing gaze lingered on Liam's hands resting on Isolde's shoulders.

"Do you think I am unaware of the king's schedule, soldier?" Liam asked, his voice laced with the authority of Captain of the Guard. "Mind who you're speaking to and keep at your post." A silent bow was the only answer the soldier provided before clicking his heel and turning back to his post. Still, Liam knew he listened.

"You have no idea what these people are capable of." Her confusing, intoxicating scent filled his head, burning through his blood. "I love you, Isolde," Liam said, willing every ounce of what he felt into the words crossing his tongue. "Please trust me," he begged. "Do as I say…and leave it alone."

Isolde's chest rose as she sighed. "I'm quite aware of what Erebus and Gage are capable of, Liam. I see it every day in the lives of those I try to help. They have no one, except me. So, as long as Erebus sits on the throne, the Hood will never stop. And if you knew me at all," Isolde said, "you would know I could never do that." Reaching up, she placed the whisper of a kiss on his lips before walking past. Halfway, she turned back, causing the intricate braid to drape over her shoulder and frame her proud, perfect chin. "Nor would you ask it of me."

Memories of his own tournament roared to life in Liam's head. He could still feel bones shattering beneath his blows, hot blood coating his hands as he plunged the dagger into the girl's chest.

"I'm sorry," he had said to her as he drove the dagger deeper, severing flesh and bone. He didn't stop until the metal guard pressed against her skin. "I'm so sorry." Tears, hot and full, fell down her cheeks, shining like rivers of living crystal. That day had morphed Liam into a creature he didn't recognize. Now, the woman he would burn the world for was about to face the same nightmares and there was nothing he could do to stop it.

With one final, fleeting look, Isolde turned back to the soldiers who waited. Her hips swung in a way she was perfectly aware drove him to madness. They broke away from the wall to follow in her footsteps. He watched as they disappeared around the bend in the corridor. Gritting his teeth, Liam's fist collided with the stone wall and a bolt of hot pain shot up his arm. Bits of rock broke free and peppered the pristine floor with debris.

As he turned to leave, his steps faltered. Looking back to the now deserted corridor, Liam realized with utter confusion he had been walking behind her nearly the entire way there. He had not led her here; Isolde had led herself.

Roars from the crowd above shook the walls of the arena. They ran up the soles of Isolde's feet as she walked with Malaki at her side. A slight limp still remained in his gait, one she knew irritated him to no end.

"Quit looking at me like that," he said, tone biting. He tried and failed to walk at a normal pace, but Isolde found her steps slowing, matching his speed.

"I have many looks," Isolde said, forcing her eyes away. "All of which are spectacular. You'll have to be more specific."

"The concerned one," he grumbled back. "The one that annoys you to no end." A small light grew at the end of the tunnel that led to one of the antechambers in the belly of the arena. "I'm fine."

Isolde's eyes swept over his hip again, the spot she knew harbored a scar much like her own. A prickle of pain ran down the length of her ribcage.

"You're right," Isolde said, her voice carrying a hint of annoyance. "That is annoying to hear."

A chuckle, deep and rich, echoed around them. "Do my ears deceive me or did Isolde Cotheran just admit I'm right about something?" A smug smile pulled at the edges of Malaki's lips, causing the dark stubble of his cheeks to crinkle. "I thought you'd share food before ever making such a declaration."

"I'm only admitting it because of your delicate condition. Seems like the kind thing to do for someone in your state."

The tunnel gave way to reveal a cavernous chamber within. Rays of the afternoon sun spilled through the small slits running along the tiled ceiling. The chamber was filled with bodies, some she recognized instantly.

Lord Milt of Harrow Hall stood beside a young male who couldn't possibly be older than fifteen. His long, scraggly black hair fell about his eyes like sheets of black night. They hung in dark contrast to his freckled, pale skin. The symbol of Harrow Hall, a stallion rearing on its hind legs, was etched across his chest in brilliant silver on a bed of emerald green.

"It looks fine, my lord," the young male said, trying not to fidget under Milt's scrutiny.

"Fine will not do," Milt said absently, his fingers readjusting another button on the young male's jacket unnecessarily. "You are of Harrow Hall. We have a reputation to maintain."

"Don't impose your sense of fashion on the poor boy, Lord Milt," Isolde said, coming to a halt beside him. "That topic is reserved for only you and me."

Milt's warm brown eyes met hers with a start. "Lady Isolde!" A look of sorrowful confusion bled into his gaze. It ran over her less than feminine attire which consisted of a cream-colored tunic, gray britches, and leather knee-high boots. "I had hoped the rumors were false."

"I'm afraid not," she said. "For once, the rumors are indeed true."

Anger flashed across Milt's impossibly handsome face. "I wish I could say I'm shocked."

"As do I," Isolde said. "Still, I suppose this gives Thornwood the opportunity to show just what we have to offer."

"I have no doubt you will," Milt said with a smile that didn't quite reach his eyes. His gaze turned to her second-in-command. "Good to see you, Malaki."

"And you, Lord Milt," he said with the bow of his head. "Who do you have with you?"

"This is my champion, Gawen," he said, stepping aside to clap the boy on the back. It was impossible to miss the fondness in Milt's eyes, in the way he said the boy's name with such pride.

"It's a pleasure to meet you, Gawen," Isolde said, with a curtsy. "I imagine you and I will have lot of fun showing the others how it's done."

A nervous smile tugged at the edges of Gawen's mouth. "I hope so, my lady." A blush spread across his cheeks and up into the lining of his hair.

"I wasn't aware a lady curtsied to half-blood trash."

Isolde whipped around to find a mountain of a man standing behind her. He was at least two feet taller than her, his shoulders broad and lined with muscle. She sensed Gawen shrinking behind her. Even Milt remained silent, his eyes guarded and jaw set.

Malaki took a step forward, his shoulders tense. "A lady can do as she pleases."

"Well," said the man, his pointed gaze looking Isolde up and down, "if she curtsies for trash, I wonder if she'll get on her knees for a real virya."

A dark chuckle ghosted through Isolde's lips as she stepped around Malaki, her hands resting on her hips. "Perhaps when I find a real virya I shall." She made a show of looking around the room only to return to him, her eyebrows rising. "It appears there isn't one present. I guess we'll never know."

A deep, menacing growl rumbled from behind his clenched teeth. "For a lady, bitch, you've got quite the mouth on you."

"Buer!" The sound of that voice gave him pause and made Isolde's lips pull back into a snarl. Volkran sauntered forward, his sneering gaze moving between Isolde and Malaki.

"His Majesty has forbidden engaging with other champions outside of the competition," he said with a mocking smile, stopping before Isolde. "But I feel quite certain you'll have plenty of time to teach this one some manners before the tournament is over. If she lives that long."

Buer smiled behind his master, a vicious grin that showed far too much of his teeth for Isolde's liking. Light from the afternoon sun glistened off his bald, sweaty scalp.

"Oh, I plan on making it to the end of this, Lord Volkran," Isolde said. "And when I win, I believe my rank will be higher than yours, will it not?"

Volkran's face reddened, his eyes glowing with a hatred Isolde knew well. "Imagine it. The Lord of Briarhole submitting to me…on *his* knees. Perhaps, my first order will be for you tell me what the ground beneath my shoe tastes like." Isolde's smiled widened. "Or I'll have you walk the streets of Elenarta in nothing but what you entered this world with. I'm generous, so I'll leave the choice up to you."

The blow of a horn cut off the growl leeching through Volkran's bared teeth. Soldiers dressed in some of the finest armor Isolde had ever seen stepped forward. "Champions, take your positions!" One of them looked pointedly at Volkran, his eyes narrowing.

"You should know," Volkran said, stepping into Isolde's space, "my wife had the same problem, speaking when she ought to have kept quiet." Isolde's blood froze at the mention of Zibiah. The cold, ruthless flames licked at her heart as his smile only grew. "Buer did an excellent job of reminding her where her place lies. So, did Lauram. Perhaps you'll get to learn the same lesson before the end."

Dread and black fury coated Isolde's heart. *Zibiah…Zibiah…*

"I've heard this same threat before from far more impressive men than you, Volkran. It never worked out well for them." She leaned in, invading as much of his space as she dared. "And believe me when I say it made what the Hood did to you look like foreplay."

A snarl ripped through Volkran's bared teeth, a light shining in his eyes. The soldiers lining the walls shifted, their hands clasping at the pommels of their swords.

"Lord Volkran!" one of them said, his eyes dark and full of warning. "King Erebus awaits."

Volkran hardly cast him a glance as he straightened. "Watching you die will be worth the trip alone." He turned on his heal and made for the exit to the tunnel with Buer in tow.

"You'll need to watch out for that one," Malaki said, his eyes trained on Buer's monstrous back.

"I'll have to keep my eye on all of them."

"Isolde!" The sound of her uncle's voice came from within the tunnels at their backs. She turned to find him perched upon his chestnut stallion. Turgon was strapped to his side and gleaming as if it had been freshly polished. Knowing Nan, it undoubtedly had been. Behind him was Versa and a new horse, one Isolde knew came from only one place.

"Hello there," Isolde said, stroking the golden snout of the palomino mare who stood at Versa's side. She nuzzled into Isolde's chest, letting out a small snicker of delight. "And who are you?"

"Loria," Alaric said, passing the reins to Malaki. "A gift from Lord Milt."

A smile, so boyish and grateful, spread across Malaki's face as he nodded to Milt who was holding the reins of a gelding Gawen was attempting to climb up on. Milt returned the nod with a knowing, pleased smile.

Versa whined and struck the ground with her hoof. Her mane tossed like the clouds of a dark storm as she pushed against Isolde's shoulder, demanding her attention. Loria's ears flattened against her head and her nostrils flared. Her mane fell about her face in shimmering, gilded waves.

"Alright!" Isolde said, breaking away to take her place at Versa's side. "I was just saying hello." She ran a hand down the length of Versa's neck in soothing strokes. "You're still my girl."

"Tell me you aren't starting a fight with Volkran and his champion already," Alaric said once Isolde pulled herself up into the saddle.

"I would never intentionally start a confrontation, Alaric!" Isolde said, placing a hand over her heart. "Wouldn't dream of such a thing."

"Hmm," Alaric said, his gray eyes narrowing. "Yes, that would be entirely out of character for you."

"He started it," Malaki retorted. "Apparently, he thinks Buer should teach Isolde the same lesson he taught Zib."

A bright light ignited in Alaric's eyes as they locked on Volkran, his gloved fingers constricting around the reins. The other champions, the leaders of their houses, and their advisors began to form a single line. Briarhole forced their way to the front, cutting off Ferden and the champion who rode at his side.

"Let's get in the back," Isolde suggested, looking from Malaki to Alaric. "Save the best for last?" Malaki grinned and tugged at Loria's reins. Alaric followed suit, his mouth set and grim. "That look is not flattering on you at all, Uncle," Isolde said with the roll of her eyes.

"What look is that?"

"The brooding, grumpy one. Malaki has coined that particular look. If you want to you use it, you'll have to ask permission from him first. I can only handle so much male brooding at once."

Alaric's jaw flexed beneath a bed of golden stubble. "You're treating this like any other job. You can't play fast and loose here." Worry chipped away at the darkness enveloping his face, softening his eyes. "You have to play to win."

"I am, Alaric. If I don't, those children, Zibiah, Thornwood …everyone I love dies. What choice do I have but to win?" The sound of drums pealed through the chamber. Each beat shot into her heart like a hammer driving a nail into place.

Alaric's face, which held the look of someone in his late twenties, appeared far sadder than she could ever imagine. He knew she was right; Isolde could see it in his eyes. Yet, something else lingered there too. Something she had fought so hard to earn…worked tirelessly to be worthy of in his eyes.

Pride.

"Then let's make sure you do." The hint of a smile pulled at the corner of Alaric's mouth as the first rays of the sun brushed their heads.

The pounding of the drums that promised blood, that promised death filled the afternoon air. Pain erupted behind Isolde's eyes as Versa moved onto the arena floor. With the protection of the stone walls now gone, the roar of the crowd pierced Isolde's ears.

After a few blinding moments, her eyes adjusted to the scene around her. Stands of towering stone and iron shot up into the air in every direction. Tips of the mountains beyond above the upper level of the arena, a monstrosity carved from the bones and heart of the mountain itself.

Gravel crunched beneath Versa's feet as she followed behind Alaric. Maroon and gold painted his back. He waved to the citizens of Elenarta with Turgon swinging securely at his side. Flowers fell at their feet, discarded by those who sat along the wall's edge. A crowd of lower level virya were huddled around the lowest section. Isolde smiled brightly at a small boy perched on his father's far too thin shoulders.

"Lady Isolde!" the boy cried, leaning over the crown of his father's head. "Father, it's Lady Isolde!" She sent him a small wave in return.

"The Bastard Prince!" someone else called, their voice filling the air. "Viributhian's Bastard Prince!"

"Traitor!" Another yelled. "Traitor!"

She looked back to Malaki who rode behind her. His eyes were looking at anything but the crowd. At the people, he had sacrificed so much for who now only looked at him in hatred.

Anger swelled in Isolde's chest. Words she wanted so desperately to hurl at the crowd who looked down at Malaki in such hatred danced on the tip of her tongue. But there was nothing she could do. She was powerless against the lies Erebus had fed the people.

Pushing the feeling down, Isolde turned back to the crowd and forced a smile onto her unwilling face. With her head held high, she continued on to the ridiculous dais that had been carved in the northern wall. A wide balcony shaded by yards of black velvet, cast a shadow over the tip of the arena.

Erebus wasn't hard to find. She could practically feel his cold, piercing stare. But she ignored him and kept her eyes on the male who lingered behind him. Liam stood at attention, his eyes forward and leather clad shoulders back. His mouth was set and mask firmly in place, the mask of a loyal soldier.

Gage hovered at Erebus' right. A knowing, charming smile spread across his face as his eyes met hers. A look of indifference held firm as she tugged at Versa's reins, bringing her to a halt beside Alaric. Malaki took up the spot on her left. Loria remained still beneath him, her ears perked and eyes wide. Erebus rose from his perch and the last remnants of the drums carried over the lips of the arena into the mountains beyond.

"People of Elenarta!" His voice rang through the air like a clap of thunder. "It is with great pleasure I present to you the champions for this Tournament of the Guard!" The crowd came to life. Their cries and cheers erupting from every corner of the arena.

"This year, we have devised a series of trials that will produce the finest Arnoria has to offer. And for this reason, the position up for the taking is not Captain of the Guard. But in fact, a place at my side as my Left Hand."

A murmur echoed through the people. Isolde felt their stares like fingers, poking and prodding at every inch of her—assessing, measuring, and judging. Even the champions and those who rode at their sides stirred in their saddles.

"And with this change, I am implementing a new rule this year as well." Erebus's eyes swept the crowd until they at last landed on her. "Any champion who competes and wins the tournament, will forfeit their claim to any land they may possess or would inherit in the future."

A well of nausea opened in the pit of Isolde's stomach. Blood, hot and furious, pumped in her ears, drowning out all sound except the rapid beat of her heart. Just like that, Erebus ripped away Alaric and Galaena's choice in giving up their power, to pass Thornwood onto her when the time came. He had made them prisoners, condemned to dwell in the bars of their own power, forever.

"If you are to be my Left Hand," Erebus continued, "I will not have you distracted by the needs of a territory. This is my word." His eyes bored into hers, holding her captive. "And my word is law."

Isolde caught the hint of movement to her right. Down the line, Ferden, Lord of Dolinmere, leaned over and whispered something to the male next to him. As if sensing her gaze, Ferden looked past the massive virya and locked onto her. A fire blazed in his eyes. It seemed to burn down to the very essence of who and what she was. She looked away, unease draping across her back like a cape.

"There will be a series of six trials over the course of the next few weeks," said Erebus, his voice carrying to every part of the arena. "If a champion fails to complete a task or is gravely injured, their lord or lady can buy their champion's life and place in the tournament, if I deem them worthy of such a gift."

Isolde swallowed the growl bubbling in her throat. She tried to ignore the sense of dread threatening to come alive in her chest. Of course, Alaric would pay whatever ridiculous amount Erebus demanded for her life. But Isolde wasn't entirely convinced Erebus would grant her such a mercy.

"The final task will be hand to hand combat. The last male"—his cold, pewter eyes shifted to her again, a slight grin playing on his face—"or female left standing will be crowned my champion, my Left Hand. To serve at my side until you are released either by my hand or death's."

The future loomed before Isolde. A fork in a path fate had set before her. One way leading to death, the other a lifetime of serving the man who had stolen everything from her. Isolde's eyes lifted to the sky, to the gods who dwelt there.

This is the only path fate wishes to offer me? So, be it. I'll burn a new one.

CHAPTER 14

L et the tournament begin!" Erebus's words rang with finality. They held the weight of absolution, of a truth Isolde couldn't escape. She stood firm in their wake—an unwavering, unyielding rock the merciless waves continued to beat against. The familiar deadly fire, cold and unforgiving as the dawn of a winter storm, ignited in Isolde's chest. Her resolve sharpened into a razor-thin blade.

This is no different than any other mission. She told herself. *The goal hasn't changed.* The notion calmed the turbulent storm threatening to swallow her whole.

Her eyes swept the line of champions—six men in all. Some were the usual muscled animals you would expect at a tournament such as this. Men capable of crushing a skull with their bare hands. Others were lean and honed like the weapons they undoubtedly were. Two stood alone. Their singular presence looked strange compared to the rest of the pack. They were alone, yet still incredibly foreboding. They dismounted and handed the reins over to the stable hands who ran forward.

"Those have to be Foxclove and Blackwater's champions," Malaki said, his calculating eyes sweeping the line. "No lord or lady at their sides."

Isolde let out a humorless chuckle as she slipped from Versa's back. "Of course, even as lord of both territories, Gage couldn't be bothered to perform such a minimal task like supporting the ones he placed in the tournament."

Ferden leapt from the night-black mare he had ridden at Briarhole and clasped his champion's colossal arm. Dolinmere's colors stretched across the impressive planes of muscle making his frame. A green that reminded Isolde of the deep pine woods of Blackford, along with accents of grey stone, looked marvelous against his flawless ebony skin.

Standing well over a foot and a half taller than his lord, Ferden's champion was massive. A tremor of uncertainty ricocheted through her limbs. But Isolde saw a softness in his mesmerizing sky-blue eyes; a softness that had no place in the arena. After a few words, Ferden released his grip and climbed into the saddle.

Rays of the high afternoon sun danced across the golden crown of his head as he turned his attention to her. "I thought I felt those eyes on me, Lady Isolde."

"Don't sound so flattered, Lord Ferden," she said, walking over to lay a hand on the mare's nose. Her eyes fluttered closed at Isolde's touch. "I was merely admiring this lovely girl."

"She is rather special," Ferden said, stroking her mane. A beat of silence filled the air between them. It carried the words neither of them wanted to say.

"That's your champion, I take it?" Isolde said, nodding to the man who stood apart from the rest.

"Sohan," Ferden said with a nod. "He was one of the many who volunteered."

Isolde's brow shot up. "One of many? That's interesting."

A shrug lifted from his shoulders. "My people know I have no say in the matter. By volunteering they relieve me of the burden of forcing someone to fight for a position none of them want."

"Very noble of them," Isolde said, and a newfound fondness filled her chest for the Dolinmere's territory. Sohan's strange eyes swept the arena. They landed momentarily on her before flittering away. "Sohan sounds like very brave man."

"A very selfless man." The words whispered through the air as a hint of sadness ghosted across Ferden's face. It died away just as quickly as it had formed. "I wish you the best of luck in the tournament."

"You're too kind, Lord Ferden," said Isolde, her head dipping. "I would think you'd wish me ill, given your stake in all this."

A look of contempt crossed Ferden's perfect, youthful face. The ghost of what looked to be regret flickered in the depths of his deep grey eyes. "You are one of the very, *very* few people in this world I would never wish ill upon, Lady Isolde." There was an edge to his voice, a sharpness that sounded so strange coming from him.

After offering a slight bow, Ferden rode back through the tunnel leading into the belly of the arena, leaving Isolde in stunned silence. A flicker of irritation ignited in her gut. Ferden had always been an intriguing, yet infuriating puzzle she couldn't seem to piece together.

The touch of Malaki's hand at her elbow drew her attention back around.

"No matter what happens, no matter what you face in this damn tournament, you do not cower to anyone," he said, his voice dropping to a whisper that was as sharp as a blade and hard as steel. "You are Isolde Cotheran of Thornwood, the Hood of Arnoria, the Thief of Sorrows… and you do not bow to fear."

Malaki's voice fell over her like a shield, an impenetrable wall nothing and no one could ever break.

Ice slid into Isolde's veins. "It bows to me."

"To you," he echoed, giving her arm a squeeze. "Win this," he ordered, before stepping away.

"You think I would let anything other than that outcome come to pass?" she asked, a sarcastic smirk pulling at her lips.

"I never doubt you, Isolde. In anything." Without another word, he carefully climbed onto Loria's back, his face set in stone.

"You can do this," Alaric said. A ferocious love only a father would possess shone in his eyes. "Come back to us."

"As you wish, Lord Cotheran," Isolde said, pulling the smallest of smiles from his lips. And with that, he and Malaki made their way out of the arena, disappearing into the shadow of the tunnels.

Fear rose at their absence, threatening to overtake what little bravado lingered within. But as the grates of the tunnels fell into place, sealing her in, Isolde's power stirred and the monstrous anger lashed out, suffocating any hint of fear that remained. Taking a deep breath, she looked to the only champion left standing nearby.

"Aren't you going to be a gentleman and escort a lady?" she asked sweetly. His frame was like that of a blade, lean and hard as steel. He wore a look of arrogance about him that had Isolde smiling.

Cocking an eyebrow, the stranger looked Isolde up and down. His gaze was full of appraisal and wicked delight. "What kind of man would I be if I allowed a lady to walk towards certain death unaccompanied?" He offered his arm to her. The corners of his stubble-covered cheeks rose, and the hint of a dimple whispered from his cheek.

"One who greatly underestimates me," Isolde said, lacing her arm through his. Flawless tan skin stood in delightful contrast against the grey and midnight-blue hues of Marsh Hall. Silver axes, glittering and fierce, were crossed over his chest in impeccable embroidery that would rival even Asha's talents.

"Forgive me, my manners have eluded me," he said with the hint of mocking propriety lingering in his words. "I am Kyros, the great champion of Marsh Hall."

Isolde's eyes narrowed slightly and knowing, understanding smile kissed the edge of Kyros's lips. "I see you're no stranger to the drama that exists between our houses. I personally do not hold any animosity toward Thornwood. Neither does Lady Circe. I can assure you of that."

"Thornwood holds no ill will towards Marsh Hall either," said Isolde, her eyes sliding to Kyros. "From what I understand, the root cause of the disagreement has been dealt with. Treatment of the humans and half-bloods in your territory has dramatically improved."

"Lady Circe is not her late husband," Kyros said, his tone gaining an edge. "She does not and has not ever treated the humans or half-bloods unfairly. That was left to the monster who warmed her bed for a time—despite what a certain vigilante bastard thinks." Isolde cringed inwardly. She had been the one to leave the scars of penance on Circe's face after she killed her husband so many years ago.

"Be thankful I only took your beauty," Isolde had said, leaning over Circe as she wailed on the floor. Blood seeped between her delicate fingers clutching her maimed face. "Your husband paid the price for not heeding my warning, Lady Circe. As the new ruler of Marsh Hall, let's hope you don't make the same mistakes he did."

Guilt churned in Isolde's gut. It festered like a wound refusing to heal. *Was Circe innocent?* Isolde wondered, chewing on her lip. *Did I maim her for no reason?*

Isolde opened her mouth to rebuke him, to defend the Hood for actions she now wasn't completely certain were warranted. Something in Kyros's eyes held her tongue. No deception lived in their depths. Nothing but open sincerity, along with a curious warmth, resided there. Shoving the overwhelming guilt away to deal with later, Isolde gave his arm a gentle squeeze. "My manners seem to be as evasive as yours. I'm—"

"Isolde Cotheran," Kyros said with a grin, his head leaning in. "I know who you are. We all do. You're quite the talk of the capital."

"That's not at all surprising," Isolde said. "If my beauty didn't cause a stir, my involvement in this damned tournament certainly would." They walked the length of the arena to the small group of champions congregating around a single male. Yards of velvet fabric, the color of ash and reeking of exuberant wealth, encompassed his bulbous frame.

"That's interesting," said Kyros. His eyes, so dark blue they harbored hints of violet, narrowed. "They've selected Lenox to be Master of Games." He cut her a look, one etched in something Isolde could only assume was displeasure. "You'll need to be careful."

"What makes you say that?" Isolde asked. "He doesn't look particularly frightening."

"He's worse than that, I assure you," Kyros said, his mouth twisting in distaste. "He was the Master of Keys. The overseer of the soldiers that serve in the dungeons and the mines." A chill slithered down Isolde's spine. "He's acquired quite a reputation for his creative punishments."

"I've dealt with men like him before," Isolde said, casting Lenox an appraising look. "He's no different from the rest."

Blinding rays of light danced off the impeccably styled locks of dark brown hair brushing the tops of Kyros's shoulders, his head tilting in thought. "Perhaps, but this is the Tournament of the Guard, Lady Isolde. Or Tournament of the Hand, I should say. Lenox's reputation for extracting pain is not something to be trifled with. This is not like one of your tea parties where you will be protected."

"You've clearly never attended a tea party with the lords and ladies of Arnoria," Isolde huffed, her lips curling. "They're just as deadly as this tournament but with much better clothes and good wine."

A rumble of laughter lifted from his expressive, sensual lips. "I suppose you're right."

The sound of Kyros deep chuckle blended with gravel crunching beneath her feet as Isolde took up the middle spot where the other champions had lined up. It was a warming sound, one that calmed the rapid beating of her heart.

Probably not the most helpful thought to have of a male who is more than likely going to try and kill you. Isolde thought with the shake of her head.

Pairs of eyes turned at their arrival. Some were filled with indifference, most with curiosity. Buer's, however, harbored a look that set Isolde's teeth on edge, her anger burning brighter. His teeth raked against his lower lip as his gaze traveled up and down the length of her tunic and britches.

"I do hope Lady Isolde is the consolation prize," he said, casting a glance to the other champions. "I can imagine getting between those legs would be worth putting my life on the line for."

"Oh, I can assure you I'm well worth the effort," Isolde said with a sarcastic smile. A laugh bubbled on the edge of her lips. "But I can tell you're not man enough to handle what's between my legs, Buer. Women have a way of knowing these things."

"We'll see if that mouth still runs after this tournament," he growled. "Who knows what might happen...Accidents do occur."

Isolde felt her power rush forward. The wall of self-control, the one that seemed to be growing thinner and thinner by the day, buckled under the weight of the monster's rage. It clawed beneath her skin demanding freedom, demanding blood.

"Come now, children, play nicely," Kyros said, taking a step forward, a sarcastic grin tugging at the corner of his mouth. "The first trial hasn't even started yet."

"And I suppose there's no better time than now," the male named Lenox said in greeting, cutting through the tension filling their small group. "I am, Lenox, the Master of Games. Let me be clear about one fact." His cold eyes swept them, taking time to truly look each champion in the eye. "Within these walls, my word is law. It is as binding as our good king's. And it will be treated as such."

It was impossible to fight the sigh that slipped from Isolde's mouth. Her gaze landed on Lenox to find him staring at her, his dark, beady gaze narrowing into slits.

"Consider yourselves thoroughly warned." A blatant threat lied within every word. Isolde clenched her teeth together but kept her mouth shut. "Your first trial will require a small addition to your attire." Servants, the first humans Isolde had seen within the palace walls, approached. A single pillow rested in the palm of their hands.

She instantly recoiled when she saw the burden they carried. Bands of silver were held before them. Their shining surfaces possessed a familiar hue that glowed against the ebony silk lining. Kyros visibly stiffened at her side, his eyes igniting with power.

"This task will be completed without the aid of your abilities," Lenox said. Isolde stared at the human before her. His eyes were downcast with his hand held out expectantly. She looked to the other champions. Not a single one had dared move.

"What good are we without our powers?" Sohan asked, his arms knotted across his chest.

"Many challenges will find their way to the one who wins this tournament," Lenox said. He moved like a shadow, swift and silent. "Including being without the aid of your powers."

Kyros, whose jaw was set, and eyes now darkened, was the first to yield. "Well, at least it matches." He wasn't lying. The perfectly polished silver was a stunning match to the thread of his tunic and britches. With a heavy sigh, he thrust his bare wrist into the servant's awaiting palm. A noticeable shudder racked through his body as the elithrium bracelet slid into place.

The others reluctantly followed suit. A deep rumble echoed from deep within Buer's chest as the metal met his skin. Taking a deep breath, Isolde forced her power down and slid her wrist in the man's awaiting palm.

"We just met and already here you are, showering me with gifts," she said to the man who held her wrist with surprising gentleness. "I shall have to bring something for you next time." His lightless eyes brightened in shock and a blush of red blossomed across his cheeks as the elithrium bracelet locked around her wrist.

The cold metal settled against her skin, and instantly Isolde felt trapped, as if the power, the very essence of who and what she was had come undone and was no more. The beast, now subdued into submission, only managed the hint of a growl echoing in her mind.

Lenox held up a finger and pointed to one of the snowcapped peaks cresting the eastern rim of the arena. "His Majesty has left something on top of the Olos Peak, the smallest within range of the arena. Six items in total. Each of which holds a great significance to him. You are to each retrieve an item and bring it back here. The champion who returns empty-handed…will be eliminated."

Isolde glanced up at Olos and the Oronilma Mountains beyond. Each pass she knew was treacherous. They were deceivingly beautiful. Past the forest of trees skirting their base, lay a labyrinth of jagged, razor sharp rocks and bottomless ravines. Their towering heights left only two possible avenues of reaching the summit. One in particular housed the bones of so many who tried to conquer it and failed.

"You may not intentionally kill or harm another competitor," Lenox said, his eyes locking on to Isolde. "But as we all know, accidents do happen." She merely shot him a cocky grin. "You may only retrieve one item from the peak and one item only. If you are caught bringing back more than one, you will be eliminated. Any questions?" When silence was his only answer, Lenox smiled and rubbed the palms of his small, pale hands together. "Excellent. Take your places."

Gold and blood-red gravel crunched beneath Isolde's feet as she took her spot in line. Lenox came to stand before her. He wasn't particularly large, standing less than an inch taller than she did. But something in his eyes had her on guard. A darkness lurked in his gaze, and a cruel smile pulled at the corners of his thin, cracked lips.

"Lord Gage, asked me to remind you of what you are fighting for, Lady Isolde." Lenox nodded behind her. She followed his gaze to the dais, to the throne, and the boy who stood behind it.

"Tanor!"

His name felt like a blade in her mouth. He looked nothing like the boy she remembered. His cheeks were hollow and terrifyingly pale. Fear lingered in the depths of his downcast eyes. Gage gripped his shoulder and leaned in to whisper something in his ear. Isolde could see him tremble at whatever that monster said, earning a smile from his handsome, deformed face.

"I hope we have an understanding of what's at stake," Lenox said, drawing her attention forward. The power of the elithrium bracelet blanketed the furious rage swelling inside her. The monster within tried again and again to rise. Each time it was knocked back down, buried once more.

When she didn't respond, Lenox smiled. "Good."

Isolde tried to force the waves of terror down. But she had no time to ponder, no time to let worry burrowing its fangs deeper than it already had. A moment later, Lenox's commanding voice rang through the air. "Let the tournament begin!" The sound of a gong pierced the air, and the crowd roared.

Buer wasted no time in shoving Isolde aside and sprinting ahead. Gravel dug into her shoulder, causing beads of blood to swell to the surface. He looked back at her with a savage grin, his massive arms pumping at his side.

A growl ripped through Isolde's teeth as she shoved herself up and started to run. Just before disappearing into the tunnel leading to the mountains, the sound of Malaki's voice carried over the wind, undoubtedly by the aid of Cillian's power.

"Not the main road!" Malaki called, his hands cupping his mouth. "Take the Pass of Mordith!" She nodded, hoping he saw she understood. Half of the pack had already disappeared through the tunnel and was heading towards the city.

Already her muscles felt different, as if a piece of her was missing, a part that was just out of reach. It made her feel sluggish and off balance with every step she took. Once she breached the gate, she took an immediate right. The path wound through the buildings lining the mountain's base, some of which were embedded into the face of the rock itself.

"Lady Isolde!" Her name chased her through the streets, following her down every alley, and around every corner. Her teeth gritted but her lips tugged up into what she hoped was a convincing smile rather than a grimace. Up ahead lay the path she knew most of the others took; it was wide and easily accessible. But it would take twice as long as the one she intended to follow.

The Pass of Mordith, the path of death and light, was a far more difficult climb. Filled with densely packed forests, rocks sharp as blades, and only a crack a few inches wide to serve as a hand placement for the three-hundred-foot, vertical climb to the summit, the Path of Mordith was littered with the bones of those who had foolishly tried and failed to conquer it.

Sweat poured down Isolde's face as trees sped past in a blur. Fire burned through her legs and chest with every step she took. Heavy breaths filled the silence as she dodged trunks, roots, and boulders invading her path. Only when she stared up at Olos' summit, free of the pine and branches, did Isolde dare pause.

The cool touch of the elithrium bracelet brought a scowl to her face. Black diamonds glistened in the bed of elithrium laced silver encasing her wrist like a delicate shackle. Thinking back, she was the only one who had been gifted such a fine-looking piece. The others had been nothing but a band of plain silver.

"How lucky I am," Isolde said, tugging the end of her sleeve over the priceless prison. Taking a deep breath, she made the trek up to the vertical rock face to the final three-hundred-foot ascent to victory. A lone crack maimed the surface, not offering more than two inches of room at any given point. Steeling her nerve, Isolde pushed out a heavy sigh, wedged her hands into the crack, and began to climb.

One step…one pull…keep contact…don't look down. Pebbles fell away beneath her touch, causing the back of her hands and the pads of her fingers to groan in pain. She took another step, and the sole of her boot slipped down the rock face. Panic flooded Isolde's gut as she wedged a fist into the crevasse and her body swung out. Pain sliced through the skin covering her knuckles as her back slammed into the mountain. The open flesh stung in the bitter, cold air, and a river of crimson ran down her wrist, coating the bracelet's irritating beauty.

A cry that had managed to break past the lodge of fear in her throat, ripped through Isolde's teeth. She was nearly halfway there and with nothing but air and death's welcoming arms beneath her feet. Isolde knew, even if she didn't have that damn bracelet in place, she would be dead on impact. Being a virya granted many things, but salvation from a three-hundred-foot drop wasn't one of them.

Shoving the fear down, Isolde thrust her knuckles and forefingers back into the crack and braced her feet against the rock. "Move your damn feet!" she growled to herself. Her teeth were bared as she climbed, refusing to feel the pain settling into her bones and torn flesh. "Don't stop!" Drifts of snow carried with the wind, stinging Isolde's exposed cheeks the higher she climbed.

Six small flags, all bearing the House of Tenebriath's signet, snapped in the frigid breeze just over the crest of the cliff. Keeping her eyes up, Isolde forced herself to keep the same rhythm. *One step...one pull...one step...one pull.* Blood ran down the backs of her hands, soaking the sleeves of her tunic. The faces of those whose lives hung in the balance filled her mind with each agonizing pull she extracted from her exhausted hands.

Nyla, Insil, Tanor, Zib... *You have to keep moving...You can't stop!*

Using every ounce of strength left in her torn, bloody hands, Isolde hurled herself over the edge. Skin peeled away from bone grew numb as blood leeched into the snow, staining it red. A cold, sweet agony settled over the open wounds covering the backs of her hands.

Before relief could find its way to her, Isolde felt the chill of a shadow fall across her back. A pair of boots came to rest inches from the tip of her nose. Slowly, her eyes rose to see Buer. A menacing, evil grin was spread across his face and a golden chalice, one of Erebus's treasures, was clutched in his hand.

"I had hoped to play with you a little more," he said with a sigh of mocking regret. His wide shoulders shrugged in indifference. "Oh well." In one quick thrust, the heel of Buer's boot slammed into Isolde's face.

She didn't register the pain or the molten anger burning through her blood. The only thing that mattered was the horrible sensation of falling. It hit her stomach like a punch as she was thrown back over the edge. A strangled, terrified cry lifted from her now split, bleeding lips.

Death rose to greet her like an old friend. It opened its arms ready to catch Isolde as she fell...and fell...and fell.

CHAPTER 15

Trails of pain blazed across Isolde's skin as her back collided with the mountainside. Flesh tore and muscle shredded from every part of her that struck Olos. Her bloody fingers desperately clawed at the rock's merciless face. Sharp stings of pain scorched their way across her fingertips as her nails were ripped away. As terror began to set in, Isolde desperately threw her hand out and lodged it into the crevasse.

The snap of her bones echoed through the Pass of Mordith. More skin peeled away, turning her left hand into pure fire. A roar of pain and fury exploded from Isolde's gaping mouth. The sound carried across the Oronilma Mountains and beyond, leaving her throat raw. Wave after wave of nausea rolled through her like the tide of the sea. With a strangled gasp, Isolde hauled herself up and wedged an elbow into the crack. Blood trickled down her ruined hand in a steady stream, steam rising from its surface. Freezing air caressed the exposed bones and tendons, stark white against a bed red.

Isolde squeezed her eyes shut, her forehead pressing into the cold, unyielding mountain. *Breathe…breathe. You've felt worse. You've been through so much worse!* Tremors ran up her arm, making her hold unsteady.

Fatigue's dangerous touch set into her arms and legs the longer she lingered. The open air at her feet felt so wide and vast. If she didn't move soon, death would have its way. Taking a deep breath, this time using her elbow and right hand, Isolde forced herself to climb.

The ring on her finger winked in the light of the afternoon sun, a mockery of the power she had at her maimed fingertips. She tried calling to it. Tried reaching out to the endless well of power wanting to swallow her whole. At this point, she would have welcomed that oblivion with open arms. But when she reached out, only a well of silence and darkness answered her call.

Shoving every ounce of the energy she had into each pull, Isolde finally made it back up to Olos. A cry seeped from her teeth as her ruined hand plunged into the snow drift rimming the cliff's edge. Tremors of exhaustion racked through her body, causing her teeth to chatter. She collapsed into the drifts and her eyes closed to the rays of blinding light shining from the snow's surface.

Adrenaline finally gave way, leaving room for the real pain to set in. It was everywhere. Not a single piece of her had been spared by Olos' wrath.

"Fucking Buer!" Isolde rasped.

The sound of footsteps brought her up short. Looking up, Isolde spotted the champion from Blackwater. He plucked the only remaining item from the velvet-lined table. A necklace, adorned with pearls and sapphires surrounded by pure silver, shimmered in his callused, tanned hand. He looked down to where she lay in the blood-tinged snow, his expression morose.

"I am sorry, Lady Isolde." His voice, a deep, rich baritone soothed the words it carried. A faint wheeze accompanied every breath he tried to force from his chest. The tanned skin that covered his brow bunched as he took a step back. "So sorry." And with that, Blackwater's champion took off down the mountain, his pace slow but steadfast.

Panic blocked out the pain, propelling Isolde up. Her steps were careless and unsteady. Every foot gained was torturous, but she hardly felt the agony anymore. Only the rising terror of failure filled her mind.

The sound of her approach brought Blackwater's champion up short, and he whipped around to face her. Isolde could have sworn it was the ocean staring back at her. His eyes, a marvelous aqua blue, harboring hints of green, narrowed in warning.

"I can't let you take that," she said, blood coating her chin. She could feel the tear along her bottom lip open anew. A tear made by the heel of Buer's boot. "It's not only my life at stake if I return empty-handed."

"You think you're the only one with someone to lose?" he asked. "Stories of the great maiden of Thornwood have reached Blackwater's shores, Lady Isolde. I've heard of all you have done for the humans and half-bloods. It's noble, and I commend you for it. But make no mistake. You aren't making it past this round."

"Give me the damn necklace and run," she snarled, taking a step closer. A flicker of her power surfaced, the animal within stirring, fighting against the elithrium.

Silence stood between them. Only the sound of the mountain air snaking its way across the peak dared make itself known. The male looked at her in fear, his eyes wide in disbelief. "That's not possible," he said. His eyes flickered to the blood-covered bracelet on her wrist. "It can't be—"

Moving as fast as her powerless body would allow, Isolde launched into the air. She jumped from one side to the next and came down on his face with her good hand curled into a fist. Bare knuckles collided with his cheek, sending him flying back to bounce off a lone boulder standing at the edge of the path.

Flakes of snow dusted his golden locks as he rose to his feet. Anger, a look that didn't suit him at all, filled his gaze. A growl of frustration sifted through his bared teeth. Isolde came at him again. He dropped into a crouch, and his long leg swept out across the snow-covered ground.

But years of training with Malaki and Galaena had prepared her well. She leapt over the attack with ease and brought her fist down again. The feel of her knuckles colliding with his jaw filled her with smug satisfaction. Every blow, every strike the other delivered sent them closer and closer to the edge.

Isolde's foot slammed into the center of his chest, the impact jarring her already exhausted body. He landed in a heap of snow at the mountain's edge. Isolde wiped the back of her hand across her bloody chin. "This could have been far less painful, you know." Fear ignited in his eyes as he shoved himself away, sending snow tumbling down into the darkness below. Isolde charged at him again, refusing to give him a second of reprieve. But he merely pushed himself to his knees and raised his hands in surrender.

"Please," he begged, blood dripping from the corner of his mouth. The priceless necklace was clutched in his grip. "I have a son… a wife."

Isolde's footsteps slowed, her gaze narrowing. She searched for any hint of deception, but nothing dwelt in his gaze except pleading and desperation. Death was the last thing she wanted for him, for any of them—besides Buer. He was no different than she was, just another victim in Gage and Erebus's games. Cautiously, Isolde straightened from her fighting stance and willed her fists to uncoil. The soles of her boots crunched against the fresh snow as she extended her unmanned hand forward. Blackwater's champion stared at it for a moment before slipping his palm into hers.

His penetrating, mesmerizing gaze lifted, and all that remained was shame. "Forgive me."

Shocked rage burned through Isolde's blood as her body was yanked forward and pitched over the side. But as she fell away, Isolde latched onto his coat sleeve, giving him no choice but to follow into the abyss. Isolde tumbled down the steep incline with Blackwater's champion at her side. Dizziness danced with the pain in a horrible duet. Up was down and down was up. The unmistakable sound of stone upon flesh rang in her ears.

When it felt as if her body couldn't take anymore, the world came to a screeching, agonizing halt. A blanket of snow encased Isolde's beaten, battered body in its cool embrace. Pain seeped through every breath trying to fill her chest. The scar on her side burned with every cough fighting its way to the surface. Warmth spread through the golden ring encasing her finger, but not a breath of wind brushed her bloodied lips.

Nothing would move save for her eyes. Snow covered the edges of the mountain that shot up in every direction. They had landed in a ravine belonging to the Gap of Duron on the far side of Olos, west of the Pass of Mordith.

A groan of pain echoed from where Blackwater's champion lay a few feet away. Wheezy, wet breaths slipped over his lips. Agony pelted every part of Isolde's body as she forced herself to roll over. A wet, sticky warmth that sent a ripple of apprehension to her gut, painted the skin beneath her tunic.

"You say you know what I do for the humans and the half-bloods," Isolde said, willing her hands beneath her chest. Something sharp pressed against her palm. Beneath a layer of soft, fresh snow, Isolde pulled a piece of rock from its icy depths. It fit perfectly in her palm. The pad of her thumb ran over its sharp, deadly edge.

"I do," he said, pushing himself to his knees. Blood ran down the side of his face in a steady stream. Drop after drop fell, coloring the snow around him.

"And you claim to be so sorry for trying to kill me."

"I am," he said. "Deeply."

"Why don't I believe you?" Isolde asked, straightening to her full height.

"I don't care if you believe me or not," he said, anger burning in his eyes. "I never chose to come here, I was forced to. A half-blood like me," he said, lips pulling into a sneer, "we're expendable to people like you. *Pure bloods.*"

Isolde froze where she stood. "Gage, ordered a half-blood to compete?" The absurdity of it was unheard of. "That can't be right. He...he would never risk—"

"Someone like me winning?" A humorless chuckle fell from his lips, exposing a row of now gleaming red teeth. "You're quite intelligent, Lady Isolde. Or at least claim to be." Isolde raised a single brow, her grip on the rock tightening. "Do you really think Gage or Erebus would have allowed someone like me to even come close to winning?"

Isolde's teeth ground painfully. He was right. Of course, he was right. "What's your name."

"Arlo," he said, resting his palms in his lap. "Not that it matters. I highly doubt Gage would part with the coin Erebus would require for my life to be spared. Still, if it's not too much trouble, after you kill me, would you send a letter to my family?"

Isolde stood dumbfounded in the wake of his request. "A letter?"

"To my wife and son," he said, throat bobbing. "Tell them I tried. Tell them...I love them—more than my own life. I don't want my boy to remember me as the villain who left him and his mother or the coward Gage will undoubtedly make me out to be. I still want to be the hero in his eyes."

Isolde's mouth went dry. The makeshift blade in her hand suddenly felt far too heavy. She doubted she could wield it now even if she wanted to. Arlo's limbs shook. His lips, now bloody and trembling, were drawn into a tight line. Sorrow and regret filled his face.

"I'm no stranger to being a villain," Isolde said. "And believe me when I say, you have no right to such a title."

"Villain…you?" Arlo said, his voice heavy with humorless laughter. "From what has reached the shores of Blackwater, you are nothing short of a hero, Lady Isolde."

"The heart of a villain isn't so different from that of a hero," Isolde said, her eyes dropping to the blade in her hand. "It's just willing to take on the burdens a hero's heart can't. Burdens…that are best left in the dark." Shifting her feet, Isolde took in the man before her. "You might be many things, Arlo of Blackwater, but a villain isn't one of them. Those, I know all too well." A loaded, painful sigh filled and left her chest. "Blackwater is a rather long way from here," she said, a grin whispering at the edge of her mouth. "I'd rather give you the pleasure of making that journey."

The pads of Arlo's fingertips dug into his thighs. Those strange, oceanic eyes were wide and full of hopefully uncertainty. "I don't…I don't understand."

"Too much blood has already been spilled by my hands," Isolde said, letting the rock hang loose in her grasp. "And I'm sure more will stain them before the end. But I'd rather not spill anymore if it's all the same to you." She forced a weak smile onto her battered face. A smile she hoped would hide the pain she felt grow with each passing second. "Not today, anyway."

Arlo's throat bobbed. His hands began to move up and down the lengths of his ripped, leather pant legs in nervous strokes. "You're…you're letting me go?"

"For the price of…" Isolde tapped the tip of the blade on her chin, her face scrunched in sarcastic thoughtfulness. Her eyes dropped to the prize still held tightly in Arlo's hand. "One necklace."

A sigh of shocked humor pushed through Arlo's lips. He looked down at the necklace that represented so much more than monetary value. It represented life itself, priceless in every sense of the word—for one of them, anyway. A stream of light caught the face of a sapphire as he held it out to her. The necklace that ensured she, along with everyone she loved, would live a little longer.

"Seems like a fair trade to me."

Isolde stepped forward and plucked it from his grasp. It was heavier than she expected. Although, Isolde felt quite certain a leaf would feel heavy to her in that moment. "And as an added bonus"—she nodded to a break in the ravine on the left—"that part of the Gap of Duron will lead you east, to the Sea of Calca. From there you can follow the coast until you reach Blackwater. Stick to the shadows and try to only travel at night." Her eyes fell to the elithrium bracelet still locked around his wrist. "And get that thing off as soon as you can."

"I owe you my life, Lady Isolde," Arlo said, fighting to stand.

Isolde stepped forward and extended her good hand to him once more. Arlo flinched at the movement, and Isolde flashed a challenging smile. "And here I was thinking we were beginning to trust each other." Uncertainty melted away, and Arlo reached forward to slip his hand into her palm.

"As tempting of an offer as your life is, Arlo," she said, pressing the handle of the makeshift blade into his hand, "your friendship will suffice." Isolde felt his hand squeeze around hers as a thankful, handsome smile, broad and unrestrained, stretched across his bloodied face. A glimpse into the male he truly was broke through, a male, she would be lucky to call an ally.

"It's yours. Whatever you may need, whenever you may need it, my service is yours."

Isolde offered him a smile and nodded to the path. "You better get started," she said, dropping his hand. "I can imagine Erebus will send his lap dog to hunt for your broken body before too long."

With one last nod of appreciation, Arlo made his way to the bend. "Until we meet again, Lady Isolde." He disappeared around the corner, leaving behind only footprints and a trail of blood in his wake. Isolde smiled and found herself holding onto the fleeting hope that she would cross paths with the champion of Blackwater again.

"Until we meet again," she said to the sound of his dying footsteps. When they finally faded away, leaving her in silence, Isolde turned back to the only path she had left to follow. A cut in the ravine took a sharp turn towards the right, to the west heading to Elenarta.

Without any other choice, Isolde took in a steely breath, and began making her way back. She took her time, not caring how late she was in completing the task. The kiss of the cold mountain air sent waves of pain through her hand, forcing her to clutch it to her body.

After a while, a sound faint but not belonging to the mountain whispered through the pass. It was a sound she had heard countless times across Arnoria. Each step she took brought her closer and closer. It bounced off the rock walls, echoing along the path.

The ravine diverged into a fork. Based on the position of the sun, the arena was down the one on the left. But the one on the right carried that horrible sound. A sound Isolde could not ignore. She gave one fleeting look down the path on the left before tucking the necklace into the lining of her britches and turned right.

The path grew wide and opened into an outcropping in the mountain. Fresh snow, undisturbed and flat, blanketed the ground. A small imperfection stood out from the rock face at the far end. It was covered with a metal grate, the square holes far too small for her to fit her hand through. Peeking in, Isolde caught a glimpse of a hallway that led to a metal door standing open to the far right.

Beyond the door, the sound of a whip cracked through the air like a clap of thunder. A bellow of agony wasn't far behind. Isolde instinctually gripped the bars and pulled. A hiss of pain ripped through her teeth as the broken bones in her hand refused to move and the now dried torn flesh pulled at her knuckles.

"The mines," she said, taking a step back. "That bastard has reopened the mines of Helecdol." Isolde's worst fear grew as she realized exactly where she was. The dungeons of Elenarta lay in the belly of these mountains. Its walls were far too thick and passageways too numerous to navigate, making an escape nearly impossible. Meaning Erebus had connected them. He had created two hellholes in one. She staggered back, her eyes sweeping, desperately searching for another way in.

"This is new," she said with a deep breath, running her uninjured hand over the cuts and groves of the gray stone. It was perfect. Far too perfect to have been made by anything other than magic. "You were made by a virya."

Guilt, savage and hot, burned through her as she made a silent promise to those she had heard. To those who dwelt, who suffered beneath her feet. "I won't leave you," she swore. "I'll come back." Forcing herself away, Isolde turned and followed her footprints back to the ravine.

She lost track of time, hardly noticing where her footsteps led as she made the trip back to the arena. The sound of the whip and the cry that followed filled Isolde's mind, making it impossible to think of anything else. The people's cries filled the air when she finally emerged from the tree line and onto the streets of Elenarta. She tried and failed to smile at the onlookers who lined the streets.

When she at last stepped out into the open air of the arena, the crowd roared. The loudest shouts came from those who sat in a sea of gold and crimson. Broad smiles shone down from where her cadre stood cheering. But it was another's voice who drew her attention.

"Lady Isolde," Erebus said, a satisfied smile forming on his face.

"You took your time completing my task. I was beginning to worry."

"Your concern is unnecessary, Your Grace," Isolde said, claiming her spot among the champions who lingered at the base of the dais. Trinkets of various kinds were clutched in their hands. "And from what I recall, you did not give a time limit on this trial," she said, with a smile that hid the pain raging through her body. "If my presence was required sooner, His Majesty should be more specific next time."

A collective hush descended over the arena. Gage stood stock still at Erebus's right side. His eyes darkening in warning.

"You're quite right, I did not give a time limit." Erebus leaned forward on the throne, his eyes piercing and glowing with fury. "But make no mistake. You will have no doubt in what I demand of you in the trials to come."

Fear cascaded down Isolde as if she had been drenched in ice water. She bit her tongue and forced herself into a stiff, passable bow.

"Now," Erebus said, leaning back, "we seem to be missing one."

"Arlo, Your Majesty," answered Gage, his shoulders square and back straight. "From Blackwater."

"Yes," Erebus mused. "One of your champions, Gage. Well, where is he?" His eyes were locked on Isolde and the blood she was covered in.

"He fell." The words tumbled from her lips as if she was stating a fact that needed no other explanation.

"Fell?" Erebus asked, his brow raised. "All on his own?"

Isolde kept her face neutral, her gaze unwavering. "The mountains are a treacherous place, Your Majesty."

"I see," Erebus said. "Well, accidents do happen, I suppose. Unburden our champions from their bracelets." The servant from before moved forward and carefully removed the despicable jewelry from Isolde's wrist.

"Taking back your present already?" she asked. The poor man

allowed only the ghost of a smile to form on his lips before promptly stepping back into formation. Power crashed into Isolde like a bolt of lightning. Claws racked down the cage in her mind. Its teeth sank into her resolve, forcing her to take a deep breath.

"Mentors," Erebus announced, "see to your champions. There are healers available if you did not bring one yourself. There will be a feast within the next few days to celebrate the first trial and the champions who completed it." Erebus rose, followed by members of court who sat in attendance. "Gage, find the body and dispose of it."

"As you wish, my king," Gage said with a bow, and Erebus swept past him. Isolde waited for the other champions to pass her before following. The hum of her power and pain in her body was becoming too much. It took all her effort to keep moving, to put one foot in front of the other.

"What of these?" Buer asked, holding up the goblet to Lenox, who stood nearby.

"A gift from His Majesty," Lenox replied, with the lift of his chin. "For having completed the trial."

Isolde wanted nothing more than to tell Lenox where Erebus could shove his so-called gift. But as she looked into the crowd, to her family, she thought of a far better use for it. So instead, she shoved the necklace into her pocket and kept moving.

Liam met her at the mouth of the tunnel, his face cast in shadow. A muscle feathered in his paling cheek as he took in the blood and maimed flesh decorating her body.

"Oh, my gods, Isolde."

Isolde couldn't bring herself to smile, to reassure him it wasn't as bad as it looked. Pain consumed her every thought, making it impossible to think of anything else.

"Liam…"

The second she was out of view, Isolde felt all her will power evaporate into the cool air of the tunnel. She fell forward and Liam's arms instantly consumed her. He wrapped an arm around her waist like a rope of solid iron. Slowly, Isolde let him help her out of the arena, smearing his clean, black uniform with blood.

"I'm alright," she said between breaths—more to herself than to him. "I'm…I'm alright."

Liam's voice filled the tunnel like a breath of night. "No, you're not."

CHAPTER 16

"We need to go now," Isolde argued, pacing the length of their ridiculously lavish chambers. Each step sent a bolt of painful remembrance through her sore muscles. While she had healed, hints of the first trial still lingered.

Rays of the setting sun pierced the archways lining the western wall. Their warmth penetrated the sheets of delicate fabric covering her body. Intricate patterns of beads and jewels of every shade of blue ran along the length of her collarbone and descended over her breasts to hug the voluptuous curve of her hips. It wasn't the first dress she had been presented with.

"This arrived for you," Nan had said, trying to balance the finely wrapped package. Earlier that day, Zego had arrived bearing the gift from her unwanted future husband.

"Lord Gage said to inform you he is most anxious to see you tonight." Light from the sun danced across his yellow teeth as a grin filled his rodent-like face.

"Consider your message delivered," Isolde had said, taking the package from Nan. She planted her foot against the door and looked over her shoulder. "Be sure to ask Gage for a treat." The door rattled on its hinges as Isolde slammed it shut in Zego's reddening face.

"The fire looks a little low, wouldn't you agree, Nan?" Isolde had asked, not giving the package another glance as she tossed it into the flames.

The newly healed flesh of her palm grazed over the silken fabric clinging to her stomach as she paced. Malaki had focused on healing her hand first. "You need to be able to defend yourself," he had argued, ignoring her protests entirely. Beads of perspiration had trickled down his face and disappeared into a line of sweat ringing the collar of his tunic as he poured his power into her. Despite Isolde ordering him to stop, to rest, Malaki had worked until a new layer of soft, pink flesh covered her hand.

"I don't remember having a choice in Liam healing me," he had argued, his eyes flashing. "I don't see why you should get to make this one for me too."

She looked to where he lay now. His massive form was sprawled across one of the oversized ottomans near the balcony. His chest rose and fell in slow, even breaths and a soft breeze brushed tendrils of ebony hair across his forehead.

"Stubborn ass," she murmured, a loving smile tugging onto her face.

Rays of the dying sun fought for dominance over his features. They did battle among the ink etched across his russet skin marked in eternal penance. Isolde, for a moment, simply looked at him. Her dearest friend, her dark angel of vengeance had been gazing out at the mountain range, at the land, the home he had given so much for. He fit this place like sand to the sea, like trees to the forest. It was impossible to have one without the other.

Peace softened the harsh, defined angles of his brow and the firm set of his mouth. It was a look that rarely made an appearance. He was tired. So…so tired. Her eyes fell to his hip. To the spot housing the scar that was healing but still left him far too vulnerable.

"This is ridiculous," she grumbled. Zibiah drifted through her heart on wave of worry. It collided with the faces of those she had seen the night of the ball. So many little faces. "I know where they are. We need to get them out!"

"And what plan, dare I ask," Cillian said, leaning back in one of the chairs along the wall, "has our brave, fearless leader come up with for getting not only them out of here, but us as well?"

Isolde's eyes narrowed as she passed before him. "Still working on it. Brilliance, much like beauty, takes time."

"For some, perhaps."

A smirk, one that brought a growl to Isolde's lips, spread across Cillian's face as he tossed a peppermint candy into the air. She watched it disappear into his open mouth, then another…and another. Her mouth watered at the sight of the stash of white-and-pink sweets clutched in his hand.

"Don't even think about it," he warned, cradling the hoard to his chest. She took a step forward, and a faint glow echoed in Cillian's eyes. "These are mine. You have your own!"

"Mine have miraculously disappeared if you call," Isolde said sweetly. "Besides, I just want one!"

"That's most unfortunate for you, *Lady Isolde*," Cillian said, his hand balling into a fist, a hint of warning coating his tone. "Besides, you never want just one and you never share."

Anger flared in Isolde's eyes as he stuffed another piece into his mouth. Cillian's teeth ground the candy into dust. Each crunch only stoked Isolde's irritation more. As she took another step, fully intent on tackling him to the ground, the whisper of the evening wind broke through the archways and kissed her cheeks. Isolde looked to the balcony and smiled.

"That's how you want to be?" she said with a shrug. "Fine." She made her way to the balcony, her bare feet padding on the cold marble floor. The snowcapped mountains stretched beyond the horizon, their tips kissing the early evening sky that held a sea of stars. But Isolde knew it was the sheer drop that would fill Cillian's candy-stuffed gut with dread.

"Are you sure you don't want to share with me, Cill?" She leapt and teetered on the edge of the balcony's thin, stone railing. A smile pulled at the edge of her lips at the sound of Cillian's strangled gasp.

"Get down!" Cillian's voice boomed through the air like a command as the front two legs of his chair slammed into the marble floor. "Now, Isolde!" Light shone in his dark eyes darting from her to the edge and back up.

Hundreds of feet of air lingered between the ground and the bare tips of Isolde's toes. "Why?" she asked. "Do I make you nervous?"

A cool breeze drifted through her fingers hovering at her sides. A smell lingered in their embrace, delicate and pure. It stirred memories she immediately pushed back, locking them away inside a part of herself where not even the light of day could touch them.

"You know damn well it does!" Cillian said, taking another step towards her, his teeth gritting. "Get your spoiled, murderous ass off that railing, Isolde Cotheran!"

"It's going to cost you," she sang, lifting one foot to hover over the abyss that lay below. A stream of steady air placed itself beneath her bare foot, helping her to stay balanced. There was no fear of falling…but Cillian didn't need to know that.

"Damn it, fine!" he growled, tossing the bag of remaining candy at the floor beneath her feet. "Just get down!"

Isolde chuckled with delight and plopped down to the floor. A sigh of relief pushed through Cillian's lips and a look of irritation met

Isolde's smug grin. "You know you're not allowed to give me a heart attack! We agreed those were only for Malaki."

Malaki's deep, sleepy chuckle filled the room. "Your own medicine doesn't taste good, does it, Cill?"

Cillian rolled his eyes but took up a seat on the couch. "You better keep an eye on your stash as well."

"She knows better." Malaki rose and glanced out the window, his smile fading into a frown of frustration. "You shouldn't have let me sleep so long." He shoved up from the couch, trying to hide the pain still lingering in his bones. "Especially not tonight."

"The time you require to get yourself ready is laughable," Isolde said, popping three peppermints into her mouth. The sugar and mint melted on her tongue, drawing a moan of satisfaction from her. Without waiting, she shoved in two more.

"I hope you get a stomachache," Cillian grumbled from where he sat beneath Blyana's perch on the back of one the couches. Isolde shoved another piece in for good measure and shot him a candy-filled grin.

Cillian's arms knotted over his chest. "You're such a child."

"That's not the point," Malaki said, ignoring them as he splashed the contents of the freshly filled wash basin across his face. Rivers of cold water cascaded down his bare back, snaking along the scars and names of the dead lingering in the rivets of muscle. "These events are just as dangerous as the trials. We can't be complacent."

"Nor can I have my second-in-command exhausted to the point he can hardly stand," said Isolde. "Let alone hold a blade if the occasion called for it." He shot her a heated look in the mirror reflecting over his broad shoulder. "We shouldn't even be going tonight."

"You can't miss this event, Isolde." Alaric's voice echoed from across the room. The golden handle of his cane glistened in the light of the fire. It hadn't escaped Isolde's notice that Alaric had been unusually quiet the past few days. Silent, even.

He hadn't gotten any sleep since their arrived, or very little. Isolde had been awoken more than once by the sound of his cane clicking against the floor. Her uncle paced through the night, his mind never quiet, his worry never ebbing. Dark shadows hung beneath his eyes as a result.

"As much as I hate to say it, you are expected to attend." He sighed. "Erebus has demanded the attendance of all the champions and their houses. Not to mention your…*betrothed*." The word fell from Alaric's mouth like it was poison. "Your absence will not go unnoticed."

"He's right," Galaena said, her hand resting on Alaric's shoulder. He seemed to sag beneath her touch. "You have to go. We all do." Her worry-filled gaze flickered to Malaki who was tugging on a clean maroon tunic.

Isolde reconvened her pacing, her irritation growing. Ever since the trial, her power had been restless, viciously alert. The memory of the elithrium bracelet, and its horrible confinement, festered in Isolde's mind like a wound. Unease spread through her at the thought of having to wear the damn thing again. Her power snarled at the idea.

"The elithrium bracelets Erebus put on you aren't unlike the ones you cut from me and Cinta," Blyana had explained after the trial. She had sat by Isolde's bedside, attempting to distract her as Liam and Malaki worked, forcing her wounds to heal.

Isolde's eyes had traveled to Blyana's hands, to the permanent mark residing on the right wrist, just below her delicate, prominent wrist bone. Another scar, another reminder of what Vara had done to her. An eternal token of what her time in the House of Pleasures was still doing to her.

"Will it leave a scar?" Isolde had asked. Not that she truly cared, but still she'd prefer to know.

Blyana's forefinger scrubbed at the tattoo on her left thumb. "Vara didn't see the need in using more silver than necessary. It was only coated elithrium, not combined. Eventually, the silver wore down enough to leave its mark." Blyana's nails dug into the tattoo, leaving behind small crescent-shaped indentions. "If it had been combined properly, like yours, it can't cause physical injury just by touching your skin. Not that Vara cared to take the extra step."

A haunted look had crossed Blyana's face at the thought, her eyes still lingering on the scar. "But it can force us to hold in our power. It's like putting a storm into a bottle and sealing the cork shut. Although, in your case, it'd be like trying to bottle a hurricane."

Isolde felt the weight of that storm. It had left a hollowness inside her heart. A dark crevice, cold and full of fear. Vulnerable … weak … exposed. That was what the damn bracelet had done to her. She looked at Blyana, who was busy brushing Cillian's hair from his face. A soft, content smile pulled at the corners of her lips. How different she was from the broken, bloody girl she found in the mud. So, different from the woman who had been forced into such hell for years. *Years.*

Anger, cold and hard as ice, spread through Isolde's heart. She had had but a taste of that torture. And as she watched her friend, her sister, pull a pair of silk gloves onto her hands, Isolde made a silent vow that Vara would pay for what she had done. That her blood would flow under Blyana's blade and by Blyana's blade alone. No matter the cost.

Shaking herself free of the memory, Isolde sighed and tossed the nearly empty bag of sweets to the side. "Well, if Malaki is done prettying himself up, let's not deprive the fine nobility of Elenarta of our company any longer."

"You're one to talk," he said, securing Secrettaker to his belt. "What time did you start getting ready today? Noon?"

"Why is it such a hard concept for you and Cillian to understand?" asked Isolde with a smirk she knew dug into his skin. "Beauty and brilliance take time. Although, I don't know why I bother. My beauty is already perfect."

She could practically hear Malaki's eyes roll. "Gods spare us."

A hidden smile lurked on the edges of Liam's mouth from where he stood at the bottom of a sweeping staircases. He wore his usual uniform, a black leather tunic and britches, all made of the finest quality. Isolde tried not to cringe at the sight.

He was still Liam, her Liam. She pressed her fingers into the length of his forearm at the thought. The cords of steel tightened, and the hint of a smile grew on his freshly shaven cheek. His ebony curls had been swept back, giving her an unhindered view of his face.

"I like this look," she said. "Less soldiery. More like you."

Liam's gaze slid to her, his brow arching. "You used to love the stubble. For more reasons than one." Heat flooded Isolde's cheeks, her fingers tightening on his arm at the memory.

Malaki walked beside her, and a faint sheen glistened from his brow. It had taken a toll on him, using the power he wielded to heal her. And while the wound at his side had healed over, she could still see a small limp, a slight catch in his gait. It didn't help he had refused to let Liam aid in healing her until he was nearly unconscious and didn't have a say in the matter.

"I feel the same way about being stared at as you do about being told what to do," Malaki said, forcing his shoulders back. A hint of annoyance lingered in his tone.

Isolde rolled her eyes. "You pushed yourself too hard, stubborn ass." There was no hiding the worry in her voice as they turned the corner. "Besides, you call me out on my bullshit all the time."

"Because you usually deserve to be called out." The sound of a piano and violin filled the corridor. It mingled with the laughter and idle talk floating in the air at the ballroom entrance. "I'll survive," he said, doing his best to force his feet to move. "I just need some rest is all." He tried to hide the shaky sigh pushing past his lips. Before Isolde could respond, the entrance to the ballroom opened, allowing light and noise to bleed into the hallway, washing them in extravagant revelry.

Zego, whose nose couldn't possibly be held any higher, announced their arrival doing little to hide the sneer in his voice. "Lord Alaric and Lady Galaena Cotheran of House of Thornwood. And their champion, Isolde Cotheran.

Isolde never thought she would miss the title of heir. But its absence left a hole in her heart, one she had no idea existed. She felt every eye turn and hold her in their grasp. A small, smug smile spread across her face as she strolled into the ballroom, her hips swaying from side to side. The muscles of Liam's arm shifted beneath her loose grip.

"Stop doing that."

"You'll have to be more specific." Her smile widened at a female whose face held nothing but envious contempt.

"Shaking your ass for everyone to see," Liam said, his words tickling her ear. "That's only supposed to be for me. Or do we need to discuss this again?"

"You're more than welcome to look," Isolde offered, her voice filled with intent. "As for them," she said, nodding to the sea of onlookers. "I'm showing them the one thing they can't stand to see."

"I can't imagine anyone not wanting to see your—"

Liam's words died away as a growl of warning broke between them. Isolde looked back to see Malaki's hate-filled gaze aimed at Liam. "Watch what you say!"

Heat filled Liam's cheeks, his own power roaring to life. A muscle feathered in his jaw and the grip on Isolde's arm tightened. "I don't believe you were involved in the conversation, Malaki."

"When Isolde is involved," Malaki said, taking a step forward and invading Liam's air, "so am I."

"Not in this conversation, you're not," Isolde said, placing her hand on Malaki's chest. "I'd rather you not know the intimate details of my sex life, Malaki. Go find a seat, I'll be there soon." His eyes pulled away from Liam to stared down at her. Anger lingered in the depths of his hazel eyes. "Please," she said, not wanting to fight with him over Liam—not again.

Without another word, he cast a final scathing look at Liam and followed the others to the table at the back of the ballroom.

Liam sighed but forced a smile on his face. "Now tell me," he said, pulling her attention away. "What are you showing that these fine people"—his lip curling at the words—"don't want to see?"

"That I'm still here," Isolde said, her smile turning razor-sharp. "That I am not the soft, delicate lady everyone expects me to be. That I am a threat."

"If anyone underestimates you, Isolde," said Liam, his face beaming with pride, "their foolishness will be their undoing."

A flicker of movement off to the right of the dais caught Isolde's eye. The colors of Volkran's house, black and purple, clung to those who had gathered. Isolde forced the snarl down, willing herself to keep the mask of civility in place. Buer stood among them. His colossal form towered over all in attendance. His eyes turned to meet her own and froze. A cruel smile formed over the rim of the golden goblet he had acquired on Olos.

Isolde's power stirred at the challenge, its teeth baring in her mind. It too remembered the mountain peak and how he had tried to kill her. Isolde's lip curled over her teeth, a silent growl rumbling at the back of her throat.

Buer's eyes flared at the sight, his own power coming forth. A tremor cascaded down his colossal frame, and the gilded surface of the goblet crinkled beneath his unforgiving grasp.

"Please don't start a fight with the other champions," Liam said, his eyes narrowing on Buer.

"I won't start anything," Isolde said, holding up her hands in mocking surrender. "Unless they do first. Then it's out of my hands."

Liam rolled his eyes. "I suppose that's better than nothing." He plucked two goblets from a servant making his way through the crowd. Wine gently sloshed against the edges as Liam placed the cup in her hands. "To your amazing success, Isolde."

She smiled and tilted the rim to tap his own. "To not dying." Liam paused before raising the glass to his lips, a soft laugh ghosting across the wine's surface.

"Hello, pet."

Anger flared to life in Isolde's chest at the sound of his voice. Reluctantly, she turned to see her betrothed sauntering forward, his usual air of smugness wafting about him like an odor. The dark charcoal jacket covering his chest and shoulders made the blue in his eyes far more striking, much to Isolde's annoyance.

"How ravishing you look, Lady Isolde," Gage said, his teeth grazing across his bottom lip. "I see you've healed up rather well; much faster than the others anyway."

"She has an excellent healer," Liam said, stepping forward to stand at Isolde's side.

Gage's gaze hardened as a barely contained sneer played on his full lips. "Ah yes," he said, casting a look over his shoulder at Malaki. "The Bastard Prince. I've heard of his healing abilities. They will come in handy when Isolde and I are wed."

"If you're familiar with his healing abilities, Gage," said Liam, a growl weaving is way into his words. "Then you must be aware of his killing ones as well."

"If Lady Isolde wishes for the Bastard Prince to stay in her presence after we are married, as her healer," Gage said, his posture reeking of subdued challenge, "then I suggest you remember your place. You will address me as fitting of my station, *Captain*. You do recall what that is, do you not? I know it's been a trying few weeks but surely, even a spawn from the gutter like yourself can remember."

Fury rolled off Liam in waves, sending a chill of dread to Isolde's gut. Her grip on his forearm tightened and the tips of her freshly painted nails pressed into the lining of his jacket. After a moment, Liam cleared his throat, and the light in his eyes faded to reveal the rich brown beneath. "Of course, Lord Gage. My apologies."

"That wasn't so hard, was it?" Gage asked with a smile that pulled at the hideous scars. "Now run along and get yourself a treat for being such a good boy. Lady Isolde and I have a wedding to plan. Thank you for escorting her, Captain."

Begrudgingly, Liam dropped Isolde's hand and stepped aside. "Of course, sir." A chill of sadness drifted through her chest at his absence.

"Come, pet," Gage said, wrapping his fingers around Isolde's wrist. The heels of her shoes skidded across the marble floor as he yanked her forward. His cold, callused grip constricted around her waist and squeezed, tucking her in as close as he could manage. As he towed her through the crowd of sickening wealth, Gage's voice cut through the air like a sharp winter breeze. "I take it the king has informed you of the blessed news?"

"Hardly the word I would use," said Isolde, her voice flat and stomach rolling with revulsion. "Death would be preferable."

"Come now, Isolde. Surely, you see the benefit in the union. We're the perfect match, the very weapon of unity for Arnoria."

"The very weapon to bring about more suffering," Isolde said. "I have no interest in becoming such a thing.

His deep, rich chuckle carried through the air. "It's precious you think you actually have a say in the matter now. Or that you did to begin with." The tips of his fingers grazed the steady pulse of her wrist. His touch was so light and intimate Isolde nearly shared the contents of her stomach with the whole room. "Decreed by the king himself. There is no greater order. Even the gods cannot stop it. You are mine, pet."

"You are aware that pets bite, aren't you, Gage?" Isolde asked, flashing a toothy smile. Already she loathed the endearment. "And I'm well informed of where your particular tastes lie and believe me, you won't enjoy mine."

"I have a feeling you can do far more than that," Gage said, his eyes darkening. "Besides, pets also know their place and are punished when they misbehave. But there is another matter we must discuss. You were rather rude the other day." A false smile played on his face as they passed a horde of bureaucrats.

"In what way?" she asked, not even attempting to hide the malice in her tone. "I'm told I can be spectacularly offensive in so many interesting and entertaining ways."

"You dared rebuke the king," Gage said, his tone sharpening. "Very unwise of you.'

"I was merely stating a fact," Isolde said, trying to yank free of Gage's grip. "It's not my fault our *wise* leader didn't have enough sense to be clear."

Gage's fingers twisted around her wrist, causing the bones to groan. Isolde bit down on her lips, refusing to let a single sound through.

"Mind your tongue!" He said with a growl. "You will not embarrass me like that again, Isolde. Or is this another lesson I must teach you too? From what I can recall, you didn't like learning my last one. Or rather, those children didn't."

Isolde felt herself go stiff in his grip as the weight of his words fell like an anvil on stone. Their faces hammered against her head like a battering ram. Gage's smile only grew as the pain was undoubtedly playing across her face, despite how hard she tried to hide it.

Gently, almost mockingly, he said, "I know it's hard." He pulled her throbbing wrist to his lips. "But in time, you'll learn to the love the cage I've made just for you. One way or another, you will learn to obey me." To anyone else it would look like a sweet moment between two people in love. But to those who knew, to her cadre who looked on helplessly from where they perched across the room, it was torture.

"That threat won't work on me forever," Isolde said, her teeth grinding. "Those children are human. One day, they'll die. They all will. And when they do, I will make sure every last drop of your blood tastes the free air. Nothing will be left. No one will recognize you. No one will remember your name. You, Lord Gage, will be *nothing*."

Light, still luminescent and piercing, dulled in Gage's eyes. The scars stretching across his cheeks thinned as his mouth formed into a smile. "There will always be someone to hold over that pretty little head of yours, Isolde. Your heart is filled with so much *love* for those unworthy of such things." Gage's palms pressed into her hips and swung her around to face the room. She fought to push him off, but his fingers dug deeper into her skin, holding her still.

"Everyone you love, your aunt and uncle, the Bastard Prince, your lady in waiting, her lover, the children...and of course..." His lips pressed to the shell of her ear, his nose burying in locks of her hair. "We can't forget the old hag you brought with you."

A gasp slipped through Isolde's tightly sealed lips. *Nan.*

Isolde's heart raced as her eyes landed on her cadre, her family huddled around one of the tables in the back. Alaric was on his feet, his eyes flowing with fury. Galaena was at his side, and a look matching her husband's, burned in her eyes. Malaki, Cillian, and Blyana were already making their way through the crowd. Sweat gleamed from Malaki's brow, color leeching from his face. Murder danced in his eyes that were locked on Gage's hands.

"They will ensure you behave," Gage said, the tips of his fingers pressing deeper, drawing her flush to his chest. She felt him at her backside—what little was there anyway. Bile built in her throat as she tried and failed to push him away. "They will guarantee you obey me. Even Liam."

Isolde clamped her jaw tight, refusing to give even the slightest reaction. "Imagine how jealous he will be," Gage continued. "Seeing us together, side by side with the king. Perhaps I'll relocate him to guarding our chambers. He can listen to every moan, every scream I pull from those perfect lips of yours. Or should that position be given to Malaki as well?"

"You seem awfully confident for a man who was bested over and over and over again," Isolde said. Fire, cold and lethal, coursed through her blood like a frozen inferno. "Defeated and humiliated, scarred and maimed by a shadow in a mask. Remind me, how many men did it take to capture the Hood?"

Malice burned in Gage's eyes and his fingers tightened, making her skin ache. Isolde didn't care. "All while losing thousands of pieces of gold? If you couldn't even catch a lowly thief on your own accord"—her fingers trailed over the back of Gage's hand as she turned in his grip—"what makes you think you can possibly tame me? Liam has done a far better job of than you ever could, and he didn't need to hold those I love over the fire to do it. So, tell me, *Lord* Gage, what is there about you that I should fear? What I should tremble to behold?"

Undiluted fury shadowed Gage's features, darkening the crystal blue of his eyes. Isolde felt a tremor roll down her spine. An inkling of a memory brushed against her mind. A memory...a feeling not unlike the one she felt now. One of darkness...and pain.

"There is much about me that should make you tremble," he said. "Even the fair maiden of a little shithole like Thornwood, should have better sense than to start a fight she can't finish."

"For someone who has such distaste for rural shitholes, you mention them often," Isolde said. "Which leads me to believe that you, yourself, are from such a place and carry that shame you place on so many others."

"I'm from no such place." A growl lingered on the edges of his words. "I am not from the gutter."

An impassive shrug was Isolde's only response. She knew the truth. It rang with every ignorant word of contempt he threw Thornwood's way.

Gage's lips pulled into a thin, furious line. "You doubt what I say?"

"Your blatant hatred and narrow-mindedness make it hard to do anything else."

"A human," Gage said, his words spewing with hatred, "killed my mother. A worthless piece of trash from nowhere took her from me because she was different. Because she had power. Power their pathetic existence could never possesses, could never understand. A power, I now wield."

A ripple of unease cascaded over Isolde's skin, chilling her to the bone. "And what exactly is that?"

Rivets of muscle bunched beneath her hand. "My power is my own business," said Gage. "And none of your concern."

"Well, I am sentenced to be shackled to you for the rest of my existence, am I not?" Isolde asked, doing her best to keep what little was left of a civil tongue in her head. "Don't you think it's only fair I should know what it is I'm marrying? You've already seen my monster."

Tendrils of dark shadow, faint but ever-present, bled into the pools of blue staring back at her. "None who have borne witness to my abilities have lived to tell the tale. Save one." His glaze flittered to the dais. "There's a reason why King Erebus has placed me as his Right

Hand. Why he keeps me close. I helped give him that throne he loves so much. Not all power lies in strength and force. The mind and heart are just as weak as flesh. Just as easy to break, if not more so. Never forget that."

I helped give him that throne he loves so much.

A retort, one that would have yielded unfathomable consequences danced on the tip of Isolde's tongue. But before she could turn it loose, Zego stepped forward. His beady eyes were downcast, and head bent forward into a submissive bow. "I beg your pardon, Lord Gage but His Majesty wishes to speak to you."

"Very well, Zego," Gage said, not taking his eyes off Isolde. "Tell him I will be there directly." Zego cast a grimace in Isolde's direction before he scampered through a door at the end of the ballroom.

"Behave yourself," Gage said, allowing his hands to fall away. "I won't be long."

Isolde buried the growl threatening to erupt from her chest as he disappeared through the gilded doorway. The blade at her side was humming, practically begging for his blood. For just the briefest of moments, she allowed the fantasy of driving the blade into Gage's heart and twisting, to play out in her mind.

But as her gaze danced across the crowd over the rim of her goblet, Isolde noticed one person in particular wasn't in attendance. Erebus's absence filled the room like a shadow. Suspicion brewed in her mind as she continued searching. Not even Volkran or his little lap dog of an heir, Lauram, were present.

How convenient...

Isolde knew exactly where she would be going. And as the rest of the delicious, expensive wine slid over her a tongue, she smiled. Across the room, Malaki caught her eye, and a look of dread instantly filled his face from where he sat at the table. The drink that was half raised, lingered on the edge of his lips.

"I know that look."

"You should," Isolde said, taking her place at his side. "You've seen it for the past fifty-five years." Not a soul was present who cared if she disappeared…for just a little while. Circe and Kyros were standing next Ferden and Sohan, their heads bent in deep, hushed conversation. Milt and Gawen lounged at one of the tables on the far side of the room, their heads bent over a blade Milt cradled in his hands.

"If I were a lesser man," Cillian said, as he and Blyana sided up to Malaki, "I would be offended for having not been invited into this conspiring conversation."

"We aren't conspiring," Malaki said, with a grunt. "I'm attempting the impossible."

Cillian grinned. "Which is?"

Malaki nodded to Isolde. "Trying to talk some sense into our fair champion."

Cillian chuckled, his obsidian eyes twinkling, "Good luck with that."

"He likes a challenge," Isolde said, draining another glass of wine.

"And just what is he trying to talk you out of?" Blyana asked.

"Going into the mines," she said, before the words could fall from Malaki's open mouth. "Which is pointless because my mind is made up."

Malaki ground his teeth and a bell-like chuckle lifted from Blyana's lips. "I agree with, Cillian," she said. "Best of luck to you on that front."

"I just need an earth wielder to move a little bit of the mountain for me." Isolde paused, her eyes glancing over to Malaki, instantly regretting her words. "That is…if you're up to it."

He had never allowed her to go on a mission without him. But as she took in the faint sheen across his forehead and rigid set of his jaw, Isolde wasn't sure if him going was the best option.

"You should know the answer to that, Isolde," Malaki said.

"There's no way I'm staying behind."

Isolde bit her lip as she stared back at him, taking in the exhaustion painted on his face. "You said yourself you need rest…Maybe you should stay—"

"I'm not staying behind," he said again, his voice ringing with finality. How could she give him an order to stay when he had never hindered her in the past?

"There's no shame in saying you aren't up to the task, old man," Cillian said, clapping Malaki on the shoulder. "We all have our limits. Well, most of us anyway."

"I could always use your head to bash through the mountain, Cill," Malaki snapped.

"Leave his head alone," Blyana said, brushing a mutinous strand of hair from Cillian's brow. "I like it just the way it is."

"It would be a shame to ruin such perfection," Cillian said, with a cocky grin.

"I believe that's my line," said Isolde. "Anyway, stay here and frolic if you want, but I'm leaving."

"Count me in," Blyana said, hooking her free arm through Isolde's.

Malaki sighed and knotted his arms over his chest. "You and Blyana leave first. Cillian and I will follow after I let Alaric and Gal know. Someone needs to stay behind if someone asks of your whereabouts."

"Thanks, Papa Bear," Isolde said with a wink. "See you back at the room."

The gilded archway passed overhead, and a sigh of wonder slipped across Blyana's lips. "This place is magnificent," she said, her eyes fixed on the intricate carvings sprawled across the walls. "There's no way I could find my way around here."

"Don't worry," Isolde said, her grip tightening. "I know the way."

CHAPTER 17

A sense of home and purpose swelled in Isolde's heart as she tugged the hood and mask into place, hiding her from the world. Peak after peak of the Oronilma Mountains glistened above them. Light from the moon pierced the canopy of the trees they crossed under.

"Let's keep off the road," Isolde had said once they reached the tree line. "Just in case one of Erebus's soldiers decided to be thorough tonight."

Keeping a good distance away from the main pass, Isolde led them through the forest, following along the route her fellow champions had taken a few days prior—the one far less treacherous and more commonly traveled than the route that had nearly taken Isolde's hand and her life.

Not a soul crossed their path on the seemingly untouched road. Still, they kept quiet. "Sound carries different up here," Malaki warned. "So, no talking unless it's absolutely necessary, that goes double for you, Cill."

"Rude," Cillian had said, his face and voice falling flat.

With bow in hand, Isolde retraced her steps the best she could remember. Faces of the mountainside stared back at her with a flicker of familiarity. Fleeting rays of the new moon gave little help. Deceptive shadows moved along the pass, causing Isolde to second guess her steps. Embers of irritation ignited, burning through her patience like paper. Trusting her gut, she took a hard right, leading them deeper into the Gap of Duron.

After another half a mile or so, they reached a bend in the path, one Isolde instantly recognized. A sound echoed off the rocks shooting into the sky around them, their tips piercing the clear night sky. Isolde knew that sound, and she turned to the others, who had grown still. The snap of a whip…and a cry of pain that quickly followed.

Cillian's eyes glowed within the depths of his mask. "Well, that sounded horribly recognizable."

"We're close," Isolde said, her voice the ghost of a whisper in the night.

Taking a final right turn, Isolde spotted the grate. The bars, which were made of iron, blended into the rock face so well, it wouldn't be hard to miss. A black pit resided on the other side. Not a soul was in sight, but still, she kept an arrow loaded, her fingers keeping constant tension on the bow string.

Malaki stepped up to the grate and ran a gloved hand across its surface.

"Can you move it?" Isolde asked.

"Maybe," he said, eyes narrowing in concentration. "This part was forged by many virya who were earth wielders." Isolde didn't miss his hand reflexively shift to his side.

A crushing wave of guilt for having agreed to let him come in his state slammed into her chest. "We can find another way, Malaki."

"Not one like this," he said, his voice deep and muffled. "If this is the part of the Helecdol mines I think it is, then we're in an old shaft. One not used often. Secluded from the others. Otherwise, it would've been guarded. If we want in, we don't have a choice. Besides, it's not the first time I've had to move mountains."

Isolde knew Malaki's magic only went so far. That his affinity lay in his connection with animals and other living things. Earth, rock, and metal…were not his forte. A well of power lingered beneath his skin. It was vast…but not endless. And that limit was far closer than it ever had been before.

Wave after wave of nervousness slammed into her resolve, driving her teeth into the lining of her bottom lip. She ignored the familiar coppery taste of blood and kept her eyes on Malaki, ready to pull him away if necessary.

Taking a deep breath, Malaki pressed his palms flat to the rock. A deep breath filled his chest and his eyelids slowly lowered. After a moment, the rock began to shift and break apart. A spider web of fissures erupted beneath his hands and bits of gray stone littered the ground at his feet.

Beads of sweat trickled down Malaki's face and disappeared into the dark green mask tucked around the lower half of his face. Isolde's hand stretched out, ready to pull him away. As if sensing her plan, a slight shake of Malaki's head kept her rooted in place.

"He's fine," Cillian said. "He can do this." Isolde couldn't help but wonder if he was saying that for Malaki's benefit…or to ease his own worry. A moment later, a shudder rippled across Malaki's shoulders, his muscles straining with effort.

"Malaki?" His name sounded like a bell from Blyana's mouth. Worry filled her bright eyes darting between Isolde and Cillian.

After what seemed like an eternity, a crack just big enough for a man to slip through, split the cold surface between Malaki's hands. Chunks of rock fell to the ground and disappeared into a blanket of fresh snow. From what little of his face was showing, Isolde could see how pale Malaki had become. Sweat glistened from his skin like early morning dew. Each breath was a heavy, labored pant. He pitched forward and braced his gloved hands, now shaky and unsteady, on his knees.

"Malaki!" Isolde said, pressing a hand to his shoulder. Tremors ran up her arm, feeding the terror festering in her chest.

"Fine," Malaki mumbled, the word hardly a whisper. He didn't meet her eye as he tried to force himself up right. "I just…need a minute." But as he tried to stand, his knees gave out and cracked against the pebble covered ground. Isolde dove forward, catching him before he fell face first onto the cold, unforgiving ground.

"Fine my ass," Isolde grunted, forcing him to sit up. She braced the palms of her hands against his tunic. They looked so small. Like that of a child, not a killer, on the wide planes of his chest.

Cillian and Blyana each took a shoulder, their leather-clad fingers pressing into the swell of muscles lining Malaki's arms and shoulders, holding him up right. "I'm alright," Malaki rasped, his chest heaving beneath Isolde's palms. "I just haven't slept well—"

"Cut the bullshit," Cillian said, his voice low and edged. "This is more than just lack of sleep!"

Without waiting, Blyana tugged at the hem of Malaki's shirt, freeing it from his belt line. "Damn it, Bly!" Malaki hissed, trying to bat her away. But it was too late. They had all seen the ting of blood staining the white of his undershirt.

Isolde's mouth pulled into a grim line. Guilt and fury pummeled her like bits of hail in a storm. "You're staying here."

"Like hell I am!" Malaki said, jerking free of Blyana and Cillian's grips.

"I'm sorry, you must have misunderstood me," Isolde said, her fingers curled into fists at the sight of him struggling to rise. "I'm not asking you, Malaki."

Malaki forced his feet beneath him, his colossal frame shaking with effort. "Neither was I." He shot Blyana a withering look and tucked his tunic back into place, covering the blood-tinged shirt underneath. "You wanted trust from me, Isolde, and I gave it. Why can't you give me the same courtesy?"

The light of his hazel eyes brightened in the depth of the hood covering his face in shadow. Isolde could feel the power, the unstoppable force that would end worlds if need be. But she also felt something missing. Pain, no matter how hard he tried to hide it from her, was etched into the grim set of his jaw, the rise and fall of his chest, and the slight tremors running through his body like wind through the trees. It was there. And there was nothing she could do to ease his suffering.

But Malaki was right. Trust had been the one thing she had asked of him. And now, it was her turn.

Crossing her arms, bringing the bow and arrow around to her side, Isolde relented. "If you get tired, promise to tell us. We can come back."

Malaki nodded and the light in his eyes dimmed. "I give you my word." It was a promise, a bond that neither of them had ever broken. Their word meant everything to each other. It was as certain as the dawn rising in the east.

With a nod and a sigh to dispel the tension in her chest, Isolde nodded to the entrance Malaki had created. "Well, let's not waste any more time then."

They plunged into hollow, frigid darkness. The kind that made one think death itself coated their skin. Pits of black met them on the left and right. Isolde kept the bow ready, the feathers of the arrow resting along the edges of her fingers. Malaki was right behind her, then Blyana. Cillian brought up the rear, his daggers gripped in his deft, expert fingers.

The air itself felt different to the right, heavier, fouler. Tilting her head, she started walking further into the abyss. After a while, the sound of footsteps fell on her ears. Up ahead, the faint glow of firelight spilled along the floor and damp stone walls. They rounded a corner and came to a halt.

A wide platform overlooking a dark, circular cavern stretched out before them. An eerie glow, one Isolde knew intimately, hung in the air like a fog.

She inched towards the edge, and her mouth went dry as the bones littering the floor at her feet. Mounds of elithrium rested on the cavern floor. Tables of varying sizes were stationed around the dungeon's lowest level, each set with humans wielding tools meant for breaking and grinding the element into a fine powder.

Malaki took his place at her side. His eyes were hard with exhausted concern. Blyana paused on Isolde's right, and a breath caught in her throat. Her grey eyes shone from the depths of her violet mask.

Door after door lined the walls in perfect rings that ran up and down the length of the cavern; countless windows into worlds of unspeakable horrors. There were so many, Isolde had no idea where to begin. From what she could see, most of the cells were empty. The prisoners, she assumed, were in the mines. *Where else would they be besides a grave?* A spare few held bodies. Bodies that didn't stir. On the doors of each cell was a lock, the metal shimmering with elithrium's unmistakable hue.

"They have virya here," Isolde whispered, pointing to the closest cell. "Or half-bloods at the very least."

Malaki followed to where she pointed, his head shaking. "Another obstacle, then."

"We're never without those, are we?"

"No," he said. "But just this once, I was hoping for a little bit of mercy."

A series of tunnels and hallways leading deeper into the mountain rimmed the walls of the bottom level. Isolde scanned the crowd looking for a familiar face. Humans, all of them, were hunched over, eyes down and heads bowed over their work. Not a single one stood out.

Off to the right, Isolde caught the faintest hint of movement. Two figures shuffled along one of the lower levels, their steps silent and quick. They moved down the line of cells, tossing pieces of bread between the bars before moving on to the next. Strands of golden hair shimmered beneath a hood made of burlap and filth. The figure turned back to glance at her companion and air clogged in Isolde's throat.

"Bly!"

Blyana leaned forward and a gasp, one that could have made their presence known, fell from her lips. "Phontine!"

There was no denying it. The prized mistress of the king was making her way through the dungeons of Elenarta. "What is she doing?" Cillian asked, peeking around Blyana's shoulder.

"It would appear Phontine took after her older sister when it comes to sneaking around," Isolde said, watching her pushing against one of the cell doors. It swung open, and Phontine, along with her company, slipped inside.

Blyana's face, what little was showing, paled. "She's going to get caught!"

"We can't do anything about it right now, love," Cillian said, his fingers lightly gripping her shoulder.

"He's right, Bly," Isolde said. "The less attention drawn, the safer they'll be." They waited in silence until Phontine and the stranger exited the cell, replaced the lock, and disappeared around the corner.

A heavy, shaky sigh filtered through Blyana's mask. "Thank the damn gods." Her voice sounded so small, so unlike her, it gave Isolde pause.

"Let's keep moving," Malaki said, a note of unease filling his voice.

Taking a deep breath, Isolde gripped the handle of her bow and stepped out onto the ledge. A line of shadows, dark as night, hugged the balcony, making her nearly invisible.

The smell of waste, mildew, and blood filled the air. Every few minutes, like clockwork, a human pushing a cart loaded with freshly mined elithrium would emerge from the belly of the mountain. Once their cart had been emptied, the poor souls would return to the tunnel with wagons in tow.

"They've connected the dungeons with the mines," Malaki said into Isolde's ear, confirming her early suspicion.

"I'll say one thing for Erebus," Isolde said with an air of annoyance. "He's efficient."

"It's quite impressive, Your Majesty."

Volkran's voice carried through the air, causing Isolde to freeze. Looking over the railing, Isolde spotted the Lord of Briarhole as he emerged from a small door on the left. Lauram walked at his side, and the greenish hue of the elithrium played across the purple and black of their attire. Volkran's meaty palm rested on the hilt of a sword. A sword Isolde would know anywhere.

"Airendia."

The light shone off the pearl hilt of Zibiah's beloved blade. A snarl bubbled at the back of Isolde's throat. The beast inside prowled along the edges of her mind, its sharp claws racking against her control. It too remembered Briarhole. It remembered Zibiah's blood painting the side of her face as she was slung into the cage of iron and elithrium. She remembered Volkran's words about Zibiah the day of the first trial.

Buer did an excellent job of reminding her where her place lies—so did Lauram. Perhaps you'll get to learn that same lesson before the end.

"Isolde, breathe," Malaki said, his hand gripping her shoulder.

"He has Airendia!" she seethed, her hand drawing back on the bowstring. It groaned beneath her fingertips. Isolde's gaze locked on to a single spot on Volkran's bulbous neck. Even from where they hid, she could see the steady pulse beneath his skin. "I'll kill that bastard."

"Then Zib dies too," Blyana said. Her small hand gently landed on Isolde's fingers constructed around the bow's handle, holding the arrow in place. "I want him dead just as much as you, but is his death worth ensuring hers?"

Blyana's words pelted her fog of anger like arrows themselves, clearing her mind of the murderous haze. Taking a deep breath, Isolde allowed her hold on the bowstring to relax and the arrow's deadly tip to fall to the floor.

The sound of Volkran's repulsive voice drifted through the air. "Wherever did you find it?" he asked, his black eyes roaming the mounds of elithrium like a starved man at a feast.

Erebus stepped forward, his hands clasped behind his back. He looked so strange, so incredibly out of place. "Just had to know where to look, I suppose."

"And where will such a hoard be distributed, might I ask?"

"That is His Majesty's business, Volkran," Gage said, his voice cutting. The elithrium's light glistened off the waves of chestnut hair brushing his shoulders as he strolled into the center of the room. "I see where Lauram acquired his habit of asking questions about matters that don't pertain to him." Volkran's lip curled, his hand tightening on Airendia.

"A portion will go to the lords and ladies of the territories," Erebus said. "However, the majority of the elithrium is being put to use in…other ways."

Lauram's bloodshot eyes widened. "Does this have to do with the neutralizing of viryian power, Your Grace?"

Erebus exchanged a look with Gage. "In a sense," he said, not bothering to spare Volkran's heir a glance. "We've just scratched the surface of its potential." Lauram took a cautious step back from the elithrium, his throat bobbing.

"Isolde."

Her name ghosted from behind and she turned to see Malaki sag against the wall, his knees caving in. She pressed her hand to his chest, forcing him to stay up right. What little could be seen of his face was drained of blood, his eyes glassy and unseeing.

"Oh, my gods, Malaki!" Isolde said, panic coating her tongue. She turned her terrified gaze to Cillian and Blyana, who were both reaching for him. Cillian nodded to the path they had just come from, and Isolde returned it with a nod of her own.

"Let's head back to the ball," Erebus suggested. "After we pay your wife a visit of course, Volkran." A cold chill erupted down Isolde's arms as a vile laugh ghosted up from below. "I've heard she's made excellent progress."

"Very well, Your Majesty," Volkran said, his fingers caressing Airendia's hilt. "I believe her progress will be to your satisfaction."

"If you don't mind," Gage said, the light of elithrium brushing against his cheekbones, highlighting the crevasses on his face, "there's a matter that needs attending to with my fiancée. A correction of sorts."

Erebus paused. His sharp eyes narrowed on Gage before a smile that didn't reach his eyes formed. "Remember my words, Gage."

A stillness fell over the king's Right Hand. "Of course, Your Majesty," Gage said, slipping into a deep bow. "I haven't forgotten."

"Very well," Erebus said with a nod, his gaze still sharp and full of reproach. "Check the perimeters, both at the gate and the dungeon's entrance, on your way out."

"As you wish, Your Majesty." Gage turned and strode from the chamber, his steps quick and purposeful.

Not waiting a second longer, Isolde pushed Malaki's massive form down the balcony. His feet shuffled with each step as he tried and failed to make them cooperate. Once inside the safety of the tunnel, she dropped Malaki's impossibly heavy arm over her shoulder. "Take the lead, Bly," Isolde said, her chest burning and arms quaking. Blyana moved past them to the front, her knives out and ready. Cillian took up the other and together they trudged back through the dungeons.

"Did you have to be so damn heavy?" Cillian said, his words slipping through gritted teeth. He struggled beneath Malaki's frame. "You're as big as a fucking tree, old man."

At last they made it to the small opening on the side of the mountain. Blyana slipped through first, keeping watch to make sure no one was present on the outside.

"Isolde, leave me," Malaki said, his voice hardly a whisper. Cillian pushed his weight onto her and slipped through the opening. Her knees buckled, but she managed to keep them both from collapsing. "You need to make it back before—"

"Oh, shut up, Malaki!" Isolde grunted and shoved him forward into Cillian's awaiting arms. "You know I'm not leaving you."

The climb down was far easier than the one going up. With the help of momentum, they made it down the side of the mountain without running into another soul. It wasn't until they reached the gates leading into the arena that they came across a pair of blurry-eyed soldiers. Blyana didn't hesitate. The daggers flew from her hands like birds in flight. Each tip met its mark, disappearing inside one of the only weak spots the soldiers' armor allowed.

"Keep moving, old man," Cillian said, his voice a breathless rasp. Isolde felt the grip he had on Malaki tighten. "Just a little further. Even you can make that." Together, they worked their way around the edges of the deserted arena. Worry spread through Isolde when Malaki didn't respond, when only sounds of his heavy breathing filled the void. Sweat soaked his tunic, causing her grip to slip.

At last, they shoved the door to their chambers open, and Malaki collapsed onto the floor.

"What happened?" Nan asked, jumping up from her spot next to the fire.

"Not sure," Isolde said, her voice shaking, bordering on hysterical. She gently pulled the mask from Malaki's face. His copper skin was cold and glistened with sweat. "Nan, I don't understand! He used his power to move some rock around...I thought he was better!"

"Move him over to the couch," she ordered, already shuffling to grab her bags. Gritting her teeth, Isolde helped Cillian and Blyana lift Malaki to his feet and drag him over to the spot Nan was just occupying.

"Let me see his wound," Nan said.

Isolde ripped Secrettaker from its scabbard at Malaki's side and made a clean slice down his tunic and pant leg, laying his entire side bare. The newly formed scar had been ripped open. A steady stream of blood oozed from his far too thin flesh. Terror filled Isolde. Terror and rage.

"I thought you said all the elithrium was out of his system, Nan!"

"Helurtu's blade wasn't too far off from the one that cut you," she said, already mixing the antidote, confirming Isolde's fear. "The amount of time it took you to recover isn't normal. Not everyone can heal like you, Isolde."

Isolde bit her tongue until the familiar taste of blood filled her mouth. Tears stung the corners of her eyes, all of which stubbornly refused to fall. She ran a hand over Malaki's forehead, his skin chilled beneath her palm. "Why didn't he tell me?"

"And risk being told to stay behind?" Cillian said. "You know how stubborn he is."

"You need to get ready," Blyana said, tossing the gown Isolde had worn earlier through the air. "Gage is expecting his fiancée."

Isolde batted it to the floor. "Gage can get fu—"

"He'll only come looking for you," Blyana said, cutting her off. "You really want him to show up here and see this?" Her hand swept across Malaki's form, his chest rising and falling too rapidly. And every breath was far too shallow. Isolde hesitated, her fingers gripping the hem of Malaki's hood. "We'll look after him," Blyana promised.

Blyana was right, Isolde knew she was. But it didn't stop the pain, the guilt from slicing through her like a blade. He would never leave her. Not if she was in this state. But what choice did she have?

Bending down, Isolde pressed a kiss to Malaki's forehead and whispered, "I forbid you to die on me!" Quick, shallow breaths were his only response.

A growl ripped through Isolde's throat as she retreated into her chamber and hastened to exchange her hood for the ball gown she had snatched off the floor. Once dressed and looking to some degree presentable, Isolde made her way back through the palace. Towering arches and marble bridges sped past her. A paradise, once filled with beauty and laughter, now held only ghosts of a past that had been turned to ash.

She slowed to a causal pace, needing a moment to catch her breath and calm her racing heart. The sound of heels clicking echoed into the abyss as she crossed over the bridges.

"Lady Isolde."

She stopped at the sound of her name, at the voice carrying it. Turning around, she saw Ferden strolling towards her. His pale, golden hair, normally so well-kept and in place, was slightly askew. Creases decorated his usually flawless attire. A small smudge of dust brushed the edge of his well-defined cheekbones. Despite his appearance, Isolde could only marvel at how right his very presence was in the halls of Elenarta.

"Lord Ferden," Isolde said with a raised, critical brow. "You look slightly out of sorts today. And here I was thinking you were on my level as far as appearance goes. How disappointing."

A smirk played on the corners of Ferden's lips, but amusement never reached his eyes. "I suppose I can relinquish the title of best dressed to you for a night. It is an awfully heavy burden to carry. Are you heading back into the ball?"

"Unfortunately, yes."

"Then allow me to escort you. I can't imagine your fiancé, would approve of you walking around the capital unescorted."

"On the contrary," she said, linking an arm through his. "Gage might have more of a problem with you escorting me than finding me alone."

"I can't believe you're one to pass up such an opportunity." Ferden's lips curled up into a knowing smile as a light chuckle spilled over Isolde's freshly painted lips. They walked in silence for a moment. A silence that was easy and comfortable.

"I am sorry," Ferden said after a moment.

The smile fell from Isolde's face. "I never took you as the pitying type, Lord Ferden. Don't make me change my opinion of you now."

"Of course," he said, flashing a sarcastic smile. "Congratulations on your engagement to the Right Hand of the King, Lady Isolde. I'm sure it's everything you dreamed for yourself and more."

"Much better," Isolde said, giving Ferden's arm a squeeze. "I can't have you going soft on me."

Mighty waves carved from stone passed over their heads. An eternal tribute to Ceto, the goddess of water. The ball was still crowded despite the late hour. The scent of champagne and spirits filled the air. Food lined the tables as if it had never been touched.

"Wasteful," Isolde said, her lip curling in disgust. "So many would do anything for just a crumble. And here it is…untouched and unappreciated."

Ferden sighed. "Those who carry the burden of poverty are the ones who suffer the most."

The dais was empty, much to Isolde's relief. Perhaps Gage had thought twice about seeking her out and abandoned his plan. But her hope instantly died as a vice gripped the back of her arm.

"There she is," Gage said, pulling her to his side and out of Ferden's reach. "I've been looking for you everywhere, pet." His cold, hard eyes flew to Ferden whose face held nothing but a look of bored neutrality.

"I was on my way back from freshening up when Lord Ferden spotted me and offered to escort me back to the ballroom," Isolde said, fighting every instinct to not plunge the blade at her thigh into Gage's chest.

"And now that I see you are back safe and sound with Lord Gage," Ferden said with a small bow, his eyes not leaving Isolde, "I believe I have business with Lady Circe that needs addressing. Enjoy the rest of the ball." Isolde nodded but kept her lips sealed.

Gage's grip tightened as Ferden disappeared into the crowd. "If I ever see you on the arm of another man again," he said, "I'll give their arms to you on a silver tray. Are we clear?"

"Crystal," Isolde snarled. She tried yanking away from him, but Gage merely pulled her towards the dance floor. Music, lovely and vibrant, filled the air along with the smell of body odor and wine.

"Behave yourself," he warned, "and dance with your fiancé."

Isolde kept silent and danced as if she were made from a block of ice, moving like a statue. If she was going to be forced into this, she certainly wouldn't make it easy for him. Gage pulled her closer, making his body flush with her own. "I seem to recall sending a dress for you to wear tonight, did I not?"

"It wasn't my taste," Isolde said, dismissively. Not that she'd seen it before tossing the package into the fire.

"Does it look like I care what your tastes are, Isolde?" His eyes shone with a malice she knew well. "You are mine, and you will wear what I tell you to wear."

"I think not," Isolde said, her lip curling.

"I thought you might say that." He twirled her in his arms until her back pressed into his chest and wrapped an arm around her like a steel bar, holding her in place. "That's why I brought a little incentive." Gage stretched a hand forward and pointed to the dais. Erebus had regained his seat. To his right stood Phontine, the very vision of beauty in a long, flowing dress made of ebony silk. Another stood to his left.

"Tanor!" His name fell from her mouth in horror. Not even the fine clothes they had dressed him in could hide the patchwork of cuts and bruises decorating his skin.

"Yes," Gage spat, forcing Isolde back into the dance. "The king thought he was of some significance to you." With each turn, Isolde fought to look back at Tanor who kept his eyes firmly planted on the ground. "Although I can't imagine why."

"He has nothing to do with this!"

"Oh, but he does," Gage said, his hand pressing into the small of her back. "Your actions have brought him here, Isolde. You are responsible for what comes next. Remember that." Gage looked down at her dress, his gaze pointed and filled with intention. "Perhaps this will teach you to do as you're told." Gage looked over her head and nodded.

Isolde turned to see a whip clutched in a soldier's hand, fall across Tanor's back. His cry followed the crack of leather cutting through cloth and flesh. He crumbled to the ground at Erebus's feet. The long whip skittered across the floor, smearing blood across the dais. The soldier took a step forward and drew back again.

"Stop it!" Isolde cried, fighting in Gage's grip. He wrapped his arms around her waist, holding her in place. She dug her nails into his skin, drawing blood to the surface. "Stop it, or I swear I will kill you!"

"Is that a threat I hear, Lady Isolde?" Erebus's voice carried over the hushed crowd. "This filth was caught stealing food, and you dare intervene in my Right Hand's rightful punishment?" Isolde knew Tanor had done no such thing. No, this was all because she didn't wear a damn dress. Because she chose not to obey.

Erebus flicked a finger to Tanor. "Continue."

The whip came down again, striking the back of Tanor's legs. The fine velvet britches split open causing blood to spill out around him. A drop landed on Erebus's boots, marring their impeccable shine. Sobs broke from Tanor's dried, cracked lips as he curled up into a ball and waited for the next blow to fall.

"Lady Isolde," he said, tears streaming down his face. "Please!" His voice broke something in her, shattered it at the foot of the throne.

"I'll wear the damn dress," Isolde seethed, doing everything she could to keep her power in check, to not shift into the bloodthirsty beast lurking beneath her skin. "He is just a boy!"

The whip fell again.

A low, dark laugh brushed against her cheek as Gage's fingers dug into her hip, refusing to let her move.

"Your Majesty!"

Alaric's voice cut through the fog of hysteria rising in Isolde's mind. It rang with the authority of a lord as he cut through the crowd. His knuckles were bone white as they gripped the handle of his cane. "This boy is of my house. I will take responsibility for his actions."

"No." The word fell like an axe from Erebus's mouth. Alaric stood dumbfounded, his jaw tightening. "He committed the crime, Alaric. And he will pay for it."

Liam emerged from the crowd, and his dark, sorrowful eyes danced between her and Tanor. The whip fell three more times before it finally stopped. Tanor mercifully lost consciousness at the fourth strike.

"Remember this, Isolde," Gage said, tucking a piece of hair behind her ear. "You are not the only one who will suffer if you do not do as you are told."

Galaena rushed past Alaric and knelt down beside Tanor's still body. The layers of grey, shimmering fabric pooled around her feet, the hem now drenched in blood. A grim look played on her face. Liam stepped forward, his jaw tight and throat bobbing. Carefully, mindful of the open wounds, he lifted Tanor in his arms and cradled him to his chest. Drops of blood trailed behind him, painting the floor red.

"You will pay for this," Isolde swore, her body shaking with rage. "I swear on every drop of his blood that is spilled." She turned to look Gage in the eye, honing every ounce of malice into her gaze. "You will pay for all of it."

Before Gage could utter a word, Alaric took Isolde's arm, pulling her from his hold. "My champion needs her rest, Lord Gage." He didn't wait for a response as he pulled her through the crowd. Galaena followed behind, her steely grey eyes glowing with fury.

Tanor rested on a cot made of fine sheets and goose down. After a few hours, he stirred just long enough to see her. Long enough, for a single tear to fall down his face before slipping back into oblivion.

Isolde stroked his hair as the healer she had sent for, attempted to close Tanor's wounds. "I'm sorry, Lady Isolde," the girl said. Her hands trembled with exhaustion over Tanor's body, fear coating her words. "This is the best I can do." It was true; she wasn't Malaki. And asking him was out of the question. He was still unconscious in her room.

"Does it sound like I want excuses?" Isolde snarled. "I said fix him!" Her voice was devoid of kindness, of any compassion at all.

Tears of fear brimmed in the girl's bright eyes and an echo of light surfaced as she returned to the task at hand. The bleeding had finally stopped, but the wounds remained open. Galaena hovered nearby, her mouth set into a grim line.

"You need rest," she said. "The second trial starts in a few hours, and you haven't slept."

"And you think I could now?" Isolde shot back, causing the healer to jump.

Galaena took the seat next to her. "I think you need to remember that if you don't win this, Tanor won't be the only child who suffers."

The girl's hands froze, and her eyes rose to meet Isolde's.

"If you breathe a word of this conversation, I will kill you myself," Isolde growled. The girl dropped her gaze as beads of sweat formed on her forehead.

"I'll stay with him," Galaena offered, her voice far softer than normal. Isolde assumed it was for the girl's sake and not her own. "No one will touch him again. I promise. He's safe."

Her aunt held out her hand, and a stream of water from the pail resting beside the bed, floated through the air. Flattening her palm, Galaena pressed the cool wall of water to Tanor's forehead. It moved in small, gentle circles along his pale, glistening skin. The muscles in his face eased immediately and a soft sigh broke through his lips.

"Go, Isolde," Galaena said, her voice gaining an ounce of hardness.

Grinding her teeth, Isolde shoved up from the floor and stalked to her bedroom. Malaki lay sprawled across her bed. A soft, steady rise had returned to his bare chest. The harsh lines of pain had left his face at last, drawing a sigh of relief from Isolde's lips. After undressing, she slipped into a simple nightgown and stretched out on the ottoman next to the bed. Tanor's blood still coated her hands. And yet, she couldn't bring herself to wash it off.

It belongs on your hands. You're the one to blame.

Tears threatened to spill over Isolde's cheeks. She stood at the edge of an abyss of sorrow, guilt, and shame. But the cold flame of retribution ignited, luring her away from the path of despair. Hatred, cold and unforgiving, blossomed in her heart.

"They'll pay," she swore, her eyes turning to the stars looking down on her from the night sky. To the gods who dwelt among them. "I swear to you bastards, they will pay." Isolde's hands balled into fists atop the silken duvet. "And so will you."

CHAPTER 18

Isolde felt the roar of the crowd echo through her bones. Their screams filled her to the brim with every vibration making its way through the soles of her boots. The sound that was begging, demanding blood.

She, along with the rest of the champions, lingered in a new holding room. One adorned with velvet-lined furnishings and ornate tables covered in more food and drink than necessary. Flames battled within the grated mouth of a roaring fireplace. Isolde kept far away, her arms knotting over her chest as the sound of every crack of a dying branch caused her to flinch.

They waited silently for Lenox to fetch them. Except one. Isolde's eyes flickered to an empty chair at a nearby table and a swell of hope filled her chest. Arlo should have at least made it through the Oronilma Mountains by now if he had managed to maneuver the Gap of Duron and steal a horse.

Her mind inevitably found its way back to Tanor. True to her word, Galaena was still by his side when she rose the next morning. The dress from the previous night, crinkled and stiff with drops of dried blood, clung to her form.

A new healer had arrived. His obsidian eyes shone with the effort of using his power. "He was awake for a little while," her aunt said, running the cool wall of water across not only Tanor's brow, but the healer's as well. "Long enough to eat and drink a little."

Isolde swallowed around the lump in her throat. "Good." She turned her eyes to the male who was focusing on Tanor's back. "The girl from before," Isolde said. "What is her name?"

"Shaye," the male said, his eyes dark and tone hard. "They came to fetch me after she overdid it last night. Trying to *fix* him."

Isolde flinched at his tone. Regret filled her heart at the look of hatred he cast her way, at the cold reminder of how cruel she had been. Isolde knew she was no different from the rest of them in the poor girl's eyes, and now his.

Isolde pulled a small pouch from her side, filling the air with the unmistakable sound of jingling coins. "I know I have no right to ask anything of you, but please, give these to her," she said, holding the bag out to him. "No amount of gold will excuse my behavior. Tell Shaye Lady Isolde sends her deepest gratitude...and most sincere apologies. If there is anything she ever needs, I am at her disposal."

The virya looked at the velvet bag, then back to her. A softness lightened his face, and the hint of a smile brushed the edge of his sharp mouth. "As you wish, my lady."

"What's running through that pretty little head of yours?" Kyros asked, pulling Isolde from her own mind. A smirk played on his handsome face that was half turned in her direction, his impeccably maintained brow arching.

"Nothing that concerns you," said Isolde, her arms tightening over her chest.

"I was merely curious," he said with a shrug. "Thought I caught a faint whiff of smoke."

"What you smell is the scent of your burning carcass if you don't keep your nose in your own business. I'm sure you have plenty to occupy yourself with."

"My, my," Buer said, turning from where he lingered near the fireplace. "Feisty this morning are we, Lady Isolde?" His massive form seemed to take up the entire space of the western side of the room. "I hope you save that energy for the arena. I'd hate to embarrass Thornwood by killing you so early on."

"Are you sure Volkran made the right decision in picking you for a champion, Buer?" Isolde asked, hardly sparing him a glance, already bored of the conversation. "Your talents seem better suited for a jester. Seeing as you like to tell jokes, despite how early in the day it is."

"You think you're untouchable, don't you?" Buer asked, his lip curling. "Let me tell you…*Lady Bitch*. I don't care what rich prick has claimed you or how close he is with the king. In that arena," he said, pointing a finger to the ceiling, "you'll bleed just like the rest of these bastards." Buer smiled, his eyes igniting with anticipation. "And I'll take my time in doing it."

The others, apart from Kyros, kept their distance, but Isolde lounged against the cool, stone wall; her brow was cocked, and a smirk formed on her face. A butter knife glistened on the table to her right. A glob of half melted butter dangled on the edge of the dull blade.

Not sharp...but just sharp enough. Isolde smiled at the thought of how painful cutting this prick's eye out would be.

"I don't hide behind anyone, Buer," Isolde purred, her smile growing. "I'm more than capable of putting you exactly where you belong. On your knees, with your balls shoved so far down your throat, your own mother won't be able to hear you crying out her name."

Buer's lips twisted with rage, but his words fell short at the sound of footsteps breaking through the darkness.

"Champions!" Lenox said in greeting. "To the arena!"

Buer looked back at Isolde, his eyes alight with hatred. "We'll see who's left with something shoved down their throat …Lady Bitch."

"I look forward to you trying," Isolde smarted with a smile.

He cast one final look of malice her way before storming out. The others followed suit, their lips sealed and eyes forward. The faintest of lights reflected in Lenox gaze as they passed in a single file line like obedient children.

Kyros chuckled, his dark, nearly violet eyes turning to gaze over his shoulder. "Lady Isolde, your reputation was not exaggerated."

"What reputation might that be?" she asked. "I know they couldn't possibly have portrayed how beautiful I am with any amount of accuracy."

"That they did not," Kyros admitted, following behind Foxclove's champion, Demir, whose head was turned slightly towards them. "I was referring to your particular talent for trouble."

"I suppose it depends on your definition of trouble," Isolde said, her eyes narrowing on Demir. His poorly hidden curiosity grated against her nerves.

"Lack of self-preservation, a tongue that could put the sharpest sword to shame, and beauty that knows it's worth." Kyros shot her a mischievous grin. "I would say those fall under the category of trouble."

"That is the definition of someone doing what they want and not giving two shits about the opinions of others, Kyros," Isolde said, her hand coming up to shield her eyes as they stepped out into the hot afternoon sun. "And looking exceptional while doing it."

"No argument there," he yelled over the deafening crowd. "But your charming husband to be and the one who holds his leash might."

Isolde followed his line of sight to the north. There, of course, was Erebus, but his presence wasn't the one that stopped her short. Tanor stood a step or two to the left of the throne. Her eyes shot to the man lingering directly behind him like the shadow of death he was. The palm of Gage's hand clasped on to Tanor's shoulder, his fingers squeezing. A wince laced through Tanor's pale, battered face.

The beast prowled forward, its fangs bared in Isolde's mind. Power and light filled her eyes as it saturated her blood. A grin formed on Gage's face, his teeth flashing and scars stretching.

"Lady Isolde," Kyros murmured, his voice lethally low and full of seductive warning. Gone was the smile; gone was the jesting. A faint glow filled the depths of his piercing eyes. Isolde couldn't help but think she was looking at the night sky just before the break of dawn. "I believe our attention is required elsewhere."

Forcing the bars of control into place, she turned from the dais and followed to where the others were gathered in an incomplete circle at the center of the arena. A servant with an elithrium bracelet stood waiting for each of them. The beast within reared in panicked anger. It's sharp, unforgiving teeth bit into her resolved, doing everything possible to seize control. To not let that horrible piece of jewelry, touch her skin again.

Malaki's calm, reassuring voice filled her head. *Breathe, just breathe.* It was all she could do, all she could focus on when the poor girl slid the shackle into place. A growl died on her lips as the elithrium took hold, taming the monster within. The girl scurried away as if her life depended on it.

"The last trial showed us your speed," Lenox said. "Now, we will test your knowledge of weapons." A drop of relief trickled down Isolde's spine. "One at a time, you will each be tested on various forms of weaponry, ranging from the longsword to the bow."

Isolde could practically hear Malaki and Liam begging her not to smile. But she couldn't stop the tiniest tilt of her mouth from breaking free. "Today, you will be facing the prisoners of Elenarta. Ones that have been given the chance of freedom if they manage to disarm a champion. It is vital to showcase all of your skills," Lenox continued. "For they will determine a great many things in the trials to come. You will each go in turn of the number you select from the bag." The fringe of his cloak brushed the gravel, covering the fine fabric in a layer of dust. He stopped before Buer, whose face was set in stone. "Champion of Briarhole, pick a stone."

Buer's hand slid into the bag. But on the way out, he cupped something in Lenox's pale, papery hand. In it sat a single stone. A number six written in blood red was painted on its surface. The final spot for the day.

Isolde shot a glance to the sideline, to the section covered in purple and black. Lauram and Volkran stood at the top. With Buer going last, the prisoners set to fight him would be worn down, easily beaten, making him look like a damn good fighter, whether that was the case or not.

Lenox stepped before her and shook the bag with impatience. "Champion of Thornwood," he barked. "His Majesty is busy. Select a stone!"

"Don't I get to a special number like Buer?" Isolde asked sweetly, batting her eyelashes, her voice sickly sweet and petulant. "He got one. I want one too."

Lenox balked, his pudgy face reddening. "You dare accuse—"

"Oh, you misunderstand," Isolde said, cutting him off. "I wasn't accusing, I was stating a fact. But don't worry." Her gaze slid to Buer as she thrust a hand into the bag. The tips of her fingers curled around the cool surface of a stone. "I plan on winning this either way. And I won't need to cheat to do it."

Red bloomed across Buer's face, the muscles of his arms and neck straining.

"Careful now," Isolde said. "You'll give yourself a headache." His lips pulled back over his teeth, allowing a growl to echo across the arena. But he stayed rooted to the spot, not daring to break Erebus's rule.

Kyros chuckled as he shook his head. "Like I said…trouble."

"Only I'm allowed to cheat," Isolde grumbled, unfolding her fingers around the stone to reveal a number four.

Kyros nodded. "Not bad." He held up a number one. "Looks like I get to break them in for you."

"Try not to show off too much," Isolde said, with a wicked smile. "Save some of the glory for the rest of us."

Off to the side, Sohan shook his head, doing his best to hide the hint of a smile on his face. Gawen, who stood just to his left, looked petrified. His eyes swept the various weapons stationed around the arena floor. He had his sights set on the trident and spears residing at the southern end of the arena.

"Used one often?" Isolde asked, tossing the stone from one hand to the other. "Not a common weapon for those who live in Harrow Hall."

"On occasion," Gawen said. "Probably not enough to be dangerous…but enough." A hint of light shone in the pools of rich brown that held flakes of brilliant green. "What about you? What gifts do you have that make you as dangerous as everyone says?"

"Dangerous, am I?" Isolde chuckled. "I'm good at all of them, Gawen," she said, waving a hand casually around the arena. "This is merely a formality before I take on the role of the King's Left Hand."

Gawen chewed on his bottom lip. "Is that…is that what you want?"

"It doesn't really matter what I want, does it?" The words fell from Isolde's mouth before she could stop them. "Or what any of us want."

"I suppose it doesn't," he said, with a slight frown. "Although I have a feeling you find a way to get what you want, more often than not."

Isolde smiled, truly smiled. Gawen's blush deepened and raced to the tips of his ears that were half-hidden in a bed of dark curls. "Call me resourceful," Isolde said, a fondness forming in her heart. "What number are you?"

He raised the stone bearing the number three. "Would you like to trade and get your turnover quicker?" he asked, holding up the stone between them. The offer was out of sheer kindness, an act of chivalry he had undoubtedly learned from the man who brought him here. Her gaze swept to a sea of emerald and gold, to Harrow Hall. Milt's towering form hovered at the edge of the railing, his arms crossed into a tight knot.

Gawen's lanky form and obvious lack of defensive skills meant he needed every advantage he could get. And she had a feeling ending this sooner rather than later was exactly what Gawen needed.

"I'm already going to beat Buer in every other event. Let's not embarrass him too badly with this one."

Gawen smiled nervously, a set of dimples forming on his freckled, pale cheeks. "I'm sure the gods will reward you for that."

Isolde rolled her eyes. "The gods have never rewarded me. Not that I have done anything to deserve their...*charity.*"

"The champion from Marsh Hall, Kyros, will be our first trial of the day!" Lenox said, his voice booming off the walls of the arena. "The remaining champions will wait along the lining of the tunnels." Isolde looked down the row of champions. Each one wore the same look of confusion she did.

"What fun would there be in having you know each other's strengths and weaknesses?" Lenox asked, his yellow, cracked teeth glistening.

"Oh yes," Isolde said, her arms crossing over her chest. "Our deaths must be as entertaining as possible. Isn't that, right?"

Lenox's grin turned into a malicious grimace. His mousy eyes narrowed. "What good is a Left Hand who can't anticipate their opponents' moves, Lady Isolde?" Isolde merely rolled her eyes and turned with the others, making their way to the tunnels.

"I'll try not to wear them down too badly for you," Kyros said as he passed.

"I'd hate for you to take it easy on me," Isolde shot back, over her shoulder. Kyros's soft chuckle followed her into the shade of the tunnel. They walked down the incline and halted at the line of soldiers stretching across its base.

"You are to wait here until you are announced," a soldier said, his voice deep and completely lacking emotion.

"And what if I need to use the privy?" Isolde asked.

The soldier pointedly ignored her, the grip on his elithrium spear tightening. She merely sighed and selected a spot on the wall to wait. The others spread out, keeping a healthy, respectful distance from each other.

The first unmistakable clash of metal rang through the tunnel as cries for blood filled the air, signaling the start of the second trial. Isolde closed her eyes and tried to imagine it. The strikes were far too often to be anything another than four blades, each one baying for blood and desperate to find its mark.

"What are you doing?" Gawen asked, sliding into the spot beside her.

"I'm watching Kyros's trial," Isolde said, keeping her eyes closed. "He was using two blades...but now..."

It changed suddenly. Heavy echoes of striking blades drummed down the tunnel, each one more drawn out than the last. Lengths of time filled the spaces with each blow. "Now, it's axes. Or longswords."

"How can you tell?" Gawen's words held a note of fascination, and the sound brought a smile to her face.

"Listen," she whispered. "You can tell by the number of times the weapons meet...how often...and by what kind of sound they make."

"Or if there's no strike at all, just silence," said Sohan from where he lounged across from Isolde. "Could be an arrow or a spear. Far safer, more efficient."

Isolde turned her appraising, critical gaze to Ferden's champion. "I would have pegged you for a man who likes a longsword. Interesting."

"For a well-bred lady," he said, fixing her with his mesmerizing eyes, "you seem to know an awful lot about matters with a blade."

"As do you," she said. "Although, I'm not the least bit surprised. Ferden never enters anything without the intention of winning. Seems like he picked the right man for the job."

"He didn't *pick* me, as you well know." Loyalty rang in his voice. "Lord Ferden would never force someone into this. I chose to come here."

She would have been disappointed otherwise. From the nights she'd spent across the table from him, hood and mask in place, Isolde could tell Ferden was different. She could see it in the way he talked to the people under his care, the way he treated them. Human, half-blood, or virya, it didn't matter. Ferden loved his people, and they undoubtedly loved him in return.

"I can't say that surprises me."

"It shouldn't surprise you," Sohan muttered, withdrawing back into the wall. A hint of a smile flickered across his face only to disappear a moment later.

"You can tell by the sounds they make," Isolde continued, turning back to Gawen. "The rhythm of their breathing. The heavier the blade, the slower the strike. Rapid breathing and rapid strikes mean a lighter blade, something far easier to wield."

Another cry erupted from the arena. A moment later, Lenox's voice followed behind. "Well done, Kyros of Marsh Hall! A performance fit for the court of Elenarta." The crowd cheered once again, their lips crying out his name in a chant. "Our next champion is Demir of Foxclove!"

The clash of blade after blade echoed through the late morning as Demir worked his way through the series of weaponry. His time bled into the afternoon like sand through a shattered hourglass. Passing into the shadows of the tunnel at the end of his trial, Demir chucked the bloodied mace away and stalked towards them. He ripped a cup of water from the hands of one of the servants off to the side, sending ribbons of water down his face speckled with blood.

Isolde's lip pulled into an involuntary snarl as he passed. "The sign of a gentleman always lies in his manners. Or in his inability to possess them."

"Manners are for those worthy of them, Lady Isolde," Demir said, pressing the rim of the goblet to his lips, his stare cold.

Lenox's voice cut through the air. "Next!"

Beads of sweat poured from Gawen's face as he shuffled to Lenox's side. A twinge of concern echoed through Isolde's mind when he disappeared into the blinding rays of the high noon sun. She could only imagine Milt's worry. She wasn't sure what the boy was to her dear friend, but he was most certainly someone Milt held close to his heart.

She didn't acknowledge Kyros when he claimed Gawen's seat for his own. Every ounce of her focus was trained on listening to the song of blades drifting through the tunnel. She could tell by the sounds of his movements, the strike of the blades and shuffling of feet, Gawen was doing well. A smile broke out onto her face as the sound of a sword striking the ground filled the air.

"He won, I take it," Kyros said, taking a sip from the goblet in his hand. The familiar scent of wine filled Isolde's head, making her crave just a taste.

"Not quite." She plucked the goblet from his hand and draining the contents. It was fresh and earthy with the delicious hint of blackberry. A taste reminding her of Blackford Forest. "But he's alive." With a satisfied smile, Isolde tossed the empty goblet back into Kyros's hand still held aloft.

He looked into the empty goblet and raised a single brow. "A lady would have asked," he grumbled, waving the servant over. The young man rushed forward, the pitcher of wine filled and ready.

"A lady shouldn't have to ask," Isolde said, still enjoying the sweet after taste.

"Well, I don't suppose the word 'lady' fits you quite right," Kyros said, giving the boy a kind nod before taking a sip from the precariously full goblet. "Now does it?"

"I'm known for many things, Kyros," Isolde said, her voice blending in with the cheering crowd and Lenox, who announced the end of Gawen's second trial. "But a lady is the least of them." Gawen's silhouette breached the lip of the tunnel's opening. Relief filled her chest when only a minimal amount of blood painted his figure.

"I was taken out," he said. A look of disappointment filled his face. "I could have done better—"

"You did fine," Isolde said, doing her best to wear an encouraging smile. "I heard it all."

A nervous chuckle lifted from Gawen's lips. "Truly?"

"Truly," Isolde said, giving his shoulder a squeeze.

"I believe it's my turn," Isolde said, her eyes shifting to where Kyros lingered. "Do try to not drink all the wine until I get back."

"You ask far too much of me, Lady Isolde."

Lenox stepped forward and his bulbous form blocked out the sun as he opened his mouth. "I'm here, Lenox, no need to waste your breath," Isolde said, cutting him off. "You do far too much of that as it is."

A great cheer rose to meet her as Isolde stepped out onto the arena floor. She pushed the elithrium bracelet up her arm. The gaping hole her silenced powers left behind made her lip curl. The Master of Games stood at her side, his nose pitched high in the air. "Begin wherever you see fit, *champion*," he said. "Disable your opponents until they are no longer a threat to the king."

Isolde looked around the arena, her gaze landing on the table covered with throwing knives. Their blades winked in the sun's piercing light. She stalked toward them, her hips swinging back and forth. Running her fingers across the handles, Isolde searched the crowd until she met the eyes of her cadre.

Cillian's face held a smile matching Blyana's. Malaki sat beside them. His arms were folded over his chest, but his ghostly pale face held a look of determination. The same one he wore when they trained. The one that said *focus*.

Her fingers curled around the handles of the throwing daggers. They were medium length and perfectly balanced in her hands. From the depths of one of the tunnels lining the walls, a sea of bodies spilled out onto the arena floor. Humans and half-bloods covered in the plates of makeshift, second-hand armor sprinted forward.

"Disable your opponents until they are no longer a threat to the king."

Isolde smiled inwardly at Lenox's words, at the holes residing within them. Blade after blade cut through the air. Their razor-like edges grazed the side of a knee, disappeared into the thigh of another, or sank into an exposed shoulder. Bodies fell at her feet. Each one possessed a wound not lethal but just enough to disable.

Isolde moved through the rest of the weapons with ease. Arrow after arrow found its mark. Trident, mace, spear—she wielded them all well enough to disarm every prisoner who crossed her path. The longsword was the only weapon to give her pause. The blade was far heavier than the ones she had trained with. Its pommel was crafted from new metal as opposed to the battered ones she was used to.

The prisoner she now faced must have been trained in the weapon as well. The blade practically sang in his grasp. It obeyed his every command as if it were an extension of his body. Isolde couldn't help but marvel at the beauty of his movements, like an artist wielding a brush across a canvas. Every blow Isolde delivered was met with an equal if not better parry of his own. Soon, she was put on the defense, forcing her to move backwards on the uneven gravel terrain.

Each strike sent a jolt of painful vibrations through her arms. Isolde reached for her power on instinct. She grasped for the strength she had relied on her whole life. But the monster inside was silent. It lay dormant within the confines of her skin.

The prisoner struck again this time, knocking the sword from Isolde's hands. It skittered across the gravel and stopped well out of reach. She lunged forward, her hand already reaching out. But the unmistakable kiss of a blade touched the tip of her chin, bringing her to a halt.

Irritation crept into her limbs as the blade forced her head up, laying her neck bare. Lenox's voice filled the air, and fury burned in her veins.

"Time!"

The blade hovered for a moment longer, its edges pressing into her skin. When the man finally let the sword fall to his side, Isolde took a deep breath. She turned to see a smile, one only the promise of freedom could provide, grow on his face.

"You're a good fighter," Isolde said, extending her hand. The man's eyes narrowed in suspicion. Not that she blamed him. "It's not often someone bests me," she said, her hand still hovering between them. "It's even rarer for me to not hold a grudge when I lose."

Cautiously, he stepped forward and slipped his hand into her open palm. A silver bracelet encased his wrist. Its faint glow matched the one residing in Isolde's. "It's not often a half-blood has the pleasure of fighting a lady," he said, the harsh lines of his face softening. Faint scars decorated the skin of his cheeks and continued above his brow. "Let alone beat one."

"Savor it," Isolde said with the smirk. She gave his hand a tight squeeze before releasing her hold. "Enjoy your freedom."

Isolde grinned as she crossed beneath the tunnel's entrance. The cool touch of the shade chased away the burn of the hot afternoon sun, drawing a sigh from her lips. She smiled to one of the servants lingering to the side and plucked a goblet from the tray. Clear, cool water stared back at her.

"No wine?" Isolde asked.

"I'm sorry, Lady Isolde," the servant said, her eyes suddenly fearful. "But the champion of Marsh Hall drank the last of the wine supplies we brought for the day."

Isolde cut her eyes to Kyros who leaned against the wall. A lazy, stained grin tugged on his mouth as he tipped the goblet to his mouth.

Rivers of wine fell down either side of his lips, staining the fine, sweat-tinged tunic. Isolde couldn't help but follow those rivers of delicious wine as they ran down the planes of his chest, soaking into his shirt. She bit her lip as the wine clung to the rivets of sculpted muscle beneath. Her mind drifted to Liam and a fantasy began to unfold in her mind. One of wine and his bare skin beneath her tongue.

"Now I've drunk the last of it," Kyros said, yanking her back into reality. "If it's any consolation, it was exquisite."

"So happy *you* enjoyed yourself," she grumbled.

"Care to help me clean up?" he asked, with a smile she knew had gotten him out of trouble on more than one occasion. "I'm sure you can get a mouthful if you work hard enough."

Isolde bit back a chuckle blossoming on her tongue as she drank down the cool water. "Oh, I doubt that," Isolde said, wiping her mouth with the back of her hand.

A sense of ease and wine-infused bliss fell over Kyros as he listened to the roar of the arena. His eyes scanned the tunnel's opening as if he could actually see what lay beyond. She had the distinct feeling, if given different circumstances, she and Kyros could have actually been friends.

"So," Isolde said, finding herself bored enough to strike up a conversation with her wine thief. "Marsh Hall."

"Is that a question or a statement, Lady Isolde?" he asked, humor dancing across his face.

Isolde fought a laugh tinged with irritation breaching her lips. "How did you become Circe's champion?"

A note of sobriety filled his eyes at the question, forcing a fraction of the smile to fall away from his infuriatingly handsome face. "I suppose you could say we have a…complicated history."

Isolde's eyes rose with interest. "Is she your lover?"

A wicked grin pulled at the corners of Kyros's sensual mouth. "Would you be jealous if she were?"

"Hardly," Isolde said, holding the cup out while a servant filled it. "Circe is not my type. And you…Well, you would be so lucky to snag my attention."

"But I have it now," said Kyros, his devilish grin growing. "Don't I?"

Isolde stared him down over her goblet. "Answer the question."

Kyros nodded, causing a tendril of chocolate brown hair to fall across his brow. "No, Lady Isolde," he said. "She is not my lover. Just someone I care a great deal about. That's all there is to it."

Isolde heard the underlying meaning in his tone. The subtle warning that said, *"Leave it alone. This is none of your business."*

"Fine then," Isolde said, taking another sip. "Keep your secrets."

Out of the corner of her eye, Isolde saw the ghost of a smile form on Kyros's face. A moment later, the roar of the crowd erupted. The clash of metal had ceased, signaling the end of Buer's trial.

Demir jumped to his feet and straightened the creases of his tunic. Gawen, who had been munching on a bowl of fruit, followed suit. Sohan remained where he was, buried in the shadows. He had gone after her, completing the trial nearly as quickly as Buer.

"To the arena, champions," Lenox ordered, with a clap of his hands.

"Finally," Isolde said, setting the cup down on the ground. "I'm starving." Her stomach growled with each step of the incline, her mind already focusing on the pan of hot cinnamon rolls waiting for her back at her chambers.

"Not one to go hungry, are you?" Kyros asked, following into step beside her.

"Not if I can help it," Isolde said, shutting her eyes to the blinding sun. "I'm not my usually charming self if I haven't eaten."

Kyros opened his mouth but was immediately cut off.

"Champions." Erebus's voice filled the arena, silencing every voice present. "You have shown exceptional skill in various forms of weaponry. Tonight, we celebrate your vast talents and accomplishments. Many of which are worthy to be called my Left Hand."

Erebus raised his arms to his sides, and the crowd erupted. He smiled at them, a serene, charming grin that sent a shiver of revulsion down Isolde's spine.

"Go and rest, for the third trial will take place three days from now." *Three days!* Isolde thought, her mind already reeling. *So, little time.* Her gaze shot to the others and landed on Malaki. He was still far too pale, far too weak. How could she possibly hope to accomplish this without him at her side?

"Champions, this way, please," Lenox instructed, interrupting her thoughts. He ushered them out the way they'd arrived. Isolde filed in behind Gawen, with Kyros at her side and Sohan at her back.

"And a special thank you to the volunteers for assisting our beloved champions in showcasing their skills," Erebus continued. "But the law is the law, and nothing can pardon you from that fact."

Pleas and cries caused Isolde's feet to sputter. She twisted around to see a garrison of soldiers' spill from the mouths of the tunnels directly below the dais. Their swords glistened like rays of blazing light before disappearing into the chests and backs of the prisoners still remaining in the arena. The prisoners who had played by Erebus's rules and won their freedom in blood, only to have it ripped away.

The half-blood male who had bested her looked to Erebus. His eyes once filled with such hope, now only showed betrayal. He turned to the soldier before him, his mouth twisted in bitter fury. His eyes never wavered as the soldier drove the blade through the center of his chest.

Fury, cold and blinding, consumed Isolde's mind. It slammed against the impenetrable wall the elithrium bracelet had placed on her power. But before she could set one foot back into the arena, Sohan's strong hands wrapped around her shoulders and pushed her back. Their elithrium bracelets clinked together as she struggled.

"Let go of me!" Isolde snarled.

"You can't help them!" Sohan said, his grip tightening. With the bracelets still in place, it was useless to fight. He towered at least a foot and a half over her. Mounds of lean muscles sculpted his frame. But she didn't care.

"He led them to be slaughtered!"

The rock bit into her wrists as Sohan's impossibly strong hands pinned her to the wall. "And what do you think will happen if you intervene?" he demanded. "Do you really think you can save them? Because you can't! All that will come to pass is your blood being spilled in that arena alongside theirs. What good will you be to anyone then?"

"He's right, Isolde," Kyros said, his jaw flexing. Mournful anger filled his eyes. "There's nothing you can do."

The last of the screams echoed down the tunnel. A sickening bellow of joy that turned Isolde's stomach rang from the crowd. She ripped herself away from Sohan's grasp and allowed a servant to remove her bracelet. Power filled every muscle and burned through every thought passing through her mind. Only when the bars of confinement were firmly in place did she dare turn back to Sohan and Kyros.

"I do have people who rely on me. But if either of you ever try to stop me again, Ferden and Circe will find themselves without a champion." Isolde's voice was low and full of deadly promise. "I'll gut you where you stand."

CHAPTER 19

Black lace, what little there was to begin with, rode up the side of Isolde's thighs as she ascended the steps of the Renaylie Orelena Opera House. The silken trim brushed against her back, giving her at least a taste of comfort.

"Gage said nothing about altering it," Nan had said, her worn, withered hands tugging at the final stitch. "No one will see them."

Tanor's blood stained the fine marble floor beneath her feet. It served as a permanent reminder of what the cost of refusing to wear a dress would bring. Tears lined the rim of Isolde's eyes as a lump of guilt lodged itself in her throat. Nan kissed her cheek and cupped her chin, forcing Isolde to look into her warm, familiar eyes. "The floor might bear his blood, my rose," she said. "But not your hands."

Nan's words filled Isolde's mind as she walked through the ornate doors. It was a miracle such a wondrous creation had survived so long under Erebus's reign. Bodies of bureaucrats filled the intricate, lavish lobby. Marble, gold, and rich velvet furnishing lined every inch of the room.

Isolde ignored them all. There wasn't a soul there she cared to pass pleasantries with. The marble clicked beneath the stiff heels of her highly uncomfortable shoes. The suede carpet covering the sweeping staircase flattened beneath her feet. Memories flooded Isolde's mind with every step she climbed. Faces of the past that haunted the darkest corners of her heart stepped into the light once more.

She entered Erebus's box and took her seat in the middle of the lowest row. Hardly anything had changed. The same crown molding decorated the ceilings and banisters of the boxes lining the sides of the theater walls. The scent of sheet music, fresh linen, and wood polish lingered in the air.

The only alteration she could see was the great carving hovering over the stage. A serpent's eye cast in a gilded triangle, the symbol of the Tenebriath house, looked down at the audience slowly filing into their respected seats. A growl rumbled through Isolde's chest, her fingers twisting the program in her lap.

"That's not the Tenebriath family symbol," Alaric had told her. The pad of his finger brushed over the emblem etched into the wax seal of the invitation she had received earlier that day. He had told Isolde all there was to know about Erebus. At least, everything she wasn't already aware of. "Erebus changed it after he seized control."

"What was it before?"

Alaric plucked a piece of parchment from the desk. "The Tenebriath line hails from the Wilds of the North," Alaric said, dipping a quill into the vat of ink. "Seems only fitting their symbol would represent that notion too." After a moment, he pushed the paper to her.

In the center was what she assumed to be a four-pointed snowflake. Its edges were razor-sharp, anything but delicate. Alaric tapped the quill to the four points. "Erebus's father, Zelos Tenebriath, had a plan, an ambition to rule Arnoria, in every direction."

Isolde's brow rose. "A compass," she said. "Not very subtle on Zelos's part."

Alaric grimaced. "He was a prideful man and a cruel one."

"And I suppose this," Isolde said pointing to the figure eight dominating the middle, "is meant for infinity?"

Alaric's mouth thinned. "Precisely."

"Why did Erebus change it?"

Alaric sighed, and the tips of his fingers hovered over the letter. "Erebus is many things, but self-deprecating isn't one of them. Whatever reason he had for forsaking his family seal, I can imagine it must have been something worth losing everything for. Something worth far more than his own legacy."

Fingers, warm and familiar, encased Isolde's fidgeting hands. She blinked and turned to see Liam beside her. His dark gaze was shadowed in concern. "It's going to be fine," he said, sending a plume of his scent her way—midnight and orchids. Isolde took a deep breath and allowed her hands to unfold from the mess she had made.

He slid into the seat beside her, and she couldn't help but take him in. Gone was the uniform of a soldier. Instead, he wore a suit of matte black fabric. A mountainous design had been sewn into the collar of his lapel, a tribute to his abilities as an earth wielder. A pair of black trousers hugged his thighs and Isolde drank him in like a woman who had been parched for far too long.

"My eyes are up here, Lady Isolde," Liam said, his tone deep and filled with meaning. Her gaze snapped to his to find the cheeky, boyish grin she adored. And she couldn't help but smile back.

"Ah! There you are!" The sound of Gage's voice was like being dunked in a bucket of ice water. Isolde couldn't stop the snarl ripping through her teeth. He took up the spot on her left, jarring the row of seats with his weight.

"You look lovely, pet," Gage said, pressing his lips to her cheek.

The scent of brandy and cherries filled the air and Isolde's stomach turned. He inhaled deeply, running the edge of his nose along the side of her jaw. "See how easy it is to just do as I say?"

"It's either that or you hurt people, Gage," Isolde said, scooting as far away as the seat would allow. "I wouldn't really call that much of a choice. Must be sad having to force a woman into your presence. Doesn't speak very much for your charm."

Gage's hand landed on Isolde's bare knee and squeezed. She stifled a moan of pain, refusing to give him the satisfaction. "We still need to work on that mouth of yours, I see." His voice was filled with a dark promise.

"Good evening," Erebus said from behind. He was clad in a pair of finely tailored britches and jacket that shone like dull metal. Every stitch was black as night and in absolute perfection.

"Your Majesty," Gage said, as he rose from his seat, squeezing Isolde's arm until she stood as well. "I trust you're having a pleasant evening."

"I am," Erebus said, his eyes shifting to Isolde. "Especially now that I see our lovely Lady Isolde has joined us. And I believe you know this young man as well." Erebus gestured behind him, and Isolde couldn't hold back the gasp.

Tanor stood still as a statue behind Erebus, his eyes were downcast and ringed in shadow. It had only been a few days, and already she could see the changes. There was hardly any muscle left. His skin, once tan and youthful, had turned an ashen yellow.

"I thought it might be good to have some young blood in our midst," Erebus said, drawing Isolde back from the mist of rage building inside her. Swallowing her pride, Isolde forced her knees to bend.

"An excellent idea," Isolde managed to say, the words finding their way around her teeth. "Your Majesty."

A satisfied smile stretched across Erebus's face as he took her in. "I must say," he said, his voice low and drawn, "that dress is a most interesting choice for you."

"Not exactly of my choosing or my taste," Isolde said, yanking her arm from Gage's grasp to run a hand down the length of the bodice. "But I suppose it will do." The grin on Erebus's mouth fell into a hard line at the sight of her arm. While no bruise had formed yet, Isolde knew Gage's fingerprints certainly had.

"I'm sure Lord Gage went to great lengths to pick it out just for you," Erebus said, his piercing attention cutting to Gage. His eyes, like liquid silver, were brimming in subdued fury. A smile, false but wholly believable danced across his face.

"I would have thought my intended would preferred me all to himself, Your Grace," Isolde said, her eyes cutting. "But perhaps not."

Amusement flickered across Erebus's face and rage burned from Gage's eyes. The lights flickered overhead, signaling the play was about to begin. It cast them in shadow, making Gage's eyes glow all the more.

Liam cleared his throat, bowing behind Isolde. "I believe the show is about to start, Your Majesty."

"Yes," Erebus said, plucking a goblet of wine from the silver tray offered to him. "Do save this squabble for after the show, Gage."

"Of course, Your Majesty," Gage said with the bow of his head. He gripped Isolde's arm again and forced her into the seat. "I will kill every one of those little shits if you ever embarrass me like that again, Isolde," Gage hissed, sliding a hand up her thigh. "And I'll make you watch."

Anger blossomed in Isolde's chest as his fingers pressed into her flesh. But a small gasp had her turning back. Tanor's face was contoured in pain as he slowly lowered himself to the chair directly behind Erebus.

His eyes met Isolde's, and she felt her heart shatter. Sorrow and despair lingered in his hollow gaze. Fine clothes might have covered him, but they did nothing to hide the scars within, the ones lingering in his eyes. Isolde felt her power stir, the animal lurking beneath her skin raked its claws down her resolve. And just as she was about to give in, she felt the back of a finger caress the side of her right thigh. Opposite to the one Gage's paw had laid claim to, Liam ran his finger across her skin, leaving a trail of fire in its wake.

It was his only way of comforting her. The only way for him to say, *I'm here. I'm with you.*

The lights dimmed, casting the opera house in darkness. Slowly, the velvet curtain was drawn back, and the Renaylie Orelena came to life. Swallowing back the lump in her throat, she faced the stage, and endured.

Isolde felt every note drifting through the warm, scented air. Each one carried an echo of the past, an ember of memory, dim but ever glowing. The piece was one she had heard as a child. One her father had sung to her every night as she fell asleep.

Emotion, savage and suffocating, found home at the base of Isolde's throat. Air refused to move as the music swelled and unwound around her. It moved through her like nothing else ever had, like nothing else ever could. The story and the music carrying it, wove their way into every part of Isolde's soul. Drifting like wind through the trees of a forest, they left nothing in her heart untouched.

Decades had passed since Isolde had allowed a single note to cross her lips. A lifetime ago, in the meadow that belonged only to them, Isolde had held Kamden close and sang her final song for him. The song she had agreed to sing on their wedding day.

Now, it all came roaring back. A torrential outpour of emotion she could easily drown in. Isolde thought she knew torture, but this was far worse. Not even the grip Gage kept on her thigh could shake her from the memories flooding her mind.

One in particular was of her youngest brother playing the piano. His music blended with her voice as they shared the stage. They had crafted pieces of music together. Little plays their parents watched lovingly from the wings. Even at a young age, they were both prodigies. His thin, long fingers moved across the ivory keys like he was born for such a thing. Like the gods had created him for this sole purpose in life. It was effortless, and it was beautiful.

The ghosts of the past filled the opera house as the piece unfolded before her. Ghosts Isolde had loved more than her own life came back like the phantoms they were. She had tried to bury them beneath decades of grief, pain, and anger. Tried to forget, tried to not feel the endless well of sorrow carving into her chest. Yet she could never bring herself to fully erase them—not entirely.

How she wished to see them. To hold them all once more. To hear their laughter, see the smiles shine from their faces, and feel their warm, safe arms around her. But only the sounds of their screams filled her head. An image, brutal and vivid, filled her mind. Her father's face, handsome and so full of life, was beaten beyond recognition. Her mother, Isolde's strong protector and idol, lay beside him in a pool of blood, her throat laid open.

It was a memory she fought to forget nearly as hard as the one of when she found Kamden's mutilated body. In that moment, she wanted nothing more than for the past to die. To let that one piece of herself disappear forever. For the memories to fade into oblivion along with her pain.

The music ebbed and flowed, cutting into Isolde's heart. The performers moved across the stage, feet silent beneath the sound of the orchestra. Every note, every word pierced her already battered heart like a quiver of arrows. Each one broke away what little she had left, what little of her resolve to stay strong remained. But it was no use. Her father's favorite piece rose over the crowd and held her in its loving, thorny embrace. Tears swelled and threatened to cascade down her cheeks, unrestrained and unapologetic. The music filled her heart until there was simply no room left. It was music she remembered from so long ago.

Her father's music.

His face grew in her mind. A smile of his own, spreading with such reckless abandonment, was shining from his handsome, youthful face. A dark brown beard, always well-kept and trimmed, glistened in the dim lights of backstage.

His colossal form stood above her like a shadow of protective darkness. She remembered thinking he was a giant, a legend made real. He was nearly as tall as Malaki, and just as broad. Yet nothing but gentleness filled his gaze as he cupped her cheek in the palm of his hand.

"Listen, my little elenmair," he said, squatting down to whisper in her ear. That was his name for her, his precious little star. "Listen to the music."

Isolde remembered something stirring deep within her heart. The music, his music, filled the air. It was a marvelous melody created by his hand, by his own brilliance she partook in, that she cherished. Even then she had cried openly. It was all too much. Too much beauty for her small, sensitive heart to bear.

"Do not be ashamed of your tears," he said, tugging her hands away from her face. "Tears are a soul's way of speaking when we have no words for what lies within." Her father always knew what to say and how to make a smile return to her face. Even as the howl of a wolf breached the notes hanging in the air, Isolde had felt no fear. Her father looked to the door leading to the back alleyways of Elenarta, a muscle ticking in his jaw.

"Papa," Isolde had said, her hand gripping his strong, callused finger. The wolf howled once more, this time much closer. Then another…and another. "Papa, is—"

"Everything's alright," he had said, the side of mouth quirking into a grin. "Nothing for you to worry about. They're just enjoying the music too." Isolde had taken him at his word at the time. But looking back, she understood he had spared her the hard, dangerous truth.

"Can I sing one day too, Papa?" she had asked, already stirring with notes that wanted to burst from her tongue, the ones her soul longed to sing.

"Yes, elenmair," he had said, his warm, amber eyes shining with pride. "One day, you will sing for us all."

"Can we always watch from here?"

A chuckle had rumbled through his chest as he lifted her into his arms. "This will always be our spot, elenmair. Always."

The memory faded like a wisp of smoke in the wind and a hollowness carved its way into Isolde's chest. Darkness and pain filled with a familiar cold fire burned through her like an inferno. How desperately she wanted to walk straight into the darkness, to let the shadows swallow her whole. To not feel…to not care.

But Isolde knew, even with her toes brushing the fine line between sanity and sweet oblivion, if she dared take that final step there would be no coming back. That no one, not even Malaki, could reach her. A bitter sadness spread through her heart and turned her sorrows into molten anger.

The sound of Gage's yawning froze the tears of remembrance threatening to spill over onto Isolde's face. A protective coat of numbness descended over her shoulders, and the ghosts faded back into her heart once more. Back into the place where no one and nothing could touch them. Vengeance, black and hot, bubbled to the forefront of Isolde's mind. Her power stirred awake as her eyes rose to the symbol looming over the stage.

Soon. She thought to herself, to the horrible creature she had been forced to keep locked up for decades. *Very soon.*

It's sharp, deadly teeth glistened in her mind. There would be no saving them from what was to come. No matter how well guarded, how untouchable Gage believed himself and Erebus to be, she wouldn't stop until they both lay dead at her feet. Never would she yield.

Isolde smiled at the thought, and the monster within smiled back.

"Until we meet again," he said, his pale eyes shining with anticipation.

CHAPTER 20

"Damn it!"

Pain, sharp and annoying, shot across Malaki's hip. Each step sent a whip of fire scorching down and across the crevasse of ruined flesh streaking across his hip and thigh. The chilled evening air rustled the stray tendrils of his ebony hair as he passed one of the many balconies that lay along the walls of the palace. Still he refused to show even a hint of discomfort.

Not only did thinking of the pain make it worse, but it also brought something, or *someone*, back into the forefront of his mind. Someone with strands of shimmering white hair, a voice that caressed his mind like fingers of delicate silk, and eyes as sharp and endless as the purest night.

"I can't wait to see you again," he said to himself, the sound of his voice echoing into darkness beneath the massive stone bridge he trudged across. The wild woman, Helurtu, who had cut him played in his memory, burrowing further beneath his skin. The anger stoked his power within, pushing it to fight against the chains he had expertly placed around them.

Helurtu had been invading Malaki's thoughts far more often than he cared to admit. The strange pause that had occurred between them, the way her blade stilled over his heart as if the gods themselves had held it at bay. And her eyes…Pools of crystal midnight sky, seemed to cradle an eternity of cold starlight. A beautiful, violent darkness.

Shoving the memories out of his mind, Malaki placed a tentative hand to his side. The ruined flesh flared beneath his touch, his own magic useless to repair the damage she had left behind. Something that had never happened before. "Next time you'll be the one left bleeding."

As he walked the hallway, mindful of keeping his head held high but eyes averted from all who crossed his path, Malaki found his way to the one place he had longed to see. Each step up the familiar stone, spiral staircase sent a joint of fire burning through his muscles and newly formed skin. He was healing, but not nearly fast enough.

Of all the times to be injured when Isolde needed you most. Malaki shook his head, shoving away the sweltering waves of guilt and shame.

At least, Isolde didn't suffer this long. He thought to himself, grateful yet again, for her unnatural healing abilities. Even as a child, she could heal from the most devastating of injuries in no time at all.

A door, one familiar yet incredibly worn, greeted him on the landing. The handle was rusted, covered in decades of dust and forgetfulness. Carefully, Malaki wrapped his fingers around the rough surface and twisted. The door gave way easily, but a traitorous squeak rang from its hinges. Malaki looked back down the stairway, listening for anyone who might have heard.

It wouldn't be outrageous to assume he was forbidden from venturing out unattended. He couldn't imagine Erebus would take too kindly to him snooping around. And that would only result in pain for Isolde, Zibiah, or the children. But with her being forced into accompanying Gage to the opera for the evening, it was now or never. Malaki made a note of how relaxed the security became in Erebus's absence. A fact that never would have stood if he was still in charge of Elenarta's defenses.

When no sound of hurried, curious footsteps came up the stairwell, Malaki took a deep breath and crossed the threshold. It was as if time had frozen, halted in a single moment of existence. A pair of boots, his boots, lay beside a small bed. One far too small for him, but just the right size for a child. It's duvet, once the color of an early morning sunrise, fit for a princess, had disintegrated into bits of charred fabric.

Books littered the ground, their pages crinkled, and ink faded into nothingness. Fairytales lost to time. An ornate rug, once beautiful and soft, crunched beneath the soles of his boots.

And the walls...

Malaki's blood chilled and his throat tightened. Scorched stones, ones covered in burn marks, filled the walls of the playroom. Lashes of flame licked at the surface like horrible scars. An image entered his mind, and Malaki shut it down before the echoes of her screams could make their way to him. It was the worst of his nightmares. The one that tore his soul in two every time it visited him.

Taking a deep breath, steeling himself for the pain that would find its way to his side, Malaki knelt and rapped his knuckles against the dusty floorboards. A dull echo answered back. He continued on, hoping no one else had found what he'd hidden nearly fifty years ago.

Malaki paused as a hollow thud answered his call. Plucking Secrettaker from his belt, he drove its tip between the planks of wood. They popped up with ease to reveal a hidden compartment. Inside was an assortment of trinkets and small treasures he and Bron, his brother in arms and true king of Arnoria, had left as boys and men. He rummaged through the worthless bobbles until at last, he felt it.

The surface was cool and grimy with neglect. But he would know it anywhere. With his prize held securely in the palm of his hand, Malaki rose and turned towards the light bleeding in from the window. Carefully, he unfolded his fingers, and a gasp broke across his lips. Tears sprang to Malaki's eyes as he looked down at the small amulet resting in his callused, scarred palm. It was something he had left behind the night everything changed. The night the Viributhians —Bron, Rey and their children—were taken from him.

Delicately, he wiped the decades of dust from its surface. In the center, was the symbol of the House Viributhian. A row of sharp, unforgiving teeth was etched into a silent snarl on a bed of priceless silver. Sapphires, mined from the depths of Oronilma, formed a ring around the amulet. The wolf was the symbol of their great house, of Queen Reyna Viributhian's birthright. She had intended to pass the heirloom down to her eldest son, Callum, when he ascended the throne.

"Why a wolf?" Malaki had asked Bron once on their many visits to the capital.

"According to Rey, it's because the wolf endures as a silent protector; always watching, always guarding. It is the most powerful of all the virya." Bron had smiled as his long, lyrical fingers brushed over the signet ring bearing the same symbol adorning his left hand. "And only a direct descendant of the Viributhian bloodline can possess that power. It's their family legacy, their dynasty."

Malaki had laughed at the time. But it wouldn't be long before Bron's words were proven true. He had seen Rey herself use that power, more than once. In the early days, they had stood side by side in battle, and the sight was terrifying. At her full height, the tip of her shoulder blade stood a good foot above his head. Secrettaker looked as harmful as a toothpick compared to the fangs she wielded. Her fur had been the color of a burning sunset, rich and blood red. It was a power his queen had passed down to her children, making them the most powerful family in Elenarta.

Until they weren't.

A single tear fell from Malaki's face, and he immediately closed his hand. The cool sigil of the Viributhian house pressed into his skin. It was priceless...and it was dangerous. He knew it would be a death sentence if it was ever discovered in their possession. The past followed Malaki as he descended the long staircase, the amulet safe in his pocket. The ghosts of his failures trailed his every step as he walked through the halls that had once been his refuge, his home.

Light from the thin moon sliced through the stained-glass windows magically embedded into the walls. The beauty of this place never escaped him. But as his feet carried him on, lost in thought, Malaki found himself in an entirely new place. One he had had no intention of treading.

When realization finally dawned, a shuddered breath racked through his chest. It was in another part of the palace. One that clearly had not been used since the time of the siege. Dust covered the ornate flower handle on the door before him, its petals dull and lifeless. Fear, laced with remnants of mournful pain, stilled Malaki's heart as he slowly crept forward. He paused, not out of fear for his physical self, but for the torturous memories that were about to be unearthed.

He listened intently before grabbing the handle and twisting. Its touch was so familiar, so agonizingly recognizable in his hand. As he pushed the door in, Malaki felt a small piece of that hardened exterior crack. Much like the room he had played in as a child, nothing had changed. He had half expected it, like everything from the previous reign, to have been burned to ash. But this room, much by his design, had been kept separate from the other chambers. By some miracle or an act of mercy from the gods, it had been spared Erebus's touch.

"Small mercies," he said to no one at all.

As general to the royal family, Malaki had longed for one thing.

Privacy.

Especially with her.

Aurora's face, his wife's face, filled his mind as he stepped into the past. Even after all this time, he could still recall the sound of her laughter, the smell of her hair, and the full, loving smile she always wore.

Dust covered the duvet of their four-poster bed. Two tables sat on either side. An empty, dry vase, one Aurora loved to fill with flowers every morning, sat on the right. Nothing but mold and a thick layer of grime covered the one on the left.

"You need something there," she had said, pushing a daisy into the vase. "Something to brighten up this room."

"I have you." Malaki had smiled, his arms wrapping around her waist from behind. "You are all the light I need in my life."

Aurora had never been as beautiful as she was that day. The day she had pressed his hand to the small swell of her stomach and told him the news with tears of joy streaming down her face. "You're about to be very busy, General."

Malaki could remember the shock of pure elation, the feeling of undiluted joy when he finally grasped what she meant. It had been here in this room when she had told him the news of their child. He looked down at the floor, at the spot he had picked her up and twirled her through the air, kissing away her tears that were matching his own. Nothing remained of that day now, except the memories he had stored up like the treasures they were.

A lump formed in Malaki's throat, his eyes stinging with tears. He approached the vanity residing near the window and with a trembling hand, he pulled open the top drawer. Inside was a small hair pin he had given Aurora during their courting. It was solid gold, set with pink diamonds in the shape of peonies.

"I want you to have everything," Malaki had said, gently pushing the pin into the side of her golden hair, drawing it back from her flawless face. Her elegant, long fingers grazed over the stones he had handpicked himself.

"This is too much," Aurora had said, her eyes down cast, "for someone like me. This is far too much, Malaki."

He sighed at the memory, at remembering how little she thought of herself because she was a human. Even now, it broke his heart. "Nothing is ever too much for you," he had said, cradling her face in his hands. "And nothing will ever be good enough for you, Aurora. Nothing."

The pad of Malaki's thumb grazed over the golden surface. A small flicker of hope sparked in his chest as he brought the priceless gift to his nose and drew in a breath. He wasn't sure if it was wishful thinking, but he could have sworn the faintest hint of jasmine and rain still lingered on the metal.

Taking another deep breath, Malaki let his gaze drop back down into the drawer. A sob broke free from his lips as a stream of fresh tears fell down his face. He reached in and pulled out a set of booties. The yarn, once fine and incredibly soft, was now moth eaten and brittle. Gently, Malaki cradled them to his chest.

"My little dream," Malaki cried. "My little light."

A virya and a human producing a child was unheard of, deemed impossible by most. The healers and scholars didn't know what to make of it. Malaki had chalked it up to luck, that perhaps a virya or even a half-blood resided somewhere along Aurora's distant lineage. Too far back for her to have inherited power but still possessed the ability to bear his child.

But his sweet wife had turned to the stars, to the gods. "What a blessing," she had said, tears of happiness streaming down her cheeks as she placed a hand over the swell of her belly.

It was then Malaki had made a decision. It was then he had decided to give up his power, his immortality, in exchange for a life with her and the precious gift she now carried.

Bron and Rey had understood and wholeheartedly accepted the news with nothing but joy. Aurora had been a part of their lives for so long they thought of her as a sister. She had been Galaena's lady-in-waiting, making her a part of their family too.

Malaki pressed the hairpin and booties to his lips. A shaky, agonizing breath rocked through his chest. The sweet sense of pain pierced his side as he fell to his knees. But he hardly felt it. This might as well have been their graves. Nothing was left of his wife and the child he never got to meet. Nothing except the priceless pieces of them he cradled in his hands.

"I'll find somewhere," Malaki said. "I'll find you both a place to rest. I promise."

He hadn't been there when they died. It was only after, when the Viributhians fell, that he had learned of their deaths. He could still remember the pain, the shock, the disbelief…the rage. There had been nothing to prevent his power from breaking forth and spilling so much blood he shuddered to remember it. Nothing, save one little voice.

Forcing a shaky breath through his lips, Malaki carefully placed the last reminders of his family into his pocket, alongside the amulet, before turning and walking to the door. His fingers gripped the doorframe, and he cast a final look at the place that had once held so much joy.

"I love you both."

A wave of agony followed in Malaki's wake as he made his way through the nearly deserted palace. He passed a window, and the light of the moon caught his eye. It was silent and as mockingly cold as the stars surrounding it.

Never had the gods granted him peace. Never had he been gifted joy without it being destroyed in one way or another. His gaze flicked to the city below, to the golden dome of the opera house nestled in the heart of the capital. The faintest hint of music carried through the night air.

"I'm sorry I'm not there," he said into the wind. As if it would carry his words through the streets of Elenarta and find Isolde. He could only imagine what she was enduring. What that bastard and her future husband were putting her through. Merciless anger burned through Malaki like wildfire, giving life to every way he wanted to bring death to Erebus and Gage. A satisfied, wicked smile pulled on his lips and plan after plan began to form in his mind.

With a heavy sigh, Malaki shoved the murderous, bloody thoughts away before they could take root, and forced his feet to move. He had been asked one thing for tonight and he'd be damned if he failed in this simple request.

"Bring me some books," Isolde had begged as Nan helped her into the hideous dress Gage had sent for her to wear. It had taken them hours to correct the pattern, adding bits of cloth to the back and sides, hiding away what lay beneath.

"You have plenty of books here," Malaki had said, waving a hand at the sizable stack lingering in the corner. "Plenty to occupy yourself with."

"None that have what I'm craving," Isolde whined. A cheeky grin pulled at her freshly painted lips. "They lack...*substance*."

Malaki rolled his eyes. "By substance, you mean romance."

"Don't act like you don't enjoy them just as much she does, Malaki," said Nan, her withered, nimble fingers fastening another button along Isolde's spine. "Especially, the more inappropriate ones."

Isolde whipped her head around, the light of the dull fire catching the black diamond earring dangling from her ears. "As much as I do?" Her mouth dropped open, and her hand quickly rose to cover the shocked laugh that came forth.

"That was our secret, Nan!" Malaki growled through gritted teeth. Heat spread across his cheeks like a wave upon the shore.

"What's there to be ashamed of?" Nan asked, fighting a smile. "You certainly don't have any when reading them. There's nothing wrong with Isolde enjoying a little—"

"Don't finish that sentence, Nan," Malaki had said, already heading for the door.

His teeth clenched at the memory of Isolde's smug smile, her hands clapping beneath her chin like an excited child. "Bring me some of your favorites!" she called after him. Excitement poured from her like little annoying rays of sunshine. "The filthier the better!"

"I'm bringing you a book on gardening," he had grumbled, tugging the door open, face burning. "Thanks for that, Nan."

Not a single soul guarded the library of Elenarta. It sat quiet as the dead, still as a tomb. But Malaki was relieved to see the books, most of them anyway, had been left untouched. Stone towers, covered with shelves that had been carved into the rock itself, spiraled to the ceiling standing nearly two hundred feet above his head.

"It was made by one of Rey's ancestors," Bron had told him. "He wanted to make a library for his wife. She was a powerful air wielder, who could use her abilities to lift herself up to the highest shelves. Rumor has it"—Bron had smiled, his eyes twinkling with mischief—"that's where she stored all of her favorites. Her *private* collection."

Malaki shook his head at the memory, a hollow echo of loving pain following the ghost of a laugh on his lips. "I'm not climbing all the way up there. Isolde will have to make do with what I find on the ground."

His fingers grazed the spines of the stories lining a shelf at eye level. Some he knew well. Some he found himself desperately reaching for. After a few moments, he reluctantly picked a handful of his favorites for Isolde and a few for his own use.

Nan hadn't lied. While war and epic quests interested him greatly, it was the tales of love that drew him to the written word. The hope and beauty found within the promise it carried, made his world a bit brighter.

"Not what I would have picked for you myself."

A snarl ripped through Malaki's teeth as the monster within raced forward. But through the cloud of surprise, he registered a single figure standing before him.

Lord Ferden of Dolinmere lingered in the depths of the bookshelves. His gaze, free of light, dropped to the book clutched in Malaki's hand. A smirk quirked on the corner of his mouth, the pale, golden mustache twisting. "Romance...interesting choice for a warrior of old."

Taking a deep breath, Malaki placed the book on top of the already ridiculous pile covering one of the nearby tables. "It's for Lady Isolde," he said, his voice devoid of kindness. "She needed a new selection. In case she's forced to be bedridden for a week to heal yet again."

Ferden took in the stack of books, and a haunted look crossed his face. "That's very kind of you," he said. "Do let Lady Isolde know I eagerly await her literary recommendations. Or if you have any to offer—"

"I do not."

The words fell from Malaki's mouth like a hammer, hard and unyielding. He ignored the faint chuckle slipping past Ferden's grinning lips. "I thought you would be at the performance tonight," Malaki said with an air of dismissal. "Seems like the sort of thing you would enjoy."

"It's nothing I haven't heard before." Ferden shrugged with an air of indifference. "Besides, there's only one voice I wish to hear, and that's beyond the realm of possibility at the moment."

"What are you doing here then?"

"I'm doing my own personal inventory of the king's library." The tips of Ferden's fingers brushed the spines of the books as his gaze lifted to the shelves above. "Normally, I'm left in disappointment. Looks like this trip will be no exception."

"What exactly are you looking for?" Malaki asked, placing another book he thought Isolde would like onto the pile.

"Our *great* king seems to be under the impression that removing all traces of history will indeed erase it completely. Not a single book remains of the events from long ago. Not a scrap of parchment detailing our very bloody, very relevant past."

Malaki paused, his guarded, disbelieving gaze shifting to the Lord of Dolinmere who continued down the aisle. "Are you questioning King Erebus, Lord Ferden?"

"I wouldn't dream of questioning the king, Malaki." The corner of Ferden's lips shifted into a grin. "Judging him on the other hand, is an entirely separate matter."

"What particular history are you referring to?"

Ferden's smile faded. "The Viributhians."

The name echoed through the space between them like the toll of a bell. Malaki's power stirred, forcing the hint of a growl to rise in his throat. "Interesting subject matter," he said, carefully placing the book in his hands onto the stack.

"They're a part of our history, are they not?" asked Ferden, never taking his eyes off the shelves. "They deserve to be recognized. No matter what the one who murdered them says. You were close to Viributhians, weren't you?" Malaki could practically feel Ferden's scrutinizing gaze on him. "You were their general, their family—the Bastard Prince."

"You know just how close I was to them, Ferden!" Malaki said, his voice a harsh rasp. "You know exactly what they meant to me, everyone does. Don't pretend otherwise." Malaki's hands balled into fists at his side. He felt their names on his skin. They burned just as much as the day he placed them there. An eternal reminder of his failure, a vigil that could never be erased.

Ferden paused for a moment, his pale eyes shifting back to where Malaki stood. "You grew up with Bronomir. His father, Cethin Histavilar took you in. An orphan from…" Ferden's head cocked to the side. "Where exactly?"

"I wouldn't know," Malaki said, his voice flat and cold. "I was never told of my origins, nor did I particularly care. If they didn't want me, then what makes them worthy of my time?"

Ferden searched Malaki's face, hunting for something deep within the foundations of who he was. Malaki felt naked beneath his gaze, exposed.

"And I assume you're aware of the rumors."

"There are so many," Malaki retorted, tossing another book onto the pile. "You'll have to be more specific."

"That one referring to Queen Reyna and King Bronomir's children, or one of them anyway, possessing powers unlike any others. Callum, Riven, Asher, and Odette, all gifted in their own right. Two of which were exceptional in battle, warriors much like their mother. The other two were kind souls, gentle children. Blessed in other areas, particularly music—if I'm not mistaken. But there was one who stood out from the rest. They were rumored to have possessed power unlike any other, to wield more than one element." Ferden's eyes cut to Malaki. "And could change into anything their power demanded."

"That's impossible," Malaki said, scanning the shelves.

"Is it?" Ferden pressed. "I'm not a scholar, nor do a I claim to be, but I can't imagine it's beyond the realm of possibility."

"You've been listening to far too many fairytales, Lord Ferden," Malaki said, plucking another book off the shelf. "Besides, if any of them were going to possess such power, it would have been Callum. His power and fighting skills nearly matched mine."

"I don't believe this was any fairytale," said Ferden. "How could it be? Fairytales, from what I understand, have happy endings. None of Virbuthian's children were blessed with such a mercy. Especially not the youngest. Odette, I believe she was the youngest. Her death—" Ferden's jaw tightened as he looked to the window. Sorrow and fury shone in his gaze. "Her death was particularly horrible. Volkran made sure of that. He never forgave her for making him look like a fool."

"She was an innocent child," Malaki said, his voice laced with a growl. "She didn't deserve what happened."

A shadow fell over Ferden's face, and a glimpse of the monster beneath echoed in the depths of his eyes. "At times, death is the kindest gift fate has to offer. Especially to those who have known true suffering."

Malaki shivered at the memory. At the sight of what was left of his world, of his family. The bodies of the children he had known since they were born had been mutilated, ripped apart, and burned. They haunted in his mind, refusing to leave. Every face visited him. Day and night, they were there. The places on his body that bore their names burned across his scarred, russet skin.

"Why did you bring this up?" Malaki asked, his voice hardly a whisper.

"Because even though our history is a terrible one," said Ferden, forcing his shoulders back. "it is ours nonetheless and is worth remembering. I will not leave the next generation to suffer such a reoccurrence because we were too weak to remember. Too cowardly to acknowledge it. And if we do not wish for it to happen again, we all must stop hiding from it. We must remember them."

"Dangerous words whispered in dangerous places, Lord Ferden," said Malaki. "Some of which are bordering on treasonous."

"Only if heard by the wrong ears." Malaki remained silent as Ferden strode past him. "Eventually, change must happen, Malaki. And I believe we have come to such a time."

Ferden's hand brushed Malaki's arm, his touch hardly noticeable, like a breath of wind.

A gasp of air exploded from Malaki's gapping mouth as what felt like pure light and power filled him. It ran through his body, penetrating his blood until it found the wound at his side. A moment of excruciating pain erupted down the scar, leaving him panting on the library floor. Just as quickly as it came, the pain was gone, giving way to splendid painless relief.

He shot to his feet with a start and scanned the library for Ferden, demanding to know what he had done to him. But as he twisted, Malaki felt not a single echoing reminder of Helurtu's blade lingered on his skin. Ripping the tail of his tunic loose, Malaki's eyes widened. A smooth, aged scar was in place of the hideous wound that had marred his flesh. Gingerly, he pressed against its edges. Not an ounce of pain answered back.

"What the hell did he do to me?"

Looking to the table, Malaki noticed a new addition to the stack he had collected for Isolde. Its pages were laid face down, frail and creased with time's unforgiving touch. Faded handwriting met his eyes as he held the book gingerly in his hands. It sprawled across the withered parchment in beautiful, forgotten eloquence. Malaki squinted, hardly able to make out the words:

When the blessing of the gods
has reached its peak,

an heir of sacrifice you will seek.
Their power beyond all measure,
a rare, one-of-a-kind, treasure.

Four in one, a might will grow,
to a power no one being can match or show.
But this will be the end of their story,
for death is the price of their glory.

"Four in one, their might will grow…death is the price of their glory." Malaki's voice trailed off as the words sunk in. Savage fear filled his veins. He snapped the book shut. "Nonsense," he snarled, tossing the book back onto the table. He scooped the stack up into his arms and made for the exit. But just as he passed the first bookshelf, Malaki felt himself stop.

Turning back, he glanced at the book Ferden had left behind. It seemed to call out as if a part of him knew it was important. That there was more hiding within those pages. With a heavy sigh, Malaki strode back to the table and tucked it into the lining of his britches.

The intricate archway of the library passed overhead, and Malaki couldn't fight the temptation to run his trembling fingers over the fully healed scar. He had never seen anything like it or felt the effects of such vast power before. Ferden's abilities had always been a mystery, much by his own design. Not even Alaric knew what lurked beneath his skin. Malaki knew one thing for certain.

Ferden was an earth wielder.

The most powerful earth wielder he had ever come across. A twinge of unease stirred in Malaki's gut and an unsettling question took root in his mind.

"What else are you hiding, Lord of Dolinmere?"

CHAPTER 21

The last remnants of the music died away and the bowing actors disappeared behind a curtain of fine, red velvet. Isolde's chest was impossibly heavy and filled with the remnants of the last notes filtering through the air. She clapped in applause and the ghost of a smile tugged at the corner of her mouth.

"What a waste of time and money that was," Gage said, rising to his feet. "Wouldn't you agree, Lady Isolde?"

"Someone with no taste at all would hold such an opinion," Isolde bit back as her anguish hardened into stone. "The world needs beauty. Otherwise what else is there to live for?"

The pads of Gage's merciless fingers gripped Isolde's arm and yanked her to her feet, his jaw flexing. "Is that an insult I heard, Lady Isolde?"

"Not at all," she said, willing herself to not flinch. "I was merely stating that art is a crucial part of society."

"I couldn't agree more," Erebus said, rising from his seat. Gage's hand fell away from her arm, leaving behind only the subtle ache of a bruise yet to form in its wake. "It's for that very reason I allowed this place to remain open after I seized control, along with the palace library."

"How very wise and cultured of you, Your Grace." The words felt wooden in Isolde's mouth, and she knew they sounded just as much.

"The late king was rather fond of the arts, especially when it came to music. I suppose that's why they spent such an extraordinary amount of money on such things and why he named the opera house after his late sister, Orelena," said Erebus, his sharp eyes scanning the stage. "Tell me, Lady Isolde. Is music among the list of talents you possess?"

"No, Your Majesty," she said. "I didn't have the patience as a child to sit still long enough to learn."

A chuckle rumbled from Erebus's lips. "I can believe that entirely."

Gage forced his scarred face into a grin and his cold eyes turned to her. "My fiancée is quite spirited, Your Majesty."

"That she is." Light from the sconces danced across the obsidian band perched on Erebus' brow. "Would you mind if I had a word with her alone, Gage?"

"Not at all, Your Grace," he said, his eyes sliding to Isolde. They said one thing and one thing only. *Behave.* He made to move past her, the planes of his chest brushing her aching arm.

"Oh, and one more thing," Erebus said, bringing Gage to halt. His hand lashed out and constricted around Gage's windpipe. Isolde moved out of the way, pressing against the railing as Gage fell to his knees before Erebus. His face reddened, and power, dark and terrifying, filled his eyes.

"Lady Isolde might be your betrothed," Erebus said, his words laced with frigid malice. "But that doesn't give you the right to lay your hands on her." Gage struggled for air, his mouth gaping open, hungry for the air Erebus was denying him. "If I see another mark or one more bruise, Gage, even after you are married…I will be very, *very* disappointed. Am I in anyway unclear on this matter?"

Erebus thrust Gage's blanching form into the seats, shattering their wooden frames. Cough after cough erupted from his chest, his mouth gaping wide and desperate for air. Heat rose to Gage's cheeks, replacing the purplish tints painted across his face. Splintered wood peppered the fine jacket stretching across his chest and shoulders.

She couldn't hide the shock on her face. The disbelief in what she had heard. But as Gage straightened and forced himself into a bow, she couldn't help but smile inwardly.

"I understand, Your Grace," Gage said, a garbled, strained tone accompanying his voice. "It won't happen again, I assure you." A pointed stare, one signaling his dismissal, was Erebus's only response. A look of hatred, of retribution, spilled from Gage's gaze as he turned and strolled from the theater box.

Liam followed behind, leaving her with the gentle brush of his fingers as he passed. He, along with the others, disappeared into the crowded hallway. Erebus stood at the edge of the balcony, his eyes fixed on the stream of people making their way out of the opera house.

"I have not kept my word to you, Lady Isolde," he said, not turning her way. "And for that, I apologize."

"I'm not sure I understand, Your Grace."

"I assured you Gage would behave himself." Erebus tilted his head towards her, his eyes staring at the doorway. "It seems my warnings went unchecked. Just because you are betrothed to him, does not mean he has the right to treat you in such a manner."

"And yet you condemn me to a life at his side," Isolde retorted. "A lifetime in his bed."

"You condemned yourself," Erebus said, his cold eyes cutting to her. "Words are powerful weapons. More damaging and deadly than a blade could ever dream of being. And you wielded yours with a killer's intent the night of the ball."

The edge of her teeth bit into the lining of her tongue. *Your words have consequences!*

"But even when you are married," he continued, "that behavior will not be tolerated. Especially not when my Left Hand is on the receiving end of such treatment."

"Awfully confident of you to think I will be the victor."

"You have done well, Lady Isolde," Erebus said, his words echoing a hint of calm satisfaction.

"How pleased I am to hear of your approval," Isolde said, her words laced with annoyance. He might have disapproved of Gage's treatment of her, but that didn't erase the decades of despair staining his past.

"I highly doubt that," Erebus said, the hint of a smile peeking over his shoulder. "I invited you here tonight to serve as another trial in your games."

"I thought I was here as Gage's guest. I must be truly special to get a trial of my very own," Isolde said, her guard rising instantly.

"You are special," Erebus said. He turned to look at her and his silver hair glistened in the light of the massive chandelier dangling over the now deserted seats below. "Tell me of your parents."

Nothing could have prepared her for that—especially, not from him. "My parents are of little consequence." The words felt like blades as they tumbled across her tongue.

"Even so," Erebus said, fixing her with his gaze. "Tell me."

Isolde licked her lips and let the words flow. "They were wonderful people. Kind, courageous, and selfless. Everything I have ever dreamed of being. They were killed when I was very young."

The theater was now vacant, save for the few souls who stayed behind to clean. Leaving behind a vast silence that seemed to grow thick in the small theater box. The tips of Erebus's finely polished fingers grazed over the ornate railing. The facets of the ruby ring shimmered on his left hand. "They perished in the siege?"

Isolde let her silence answer for her. The fury burned through her, spilling into a deeper hatred than she had ever felt before. It was a black abyss and all-consuming.

"Lord and Lady Cotheran took you in after the fall," Erebus said. An arrogant smile danced on the corner of his mouth that was far too expressive, far too sensual. Whiffs of Erebus's scent drifted through the air. Steel and rosewood. "I must not have had the pleasure of meeting them. Not that it's a great loss. They were traitors, after all. Deserving of such a fate."

Without a second thought, Isolde let her fist fly. The only thought running through her mind was breaking the smile clean off Erebus's face. Her knuckles collided with a broad, cold palm. Her bones groaned as he squeezed. Not painfully, but enough to let her know she was at his mercy. That he was fully capable of inflicting pain, if he so chose.

"Striking a king, Lady Isolde," Erebus said, looming over her, forcing her back to bend. "Not your brightest move thus far."

"Don't you dare insult my parents!" Isolde seethed. Only a hint of a tremor lingered on her lips as she stared at him in pure, unrestrained hatred. "They were good people. Far better than the likes of you."

Erebus looked into her eyes, and something crossed his face. It was a look of disbelief, of hope, and something else. Light, subtle but ever-present, pierced his cold, steel-gray stare.

"You have passion," Erebus said with a smile that made Isolde's blood run cold. "Passion...spirit....*fire*. They can bring about a great many things...or burn everything you love into ash." The tips of Erebus's fingers tightened around Isolde's closed fist. His fingertips glistened with flakes of frost forming across his skin, invading her own.

A fiery sensation, much like the one from long ago, ignited in her hand. Memory after memory, agony after agony, tumbled through her mind. The beast within, that unstoppable force of sheer power and fury, roared to life. It too remembered, and it shook with fear. Isolde forced herself to be still, to not let the terror show in her eyes.

"You are not the only one your passion might burn. Be careful with how you wield it."

"You almost sound like you know from experience." Erebus's eyes narrowed. The fine shadows of his flawless cheeks ticked as his teeth ground together, accentuating a strong, perfect jawline. He was beautiful. There was no denying such an obvious fact. But a darkness lingered about Erebus. Like a disease, a rot that no amount of time or love could ever remedy.

"What happened, *mighty* king?" Isolde asked, her tone mocking and full of sarcastic sweetness. "Did you fly a bit too close to the sun?"

A growl slithered through Erebus's teeth. Flame and ice merged across her skin as the memories of the past collided with reality.

"My power is infinite," he said, forcing her flush to his chest. It was hard and cold as ice. "It has no limits." Pain crept along her spine, but Isolde kept silent, her anger burning all the more as she stared Erebus down. "If you become my Left Hand, you will bend the knee to me, Isolde." Her title-less name on his tongue felt wrong, so stripped and bare, she shivered at the sound. "You will submit to me! In any way and every way, I see fit."

"Men like you have tried to tame me," Isolde said, yanking her hand away. The touch of his wintery grip clung to her skin. "Your Right Hand is trying right now and failing quite spectacularly at it. None of them lived to tell the tale."

She turned on her heel and headed towards the exit. Her shoes clicked against the marble floor, and her hips swung left and right. She knew exactly what he wanted, what he had planned if she won. And it made her infinitely happy to showcase exactly what would never be his.

"There are no men like me, Isolde," Erebus warned, moving past her. A chill hung in the air as he went, a cold warning for what truly lay beneath. "It would be in your best interest to remember that. Come." The word hung in the air like a command, as if she were being summoned to her master's side. But it was an order, nonetheless. One Isolde could not afford to ignore, even if she wanted to.

Gage and the others who hovered just outside, followed in line as they descended the massive winding staircase. A group of soldiers lingered at the bottom step, each bearing their elithrium weapons to a small group of citizens who had gathered in the lobby.

"Death to the false king!" one man chanted, his viryian eyes glowing.

"False king!" another called.

"Do something about this rabble, *now!*" Erebus growled into Gage's ear, his lip curling into a snarl.

A male pushed his way to the front of the crowd and his hand disappeared into the lining of his cloak. "Traitor!" Twisting to the right, his hand snapped out and a metallic glint caught Isolde's eye.

A dagger cut through the air, its blade sailing past her face, heading straight for Erebus. For a split second, she paused. She could just let the dagger find its way into his beating, cold heart. But then, that would leave no one and nothing standing in the way of Gage killing Tanor and the others.

Reluctantly, Isolde sent a blast of air behind her, knocking the blade aside. Its tip embedded into the wall a mere inch from Erebus's face.

"You dare try to kill me!" He roared. His eyes ignited with a fury, sending a trickle of fear cascading down Isolde's scarred spine. "Traitorous trash."

No warning came as spikes of ice erupted from the floor. Their tips stretched to the ceiling, impaling those who stood in their path. Blood dripped down onto the fine marble floor, freezing where it landed.

"Father!" The lone survivor cried, his eyes swimming with tears. He cupped his father's face in his hands, blood trickling between his fingers. "No…no…no…Father!" But not a sound lifted from his blood-stained lips, and no light lingered in the depths of sightless eyes. "Father, please!"

"Take care of that one won't you, Lady Isolde," Erebus said, straightening the cuffs of his jacket.

She wasn't entirely sure she had heard him correctly. Tendrils of her dark hair brushed the side of her cheek, her eyes darting between Erebus and the male standing in a pool of his father's blood.

"I don't like to repeat myself," Erebus said, and his silver eyes shone with a murderous light. "Kill him *now*!"

Dread boiled in Isolde's gut as she looked back to the male still clinging to his father's corpse. Hating herself with every step she took, Isolde descended the grand staircase.

The male turned his gaze up to her and light filled his eyes, giving Isolde pause.

"Stay out of this," he said, "My fight is not with you!" A hiss carried with his words as she took another step.

"I'm not your enemy either," Isolde said, allowing an ounce of her power to come forward. The ring on her hand felt warm against her skin. "Your life is not worth it. Surrender…please."

His only response was an earth-shattering cry as his hands extended to the bar on the right and curled into a claw. There was no warning for the endless streams of water, wine, and spirits rising from behind the marble countertops. Their tips turned her way and struck. Isolde launched a shield of air in front of her. Liquid of every color rained down, soaking through the layers of her dress.

Isolde hardly had time to breathe before a ribbon of water broke through her defenses and shoved its way down her throat. Her chest instantly filled with water, her eyes bulging in panic. She fell to the ground, her knees striking the marble steps in a painful crack. The sting of pain radiated across her skin that had split open.

"Your Majesty, she needs help!" Liam's voice cut through the fog of noise. "Help her—" A grunt of pain followed.

"You dare order the king?" Gage snarled. He slammed his fist into Liam's stomach again, forcing him to his knees.

"If Lady Isolde wishes to be my Left Hand, Captain," Erebus said, "this filth should be no problem for her."

Panic rose, and every instinct roared to life in Isolde's chest. A gust of wind, solid as stone, shot out from her open palm. It slammed into the male's chin like a punch. Debris rained down on their heads as he collided with the ornate walls she loved so much. The contents of Isolde's stomach spilled out onto the floor, making way for the choked bits of air to slowly return to her lungs.

Children, pureblood by the looks of them, were huddled against the walls. Their tiny eyes, filled with fear, were glowing with a power some of them had yet to harness, had yet to understand. Aside from a virya who had lost control, there was nothing more dangerous than a child who had yet to learn how to control the power lurking beneath their skin.

The soles of Isolde's feet planted on the slippery, marble floor, and she forced herself up right. Under a pile of shattered stone and wood, the water wielder rose to his feet, his eyes simmering with rage. More ribbons of liquid formed and rose in the air at his command. Their tips found their way into the eyes, noses, and mouths of the soldiers' present. A shield of ice erupted around Erebus, severing the ribbon of red wine poised to strike. It painted the floor red like a river of blood at his feet.

"Kill him, Isolde!" Erebus ordered, his eyes burning with molten steel. "As your king, I command it!"

The male's gaze turned to Erebus and erupted with power that set her teeth on edge. With hands curled inward, he forced the water and wine alike to bow to his command.

"Enyalmen damor!" he cried and shoved the might of his power in every direction. The impact threw Isolde backwards. The sensitive, ruined tissue covering her back screamed in pain as she collided with the edge of the stairs. The unmistakable sound of shattering glass rang through the air. Water trickled from the broken windowsills of the lobby entrance and shards of rainbow glass shimmered across the opera house lobby floor.

Isolde forced her feet beneath her, ignoring the barking pain radiating down her back. "What are you waiting for?" Gage said, his teeth bared in rage. "I believe your king gave you an order."

Isolde's eyes shot to Liam who lingered on the top step, his hand still cradling his midsection. Tanor stood behind him. She knew exactly what would happen if she refused. Swallowing the bile building in her throat, Isolde kicked off her ridiculous heels and launched herself into the streets of Elenarta.

Trails of chaos snaked their way through the capital, giving her just enough of a trail to follow.

Perhaps, I can talk some sense into him. She turned left. *Maybe I can sneak him out of the capital…Maybe he's not too far gone.* But all hope disappeared as she veered right. Bodies littered the length of the street. Their eyes were fixed and unseeing. A shade of purple covered their wet lips.

He drowned them all…

House after house passed in a blur. Empty windows and empty doorways. Not a soul dared peer out at the virya sprinting through the streets. Up ahead, Isolde caught sight of the male as he turned left, the light of the moon catching the locks of his ebony hair. She took the turn harder than anticipated, her bare feet skidding across the wet, slick cobblestone.

Before Isolde could right herself, a shot of water collided with her face. Pain ripped through her jaw and neck like the lash of a whip. Blood's coppery taste coated her tongue and trickled down her face. Anger flared to life but instantly dissipated into fear as dirty, filthy street water pushed its way past her lips and filled her mouth.

The male stood above her, his hand outstretched, fingers curled inward. Pain and fire filled her lungs as she tried and failed to catch her breath. Panic rose and spread, blurring every sense of thought trying to cross Isolde's mind. The ring's power charged forward like a stampede. It burned against her skin willing her to use it.

And for once, Isolde didn't hesitate.

Wind tore down the street in an unstoppable gust of fury and might. It slammed into the water wielder, forcing him to drop the hold on the water spearing its way into Isolde's chest. Windows shattered, covering the streets in glittering shards of glass. She dropped to the ground and vomited. Glass bit into her hands, knees, and feet, but she didn't care. Brown water rolled across her tongue in a wave of filth. Disgust and outrage seared through Isolde like wildfire as a final cough racked through her chest.

Forcing herself to stand, Isolde sent a gust of wind across the street, pushing the shards of glass to the side. Making a path for the bringer of death she was about to become.

The stream of blood looked strange against the pale skin covering his cheek and jaw. The light filling his eyes only seemed to grow brighter as he rose. Spiral pillars of water erupted from the Adriam River at his back.

"If death is to be our end," Isolde said, "at least give me the pleasure of your name. I might wish to pay a tribute to the gods on your behalf."

"The gods," the male spat. "What have they done for me or my family except bring misery?" He shook his head, causing droplets of water and blood to pepper the wooden planks at his feet. "I suppose even the whore of the king should know the name of the man who took her life." Isolde simply cocked a brow, her lips set. "I am Piran."

"Quite the confidence you have, Piran," Isolde said. "But I see no value in killing you. That would be a waste, and it's something Erebus wants." Isolde dragged the back of her hand across her mouth. Dirt, blood, and grime coated her teeth, the smell of the water lingered like a foul reminder. "Don't give him your death. Let me help you get out of here!"

"Fine words from Erebus's puppet," Piran said, his teeth flashing into a vicious smile. A strangeness lingered in his voice, one that said he wasn't himself anymore. He was on the cusp of tipping over the edge of no return. "What pretty words you say. Pretty words…pretty face…but false nonetheless."

"I've been called many things," Isolde said. "But false isn't one of them. Erebus is not worth your life."

"And yet you serve him," Piran shot back. "Does that make him worthy of yours?"

"My life is not his," Isolde said, her voice cold and hard as steel.

Piran's smile widened, his eyes glowing with power and madness. "Then why are you chasing me like a bitch who heels on his command?"

Piran moved like the waves of the sea, strong and unrelenting. Spears of water filled the air, their tips pointed directly at her heart. Instinct alone forced Isolde's power forward. A shield of pure, impenetrable air rose around her. The sharp points of the frigid river pelted its impenetrable surface, driving Isolde back along the docks of the harbor.

Exhaustion filled her bones, giving the monster beneath room to stretch, to move, to break free. The ring hummed with power. Its metal warmed against Isolde's wet skin, forcing more, taking more, demanding more. Darkness, cold and irresistible, crept into Isolde's heart as she continued to take each of Piran's blows.

Kill him…kill him!

"Piran!" Isolde cried, over the roar of the wind she forced against the spears of water pummeling her power. The spears that would shatter bone and tear flesh. "Stop this!"

"Defender of the false king," Piran cried. "Death is what you bring!"

"Piran, please!" But her pleas went unanswered. All that remained in Piran's glowing eyes was the need to kill. The haunting realty of a virya who had lost themselves to the savagery of their nature.

"While a wielder cannot transform, they can lose themselves to their power just like we can," Alaric had explained not long after he and Galaena had taken her in. "The power belongs to the gods. To the curse they put upon our kind so long ago."

"Fight it, Piran!" Isolde called, her strength dwindling. "Don't let it control you!"

"You're not like the rest of Erebus's men," Piran said, his cold, calculating eyes narrowed. "You're different."

"I am rather extraordinary."

"And yet you stand at his side." Piran's hands curled into claws at his side, striking Isolde's shield harder. "You do *his* bidding."

Isolde shook her head. "Not willingly."

A sharp hiss sliced through the air. 'Says the girl dressed in a such finery. Says the girl who saved the king's life!"

"It wasn't for his benefit." Isolde's words carried on the back of a punishing gust of wind. "It's not only his life I saved."

It collided with his jaw, shattering the teeth within. Piran coiled into himself as a trail of blood leaked out from his open mouth. Reality hit Isolde like a punch. She knew what kind of threat Piran now posed. It left her with no other choice than to obey Erebus's command.

Piran rained down his fury. Arrow after arrow of water struck the shield. Black spots formed before Isolde's eyes. Tiny fissures snaked their way through her defenses, fracturing pieces as they went. Piran's power swelled, causing a towering wave to rise from the depths of the river.

Shoving against the fear, Isolde pulled from the new, infinite well of power buried within. It spread through her bones, infecting her muscles, and saturating her blood. The wave rose above the dock's railing. It loomed over her, blocking out the light of the moon, casting her in darkness.

"You're quite powerful, Lady Isolde," Piran said, his voice devoid of sanity. "Let's see how deep that power actually goes."

His hands rose above his head, leaving his chest exposed. Isolde struck without hesitation. A wall of air exploded from her palms and hit Piran's exposed chest. A grunt of shocked pain slithered over her skin as he finally relinquished his unforgiving hold on the Adriam River. The wall of water returned to the depths below, bathing Isolde in moonlight.

Piran's fingers clutched at the crushed bone in his chest as he fell to the ground. A new, steady stream of blood breached the corner of his lips and ran across his pale cheeks. She knelt at his side and took in the blow that had destroyed his heart beyond repair.

"I'm sorry," Isolde said, reaching a shaky hand forward. The ribbons of air once filling Piran's lungs worked their way through her fingers and around her wrist. When only a tendril of air remained, Isolde leaned forward and gently laid a hand on the side of his face.

The light flickered in Piran's eyes, giving a glimpse at the man who once resided there. "Enyalmen damor!" he said. His fingers constricted around her wrist, drawing her closer. "Enyalmen damor!"

There it was again. The same phrase the human had used in the village. "What is that?" Isolde demanded, her palm pressing to Piran's face. "Tell me!" But a moment later, the monster within Piran turned its head, and light filled his eyes once more. Blades of water shot up from the side of the dock, their points aimed at her throat.

"Forgive me."

In one fluid jerk, Isolde ripped away the last remnants of air in Piran's chest. The daggers of water fell to the ground with a splash. Lightless pools of soft green looked past her to the sky above. A softness, peaceful and content, lingered on the edges of Piran's face. Guilt, burning and suffocating, swelled in her chest.

"He'll pay," Isolde said. With a shaky breath, she ran a hand down Piran's face and closed his eyes to the world. "I swear to you, I'll make Erebus pay for this."

CHAPTER 22

"I hate the damn snow," Cillian grumbled. His voice, while maimed by the mask covering his face, was still the most beautiful sound in the world to Blyana.

"It's not that bad," she said, slipping through the hole Malaki had made in the side of the mountain face. Fresh snow dusted the opening, leaving behind a powdery white trail. "I rather enjoy it actually."

"You're the one with the second skin of fur. The rest of us are left to suffer."

A chuckle, muffled but still bell-like, bled through the finely tailored mask covering the lower half of Blyana's face. It echoed off the darkened hallway stretching from the left and the right. "So dramatic!"

Cillian's eyes narrowed. "I'm not being dramatic," he said. "I just don't care for the cold is all."

"Thankfully, the snow seems to stay up in the mountains," Blyana said. "At least this time of year. Did you not have winters where you're from?"

Silence hung between them, and regret instantly filled Blyana's gut.

"No," Cillian said, the familiar, haunted tone filling his voice. She knew how he felt about his past. It was a time he would rather forget, much like her own. "Where exactly did Isolde ask us to start, love?" He asked, changing the subject.

"The guards," she said, forcing the guilt away. "Liam said most of them had a universal key at their disposal. If what he said can be believed."

"If Isolde can trust him, so can we, Bly." Her eyes narrowed in annoyance at his petulant tone. "Besides, we got the easy assignment tonight. Find another way into this hellhole and acquire a key. At least we're spared Gage and Erebus's company for the evening."

"Fair point," Blyana said with a shrug.

"We can't use the main entrance," Alaric had said. "Guards are stationed at the gate around the clock. It's more heavily secured than any other place in Elenarta. Apart from the royal chambers in the west wing."

"So, as it stands," Malaki had said, crossing one foot over the other, "we only have the entrance in the Gap of Duron as a means of getting in and out. We need another point of entry."

"Sounds like the perfect project for us, Cill." Blyana's power had stirred with excitement.

"Try to not get yourselves killed." Isolde had sighed, slipping the hideous dress Gage had sent her to wear into place. "Just find a way in if you can. Or someone who can get us a key to the cells."

"We're experts at avoiding death at this point, Isolde," Cillian retorted, the tip of a dagger balancing on the pad of his forefinger. "You're the one going into the den of vipers."

"Don't remind me," Isolde said, tugging at the layers of silk and lace. "Take the main road and keep out of sight."

"What if we want a little excitement?" Blyana asked, a mischievous grin pulling onto her face.

"If you do happen to kill someone," Isolde said, returning her smile—a sight that made Blyana's heart sing—"clean up after yourselves."

"We weren't raised in a barn, Isolde," Cillian smarted, tossing the blade in the air. The hilt landed in his awaiting palm. "Despite what others might think."

Taking a breath, Blyana stepped out onto the ledge and kept to the shadows moving across the stone walls. Echoes of pain filled the putrid air. The sound of cell doors slamming shut bounced off every surface, causing Blyana to flinch. Her hand gripped the hilt of the dagger at her side, and the leather encircling her fingers strained against her hold.

"Choose carefully, love," Cillian said, his lips brushing the side of her cheek. "Every person you kill is another body we have to hide."

"Some might be worth it," Blyana said over her shoulder. "Where should we begin?"

"I suppose from the bottom and work our way up?" Cillian asked, nodding to the railing. "There can't just be one way in and out of this place."

Floor after floor of cells passed by. Blyana kept waiting for one of the prisoners to call out, to make their presence known. But even if they had been seen, not a soul dared or bothered enough to bring attention to them.

At last, Blyana's foot struck the bottom of the pit. A greenish hue, one that seemed to permeate the air itself, sent a shiver down her spine. The mound of elithrium, that seemed to have grown since their last visit, sat fifty feet away. It branched out across the ground, the summit reaching nearly thirty feet high.

Cillian's hands balled into fists at his sides, the leather groaning. "There's no telling how many lives were lost getting this here."

"I'd rather not know," she said. "It might make me more inclined to kill more people than I care to hide."

"Hasn't stopped you before, has it?" Cillian asked, his obsidian eyes twinkling with mischief.

"Not yet."

Off to the left, one of the many doors lining the walls swung open. Red covered its surface, making it appear as if it were covered in blood. For reasons Blyana couldn't understand, a wave of cold dread fell from her spine.

A lone figure emerged from the darkness within. His shoulders, not much broader than Cillian's, were draped in a fine cloak of rich brown suede. A hood was draped over his head, shrouding his face in shadow. Even his hands were covered with a pair of fine leather gloves.

Cries of agony, ones that chilled Blyana's blood, followed in his wake. The shrouded figure turned back to the door, hands trembling at his side. Slowly, they curled into fists that were undoubtedly hard as stone. After a moment, the stranger pushed the door closed, cutting off the unanswered cries ricocheting through the dungeons.

He slid a key into place, his hand bracing against the door. The faintest hint of a whisper carried through the air.

"What did they say?" Cillian asked, tracking the figure now retreating to the main entrance.

"I can't be sure," Blyana said, "but it almost sounded like…'forgive me'." Blyana shook her head. Surely, she hadn't heard them correctly.

"Well," Cillian said, his voice hard. "If he had anything to do with the sounds coming from in there, he has much to be sorry for."

Blyana cast one final look at the door before following Cillian back through the shadows. As they moved, they tried every door they came across. But only the infuriating feel of an immovable lock met their attempts.

"That really might be the only way in," Cillian mused as they reached the tenth floor.

"If it is," Blyana said, her temper flaring. "Erebus might be smarter than we give him credit for. There has to be something else. We have to find…" Her voice died away as a familiar sight caught her eye. A wave of golden hair glistened in the depths of a hood that moved from cell to cell four floors down.

"Cill," Blyana said, tugging him closer to the edge. She pointed a finger to the two figures moving along the dirt-covered floor. Their hands shot out from beneath the confines of their burlap cloaks to toss pieces of bread into the depths of the darkened cells on their right.

"Bly," Cillian said, "is that…?"

"Phontine."

Her sister's face turned, and the light of the torches hanging on the wall caught the planes of her beautiful face. It was her. There was no denying it. The grey eyes, matching her own, burned with a hint of subdued power in the hood covering her head.

"The apple most certainly doesn't fall far from the tree," Cillian murmured.

Terror laid siege on Blyana's heart as a pair of soldiers emerged onto the sixth floor. Weapons, sharp and lethal, gleamed from their sides. Blyana was powerless, utterly useless from where she crept four stories above. Without thinking, she ripped the daggers from her side and turned to the stairwell.

"Bly!" Cillian rasped, his arms constricting around her, wielding her arms to her sides.

"Get off me, Cill!" she snarled, fighting against his hold. "I have to help her!"

"From what I can see, your sister doesn't need our help." Cautiously, he extended a finger forward and pointed. Phontine and her companion shuffled along the shadows clinging to the walls. They slipped into one of the cells that had been left open and closed the door behind them without so much as a sound.

Blyana held her breath, her eyes glued to the soldiers walking past.

Tendrils of power trickled through her body, coating her skin. If Phontine were in danger, there would be no stopping her. Not even Cillian.

But the soldiers kept moving, not giving the cells a second glance. A sigh of relief spilled from Blyana's chest and Cillian slowly loosened his hold, leaving her arms trembling.

"Forgive me, love," he whispered, regret filling his voice. He knew how she felt about being grabbed, about being touched without permission. But she had given him little choice in the matter.

"There's nothing to forgive," Blyana said, raising a hand to cup his face. Even through the layers of fabric, she could still feel his warmth. It radiated from him like the desert sand. But she could also feel the lines of regret cutting across his face. Stretching up, she placed a gentle kiss on his cloth-covered lips then the scar running down his right eye.

"Let's see what my sister's up to."

Upon reaching the landing of the sixth floor, Blyana hovered by the corner of the stairwell and waited. It didn't take long. Quiet as the dead, Phontine and her phantom slipped from the cell. After casting a quick glance around, they continued on their way, tossing scraps of bread as they went.

"I'm betting they didn't walk in through the front door," Cillian said.

Blyana's lips quirked into a knowing grin. "And with that key," she said, nodding to the golden trinket clutched in Phontine's fingers, "they won't need to." The key's golden surface twinkled in the dark like a beacon, filling Blyana with hope.

Cillian's thieving, covetous eyes sparkled. "A one size fits all from the looks of it. Isolde had better get me a new bag of candy for this."

"We need to get back." A voice pierced the air, bringing Blyana to a stop. It was wholly male, soft and melodic. "I'll be missed in the kitchens, and you—"

"Shh," Phontine said, her voice like a knife through Blyana's heart.

"Erebus is at the theater tonight. I have time."

"I don't want to risk you getting caught," the man pressed. "We take enough risks as it is, Phontine. If anything were to happen to you—"

"I'm more than capable of making that decision for myself, Frey," Phontine said, her tone hard and filled with a stubbornness that brought a smile to Blyana's lips. Carefully, she tilted the edge of the blade around the corner. Phontine and the male beside her reflected across the polished surface.

"I know you can care for yourself," Frey said, his lips quirking. "You've proven that more than once." His fingers threaded through her own. "I love you, Phontine. But my love doesn't come without fear for your wellbeing. No matter how annoying it might be." A smile, crooked and charming, tugged at the edge of his lips.

Phontine's hands splayed across his chest. "And that is something I will never take for granted." Light filled her gaze as she looked up at him, into the pools of warm, honey brown that held not a breath of light in their depths.

"He's a human," Cillian whispered. "She's in love with a human."

A torrent of fear and utter happiness waged war in Blyana's heart. Joy for her sister having found someone who would be a light in a world that had only shown her darkness. But also fear for what it would mean if Erebus, or anyone, discovered their secret.

"We've done what we can for today," Frey said, his cautious, lightless eyes sweeping across the dungeon. "Let's not push our luck any more than we already have."

Phontine released a heavy sigh. "Fine." She took a step back and pulled the gilded key from the folds of her cloak. It hung on a stunning chain secured around her neck. "But we get to stay twice as long next time."

"Whatever you wish," Frey said, his lips pressing to Phontine's forehead.

They moved across the blade's surface and disappeared into the dark. After a moment, Blyana followed after the sound of Phontine's fading footsteps until only silence filled the air. Taking a right, she was met with a wall of solid rock.

"A trap door," she said, her fingers grazing across the surface. "A well-hidden one from the looks of it."

"Your sister's just as crafty as you are," Cillian said. "Is this a family trait I should be concerned about passing on?"

"Hardly," Blyana said. "Our parents were farmers who devoted their lives to serving the gods. Craftiness wasn't in their nature." Her heart warmed at his mention of children. Raising a family had always been a desire of hers. To give someone the unconditional love only a parent could. "Apparently many things weren't."

Her past was no secret to Cillian. She had shared her story in what detail she could bring herself to burden him with. He had wanted to know it all. Every dark secret haunting her mind and heart. But there were some nightmares, some memories not even she could bear to relive.

After a time, she had opened up to him about her father bartering her life away like she was nothing but cattle. Using her body, her life, her soul as a means to pay a debt that wasn't her own. The same black hatred that always rose at the mention of her father hardened the lines of his face.

Cillian cleared his throat. "We still need to get the key from your sister, and I would prefer to do it before Erebus returns."

Blyana kept pace as they raced back through the dungeons. Only when the touch of the cool night air kissed her cheeks and the shadows of the palace loomed overhead did Blyana breathe a sigh of relief. Each step was a silent whisper across the marble floors as they made their way through the palace. A small smile played on Blyana's lips, crinkling her eyes.

"What's that smile for?" Cillian asked.

"I was just thanking the stars for blessing me with a mate who knows how to keep quiet," she said, shooting him a look.

A dark, lustful shadow fell over Cillian's face and a grin that had her melting grew. "Only when necessary, love."

A blush spread across her cheeks. "Not as many out and about as usually," she said, her ears straining for any sign of a lone servant or soldier heading their way. But only silence answered back.

"Hmm," said. Cillian, "I suppose with Erebus gone, people are free to do as they please."

"Amateurs," Blyana said.

"Or overly confident, pricks."

"That too," Blyana chuckled.

She took a sharp right and felt Cillian's hand brush her palm "The servants' quarters are this way," he said, nodding in the opposite direction. "Shouldn't we start looking somewhere that's close to Frey?"

"We can't very well approach Phontine dressed like this," Blyana explained, waving a hand at the mask covering her face.

"And you think a pretty dress will make your headstrong sister hand over that key more easily than a mask will?" Cillian asked, his arms knotting over his chest. "At least this way our faces are covered."

"No," Blyana said, fighting the dread of having to see her sister face to face again. To stare into the hatred of one she loved so much. "But I'm not contributing to her nightmares any more than I already have, Cill."

His dark eyes softened in understanding. "Very well," he said. "Real clothes it is then." They burst into their chambers, startling Nan from where she lounged on one of the spare couches. A book was pressed to her chest, one Blyana recognized instantly.

"Don't mind us, Nan," Cillian said, with a wave. "Just breaking into the royal quarters and what not."

"Oh," Nan said, resting back into the overstuffed cushions, her eyes already scanning the pages once more. "Nothing out of the ordinary then." She reached over and grasped the glass filled with an amber liquid from the table.

"What chapter are you on?" Blyana asked.

A coy smile tugged on her withered face. "Seventeen."

"Oh my," Blyana grinned, her face warming. "Wait until you get to twenty-six."

A warm blush spread across Nan's cheeks as a knowing chuckle filled the room, her eyes falling to the page. "Do come back in one piece, or Isolde will kill you both."

"Noted," Blyana said, hurrying to strip out of the cloak and hood. Once dressed, she and Cillian bid farewell to Nan and hurried toward the west wing of the palace.

"Chapter seventeen?" Cillian mused, his brow quirking. "Twenty-six?"

"You already know," Blyana said, her cheeks flaming with memory.

Cillian's teeth raked across his bottom lip, and a wicked, delightful heat filled his gaze. "I might need a reminder later."

Peeking around the corner, Blyana spotted Phontine crossing one of the countless stone bridges. Gone was the cloak and trousers. In its place was a ravishing dress, one made of velvet and black as midnight. It shimmered beneath a line of torches hugging the pillars at the end of the bridge. Waves of golden hair cascaded down her back, brushing the base of her spine. She looked so different from the little girl who used to play in the creek with her on hot summer days. The one who could paint a masterpiece from mud and juices of berries.

How beautiful you are, little sister.

The thought withered and died just as quickly as it blossomed. Phontine's beauty, much like Blyana's, was just as much a curse as it was a blessing. Perhaps even more so.

Phontine paused at a set of pearl-plated doors. Carvings, more beautiful than any Blyana had ever seen, decorated the walls like living art. The Oronilma Mountains had been carved into the flesh of the stone. The entire mountain range spread across the walls running down the length of the corridor. A line of soldiers stood at post, ten to the left and ten to the right. Their elithrium swords were held tightly in their grip. Moving as one, they stepped aside, allowing the king's mistress to pass.

"Not that I'm doubting your impeccable skill set, love," Cillian said. "Or mine for that matter. But twenty soldiers are a rather big ask."

Blyana looked over Cillian's shoulder to an archway leading to a balcony and her smile widening. "We don't need to kill them."

Cillian followed her gaze, and his head shook from side to side. "Please tell me you don't mean—"

"I think you know the answer to that," she said, unable to hide the excitement in her voice. Stepping out onto a nearby balcony, Blyana searched the mountain side until she found it.

"There!" She pointed to another balcony, one she hoped would lead to the west wing.

Cillian stilled beside her, his eyes growing wide as he looked over the edge. "I think I'll take the twenty soldiers."

"It's not that far," Blyana said, her sharp eyes already mapping out where to climb. Balcony after balcony jutted from the mountain's face, serving as their own personal steppingstones. "We'll just need a boost, air wielder."

Cillian's face paled, and she could feel the trepidation. The depth of his fear ricocheted down the bond. She felt it as if it were her own. "Bly, I…I can't—"

"We need that key, Cill," she said, gripping his arm. "It's our only way of getting the others out of here. This is no different than Briarhole."

A humorless laugh lifted from Cillian's lips. "I didn't particular care for that little adventure either." His eyes followed the sheer drop that led down to the river snaking its way through the city, several hundred feet below their feet. "This is not what I had in mind for this evening."

"What, pray tell, did you have in mind?"

"Something with far fewer clothes," he grumbled. "Certainly, not this."

"What was it you said to Malaki?" Blyana asked, her lips turning up into a knowing smirk. "Spontaneity is the spice of life?"

"That was meant for Malaki," Cillian said, his voice flat and filled with indignation. "Not me!"

Blyana rolled her eyes. "It sounds like great advice for you as well. Should I start calling you Papa Bear too, or would you prefer old man?"

A growl rumbled through Cillian's teeth, sending a shiver of delight down her spine. "I am not old, Blyana."

"Of course, you're not," she chided, taking a few steps back. "Just follow me and you'll be fine." She didn't hesitate as she took off into a sprint. Power filled her limbs, driving her forward. Without breaking stride, she launched over the rail and into nothingness. The night air raced over Blyana's skin, bringing a true smile to her face. Danger gave the sense of absolution she craved. Here, her life was her own.

Far too soon, the edge of the next balcony struck her feet, and she rolled into a crouch. She looked back to see Cillian still pacing back and forth. Even from fifty feet away, she could feel the fear echoing down the bond. She raised a hand and beckoned him to follow.

The faintest whisper of his voice carried on a gust of wind. "Damn woman!"

Keeping his eyes on her, Cillian's shoulders rose and fell as a deep breath filled his chest. He took off across the balcony, arms pumping at his sides. Wind rushed past Cillian's face as he leapt into the night air. It wove its delicate fingers through his hair, giving her an unhindered look at his face.

A smile broke out on his lips. It was a smile Blyana had never seen before. She felt his emotions down the bond and her heart swelled. Fearless freedom throbbed between the chain linking them together and Blyana's face split into a grin.

But the smile faded the moment understanding took hold. Terror filled Blyana's heart as Cillian continued to fall. She could see the tips of his fingers would come up short, missing the balcony entirely. There were no words. Only sheer panic echoed down the bond and filled the depths of Cillian's eyes as he reached a hand out to her. A hand she would have no hope of catching.

"Cillian!"

His name fell from Blyana's lips like shattered glass as her mate disappeared beneath the railing.

CHAPTER 23

Isolde took her time in making her way back to the opera house. The last thing she wanted was to return and see the look of smug triumph gleaming from Erebus's face. To see the spark of victory at her obedience.

"Damn it!" she growled, as her sliced heel landed on a stray pebble in the street. A gust of wind leapt from her open palm and swept across the ground, clearing her path of any debris still lingering on the cobblestones. She looked back to the bloody footprints she left behind. "Like a trail of bloody breadcrumbs."

The golden dome of the Renaylie Orelena glistened overhead, welcoming her back. A crowd lingered at the base of the wide, ornate steps. Erebus and his stupidly faithful men waited on the top step. Their feet crunched on the sharp edges of the colorful, broken glass littering the marble surface.

"Well?" Erebus demanded, his brow cocked expectantly. A faint light ignited in his eyes as he took her in. The dress she had worn was now soaked and held tears and nicks along various parts of what little fabric there was to begin with. Still, Isolde was thankful they resided nowhere of consequence. "I take it you took care of the traitor, Lady Isolde?"

"He's dealt with," she said, her head stooping into what could be conceived as a bow. "His body is in the harbor, on the docks."

"Your Majesty," one of the soldiers said, running up the steps. "We have identified the traitor. He is the grandson of one of the jewelers in the city."

"Kill his family," Erebus ordered, his tone as cold as the ice slithering through his veins. His piercing, glowing eyes scanned the crowd still huddled around the entrance. To the few prisoners who remained alive, their arms bound painfully behind their backs. They were held on their knees at the foot of the stairs, glass cutting into their skin. "And let this be a lesson to anyone who dares oppose me!"

Panic and anger swelled in Isolde's chest. She should have known Erebus wouldn't stop at Piran. That his anger wouldn't be slated by the death of just one man.

He stopped before her, and a satisfied smile tugged at the corner of his mouth. "Well done, my little falcon."

Bile rose in Isolde's throat as the freezing tips of his fingers trailed along the inside of her arm. Erebus stilled and his attention shifted to something behind her. Isolde turned to see his eyes following the trail of blood running up the steps—her blood.

"I can't have you injured, Lady Isolde," Erebus said, his jaw feathering. "Go to your Bastard Prince. Have him heal you. If he isn't up to the task, I will find someone who is." Erebus's eyes lingered on the blood a moment longer before his touch disappeared, and he walked away. Tanor followed behind. His sunken eyes remained glued to the ground before him.

"Tanor—" Isolde said, her hand reaching for him. Words filled her throat, words that would do little for the pain she had caused. But a vice-like grip constricted around her wrist before she could reach him, yanking her away.

"No, no," Gage cooed, his grip tight but not enough to leave a mark. "He belongs to the king now. You don't touch what belongs to the king."

"Apparently that rule applies to you as well, doesn't it?" Isolde said. "Because the way I see it, I am Thornwood's champion for now. When I win, I will be the king's Left Hand—not yours."

"Did you forget the part where you will marry me, pet?"

"By the king's order," Isolde said. "Who knows how I might persuade him." Her finger grazed the wide planes of Gage's chest, trailing along his collarbone, and into the dark bruise left by Erebus's hand. "I am quite irresistible after all. And Erebus is unwed. Sounds like opportunity to me. And I must say, he seems awfully protective."

She smiled at the fury brimming in Gage's eyes. His pulse hammered beneath her touch as she leaned in close, her lips nearly grazing his ear. "And I have a feeling bedding a king would be far more satisfying than fucking a Right Hand whose equipment, if the rumors are correct, leaves much to be desired."

Burning rage filled the blue depths of Gage's eyes. "Bitch!" Pain ripped through Isolde's wrist as his grip tightened. Erebus's order was long forgotten…or ignored.

"Lord Gage!" Liam's voice, laced with warning, reverberated across the front steps. "Allow me to escort Lady Isolde back to the palace, sir. I believe the ladies of Marsh Hall were seeking an audience with you."

Gage hardly spared Liam a glance, malice still churning in his gaze. "Very well," he snarled, shoving her away. "Do make sure my future wife gets back safely, Captain." He veered to the group of ladies hovering near the entrance. They flocked to him like a gaggle of geese with tears of fear and falsehood streaming down their painted faces.

"We don't have much time," Isolde said, pulling Liam down the opposite way. "We have to get to that jeweler before it's too late."

Isolde kept a controlled, unsuspecting pace until she reached the mouth of one of the nearby alleys. Pain tore through her feet with every step. As the shadow of an awning crossed overhead, she took off into the night. Only the sound of Liam's steps, sure and constant at her back, met her ears. Drawing on her memory of the area, Isolde took turn after turn, down the familiar streets.

The distinct sound of footsteps, ones clad in armor, echoed through the still, pungent air. She halted at the corner of an intersection, the sound of broken glass piercing the night.

"Everyone up!" A soldier's voice pealed through the night like a death toll. The heel of his boot kicked the small wooden door, ripping the hinges from its frame. A small sign hung above the door.

Mirelda Jewelry Emporium

"What are you doing?" Liam demanded, his chest heaving. Isolde glanced around, her eyes searching for the one piece of security that would protect them both.

A flicker of movement caught her eye one street over. Lines of laundry were draped across the alleyway, connecting the two buildings on either side. Isolde smiled and turned to the soldier at her back. "I'm inducting you into the cadre, Liam."

Isolde sprinted across the street, leaving Liam behind with his mouth hanging open and eyes wide with disbelief. She yanked two cloaks from the line, sending pins sprawling across the ground. Taking the hems, she pulled the silk fabric apart. It gave way to form a makeshift mask and cloak.

"Does your insanity know no bounds?" he asked. "We can't take on a garrison of the king's soldiers!"

"The Lady of Thornwood and the Captain of the Guard might not be able to," Isolde said tossing the garments into his hands. "But for the Hood of Arnoria and her cadre, there aren't not nearly enough."

She fastened the handkerchief around her face and knotted a twine of leather around her hair. The silk felt like water on her bare shoulders as she draped the rest around her back. Cries of fright reached them, pulling her attention back to the shop. One by one, the soldiers dragged Piran's family into the street.

Liam stood dumbfounded, his gaze bouncing from the cloak in his hands and back to her. "Make your choice, Liam," Isolde said, tugging the dagger she kept at her thigh free. "I'm going with or without you." She pushed past him and turned just enough to peer around the corner. Three bodies were kneeling in the remnants of the shattered door, all dressed in their nightshifts. Two girls no older than thirteen were clinging to the side of a male whose eyes were filled with terrified confusion.

"I don't understand," he said. "Lonan and Piran are good men! They work hard and pays what the king demands…We all do!"

"Your son and grandson were traitorous little shits," one of the soldiers said, raising his sword before the man's face. He cowered beneath the deadly glow of the elithrium blade. "They met a traitor's end. Just like you will too."

Power slithered across Isolde's skin, gathering in her palm like a small hurricane. Carefully, she allowed that power to grow. It swirled in her hand, sending gusts of chilled wind across her arms and chest.

The soldier stepped forward, the grip on his sword straining. It glinted in the light of the moon as Isolde shot her power forward. It collided with the soldier's legs, jerking them out from underneath him. Moving like the nightmare she was, Isolde slipped to his side and drove the dagger's tip through his chest. She twisted the pommel left and right, drenching her hand in blood.

The sound of blades colliding filled the night like a symphony of death. Gusts of wind continued to roll across her palms, each one finding its mark like the tips of one of her arrows. Guard after guard fell beneath her blow, their armor dented, and bodies broken. It wasn't long before a wave of exhaustion crashed through her body, forcing a grunt from her lips.

Liam moved like a shadow of terror, cutting through bone and flesh. Blood and death followed wherever he went. It filled the street, painting the cobblestones red. Armor cracked against the stonewalls lining the streets, sending bits of debris falling to the streets below. He moved like death itself, and Isolde couldn't help but watch in awe.

As the final soldier fell at her feet, Isolde felt her control give way. The monster stirred at the corners of her mind. The power coming from her mother's ring hummed with need, with demand for blood.

"Haven't you seen enough?" Gritting her teeth, she forced that desire away, shoving it back behind the wall of confinement in her mind. Taking a breath, Isolde turned to the family huddled together in the sea of broken bodies she and Liam had rained down upon them.

"We need to get you inside," she said, laying a hand on the man's shaking shoulder.

"Who are you?" he demanded, jerking away from her touch. Power stirred within his gaze, the distrust making it brighter. Her own responded in kind, forcing her to bite back a snarl.

"Not here," Isolde said, keeping her temper in check. "Let's take this inside."

The male took one look around at the soldiers littering the streets and nodded. Rising from the ground, he helped the two girls to their feet and led the way into the destroyed shop. Debris and splintered wood covered the floor. Cases, once beautiful and whole, had been smashed into fragments of glittering, jagged glass. It covered the fine pieces of jewelry within like drops of rain.

Isolde's eyes landed on the intricate painting decorating the back wall. Flowers with beautiful white petals surrounded the name while vines wove their way between the letters.

Mirelda Jewelry Emporium
Hayes Roarbilt, Owner

"A beautiful shop you have here, Hayes," Isolde said, running a finger along one of the only cases left untouched. Rubies, of every cut and size, rested in a bed of black satin.

Hayes bristled. "Quite rude for you to know my name but not offer yours in return, stranger."

"Who we are is of no consequence," Isolde said, deepening her voice as best she could. It was strange not having her mask, not having that extra level of security to hide behind. "All you need to know is that Erebus has marked you and your family for death. You can't stay here."

Hayes pulled the children closer. "And where are we to go? This shop is all I have. It has been in my care since the Viribu—" The name died on his lips and a look of fear filled his eyes.

"You can say the name," Isolde said, her tone softening. "We are no friend to Tenebriath, nor do we recognize him as the true king." Liam shifted at her side.

"Many have claimed such notions," Hayes said, his eyes narrowing. "To weed out disloyalty."

"Correct me if I'm wrong, but I don't believe a loyal subject would slaughter the king's soldiers, do you?" Isolde asked, her blood-covered hand sweeping out to the massacre lying just beyond his front door. Isolde didn't miss the slight flinch in Liam's frame. Nor the way his hands curled into fists at his side. "You stood with the Viributhians?"

Hayes' inclined his chin. "Yes, I stood with them. And I always will."

"Even after all this time?" Isolde asked. "After all these years, you still stand with them?"

"I stand for the queen and king who guarded those who could not stand on their own. So yes, I stand with them and their children. Children whose lives were cut far too short for the sake of another man's greed."

"They're dead," Isolde said, her voice flat and hardly a whisper. "You owe them nothing. Ghosts do not collect debts, nor can they save you now."

"Perhaps not." A sly smile took the place of the shadow of sorrow on Hayes's face. "But fate has a way of surprising you. Enyalmen damor."

Isolde stilled. There it was again. The memory of the human in the village who had repeated the same phrase in the face of death echoed Piran's final words. "What does that mean?"

"It means 'in remembrance, we fight'." Light from the fireplace still holding a breath of flame, reflected off the locks of Hayes thin, blonde hair. "It means...'we endure'."

"A noble notion."

It was all the lump in her throat would allow to pass.

A fraction of the tension still resided in Hayes's face at her words, along with uncertainty. "Why did you help us?"

Isolde looked to where Liam hovered in the corner, his eyes downcast to the blood staining his hands. "What happened was not your son's or grandson's fault. Nor is any of this your fault." Her gaze shifted to the children who were peaking around Hayes' back, their eyes filled with tears. "Are they your children?"

"Great grandchildren," he said, throat bobbing. "They are...were Piran's children. And Lonan"—tears shimmered in his eyes—"was my only son."

Licking her lips, Isolde forced the grief away to deal with at another time. "Is there somewhere safe they can go? Somewhere outside of the capital until you can form a plan?"

"I have a sister who lives just outside of the mountain range. Not far but secluded. She doesn't come into Elenarta often so it's not likely anyone would know of her. I'm shocked they knew of me."

"Why is that?"

"I'm a small jeweler, nothing of consequence. If I weren't a full blood virya or if I still owed taxes, my business would have died away decades ago. I know how to keep my head down."

"Can we get them to your sister's place unnoticed tonight?"

"I believe so," Hayes said. "But it'll be costly."

A smirk peaked over the rim of Isolde's silken mask. "I think I can help with that." She disappeared through the door and returned a moment later with bags of coins taken from the dead soldiers. "Payment for disturbing you this evening," she said, setting the bags of coins down on the counter. "Besides, I'd hate for you to part with any of these." Her hand swept to the priceless pieces covered in glass. "Will it be enough?"

"More than enough," Hayes said. He looked back to the shattered door, his head shaking. "But why would you do this?"

"Because I'm tired of seeing the innocent pay for the crimes of the guilty." Isolde said. "Because innocence and truth are still worth fighting for."

Tears filled Hayes's dark green eyes. He wrapped his arms around the girls, hugging them to his side. "How can I repay you?" Her eyes swept the shop until they landed on a piece of equipment in the far back. Moldings lined the tables, along with fragments of gold, silver, and iron.

"Do you only make jewelry?" Isolde asked, her mind turning back to the mines and the problem they now faced with getting the prisoners out.

"I'm an earth wielder with an affinity for crafting metal," Hayes said, with a hint of pride hanging in his words. "I can make anything."

"Could you make keys?" she asked.

"With a proper molding, yes. As I said, I can make anything."

"What about a sum of…let's say…two hundred or so in a relatively small amount of time?" His eyes bulged at the question. "We will pay of course, handsomely."

"I can certainly try," Hayes said. "My sister is a jeweler as well. She'll have the tools I need."

Isolde smiled beneath the mask, her eyes wandering to the small case of jewelry to her left. They were beautiful pieces. Each one unique and precious in its own way. But she had a very particular set in mind. A set Isolde hoped, would bring a spark of light into a world of darkness for someone she loved deeply. As luck would have it, she had all the materials needed. They had stayed hidden in a drawer since her first trial.

"There is something else I would ask of you, Hayes."

"Anything."

Liam kept quiet at the back of the group. His trained, sharp eyes scanned the streets as Isolde escorted the small family, now burdened with all their treasures, to the final stretch on the outskirts of Elenarta.

The soldier manning the gate took one look at the small fortune Isolde offered and let them pass by in the night without a word. A small part of him couldn't believe one of Erebus's soldiers, men he had trained, would compromise their position. All for the sake of coin.

And yet, he could feel the blood of his fellow soldiers on his hands. It had dried a while back, making his skin feel tight and ready to crack.

Isolde led the way back to the gate, and her footsteps, even barefoot and bloody, were sure and light. She came to a stop just short of the palace walls and leaned into a small alcove, her body hidden in shadow, chest heaving.

"I killed them," Liam rasped. Guilt flooded his heart, drowning him from the inside out. The mask felt too tight around his face. He yanked it free, needing the feel of fresh air on his skin. "I killed them, Isolde!"

"*We* killed them, Liam." Isolde shed her mask, and the ghost of a smile caressed her words. "You weren't the only one in that street tonight."

Liam's gaze filled with horrified sorrow and his jaw clenched until pain shot through his jaw. Before he could move, before he could even muster a thought, Isolde gripped the front of his tunic and shoved him to the wall. Her lips met his with such ferocity, with such need, he could do nothing but submit. Desire, hot and demanding pushed through his veins burning away any thought of the consequences or any notion of *what if.*

Isolde's teeth tugged on his bottom lip, unleashing a growl from his throat. The feel of her lips ghosted across his cheek, his jaw…his throat. "We can't," he said, bracing his hands against her hip, forcing her away. "What if someone sees?"

"Stop thinking, Liam." She held his gaze as the tips of her fingers tracked over his torso, his pulse beating beneath her touch. They travelled down to his abdomen …to his belt line. "For right now, the past few hours did not happen. All that matters, is this moment." Isolde smiled as a gasp leapt from his lips as her fingers gripped the bulge between his legs.

"Isolde!" Her name fell from his lips like a worshiped curse—a summoning and a warning all at once.

"Of course," she said, giving him one final squeeze before pulling her hand away, "if you're really that concerned…" He felt her absence like a wound, his skin burning with need. Her absence was a fatality he could not survive.

"Such a tease," he said, pressing her torturous, delicate hand to his sensitive flesh once more. The smug smile she wore made him crave her all the more, made her consume every part of his mind—of his soul.

"Don't think," she whispered, moving her hand up and down in slow, agonizing strokes. His head rolled back as a wave of pleasure cascaded through him, tightening at the base of his spine. He knew what she was doing. Distraction was one of Isolde's many talents, and Liam found himself falling under her spell once again. He was more than willing to fall into the gift she offered and hide from the pain and guilt that would inevitably find him.

"Isolde," he ground out, his hips meeting every stroke she gifted him, demanding more.

"Shh," she whispered in the shell of his ear. "Just let go." Her hand picked up to a maddening, unhinged speed. Just her hand alone could bring him to the brink. But her hand was the last place he wanted to come. Without warning, Liam grabbed Isolde's waist and spun her around. Her backside collided with the wall at the same moment Liam pressed his lips to hers.

There wasn't a piece of her he didn't want to claim for himself. Not a single part of her he didn't want as his own. Memories of when he first saw her filled his head as her lips moved against his. From the moment she entered his life, there was no one else. She had destroyed everything he knew about the world and made it into something beautiful, something filled with light and warmth.

Pleasure, exquisite and intoxicating, filled him to the brim as he pulled back to stare down at her. "Tell me you want me," Liam said, his voice rough and filled with a command he knew she would buck at.

Sure enough, Isolde's eyebrow cocked, and her mouth—that tantalizing, wicked mouth—pulled up into a smirk. "Bossy....bossy," she chided, teeth raking over her bottom lip. "Is that an official order I hear, *Captain?*"

A rumble filled Liam's chest and his lips crashed into hers. Desire and hot need coursed through his veins. "If I were to give you one order," he said. "one that you couldn't refuse, it would be to allow me the honor of ripping this damn dress to shreds. I want nothing of his to touch you—ever again." His hands pushed aside the ridiculous garb Gage had forced her to wear. Malice filled his heart at the thought of that bastard's hands on her, his scent lingering on her skin.

The tips of his fingers brushed the scar at her side. Liam froze as a wave of anger and revulsion crashed through him. Isolde stilled beneath his touch, her breath hitching. "I hate him," Liam growled, his thumb gently stroking her skin just below the crevice, unable to bring himself to touch it.

"Do my ears deceive me?" Isolde said, forcing the mask of humored indifference into place. "Are you confessing to hating your commanding officer?"

"With every ounce of my being."

Hooking Isolde's legs around his waist, Liam felt her deft, sure fingers tugging at the buckles of his britches. A twinge of anticipation raced across his skin, and a kiss of the chilled night air brushed his now freed, hardened flesh. A blaze of heat followed behind where Isolde's fingers treaded. Her touch was infuriatingly featherlight.

"You love to tease me, don't you?" Liam ground out, pressing her into the wall.

"Don't pretend you don't like it," Isolde said, her voice breathy. "Besides, that's what you get when you try to tell me what to do." Her fingertips grazed him again and a hiss slipped through his teeth as sinful pleasure coated his skin. "Pure frustration." Her fingers constructed around him and squeezed before retreating. "Maddening…frustration."

What little remained of his restraint broke. In one fluid motion, Liam pressed Isolde's hand to the rock wall beside her head and thrust forward, leaving nothing at all between them. Her gasp disappeared into Liam's mouth as he pulled back, giving her no reprieve, no time at all. He slammed his hips forward again and the tips of Isolde's nails pierced the flesh of his back.

"Liam!" His name on her tongue burned through him like molten steel.

"Mine," Liam growled, each thrust blossoming into a wave of pleasure. "You…are…*mine*!" He lost himself to her touch…her taste…her body…and the irresistible sounds falling from her lips. Death and shame stood by, not invading what little peace they had found outside the gates of Elenarta.

As pleasure scorched and squeezed its way through her body constricting around him, Isolde's grip tightened as a gasp fell from her open mouth. One final thrust sent them both over the edge of oblivion. Liam rested his head in the crook of her shoulder, his chest heaving, muscles shaking. Isolde shook around him, the aftershock cascading across her skin like ripples on a pond. Her scent filled his head, clogging every rational thought.

A lazy, satisfied smile perked on the corners of her swollen lips. "Admit it. You love to be teased."

Liam smiled. "Only by you."

Begrudgingly, he unwound her shaking legs from his waist and helped her readjust her gown before tugging his britches back into place.

"I wish it would take," Isolde said, her eyes darkening with disappointment. "I wish the bond would form."

That damn bond! The gap between them seemed to grow. The

vastness lying between their hearts felt like a void. Without thinking, his hands found their way to her waist.

"It will," Liam swore, holding her tighter, his fingers digging into her skin, readying himself for the moment he would be forced to let her go. When he would have no choice but to see her at Gage's side. Chained to the bastard who had left her scarred and deformed. Already he missed the feel of her. Missed her touch, her taste. A hint of the scar on her side whispered from the depths of her dress like a hideous, eternal reminder.

"Whether it wants to or not," Liam said, "our bond will take. One way or another, we will be together, Isolde. Nothing will stand in the way of that. I swear it."

CHAPTER 24

"Cillian!"

Blyana hadn't known she could feel fear like this. As if every part of her had ceased to exist.

She leapt onto the guard rail, her eyes wide and searching. If Cillian died, if she were left in this world without him…The thought was unthinkable, unimaginable. But as she looked over, ready to follow him into the depths of Elenarta, his face came into view.

Beams of moonlight caught the faint sheen coating his forehead. She could feel the tendrils of wind his power created kiss her flaming cheeks. Foot by foot he climbed up the side of the mountain, his fingers bone-white and trembling. Each step, each pull was aided by a gust of wind he pulled from his power.

"That's it," Blyana said, her voice strangled with terror. "One step at a time. Just like before."

With one final pull, Cillian latched onto the rail and Blyana dove forward. The tips of her nails sank into the lining of his tunic, refusing to let go. Panicked relief swelled in her chest as her mate tumbled over the balcony's railing, his body trembling.

"If I die," Cillian rasped, forcing himself to stand, "I blame you."

Blyana leaned up and wielded her lips to his shaking mouth with a desperation she knew he could feel. "If you die," she breathed. "I die too."

The gentle brush of Cillian's fingers dusted her cheeks. "Then I should do a better job of staying alive then."

"It would be appreciated," she said, giving him a small kiss before breaking away. "Can you make it the rest of the way?"

"I don't have much of a choice now do I, love?"

"One jump at a time," she said, giving his hand a squeeze. "This time, together."

Cillian followed Blyana as she created a path across the mountain's face, his accuracy and speed growing with each leap. She smiled at the sight of his confidence overshadowing his fear, a fear from his past. The hint of a scar peeked out from beneath his finely tailored jacket. She couldn't help but wonder if the ones responsible for their existence carried the blame for the scars lying within.

At last, Blyana's feet struck the final balcony. It was a wide space, one adorned with exquisite pieces of furniture and marble statues. Keeping close to the intricately carved archway, Blyana tugged Cillian to her side as her fingers slid along the red, velvet curtain filling the doorway and carefully pulling it back.

"There she is!" A male voice cut through the air, silencing the echo of Phontine's heels. "I was wondering where you'd slipped off to."

A beast of a man, one clad in some of the finest armor Blyana had ever seen, stepped away from a set of doors on the opposite side of where she and Cillian lurked.

"I was out for a walk, Titus," Phontine said, with a tone of bored indifference. "Not that it's any of your concern."

"As your personal guard," Titus said, stepping into her path, "where you go and who you are with is very much my concern." He was a good foot and a half taller than Phontine, but it didn't seem to dissuade her in the slightest.

"I take my orders from the king," she said, making to move past him. "Not his babysitters."

Titus shifted to block Phontine's way again. "You would do well to remember I report to him. And who knows what might fall on his ear." He reached a hand forward and pinched a lock of Phontine's hair. A crooked smile formed on his stubble covered face.

Blyana's fingers wrapped around the hilt of the dagger secured to her thigh. She felt the warm press of Cillian's hand at her back, his chest humming a vicious growl.

"And you think he'll believe you?" Phontine asked, her freshly painted lips pulling into a cocky, sarcastic smile. To anyone else, it would have appeared genuine. But despite all these years, Blyana knew what lay beneath. Fear. It was etched into the set of her mouth, the glow in her eyes.

"He has before," Titus murmured, his gaze roving over every part of Phontine before nodding to the rest of the soldiers stationed along the walls. Without question, they turned on their heels and marched through the door. It closed behind them with a deafening click. Blyana shifted to the right, moving the curtain just enough to slip through.

"When the last of his whores didn't fall in line," Titus said, stepping into Phontine's space, "I made sure another one was put in her place." Red coated Blyana's vision. The hilt of her dagger felt slick against her palm as she pulled it from the sheath.

"You are a favorite of his, Phontine," Titus said, sliding his hand along the back of her neck. Phontine stiffened, her hands pressing into his chest as he tugged her forward. "But you are replaceable. So why don't you be the good little whore Vara trained you to be and do as you're told."

And as Titus's lips crushed Phontine's, Blyana's power exploded.

The tip of her dagger sank beneath the lining of Titus's chest plate, severing his vocal cords. Cillian shifted to the right and ripped Titus's hand free of Phontine's neck. The sound of shattering bone filled the air. A mangled mess of skin and bone was all that remained of the dying soldier's hand.

"What the hell?" Phontine gasped, her dress now soaked in Titus' blood. Her eyes were wide and filled with light as she took them in. "Blyana!"

The sound of her name broke through the haze of fury. It shattered the bloodlust coursing through Blyana's veins at the sight of her sister's horrified, blood-speckled face. "Phontine..."

Titus fell at their feet, his hands grasping at the jagged wound splayed across his throat. Blood bubbled to his lips as he reached a hand to Phontine. She jerked back with a snarl. He fell to the floor, his fingers outstretched as if still trying to reach her.

"I suppose this isn't the best time to introduce myself," Cillian said, shoving a hand through his hair, his eyes still glowing with power. The same charming smolder he wore the day Blyana came to Thornwood fell into place like a mask.

Phontine's eyes blazed as they lifted to Blyana, who licked her lips, her blood-stained fingers twisting into knots. "Phontine, this is Cillian. He's my—"

"Does it look like I give a damn what he is?" Phontine spat, not bothering to give Cillian a second glance. "How did you get in here?"

"Took a wrong turn," Cillian said, his smolder shifting into a sarcastic grin.

Phontine's eyes narrowed, her teeth flashing. "And look at the mess you've just caused me," she said, waving a hand at the dead guard at her feet. "What am I supposed to do now?"

"We'll take care of it," Blyana blurted out. "You don't need to worry about that. I just couldn't stand by and watch him—"

"Watch him what?" Phontine spat.

Blyana couldn't bring herself to the say the words. To voice the horrible fate Phontine had just escaped from. "You're taller than I thought you would be," she said, her hands wringing together. The cooled layers of blood covering her hands brushed against each other. She felt the foolishness of her words even as they left her mouth.

"That's all you have to say?" Phontine let out a harsh, humorless laugh. "After all these years?"

Blyana's finger scrapped against the tattoo on her left thumb. "I just meant…You look so different than the last time I saw you…at home."

"That was a long time ago, in a life that no longer exists. I have no home." Phontine's words were as dead as the haunted look in her eyes.

"Yes, you do!" Blyana said, her voice pleading.

"Don't tell me. At your *precious* Thornwood?"

"Yes, at Thornwood," said Cillian. "You have a home there, if you want it."

"Oh, it's that simple, is it?" Phontine's nose flared. "And just how to do you propose to make that happen? Do you actually believe Erebus will just let his *gift* from Vara go free?"

"We won't leave you behind," Blyana declared, her voice ringing with promise. "I've already talked it over with Isolde and she gives you her word. There is no surer thing in this world than that."

"How can you be so certain?"

"Because it was Isolde Cotheran who saved me," Blyana said. "She took me from the House of Pleasures, from that hellhole. She gave me a home, and she wants to give you one too. I trust her without question."

Phontine's face hardened. Decades of hurt and loneliness shone in her eyes. "How lucky for you, Blyana, to have someone who cares that much about you."

Blyana stared back at her sister and realization dawned.

"You think Isolde chose to not save you, don't you?" She asked. "That we chose not to come for you?" Phontine looked down at her hands, her fingers twisting into knots. "We thought you were dead, Phontine. I was told you were killed—"

"And yet you didn't come to Vara's to check for yourself, did you?" Phontine's voice was laced with hurt, with blame Blyana could not escape from. "No, you were too busy living in the lap of luxury with that spoiled bitch from Thornwood."

"Do not speak ill of her," Blyana growled. The spotted leopard beneath her skin growled in her mind, its teeth bared. Even Cillian tensed, his jaw ticking. "Isolde is as much my sister as you are."

"Yes, the protection of the heir to Thornwood. What a prize that must be. Well, former heir, I should say." A cold laugh chimed from Phontine's throat. "You should know, if Isolde wins this tournament, she will be nothing but a minion to Erebus, wife to the Right Hand, and the plaything for both. Tell me, does she know Erebus is rather particular in how he likes to be pleased? That certain things will be expected of her? I might even have to teach her a thing or two or perhaps he will send her to Vara for a while—"

Blyana snapped and her hand slashed through the air before she knew what was happening. A fierce anger, one Blyana hadn't felt in so long, burned through her veins as she shoved Phontine against the wall.

"I haven't made myself clear enough for you, Phontine," said Blyana, the heel of her hand pressing into Phontine's throat. "I am not the same girl you remember. Don't put me in a position to show you just how different I am."

Hurtful disbelief shone in Phontine's eyes. It was a pain that tried to soften the edges of Blyana's resolve, to curve the anger burning through her veins. But she refused to yield to it.

"I meant every word," Blyana said. "We won't leave you behind. But I'm warning you now. Do not *ever* disrespect Isolde again. Have I made myself clear on this point?"

A shuddering breath broke through Phontine's rosy lips as she straightened herself beneath Blyana's hand. Resolve found its way into her eyes. "You certainly aren't the sister I remember."

"No, I'm not." Blyana let her hand drop. "The girl you remember died long ago."

"Seems like we have something in common after all."

Phontine didn't give Blyana a second look before turning her back and continuing on her way. The scent of lavender and blood hung in her wake.

"Get rid of that," Phontine called, pointing to Titus's dead body before slipping into her assigned rooms, and slamming the door.

Blyana stood frozen, completely at a loss for what she had done. Cillian was there at her side before the overwhelming wave of sorrow crushed her. His deft, gentle fingers plucked the blade from her trembling hands and slipped it into his pocket. She hadn't realized she had moved it into the opposite hand, the one that hadn't bore down on her sister's throat.

"It's alright, love." His lips pressed to her temple. "It's alright."

Blyana shook her head, causing a curtain of hair to fall between them. "I don't think so, Cill," Blyana said. "With her temper and stubbornness…forgiveness is impossible."

Cillian gently brushed her hair aside and tucked it behind her ear. "You know what I say about impossibilities."

The ghost of a smile tugged at the corner of her mouth. "Impossibilities are opportunities that haven't been given the chance to happen yet."

"That's right." Cillian's warm lips pressed to her forehead. "Let's get this cleaned up."

When their feet landed back on the balcony of their chambers, Nan was nowhere to be found—nor were any of the others. Blyana's body ached from lifting Titus's carcass. Luckily, he had fit perfectly through one of holes in the privy stationed in the west wing. Blyana had smiled as the sound of his body hitting the soiled, shit-filled water echoed up through the dark. By some miracle, the finely crafted armor and the many layers underneath, had concealed most of Titus's blood, leaving the velvet carpet for the most part, unstained.

"Productive night," Cillian said, pouring himself a drink from the bar. The warm, sharp smell filled the air, giving her a sense of home. Blyana leaned against the desk and sighed.

"Almost," she said. "We didn't get the key."

"Are you so sure?" Shifting his glass, Cillian dug into the pocket of his trousers and plucked the golden key from within. It dangled before Blyana's eyes on a fine gilded chain.

"How?" she gasped, snatching it from his hand.

"That bastard's hand wasn't the only thing I pulled from your sister's neck," Cillian said, swallowing back the contents of his glass in one gulp. "You know multitasking is one of my better skills."

Blyana smiled down at the key, her cheeks warming. "We'll need to get this back to her," she said. "Sooner rather than later."

"We will," Cillian said. "Although, I'm leaving that particular chore up to the other two in our group. And I expect *two* bags of candy for my efforts."

Blyana wound her fingers through the delicate chain, the metal cool on her blood-stained skin. She fought the sadness, fought to hide the hurt she knew Cillian would see, could feel.

"What a demanding thief you are, my love."

She ran a hand over his stubbled cheek before she made her way to their bedroom. The lavish four poster bed, covered in rich, silver satin stood in the center of the room. There was nothing she wanted more than to crawl into it and lose herself to the dark abyss of her own thoughts.

But before Blyana could take a single step, her mate stepped up behind her and plucked the golden key from her fingers. Even through the layers, she could feel his warmth. Cillian's arms constricted around her waist, tugging her flush to his chest. The unmistakable scent of the sun, wind, and warm spice filled the air. Like an afternoon breeze in the height of summer.

"You're not permitted into your own head tonight," Cillian whispered, his deft fingers tugging at the strands of her corset. Despite his words, darkness crept into the corners of Blyana's mind. Its fingers constricted around her heart, squeezing away the joy he brought.

But Cillian refused to let that happened. Refused to let Blyana stand in her own way of happiness. Refused to let the shadows have what was his. "As pretty as that mind of yours is, I want you to myself tonight." His lips grazed the shell of her ear, his warm, spiced breath spreading across her skin. "If you'll have me."

Blyana reached up and ran her fingers along his jaw. "I will never not want you, Cill."

She allowed him to pull every piece of clothing from her body. It was Cillian's way of protecting her. His way of guarding her from the thoughts and guilt that would inevitably find their way to her. He took a cloth from the table near the armoire and dunked it into a basin of cool, clean water. Gently, he scrubbed away Titus's blood.

The cusp of heartache came for her again, forcing a shuddering breath from her lips. "No, Blyana," Cillian said, his lips brushing her bare shoulder. Pebbles bloomed on her skin at his touch, at the sound of her name on his tongue. "Me," he whispered, his lips trailing her skin, his warm breath chasing away the chill of her own despair. Tendrils of love, warm and whole, traveled down the bond. "Think only of me." The tips of his fingers caressed over her lower abdomen.

Desire blossomed in Blyana, burning a trail to her core. It was still an odd sensation, even now. One that had taken years for her to trust. But with Cillian, with her mate, she could enjoy that sensation again. There was no one else she could ever be with. No one she would trust in this way ever again.

Bits of clothing found their way to the floor until nothing except air stood between them. His lips traveled over her shoulders, never straying from the boundaries she had set in place. It had been a process, one that took time and a lot of patience on Cillian's part as Blyana had shown him long ago where his touch was wanted and where it was not. He followed her lead as she led him to the bed, his fingers entwining with hers. The feel of his eyes on her made the need all the more urgent.

"Eyes only on me," he said, carefully pressing her into the bed.

There was nothing Blyana loved more than to feel Cillian's body against hers. To feel how perfectly they fit together. It was as if everything was right with the world. That nothing and no one would ever harm her again. Joy and pleasure, painted on by Cillian's expert touch, covered every part of her as he slowly made them one flesh.

A twinge of fear, old but still ever present, ever poisonous, leaked into her heart. The hint of a memory touched her mind as Cillian moved, each thrust bringing a mixture of exquisite pleasure and rising panic along with it. A face, one she feared and loathed, threatened to break through the fog of joy, to steal away this moment.

Before it could take root, a growl whispered through Blyana's teeth, and she wrapped her legs around Cillian's waist and squeezed. His obsidian eyes flared, and she twisted his hips to the right, putting him on his back in an instant. She landed on top of him, sending a spike of sheer ecstasy through her core as every inch of him embedded to the hilt.

"That's it, Bly," Cillian rasped, as he met her thrust for thrust.

"Take control, love."

A gasp fell from her mouth as her fingernails dug into his chest. This was what she craved. The power, the sense of control that had never been afforded to her before him. The kiss of Cillian's power brushed her face, and a gentle breeze pushed the strands of her silken hair back. His dark eyes stared up at her, desire burning in his gaze.

"Eyes on me, love," Cillian said with a smile, wicked and full of the most the delicious temptations. Sweat shone across his chest, highlighting his perfection. The scars glistened beneath her palms. And Blyana could only marvel at him. At the male who had endured this and could still find the will to love as he did.

Cillian's hands, callused and tender, moved along her hips, blazing a trail of fire across her skin to her breasts. Another bolt of pleasure erupted from within, driving her to move faster, working him the way she knew he liked and in a way she needed.

"Yes, Bly," Cillian growled, his grip tightening. But never painfully, never beyond what he knew she wanted. "Take what you want."

Blinding, sweet agony blazed through Blyana's core as pleasure erupted along her spine. A cry lifted from her mouth as Cillian continued to move, coaxing every bit of pleasure from her he could.

Blyana was only given a moment of reprieve before Cillian's pace picked up again, his hips thrusting and grip tightening.

The wave of pleasure ebbed and still Cillian didn't stop. "Cill!" She breathed, as the pressure built again, her heart racing. "Cill, what—"

"Did you not call me an old man earlier, love?" A wolfish grin spread across his face. "Besides, you know I never stop at one." His hands slid down to her waist and began moving her back and forth, creating a delicious friction. A gasp lifted from Blyana's lips, and her core tightened.

"Old man, am I?" Cillian's thumb grazed over the most sensitive part of her in quick, torturous circles. In an instant, blinding ecstasy shot up Blyana's spine. Her muscles quivered and tightened around every inch of him.

"Gods, Cill!"

Her name, carried by a growl, ripped through Cillian's teeth a moment later. "Bly!" His arms came to wrap around her, his muscles shaking and chest heaving. Sated and filled with nothing but joy, Blyana smiled...truly smiled. In a way only Cillian could bring out.

"I can't imagine anything better than that, love."

He moved a lock of hair from her face, and the touch of his lips brushed her brow. The palm of his hands caressed her skin, refusing to let her move, refusing to let them be anything but one in that moment.

"You're perfect," Cillian whispered, his lips trailing along the sensitive skin under her chin. It was in moments like these when Blyana actually believed him, that she was entertaining the notion she wasn't someone Vara had ruined and left unfit or unworthy of love.

"I love you," Blyana whispered, turning her head to rest over the rapid beat of his heart.

"Not as much as I love you," he teased, running his fingers up and down her spine.

"That's debatable." She laughed, turning her face to kiss his bare chest. Small scars stood stark white against his glorious, tanned skin. It had always reminded her of a sunset. "I wish you would tell me what these are." Her lips trailed over the marks she had seen so many times before. "You know all of mine. It's only fair I know yours."

Cillian's eyes darkened, and his gaze fell to where her fingers lingered. Muscles coiled beneath her touch and a sharp breath filled his chest. "One day," he said, his voice grated, as if the very idea of sharing his past pained him. His eyes turned to her, black and as beautiful as a cloudless night. "One day I'll tell you everything, love. I promise."

She wanted to press him further, to demand to know who made

those marks on him. But Cillian had never forced her into talking. Never demanded anything of her, other than honesty. She saw a similar pain echo across his face and did the only thing she knew he needed in that moment. She nodded and kissed the scar over his heart. The one that was longer and deeper than all the rest.

"In your time," she said. "Only in your time."

CHAPTER 25

Hollow.

That was all Zibiah felt from the small shards of elithrium festering beneath her flesh. They had been there for so long she couldn't remember a day without their agonizing presence. Their points burrowed so deep they felt as if they had become a part of her. Every breath was a wave of agony riding on the necessity to survive.

She tugged on the chains holding her in place. Not even the shackles at her ankles had been taken away. Not that she could escape, let alone stand, even if she wanted to. They had left no room, no chance for their prize to escape.

Freedom, the one hope she had clung to, hovered at the corners of her mind like a nearly forgotten dream. The days trickled by, and that once shining beacon of hope was now slowly fading into darkness, dying little by little. Just like her.

Still Zibiah continued to fight. Just as she always would. Just as her father had taught her.

Pain does not control you; death does not hold you. Her father's voice brushed the corners of her mind, like the waves upon the shore she missed so much.

But there was so much pain. It carved, sliced, and burned through her very being, taking piece by piece as it went. Tears, or the memory of them, stung in the corners of her eyes. A time had come and gone when she didn't believe herself capable of crying anymore. That the tears allotted to her in this life had been spilled and stained the cold, stone table beneath her.

Zibiah flinched as the door to her cell swung open. Footsteps, quiet and light, filled the darkness around her. Tremors of fear, of memory at what footsteps now meant in her world, rolled through her at the sound.

"My lady?"

Zibiah knew that voice…She knew she did. But a fog of agony clouded every thought, making it impossible to think of anything else.

"Zibiah?"

Something inside her heart stirred at the sound of her own name. She had heard it plenty since her arrival but never in this way. Never in this tone—soft and alluring. His voice was deep and rich. Like a ripe berry on a hot summer day, sweet and incredibly irresistible.

Zibiah forced her eyes to open only for them to be slammed shut again. The torch from the wall sent a bolt of burning pain through her head. They had kept her in the dark so long, a simple flame was unbearable.

The sound of shuffling feet echoed around her, along with the distinct hiss of a flame's death as the torch was thrust into a bucket of water. Darkness enveloped her again, and she breathed a sigh of relief.

"Forgive me." He was much closer now, his breath brushing her ear. "I should have known."

Zibiah opened her lips to speak but found her throat too sore and raw for words. The echoes of her screams filled her mind. They had implanted her again that day. Or was it yesterday...or the day before? Zibiah felt the cold fingers of sorrows grip her heart. She had no idea how long ago it had been. The loss of even just a shred of reality nearly shattered her.

"Here," he said. "Drink."

Zibiah felt the rim of a cup at her lips. The cool touch of water shocked her awake with an uncontrollable thirst. Her wrists fought against the shackles, her fingers reaching forward, desperate to grasp the cup for themselves.

"Easy," he said in a gentle whisper. "I don't want you to get sick."

After a moment, her dark savior pulled the cup from her still dry mouth. She felt her lips pull back into a snarl, but no sound came. Not an ember of power filled her chest. It was if a piece of her was gone or permanently silenced.

"I will come to you when I can," he promised. "With food and water."

Confusion filled Zibiah. She tugged at the chains in her wrists, rattling them in a wordless command.

"That I cannot do. Not yet, anyway."

"Who are you?" The words felt like sandpaper sliding over a fresh wound at the base of her throat.

Her phantom fell silent. Quiet darkness filled the void. She worried he might have slipped out, leaving her alone in the dark once more. But after a moment, Zibiah felt the gentle pressure of fingertips caressing her brow. She had been touched by so many she should have been repulsed. But his voice filled her with a feeling so foreign she didn't understand it.

Beauty...power...and something else entirely. A small thread tugged in the center of her chest, so small she nearly missed it. But it was there.

"I am no one." His voice was soft and filled with a quiet pain. Zibiah turned her head towards him. Her tired eyes searched the dark, wanting nothing more than to see his face. It was hidden beneath a hood. A hood not so different from the one she had worn once upon a time, in a world that seemed so far away.

"Tell me," she begged.

A heavy sigh filled the cell, and the tips of his fingers grazed the side of her bruised face. His touch was as warm and gentle as the waves of the Sea of Calca, of her home. "I am someone who should have acted when they had the chance. I am the reason for your suffering. You should hate me, Lady Zibiah."

A gasp spilled from her lips. Realization dawned like the break of a new day. It was the way he said her name. She had heard it only once before, at the library in Briarhole, from the lips of a soldier of Endurmure.

But once had been more than enough.

His face filled her mind. Handsome and kissed by the sun, eyes dark as a night sky, yet so bright and full of life they were impossible to forget. Even his scent, sunlight and dark spice, filled Zibiah's heart with a hope she had not dared to trust until now.

"Eryx!"

CHAPTER 26

Dark clouds hung over the arena like an omen. Isolde felt their weight on her shoulders with each step she took. Exhaustion filled her limbs like liquid lead. She had spent a fair amount of time the night before in the outskirts of the capital at the small cottage hiding Hayes and his family.

"It will take me a few days," Hayes had said, studying the golden key Blyana and Cillian had lifted from Phontine. "Along with the additional order you placed."

"We don't require them at the moment," Isolde had said, her hood and mask firmly in place. "Just before the final trial is to take place. However, we do need to return that particular key as soon as possible."

"I'll make the molding and a copy now," Hayes had said with a smile. "I can imagine the owner is most anxious to have it back."

He had no idea just how right he was. Once the copy had been made, Isolde followed the path Blyana and Cillian had taken and placed the key on Phontine's pillow. She had tried to ignore the sounds coming from the direction of Erebus's chambers. But even as the muted afternoon's rays shone down on her freshly braided hair, Isolde felt a well of rage settled in her bones at the memory.

Buer led the pack onto the gravel covered ground where the Master of Games waited. "Good afternoon champions," Lenox said. A dull shine highlighted the missing patches of hair on his head. "His Majesty will be with us momentarily."

The inner walls of the arena were lined with soldiers. Each one held a spear in their right hand and a shield in the other. Kyros stood to her left. His normally charismatic face was etched in stone.

"Brooding isn't your look," Isolde said.

"All looks are my looks, Lady Isolde," he said, the hint of a smile tugging at the corner of his lips. A cheer broke out from the crowd, drawing Isolde's attention to the dais. A light grey jacket and pair of finely tailored pants were molded to Erebus's form. A regal smile, both sharp and alluring, shone from his face.

"At the last trial," Erebus said, his voice carrying over the arena, "we put our champions' skills to the test. They showed their abilities with weaponry necessary for the title of being my Left Hand. Many strengths were shown, but so were weaknesses."

Isolde looked around to the others. A muscle ticked in Kyros's jaw. Gawen looked between the champions, his hands shaking. Sohan shifted his weight from one foot to the other and crossed his arms over the wide span of his chest.

"My Left Hand cannot be found wanting in any area. The life of this very kingdom could potentially depend on the rise and fall of a blade." Erebus snapped his fingers, and one of the grates to their left rose. From the depths of the tunnels, a group of humans came forward. Each carried a single weapon. Their blades were sharp but mercifully lacking in the familiar elithrium hue.

"Yesterday highlighted your shortcomings," Erebus continued as the humans came to stand before them. One for each champion.

"Today we will see how well you overcome those vulnerabilities." The poor girl in front of Isolde was holding a longsword. It was entirely too big for her tiny frame. Her arms shook under the weight, and her sunken eyes were down cast. But Isolde knew her instantly.

"Nyla!"

The little girl from Briarhole looked up through the stands of her blonde hair. A fresh scab covered a slit on her small, bottom lip. Isolde couldn't believe the change. She had been thin at Briarhole, but nothing like this.

"Nyla." Isolde's voice cracked as she inched closer, her hand outstretched.

Sohan cleared his throat, and she glanced up just in time to see him give a subtle, warning shake of his head. Hardness lingered in his gaze sweeping the row of humans before them. To the untrained eye, he would appear indifferent, passive to the suffering standing at his feet. But Isolde knew better. Anger, much like her own, lurked in his piercing gaze. The pad of his hand covered the fist forming on the other as that gaze fell on Nyla.

"You will all fight today," Erebus said, drawing Isolde's hate-filled eyes. "You will fight until the person you are facing is no longer a threat to the kingdom…or to me." His eyes scanned the line until they at last stopped on Lenox. "Master of Games."

"Thank you, your Majesty," Lenox said with a bow. He stood before Buer with a bag held out. "There are six stones, each painted one of three different colors. Whatever stone matches your own will be the one you will face in combat."

Buer's eyes shifted to Isolde. A sick smile formed on his face as he pulled his fist from the depths of the velvet bag clutched between Lenox's hands. A red stone sat in his meaty, callused palm.

Next was Demir, who retrieved a yellow stone. A small sigh of relief pushed through Gawen's chest as he pulled a pale, blue stone from the bag.

"Looks like it's you and me, Demir," Kyros said holding up the second yellow stone between his thumb and forefinger. "Do try to not get my face. The ladies of Marsh Hall wouldn't be too happy with that." Demir merely looked away from him without a comment. His eyes were forward and face neutral.

Sohan reached in next and extracted the last remaining red stone. The lines of Buer's face crinkled into a scowl.

"Don't look so disappointed, Buer," Isolde said with a smirk, plucking the remaining blue stone from the bag. "It wouldn't have ended well for you to face me anyway. I'm saving you the embarrassment."

"For a woman of such noble upbringing," Buer snarled, red finding its way to his cheeks, "you don't know how to keep your mouth shut."

"Being quiet was never my forfeit."

"Clearly," Kyros murmured, sending her a wink.

"Red, yellow," said Lenox, his eyes turning to Isolde with a sneer. "Then blue."

"As you wish," she said, with a mocking bow of her head.

Buer stalked to the human and yanked the bow and quiver heavily loaded with arrows from his arms before shoving him to the ground. The man fell with a groan as a billow of dust filled the air around him. Isolde kept her face neutral. But the echo of a snarl filtered through her clenched teeth.

"The rest of you to the sidelines!" Lenox ordered. The humans, including Nyla, migrated to the far end of the arena, their weapons in tow. The crowd clamored Isolde's name as she approached the wall. Biting back the bitterness, she sent a wave and smile to them in response. Gawen took the spot beside her, his eyes downcast.

"It's just a test," she said, doing her best to keep her voice calm. "Another trial to entertain the masses, nothing more."

A slight nod was Gawen's only reply, followed by an audible bob of his throat. It didn't escape her notice where his weakness lay. She heard it during the second trial. "The longsword's the least fun anyway."

A shy smile broke out onto Gawen's face. "It's certainly not my favorite." His eyes rose to the stands and landed on Milt. He was standing at the bottom level of the arena, not at all where the Lord of Harrow Hall should have been sitting. His hands were planted on the railing, knuckles white.

Isolde met his eye. They seemed to say only one thing. *Please don't hurt him.* She shot him a wink and a small, reassuring smile. A look of relief fell over his face, and his grip on the railing relaxed as he nodded in return.

The sound of a gong shook the air and the two massive virya in the center of the arena collided. Buer had forgone the bow and quiver. Tossing them to the side, he landed a punch on Sohan's chin, forcing him to take a step back.

Isolde looked to the crowd. So many had come to support their champion from the territory of Dolinmere. All but its lord. Ferden's absence lingered in the crowd like a blot of ink on paper. A bubble of furious irritation swelled in her chest.

Why is he not here for Sohan? she wondered, her arms crossing over her chest. *Better yet, why do I care?*

The heel of Sohan's boot dug into the gravel, and the edge of one of his throwing knives grazed the length of Buer's arm.

"You better savor that," Buer snarled, whipping away the waterfall of blood running across his skin. The cuts healed nearly instantly, leaving behind nothing but a smear of blood. He came at Sohan again, his arms jutting out to the side.

Isolde's eyes widened as a tower of earth and gravel erupted from the arena floor on either side of Sohan. A pair of jaws, filled with jagged bits of rock, cracked open into a vicious snarl.

"An earth wielder," Gawen said, his voice shaking.

Isolde nodded, unease pooling in her gut. "A damn powerful one from the looks of it."

Buer thrust his arms toward Sohan, and the towers of sharpened rock obeyed his command. Shoving his foot back, Sohan darted out the way of the first blow and extended his hands towards the banks of the Adriam River. Streams of water breached the lip of the arena and drifted through the air to form one massive column of water. It collided with the towering spiral of earth looming above. They clashed like a clap of thunder, the sound echoing through the arena.

Buer dodged the spears of water and drove his fists into Sohan's sides. Grunt after grunt of pain spilled from Sohan's lips. Protecting his head, Sohan reached out to the water soaking into the arena floor and sent it hurtling towards Buer's face. The spear of putrid water knocked him to the ground and shoved past his lips. Sohan slowly rose to his feet, his breathing shallow and labored. The sympathetic echo of pain resonated with Isolde's ribs as he clutched his side.

With a furious roar, Buer slammed his fists in the earth, forcing a tremendous amount of power into the blow. The ground cracked beneath Sohan's unsteady feet, the vibration making it nearly impossible to stand. The crater split the ground, sending gravel and dirt into the darkness below. She wasn't even sure Malaki was capable of such a feat. A huff of exhaustion spilled from Sohan's lips as he cleared the crater and landed, tucking and rolling as he went.

Turning on his heel, Buer darted for the quiver of arrows discarded across the arena floor. Sohan cleared the distance in three strides and wrapped his massive arms around Buer's middle, driving them to the ground. Sohan's iron-like fists laid into Buer's exposed ribs. Each strike echoed with the unmistakable sound of shattered bone and bruised flesh. Breaths left Buer's throat in wheezing spurts, his eyes glowing with power and fury. Isolde couldn't help but smile at the sight.

In the next breath, Sohan's fist drew back and Buer struck. The tip of an arrow pressed into the hollow of Sohan's throat, sending a bead of blood down his neck. Sohan answered with a blade of his own beneath Buer's chin. A small stream of blood echoed the one that now fell down his own throat. The two virya stared at each other, eyes glowing and teeth bared.

"We have a draw!" Lenox announced, his voice carrying over the roaring crowd. "Unless of course you wish for them to continue, Your Majesty."

The crowd answered in a roar, their fists punching the air and feet stomping the ground beneath them. "Live! Live!"

Erebus smiled from his throne, his arm resting around Phontine's waist. "I believe you have your answer, Lenox."

"As you wish, Your Grace," Lenox said with a bow. "Drop your weapons!" Neither Buer nor Sohan moved. They pressed the blades further, spilling more blood onto the gravel floor.

"I said drop your weapons, champions!" Lenox roared. *"Now!"*

Reluctantly, Sohan ripped his blade free from Buer's chin and shoved him to the ground. He left Volkran's champion lying in the dirt without a second glance. A pair of soldiers stepped forward, each one grabbing onto Buer's massive shoulders as he lunged for Sohan's back.

"To the sidelines, Buer!" Lenox ordered, his tone laced with warning. "Next, Foxclove and Marsh Hall!"

"Well," Kyros said, shoving away from the wall at Isolde's side, "I better not see a puddle of drool at your feet when I return, Lady Isolde."

"No need to worry on that account," she said, crossing one ankle over the other. "It takes far more than a pretty face to impress me."

"You think my face is pretty, do you?" He winked before turning his attention back to the arena and waved.

Declarations of love and desire filled the air as a winning smile spread across Kyros's face. He blew a kiss to a group of females huddled around the railing. Isolde rolled her eyes as a few of them pressed the back of their hands to their foreheads and fell to the floor in a swoon.

Demir and Kyros circled each other. The mace in Demir's hands looked heavy, its spikes were short but noticeably sharp. Kyros plucked two arrows from the quiver at his hip and tossed it aside. He stared at the arrow heads, his eyes gleaming.

With a quick twist of his fingers, the shafts fell to the ground at his feet, leaving the heads resting in his grasp. Isolde fought the cringe working its way up her back. He held one in each hand, their edges sharp and glistening in a lone ray of sunlight breaking through the clouds.

"Begin!"

Isolde pushed off the wall as the two virya met halfway. Their blows cut through the air like beautiful death. Each were exceptionally skilled, adept at fighting in close quarters. Their jabs and thrust were quick and lethal. But the mace was heavy and cumbersome, making Demir's strikes slow and clumsy.

They danced around each other, creating a cloud of dust at their feet. Small nicks and scratches covered their arms and the wide expanse of their chests. Drops of blood fell to the ground and painted their tunics red. Isolde couldn't take her eyes off them. A light that told Isolde their power was pushing...demanding to be turned loose began to grow in their eyes.

"Demir doesn't have an elemental ability," Malaki had said. "Neither does Kyros. They both can transform into a bird of prey of some kind. And they both know how to fight."

Demir delivered a blow to Kyros's face, sending him sprawling to the ground. "Not bad," Kyros said, spitting out a mouth of blood. "For a mercenary." The tip of Demir's shoe collided with Kyros's ribcage. He rolled across the arena floor, covering him in a layer of dust.

"Killing is my specialty," Demir snarled, a stream of blood dripping down the corner of his mouth. "And I excel at it." Kyros rose and sent a blade flying through the air. Demir's feet shuffled from side to side, dodging the blow, advancing until he was close enough to land a blow to Kyros's chest. A gasp of pain followed as the champion of Marsh Hall landed a few feet away, his mouth gapping wide, desperate for air.

"I expected so much more," Demir said. The gravel crunched beneath his feet with every step he took, the mace gleaming in his hand.

Kyros's chest heaved with every breath he tried to force down his throat. Still he did not move, not even when Demir loomed over him. Isolde felt a swell of panic engulf her as Demir lifted the mace above his head, casting Kyros in shadow. Without thinking, her fingers twitched at her side, sending a gust of air into the gravel and dirt into Demir's face. A snarl of irritation filled the arena as he fought to clear his eyes. Kyros rolled over on his stomach and looked to where she stood on the side lines. A subtle nod was all she received as he forced himself to stand and launched back into the fight.

Their attacks grew more vicious, more violent with every strike that landed. Isolde could see the subtle changes taking over their faces…their arms…their bodies. It wasn't until Demir swung wide, causing him to lose his footing, that Isolde saw an opening.

Kyros saw it too and drew back to plunge the tip of the arrowhead into Demir's neck. To land a blow that would end the trial and secure his spot in the final five. But Isolde saw the fatal flaw as it unfolded. Kyros had opened himself up as well, leaving his middle unguarded. Without hesitation, Demir spun through the air and struck.

Surprise filled Kyros's face. He immediately dropped the arrows and clutched at the piece of wood piercing his flesh. His knees struck the ground as a gasp of pain fell from his open mouth. Isolde found herself taking a step forward, her eyes locked on the discarded end of an arrow. Demir rose to his feet, the mace clutched in his grasp. Isolde knew there could only be one winner in this tournament. But still, the thought of Kyros's death made her angry.

"It appears we have a winner," Lenox announced. "Demir of Foxclove!"

Demir thrust the mace above his head, and a roar of approval erupted throughout the stands, their hands clapping and fists punching the air. Erebus nodded his approval and Demir sunk into a bow, his head practically touching the gravel at his feet. A pair of humans ran forward, a stretcher clutched in their hands, and stopped at Kyros's side.

Lenox held a hand up, forcing them to stop dead in their tracks. "What is your judgement, Your Majesty?"

Erebus's cold eyes raked over Kyros as he forced himself to rise. A faint sheen of sweat began to form across his brow and a steady stream of blood trickled between his fingers.

"Stop moving," Isolde growled, allowing her words to be carried on a breath of wind. Kyros shot her an annoyed look but took her advice and turned his attention to Erebus.

"Forgive me, Your Grace," he said, forcing what Isolde believed to be his most convincing smile into place. "I was hoping to give you a better show today. If you allow me to continue in the tournament, I guarantee you will not be disappointed."

Malice and fury filled Demir's eyes. The grip on the mace tightened.

"Well," said Erebus, "I believe Demir completed the task. I see no need in robbing the good people of Elenarta of a worthy champion. As long as Lady Circe is willing to pay the price for your life, of course."

Isolde turned to the crowd, to the section housing Marsh Hall. At the top, in the rightful place of the Lady of the territory, Circe rose. Scars, the ones the Hood had left behind, screamed from her porcelain face.

"I'm more than willing to pay for the life of my champion, Your Grace," she said, with a bow. Her dark eyes fell to where Kyros stood, and Isolde could have sworn she saw the faintest hint of love and perhaps genuine concern.

"Very well," Erebus said. "It is settled. See to your champion, Lady Circe."

Kyros bowed his head as much as his body would allow. "They will sing sonnets of your generosity for centuries to come, Your Majesty."

"Take him to the infirmary," Lenox ordered. Once Kyros was loaded up and hauled back through the blackened tunnels, Lenox turned his attention back to the crowd. "Four of your champions have now shed blood in the arena." Noise filled the air once more as Lenox turned back to Isolde. "And for our final match…Harrow Hall and Thornwood!"

CHAPTER 27

Nyla waited with sword in hand at the center of the arena. Her eyes were pointedly focused on the tips of her bare feet.

"Thank you, Nyla," Isolde said, gently taking the sword from her arms. "Are you alright?" Her eyes rose for just a moment and Isolde's mouth soured with regret. "Of course, you're not," she said, hating herself for even asking such a ridiculous question. "I'm working on finding a way to get you out of here."

A small flicker of hope ignited in Nyla's eyes. "Truly?" Her voice was so small, so incredibly hopeful Isolde felt a piece of her heart crack, allowing guilt to seep in and burn her to the core. All Isolde could offer was a small smile, hoping she understood and would hold on to the knowledge that someone was coming for her. That she was not alone or forgotten in a world that had given her every reason to believe otherwise.

"Be gone with you!" Lenox snarled. His hand flew through the air and caught Nyla on the side of the face, erasing the smile in an instant. A cry slipped through her lips as she hit the ground hard, the sound piercing Isolde's heart like a blade. Fury painted her vision and a ferocious snarl ripped through her bared teeth. Nyla slowly got to her feet and ran back to the side of the arena and disappeared down the tunnel.

"Call yourself a man?" Isolde asked, coming to stand before Lenox, her nose nearly touching his. "Putting your hands on a child?" Her voice was so calm, so cold, she knew her power spoke along with her. The blade shifted in her hand. Its razor-sharp edge rose to rest against his pale cheek. "Let's see how well you do against someone who can fight back."

Lenox paled, his eyes grew wide in fear and disbelief as they shot to the dais.

"Lady Isolde," Erebus chided, his tone light but full of warning. "Do refrain from threatening the Master of Games, would you?" Gage stirred behind the throne and his mouth pulled into a tight, angry line. Her lip curled into a sneer at the sight of him, causing his eyes to darken all the more.

"Forgive me, Your Majesty," she said, wrenching the blade away to slip into a mocking bow.

The corner of Gage's lip curled, but Erebus merely chuckled and waved a hand through the air in dismissal. Isolde couldn't fight the look of disdain painting her face as she turned back to Lenox. A touch of paleness still lingered around his cheeks and a dark line left by her blade streaked down the left side of his face.

"Be grateful it's not permanent," she whispered, before turning to Gawen. The hilt of the longsword, identical to Isolde's, shook in his hands. He was just as pale and speckled with drops of sweat as Lenox, who stood between them.

"The match is over when one of you is no longer a threat," Lenox said, his voice booming, causing Gawen to jump. His voice carried over the arena, giving Isolde the suspicion he was a wind wielder.

Gawen was shaking. The tip of the sword shifted in the gravel at his feet. Isolde looked to the stands, to the mass of emerald green and gold residing at the eastern side of the arena. Milt stood at the front, his massive arms crossed into a tight knot over his wide chest.

The crowd's roar hammered against the inside of Isolde's skull. Her fingers flexed around the pommel. The warm leather, new and unfamiliar, felt odd in her grasp.

"Begin!"

Gawen flinched and his eyes flew to Isolde who stepped forward. "Remember," she said, "this is just a test." Gawen looked unsure, as if he couldn't decide whether to trust her or not. With a smile, she slid her right foot back into an attack position and tightened her grip on the handle. "Let's entertain them for a bit, shall we?"

The monster within grinned at the feeling of her power coming forward as a small gust of wind built in the palm of her hand. She shoved another bar into place, causing it to snarl in return.

Not today…not him. She would have to be careful with just how much power she used. Teeth and fury bit into the bars in her mind. It wanted freedom. So desperately it wanted out. The power coming from her mother's ring only encouraged the beast all the more.

Not him! Not him!

Mindful of her movements, Isolde fought with the same speed and ferocity as she would if she had been sparring with Tanor. A gust of wind sailed from her hand and collided with Gawen's chest. He staggered back a step or two, doing his best to keep the tip of the blade from plunging into the ground. A tiny light ignited in his eyes, his own power coming to life.

"Use that power," Isolde said with a grin. "I won't break."

Gawen licked his lips and took a deep breath. Within seconds, Isolde felt something constrict around her ankle. She looked down to see a tiny briar curl around the heel of her boot. Its sharp points dug into the leather and scraped along her skin as it continued to climb. Irritated at the slight sting of pain, she slashed the sword through the air and severed the plant at the root. To Isolde's astonishment, two more sprouted to take its place. The sharp, thorny fangs pressed into her leg, digging for blood.

"Clever," she said with a rueful smile. "Very clever."

Gawen drew the sword back, his face shining with confidence, and attacked. While his earth wielding abilities kept Isolde on her toes, each strike he delivered was slow and easy to read. The edge of his sword crashed with the broad side of her own, jarring her grip. A look of uncertainty and fear spread through his eyes.

"Good," Isolde said, smiling over their crossed blades. "Now push me back."

Gawen didn't hesitate. He advanced with all his strength, which was considerable given his size. Isolde made a show of stumbling back a step or two before coming back at him again. This time driving her blade low, aiming for his leg.

He met her attack, parrying her move with ease. Soon, a competitive smirk bloomed on Gawen's face. Red painted his cheeks as he advanced, putting her on the defense.

"Move your feet," she said over the cheering crowd. Half chanted her name, while the other cried for only him. Gawen smiled at the sound, his eyes swimming with pride. Isolde bet he had never had anyone cheer for him before, nor take up residence in his corner. Except for Milt. His voice carried above all the others. His massive hands cupped around his mouth, sending his deep, bolstering voice across the arena.

"There you go!" he roared. "Use your momentum. Don't let her catch her breath!"

Isolde shot him a look of annoyance, sweat stinging the fresh scratches decorating her arms and legs. An infuriating grin spreading across Milt's handsome, punchable face. Soon, the crowd began to chant for an entirely different reason. Demands for blood reached Isolde's ears and unease settled into her bones like lead.

They had had their warm-up for this fight, and now the crowd wanted the arena painted red. Gawen wasn't a terrible fighter, far better than most beginners. But he was growing weary. Each strike was slower than the last. He hadn't tried to ensnare her with a vine within the last two attacks. Meaning he only had so long to maintain control until his power took over for him completely.

Piran's cries, the madness that had consumed all of who he was filled her mind. Isolde wouldn't let that happen, not to Gawen. Nor could she let him win.

"I've had a marvelous time," Isolde said over their crossed blades. "But this needs to end."

"How?" Gawen asked, his teeth gritting as he fought for control of himself.

Isolde smiled. "Do you want it in the arm or the leg?"

Gawen's eyes grew wide. "Wha-what do you mean?"

"They aren't going to let this end without a little bit of blood being spilled, Gawen," she said, making a show of pretending to shove him back. "So I'm going to place just a little nick on either your leg or arm and I'm giving you the choice of which one you'd prefer."

Gawen's crooked teeth bit his lip. "My leg," he said after a moment. "I help make the saddles for Lord Milt. I need my arms."

"Very well," Isolde said, with a wicked grin. "Try not to scream."

Before Gawen could ask what she meant, Isolde swept her leg out. It slammed against his calves, sending him crashing to the ground, pulling gasp of surprise from his lips. Flicking her wrist, Isolde brought the blade down across his thigh in one clean strike.

A grunt of pain echoed behind his clenched teeth as blood saturated his pant leg. She kicked the sword from his grip, mindful of his hand. Blood spilled between Gawen's fingertips, his face twisting in pain as he tried to push the edges of the wound together.

"A small nick," he ground out. *"A small nick?"*

"They'll patch that up," Isolde said, doing her best to hide the twinge of guilt. She hadn't meant to cut him so deep. "Besides, lovers adore a man with scars." A pained smile slowly fell as Gawen took in the Master of Games.

Isolde turned to Lenox, expecting to hear her name fall from his lips, naming her the victor. But Lenox remained silent. His hands were clasped in front of him. A look of cruel expectancy lingered in his eyes.

"I believe this is the part where you do your job, Lenox," Isolde said, her voice hard and carrying the weight of a Lady of Thornwood. "And declare me the winner."

"You have not completed the task," Lenox said, with a shrug. "Therefore, you cannot be named the winner."

Placing a hand on her hip, Isolde drove the sword's tip into the gravel and leaned against the pommel. "As Master of Games, I would think you could remember the rules. Perhaps we need a replacement."

A look of anger broke through the smugness. "I haven't forgotten anything, Lady Isolde. You have not removed the threat."

"Do you think he can stand to fight me?" Isolde asked, waving to Gawen. "Do you see a sword in his hand? I'm sure to someone such as yourself he's a threat, but to anyone else—"

"I see that you have left a weak point in this kingdom alive."

The words hit Isolde like daggers. "I don't recall His Majesty ordering me to kill my opponent." Shock saturated her blood, filling her with disbelief. The fingers on her hip dug into her lining of her tunic.

"He commanded you to remove the threat." A row of hideously stained yellow teeth flashed behind Lenox's thin lips.

"How is this any different than Demir and Kyros?" she demanded, her anger rising. The beast within snarled, its claws carving into her sanity as she straightened, her fingers lacing around the sword's hilt. "Or does *His Grace* get to make changes to the rules as he sees fit?"

Lenox's eyes grew wide, his mouth flopping open like a fish on dry land. "The king—"

"Does not need you to speak for him, Lenox."

Isolde turned her eyes to the dais to find Erebus standing, his eyes cold and hard. "And yes, Lady Isolde, if I wish it. The rules can change. You should know that better than anyone."

Isolde ground her teeth, her grip on the sword tightening. She felt the tiny fibers of the leather tearing beneath her fingertips.

"But alas, I have not changed the rules for this trial." Erebus's voice carried over the arena. "Weakness is a threat not only to the throne, but to all of Arnoria. And it will be eliminated. But make no mistake, Lady Isolde. There will be no confusion in the trial to follow. Next time, you will have no doubt in what I demand of you."

Liam shifted behind the throne. A look of worry and pleading bled across his face. His lips formed a single word. One she had heard countless times from him.

No.

A mist of red formed around Isolde's vision. She took a step forward, the tip of the sword dragging along the ground at her side. Lenox opened his mouth to scream. But another stayed her hand, rooting her to the spot. Isolde turned to the sound and her blood ran cold.

Buer stood over Gawen, the fallen sword hung loosely at his side. A trail of blood painted the ground as Gawen tried to crawl back, his eyes wide and never leaving the dust-covered blade. "The...the trial is over," he said. "It's done!"

"No, it's not," Buer said, tossing the blade from one hand to the other. "Not until one of you is dead. And I want to have a little more fun with the Lady Bitch before I run her through."

"The fight is over!" Milt's voice cut through the air as he fought to get through the group of soldiers holding him back "My king the trial is over!" Buer stopped his advance and turned his attention to Erebus who merely waved a dismissive hand through the air, ignoring Milt's pleas for mercy.

"It's over when you're dead," Buer said, bringing the blade overhead. "Not even your pathetic, bleeding-heart lord can save you now."

Isolde felt herself move, felt the well of power open up inside her as she moved across the arena floor. The broad side of her blade snapped up and caught the edge of Buer's sword. A look of shock blossomed on Buer's face as she sent a solid fist of air straight into his face, shattering his nose. A waterfall of blood cascaded down his face, filling his open mouth. Gasps of pain and fury bled around Buer's hand cupping the shattered parts of his face.

"Biiich!" he roared, the word garbled and wet.

"So, rude of you," Isolde said. "This is my trial." The icy flame ignited, shoving against what little remained of her restraint.

Buer regained his footing and held a look of unease at Isolde's approach. "What's the matter, Buer?" Isolde asked, twirling the blade around her form. It's sharp, unforgiving edge hugged her frame like a second skin. "Too afraid to take on someone who can actually put up a fight? Surely you're not afraid of me...a *woman*."

With a grunt, Buer swung the blade in a wide arch and Isolde rose to meet it. The shock racked through her arms, causing her teeth to clench.

"I'm going to wreck that pretty face of yours until not even that bastard, Malaki, can fix you," Buer growled, shoving the swords apart.

Isolde honed in on every ounce of training she possessed. Every strike was fluid as water, as effortless as the wind weaving through her fingers. After a few more strikes, she landed a blow to Buer's calf, driving him to the ground. Blood gushed from the wound, creating a pool of crimson on the ground.

Power hummed in her veins, its song irresistible and demanding death. Isolde stepped closer, her arm arching to bring the blade down on Buer's neck. "How disappointing," she said. "I expected so much more."

But the kiss of a blade touched the base of her throat, bringing her to halt. Isolde's gaze rose to meet the eyes of a soldier. The tip of his spear, sharp and covered with rivers of green, living metal, pressed into her flesh. Nine more joined him, each one holding a blade mere inches from her face. A dark, wicked smile spread across Buer's face as he rose to his feet and took a stumbling step towards Gawen. The sword trailed behind him, its tip skipping across the uneven ground.

"Please," Gawen said, his voice filled with such terror Isolde couldn't stand to hear it. Fury burned through her blood as she felt her limbs move on their own. But before she could land a blow, a strong pair of arms wrapped themselves around her shoulders and squeezed.

"Get off me!" Isolde screamed, kicking at the legs of whoever held her. "Get the hell off me!"

"Stop it, Isolde!" Liam's voice rumbled in her ear. "There's nothing you can do."

"He's going to kill him!" she snarled, driving her elbow into his stomach. A grunt of pain gushed from Liam's lips, but still he held on. "Liam, let me go!"

"Listen to me!" he growled into her ear. "All the children will die, Zibiah will die, if you don't stop!"

"Please." Gawen's voice broke through the haze of fury clouding her mind. Isolde threw her weight against Liam's hold, finding him halfway to the stands, to Harrow Hall and Milt. "Please!"

"What a waste of a champion you are," Buer said, planting his foot in the center of Gawen's chest. Isolde heard the bones snap as Buer pressed him into the dirt. His cry echoed Milt's who continued to fight his way through a sea of soldiers attempting to hold him back.

"I'll pay, Your Majesty!" Milt cried, his voice carrying over the arena. "Double…triple the price for his life! Please, I beg you!"

The air remained silent, save for Gawen's cries as Buer dug his foot deeper into his caving chest. Rivers of blood spilled over Gawen's lips and trickled down his neck to the gravel cushioning his head.

Tears streamed down Milt's face. "Please!"

The sound of Gawen's cries died with the swing of Buer' sword. Isolde gapped in horror as a mess of black hair rolled to the edge of the arena.

It came to rest at the wall, directly below where the Lord of Harrow Hall was standing. Milt looked down into Gawen's unseeing, lightless eyes, and a bellow of unimaginable anguish ripped from his throat. It carried over the silent arena and up into the sky, where Isolde knew the gods themselves could hear. Others from Harrow Hall rushed to his side, their eyes filled with the same horror and sadness as their Lord's. They clasped Milt under his arms and began dragging him to the exit.

Isolde sagged into Liam's hold. *I'm sorry…I'm so sorry.*

Only when Milt had disappeared and his wails of grief carried away with the wind did Buer turn back to Isolde, leaving Gawen's body behind. Liam tightened his grip on her shoulders and pulled her to the side, putting himself between them.

"Thank you for letting me do your job for you, Lady Isolde," Buer said. "It was a real pleasure."

A snarl ripped through Isolde's teeth as she fought Liam's grasp. "I'll kill you!" She seethed, her teeth bared and pain shining in her eyes.

"Isolde, stop!" Liam grunted, his grip slipping. A vague part of her knew he was right that there was nothing she could do for Gawen or Milt now. But still her power burned with uncontrollable rage. The only thing that would satisfy it now was Buer's death.

"Lady Isolde."

Isolde froze instantly, and she turned to see Tanor standing before her. A shudder ripped through her body at the sight of him.

"Tanor," Isolde murmured. "Oh, my gods, Tanor."

"Lord Gage sent me with a message. One he wants you to remember going into your next trial."

"Look at me," Isolde said, fighting back tears she knew she couldn't let fall. "Tanor, please look at me."

Slowly, his eyes rose to meet hers and something broke in Isolde's heart. Pits of hopeless sadness, rimmed in unshed tears, stared back at her. "He said, 'Defiance is costly,'" Tanor murmured, his lips trembling. "'I hope you're willing to pay the price for yours.'"

CHAPTER 28

"Fucking Gage!" Cillian snarled. "You should have killed that bastard at Briarhole when you had the chance."

"No argument there," Isolde said, her voice raspy and filled with regret. Liam had dragged her back to their chambers kicking and screaming. She turned to the soldiers who followed, demanding to be taken to Milt. But her demands were met with blank stares and silence. So, she continued to scream, her nails digging into the leathers surrounding Liam's forearms. They had placed elithrium shackles on her wrists, claiming she was too unstable, too wild to be trusted.

"Get them off of me!" Isolde had roared, her panic rising. "Get them off! Liam, get them off of me!"

Liam had banished them from her quarters and promptly removed them. "I'm sorry, Isolde."

Her power flooded back in one colossal wave. Wind swept through the room, shattering all the priceless decor in its path. Wood, metal, and glass littered the marble floors. Her bones had shifted, driving her knees to the extravagant floor. Only the sound of Malaki's voice brought her back to herself. The sight of his eyes through the film of red reminded her of who she was.

Isolde felt Liam stir at her side, pulling her back to the present. The pads of his fingers brushed the lining of her pant leg. Gawen's blood still coated her fingers. The dark stains stood out from her tanned, callused skin.

"Drink this, my rose." Nan's warm fingers pressed a mug into Isolde's hands. The steam from the tea kissed Isolde's cheeks. She did what Nan had asked, mostly for her sake. The faintest hint of spirits, sharp and inviting, filled her nose and stung the back of her throat with a sweet, welcomed bite.

"Killing Gage would have only brought the weight of the kingdom down on us all," Alaric said, his eyes darting to Liam before returning to the fire. "The last thing we need is more attention. We have enough of that already."

"Perhaps," Galaena said. "But it would have rid the world of one more piece of shit."

"Agreed," said Malaki.

One thought and one thought alone filled Isolde's mind. "We're running out of time." Her fingers tightened around the cup, the fine porcelain groaning. "We need to find a way to get the others out."

Malaki sighed but nodded his head in agreement. "Hayes should be done with the keys soon. It won't be long."

"We still don't know how to get into the prison besides the opening at the mountainside," Isolde said, her knee bouncing under Liam's palm. "We need another entry. One much closer to the ground level."

"We have a way in," Blyana said. "Phontine."

Isolde sucked in a breath. "Are you sure about that, Bly?" She said, her chest filling with hope she knew not to trust. "You haven't seen her in years. Do you think she would help us?"

Blyana's gaze shifted to Cillian, and a heavy sigh pushed from his chest. "It's possible. She doesn't appear to show any loyalty to Erebus, apart from the times she has to."

Isolde shook her head. "What do you mean?"

"Well, when you were enjoying your night at the opera," Cillian said, causing Isolde's eyes to narrow in annoyance, "we did some reconnaissance of our own in the mines."

"No need to remind me," Isolde said, around the rim of her cup.

"We did warn you we were going," Cillian said with a shrug.

"Not into the mines, you didn't," Malaki said.

"Either way," Galaena said, stopping a fight before one could begin, "what did you find out?"

"It seems the apple doesn't fall far from the tree," said Cillian. "We found who she's been helping take food to the prisoners. A human named Frey. Her lover."

"She was what?" Liam said, his eyes wide in disbelief.

"You have an issue with that Liam?" Blyana snarled, her eyes blazing. The back of the new couch groaned in protest as the tips of her nails ripped through the fabric.

"Of course, I don't, Bly!" Liam said, his hands balling into fists. Isolde didn't miss the way Cillian and Malaki shifted forward. "I just don't know how she would be able to do it. Those prisons are heavily guarded with very, *very* restricted access. I can't imagine they would allow the king's—" He stopped mid-sentence, his mouth open and eyes searching.

"Say it," Blyana growled. "You mean the king's *whore*, don't you?"

"Of course, I don't mean that, Bly! Your sister has no say in the matter. It's not her fault."

"No," said Isolde, placing a hand on Liam's shoulder. "She doesn't. And you know he didn't mean it that way, Bly. So, knock it off!"

Blyana rolled her eyes and slid down the back of the couch to rest beside Cillian. He casually dropped an arm across her shoulders and tucked her body into his side.

"You didn't think to mention you had found another possible way into the mines?" Isolde asked.

"You've been busy," Cillian said. "And so have we." His eyes bored into her, willing her to understand. She looked again at Blyana. There was a slight droop to her shoulders, as if she were being crushed by an unseen weight she was doing everything in her power to bear. Isolde had the sinking feeling, Phontine had something to do with it.

"So," Isolde continued, feeling the unpleasant but deserving sting of shame. "Do you think she'll help get us into the mines, Bly?"

Blyana nodded. "I think so. But persuasion will be necessary…and payment."

"Payment I'm not worried about." A small grin pulled at the edges of Isolde's lips. "Does Phontine fancy's a visit from a certain masked vigilante?"

A collective sigh echoed through the room. Alaric sat forward and buried his mouth in the palm of his hand. The light from the fire danced across the golden hair brushing his forehead. "Not here, Isolde," he said. "Please, not here."

"I'm not left with very many options, Alaric," Isolde said. "Besides, I could use a little bit of fun right now."

"Your definition of fun says a lot about your mental well-being," Alaric grumbled. "It's dangerous—"

"Only if I get caught." She was already moving to the doorway of her bedroom, her mind set.

"She won't get caught, Alaric," Blyana said, following behind, her deft fingers already pulling at the seams of the corset at Isolde's back. A satisfied sigh lifted from Isolde's lips as the pressure constricting her chest fell away. She hated wearing those damn things, no matter how good they looked.

"You're not helping, Bly," Malaki growled at the doorway. Isolde knew her nakedness was nothing to him, but still she was thankful he kept his gaze averted. The hideous scar at her side was still an adjustment. It felt tight and uncomfortable under so many eyes.

"I'm going, Malaki," Isolde said, tugging on the black leather britches and the binding that held her breasts in place. "And you are staying here."

"Like hell I am!" he growled, turning to her fully now. Tension rippled through his form, causing rivets of muscle and skin to bunch beneath the lining of his tunic. "I will not be left behind!"

"Are you fully healed yet?" Isolde demanded, placing her hands on her bare hips.

"Yes," he answered much too quickly.

"Nan, is that true?"

"I can neither confirm nor deny," Nan said from the couch next to Cillian who was stuffing his face with a fresh biscuit covered in honey and melted butter. "But he is doing considerably better. However, it wouldn't hurt to rest a few more days. Just to be safe."

Malaki's irritated growl filled the chamber. "Traitor."

"Stubborn mule," Nan retorted, causing Cillian to choke.

Isolde slipped on the black tunic and threw the light, black cape around her shoulders. "I know you think Ferden healed you, but we've never seen anything like this before. No one has. We can't be sure it's permanent." Her jaw tightened as Gawen's face filled her mind. A shaky breath drifted her over lips. "And I won't take that chance, Malaki. Not with you.

"I'll go."

Isolde turned to look at Galaena, her brow rising in surprise. "You really think I'm going to sit back and let you have all the fun?" she asked, with a smirk. "I helped train you too."

Wearing a smile, she could hardly contain, Isolde ducked back into her wardrobe and pulled out one of the spare hoods and masks she had brought.

"Gal…" Alaric said pushing himself up onto his feet, the shaft of his cane groaning beneath the weight.

"I know the mines and those dungeons better than anyone here besides you and Malaki, Alaric," she said. "It'll be fine."

"There are too many guards," Liam said. "Too many things that can go wrong."

"Well," Isolde said, sliding the mask and hood into place, "it's a good thing we have a Captain of the Guard who can pull a string or two."

The sound of heels clicking against the marble floors bounced off the finely carved walls as Phontine entered her bedchambers. The smell of lavender filtered through the air where Isolde lurked in the shadows. A heavy, defeated sigh pushed past Phontine's swollen lips as she kicked her heels to the side of the room. Erebus's scent clung to her skin and Isolde's heart ached with regret.

Terror rippled through Phontine as Isolde stepped up behind her and clamped a gloved hand over her mouth. Phontine's muffled cry filled the room and the tips of her perfectly painted nails tore into Isolde's leather-clad forearm.

"Unless you want your guards' blood to paint your room a new color," Isolde said, her voice distorted by the mask, "I suggest you keep quiet."

Phontine stilled, her nails still pressing into Isolde's arm.

"I didn't come here to harm you. Only to have little chat." Isolde wasn't sure if she believed her or not but after a moment, Phontine's breathing calmed. "Good. Now if I take my hand away do you promise not to scream?"

Phontine nodded eagerly, her fingers loosening their grip.

"Do not make the mistake of lying to me," Isolde warned as she cautiously withdrew her hand.

Phontine tugged away from Isolde's hold and turned. Her eyes, the very ones belonging to Blyana, were glowing. "How is this possible?" she demanded, taking in Isolde. "You…you were caught!"

"That's cute you and Erebus think so," Isolde said, a hint of a laugh dancing in her words. "But I'm the Hood of Arnoria. I can never be caught."

"There are other names you go by, aren't there?" Phontine said, her lip curling. "Thief… murderer… traitor."

"I go by many names," Isolde said, pulling the bow from across her back. She sunk into the velvet chair near the fireplace and draped the bow across her knee. "But most would say, exquisite… brave… charismatic… perfect…They all have a rather nice ring to them."

"I call it false advertisement," Phontine sneered. "Or self-indulgent. You might be a hero in your own eyes, *Hood*, but to those you leave behind to deal with your mess, you're a plague."

"We all can't be as perfect as His Majesty's favorite pet," Isolde said, doing her best to hide the shame in her voice. "Now can we?"

"You know nothing of it," Phontine snarled.

"I know enough." The tip of Isolde's jaw rested on a curled fist. "You might claim to hold yourself to a higher standard than me, but we both know that isn't true." Her gaze locked on Phontine. "I know you help those who cannot help themselves. At great risk to yourself…and to someone else."

Phontine stilled. "How do you know that?"

"I am the Hood," Isolde said. "I know a great many things. And I know it is no small risk you take."

"It doesn't matter," Phontine said. "I am nothing. All my value lies in the pleasure I bring Erebus in his bed. What does it matter if I die?"

Isolde stilled at her words. They were the same ones echoing through her own mind more often than she dared admit even to herself. "It matters a great deal, Phontine. *You* matter a great deal. Not only to those you help, but to others as well."

"If you are referring to my *sister*," she said, her voice dripping with disdain, "she is nothing to me. Not that I expect you to know her. She is a friend to that bitch, Isolde Cotheran. A spoiled brat who's playing pretend. The only reason she entered the tournament was for her own selfish gain—for power."

Isolde fought the urge to look to the balcony where she knew the others lurked. But she knew Blyana heard. There was no chance she hadn't. "You might be surprised."

"Erebus was rather demanding tonight, Hood," Phontine said, bracing a hand on her hip. "And I'm tired. So, do state your business and be gone."

"Very well." Isolde shot to her feet, causing Phontine to jump back. "As fate would have it, I am in need of your services."

Phontine laughed darkly. "In case it has escaped your notice, I belong to Erebus. And he is not a man who likes to share his toys. Nor would I lower my standards to spread my legs for a criminal such as yourself."

"I can't imagine Erebus is the type to share." Isolde's eyes flickered to the door. "Nor are you my type. I have someone else who tends to that particular need. Besides, I wasn't referring to those services."

"What then?"

"I need your help getting into the dungeons. The same ones you and your...*friend* sneak food into. Don't deny it," Isolde said as Phontine opened her mouth, her face pale with fear. "It's been a very long day, and I would prefer to get this done quickly. I'm sure you hold beauty sleep to the same level of importance as I do."

Phontine shifted from one foot to the other, her hands wringing before her. "Why would I help you?"

"You're a smart woman, Phontine. I believe you can guess what the consequences of your inaction will bring."

In that moment, she wasn't Isolde Cotheran, Lady of Thornwood anymore. She was the Hood of Arnoria and everything Phontine had labelled her and more. Heartless…cruel…wicked. A villain in every sense of the word.

"You never know what could happen." Phontine's lips trembled, her grey eyes glowing as the Hood took a step forward. "Erebus might find out about your little late-night adventures. Including the little side trips you take to a particular part of the palace, with a particular servant. Frey, is his name, is it not?"

Tears swelled in Phontine's eyes, and her lips trembled.

An air of false smugness coated Isolde's words as a shrug of feigned indifference lifted from her shoulders. "I can't imagine Erebus would take kindly to hearing of his little toy playing with others—especially a human. The best-case scenario for you both would be death."

Phontine's gaze widened as she leaned away from Isolde, her chest rising in quick panicked breaths. Isolde hated herself for what came next. "The worst case, would be finding yourself back at Madame Vara's House of Pleasures."

Tears of terror spilled down Phontine's face at the sound of that bitch's name. Tremors cascaded down her body and her fear saturated the room like a dense fog. Isolde's own power bled through, shining from her eyes into Phontine's. Self-hatred pressed into Isolde like a brand. She loathed using this tactic on Blyana's sister. Despised herself for playing that particular card. But she had sworn there was no line she would not cross. And if Phontine were caught, Isolde had no doubt that fate wouldn't be beyond the realm of possibility.

"Or you can help me," Isolde said, her voice softening. "And I will make sure you and Frey are taken care of."

"Taken care of?"

"I'm getting those children, another prisoner, and as many as I can out of those dungeons," Isolde said, taking a step back to give Phontine space to breath. "If you help me, I will make sure you both come with us. I will make sure, you are safe…and free."

A shuddered breath wrecked through Phontine's chest. "So, my choices are either help the Hood, a known criminal and murderer, or lay myself at Erebus's mercy?"

Isolde shrugged. "Precisely."

A fresh wave of tears fell from Phontine's eyes, and the sight tore Isolde in two. It was another stain on her soul, another mark that could never be erased. Phontine wiped the traitorous tears away almost angrily. It was weakness in her world. Isolde knew she had been trained to never cry, to never show any signs of discomfort. Beaten over and over again until there were no more tears left to spill.

But as Phontine straightened, drawing her shoulders back to her fullest height, all that remained in her gaze was pure hatred. "You really are a bastard, aren't you?"

A laugh, cold and false, bled through Isolde's mask. "The worst of them all."

Isolde poked her head out from the chamber doors and a wave of appreciation filled her heart. Only a deserted hallway was there to greet her. It had been Liam's assignment to get rid of the guards who stood post outside of Phontine's door.

"I should have known there would be more than one of you,"

Phontine scoffed as the others slipped through the window.

"Misery does love company," Isolde retorted, ushering her to the door.

"We can't get them all out tonight," Phontine muttered as she made her way down the hall. Isolde and others stuck to the shadows running along the walls.

"And why is that?" Galaena asked.

"Because there are too many guards present," Phontine answered, drawing up short to look around the corner. "You'll need something to draw them out of the mines and prisons. Unless you have an army of masked assholes at your disposal."

A growl of warning ripped through Galaena's teeth. "Mind your tongue!"

"Enough," Isolde said, placing a hand on her aunt's shoulder. "She's right. The last thing we need while trying to get them out is fighting our way through a sea of Erebus's men."

Galaena cut her eyes at Phontine but kept her mouth shut.

They followed her down corridor after corridor. Ease fell over Isolde's shoulders when Phontine took the correct route toward the servants' quarters.

"She hasn't betrayed us so far," Cillian murmured. "I take that as a good sign."

A few minutes passed before she stopped at one of the doors and pushed her way through. It was a stateroom, one intended for a servant, maybe two.

"Why are we here?" Blyana asked, her eyes sweeping the room. A pair of throwing knives danced in her hands.

"There's a secret passage," Phontine said, gripping the golden key, her fingers running over the wall. "The servant quarters are adjacent to the prisons."

On the cot was a thin blanket, hardly big enough to cover someone as small as Blyana. *How did they stay warm?*

At last, Isolde heard the subtle click of a lock, and a small section of the wall gave way. A dark tunnel loomed before them. The sound of cries echoed from deep within. Without pausing, Phontine disappeared into the abyss and Isolde followed.

The dark swallowed her whole, chilling her to the bone. Phontine's steps stopped and a moment later a small beam of light sliced through the dark. Carts of linen, old and dirty, filled the space around them. On the walls were various chains and shackles, all rusted from neglect. From within one of the discarded buckets, Phontine pulled the same ratty cloak and hood Isolde had seen her in days before.

"I'll get you a better one," Isolde said.

"I want nothing from you," Phontine said, draping the cloak around her shoulders. She pulled the hood into place, hiding her from the world. "Other than what you claim to promise."

Casting a glance through the small slit in the door, she held up her hand, telling them to wait. After a moment, Phontine waved them forward and tucked the lip of her hood further around her head. "This way."

Isolde felt Cillian's hand at her arm. His obsidian eyes were narrowed on Phontine's back. "Are you sure about this?"

"Losing your nerve already?" Isolde asked with a laugh. "We haven't even gotten to the exciting part yet."

"I'm hoping there won't be an exciting part on this little adventure."

"Are you coming or not?" Phontine's voice was a harsh whisper, but it felt like a shout to Isolde's ears.

She shot Blyana a look of annoyance, which she returned with a sheepish shake of her head. They slipped through the doorway, and Isolde realized where she was standing. They were perched on the sixth floor overlooking the prisons. The pile of elithrium was smaller than the last time Isolde remembered. It dwindled faintly in the light of the sconces lining the lowest level of the dungeons.

"And there," Cillian said, pointing up, "is our exit strategy,"

Isolde turned her hopeful eyes up to the ceiling, and there it was. The same ledge leading to the opening in the mountain Malaki nearly died creating, jutted out from the wall.

A deep growl rumbled through the air and Isolde turned her gaze to Galaena, who was deathly still. Power, terrible and absolute, shone from her eyes that were focused on the mounds of elithrium littering the floor below.

"How did it come to this?" Galaena said, her foot rising to take a step toward the landing.

Reaching out, Isolde gripped Galaena's sleeve and tugged her back in. "What are you doing?"

Her aunt shook her head. "I'm fine," she said, refusing to meet Isolde's eye. "Just…bad memories."

"We can't stay here," Phontine whispered. "There are patrols that come around every hour."

Her footsteps were light and nearly silent. Isolde marveled at how well she moved. Phontine's abilities, whatever they were, had to be powerful. She wasn't even sure Blyana knew. Phontine would have been far too young at the time for her abilities to show, for her power to manifest.

It was two more levels before Phontine finally came to a stop. "Here," she whispered, her delicate polished finger pointing in the direction of a separate set of cells. Two soldiers stood at post at the gate.

"Two for the price of one then." Isolde plucked another arrow from her quiver and notched it into place. Taking a breath, she pulled back on the bowstring and let go.

The arrows disappeared into the helmets resting on the soldiers' heads. They fell to the floor in a heap of blood and metal. Blyana reached them first and plucked the key from their belt loop.

"Test hers first," Galaena said, nodding to Phontine. "Make sure it really works for *all* the locks."

"Fine," Phontine said, thrusting the golden key into the lock and twisting. It gave way without complaint. "Satisfied?"

"Thoroughly," Isolde said before Galaena could utter the response she knew was building on her aunt's lips.

The rusted hinges groaned as Isolde pulled the door open just enough to slip through. Light from the torches welded to the outside of the cell flickered across the dirty, blood-stained floor. Small bodies lined the walls of the cavernous room.

Mindful of every step she took, Isolde picked her way through the group until she saw her. Nyla lay huddled around another child, one much smaller than herself and nothing but skin and bones.

"Insil."

The crescent shaped scar on her face looked darker, deeper than she remembered against her alabaster skin. A price she had paid for her mother's inability to pay Erebus' tax. Relief filled whatever gaps the sorrow and fury Isolde had been harboring since the day the little girl was taken from Whisper.

She's alive, Asha, Isolde said in a silent prayer of thankfulness. *She's alive.*

Nyla clung to Insil's tiny form, cradling her to her chest. A dark mark covered the left side of her face. The same one that had been bruised in Briarhole. A fresh scab covered her cheek from where Lenox had struck her earlier that day.

Kneeling down, Isolde sent a gentle breath of wind across Nyla's face. She stirred from sleep and her eyes rose to meet the Hood's. A gasp of disbelief broke through her cracked lips.

"Shh," Isolde said, holding a finger to her covered lips. Nyla carefully worked herself free of Insil's grip and threw her arms around

Isolde's neck. A shudder of emotion ripped through Isolde as she cradled Nyla to her chest. Boney prominence protruded from every part of her body. Even through her thick leather gloves, Isolde could feel them. Emotions filled her throat, refusing to let a single breath of air pass.

"Is it really you?" Nyla cried. Her voice, so small and broken, tickled at Isolde's ear. "Please tell me it's really you and not another one of my dreams."

"I'm here, little one," Isolde choked. "I'm here."

"How?"

"You really think they could keep the Hood away?"

Nyla pulled back, her eyes swimming with confusion. "But they said you had been captured. The guards, they said it was Lady Zibiah."

"There is only one Hood." Isolde said, with a grin.

"Did Lady Isolde send you? Have you come for us?" Nyla asked, her eyes wide with hope. "Please…please take us away from here."

"She did indeed," Isolde said, gently touching the side of Nyla's face that wasn't bruised and broken. And I will get you out…but I can't right now." The words felt like glass in Isolde's mouth. Sorrowful tears cascaded down Nyla's face, and her eyes fell.

"I will soon," Isolde promised, gently pulling her chin up. "But I need to make sure that what happened at Briarhole doesn't happen again. And I need to find Lady Zibiah."

"I haven't seen her since the night we arrived," said Nyla. "She's not in the mines or in any of the other cells."

Panic filled Isolde's heart. "Have you heard of where she might be?"

"People talk," Nyla said, her voice dropping to whisper. "In the mines, they say there's another place. A room deep underground where they do things to virya…to the half-bloods. Hurt them."

Isolde's gaze shot to Galaena, whose hands gripped the handles of the long daggers at her side. Horror filled her aunt's eyes that seemed to be looking at nothing at all, lost in a nightmare of the past.

Blyana knelt down on Isolde's right, her voice soft as a bell. "Hurt them how, Nyla?"

Nyla licked her lips, her head shaking. "I don't know. They *change* them. Every now and then, a virya or half-blood is taken to the door. And they never come back."

"Which door?" asked Isolde.

"It's at the bottom of the pit." Nyla swallowed. "The red one."

Isolde remembered. It had to be the same one she saw Erebus and Volkran disappearing through. That was where Zibiah was. It had to be. The urge to act now, to break apart the very foundations of the damn mountain was nearly uncontrollable. But Isolde kept herself still, kept her anger in check as she turned back to the little girl who had been so brave for so long.

"I will get you out of here, Nyla," Isolde said. "I swear it."

"Please don't leave me!" Nyla begged. "I don't want to stay here… please…*please!*" Isolde pulled Nyla into her chest, unable to take the sight of her tears.

"You have to be brave a little while longer," Isolde said, her hand cupping the back of Nyla's head as she wept into her cloak. "I promise, I will get you out. No matter what."

Pain ripped through Isolde's heart as she carefully pried Nyla's fingers from her cape and rose. "Be brave, be strong. Can you do that for me?" Tear-stained eyes stared up at her. Hope but also fear shone in their depths as Nyla nodded her head in agreement.

After gently pressing her hand to Nyla's face once more, Isolde turned back to her silent cadre. "You're sure this will work for all the locks in the prison?" she asked pointing to the key glistening around Phontine's neck.

"Yes." The tip of Phontine's finger grazed the gilded teeth. "It should work for all the cells. As I said before." Her gaze shifted to Nyla and a fraction of her icy exterior melted away.

"How can you be so sure?" Galaena asked, her eyes narrowing.

A sneer pulling past the edge of Phontine's mouth as she turned her eyes to Galaena. "I've been in this place for a long time, criminal. I haven't made it this far just on my looks and impressive skill set."

Blyana shifted her feet, doing her best to the hide the flinch. To hide a guilt she had no business carrying. But Isolde saw. As did Cillian, who brushed his knuckles against the side of her hand.

"Good," said Isolde, moving to the cell door. "Then that settles it then."

"That settles what?" Phontine demanded.

"When we give the signal, you and Frey are to plant a key in every cell in this godsforsaken place."

"And just how do you propose we do that?"

"I'm sure the fine inhabitants wouldn't mind a special ingredient added to their daily ration of bread," Isolde said with a smirk. "Wouldn't you agree?"

Phontine's eyes grew wide. "You're crazy. That will only cause madness, chaos!"

Isolde looked over her shoulder, her eyes glittering with mischief. "If there's one thing I know best, it's chaos. And the night we execute our plan, I intend for this palace to be burning in it."

Blyana smiled to herself and took a deep breath of the early morning air that held the scent of pine and dew. It reminded her of Blackford but different, lighter somehow. Warm rays of the first hint of dawn danced across her face, filling her with a hope she hadn't dared to hold since arriving in Elenarta.

Blyana's leg dangled over the edge of the balcony as her eyes moved along the streets below. It had been a restless night, one filled with nightmares of the past and new ones of the future. With a heavy sigh, Blyana rested her cheek on her bare knee and watched the city come to life.

A father and daughter were walking hand in hand down one of the cobblestone streets. A dull ache formed in her chest at the sight. Memories of a scene so similar to this one played in her mind. She had been about that same age when she would accompany her father to the market in Whisper. And for once, in so many years, she didn't stop the memories or the dreams of what could have been from resurfacing.

"Cillian will die of terror if he sees you." Isolde's voice severed her train of thought, sending her memories back into the deep, dark corners of her heart.

"Why do you think I'm sitting here waiting?" Blyana said, with a sly smile.

Isolde took the spot opposite her. "Do try to not kill my weapon's expert so early in the morning," Isolde said, tucking her legs under her. "He might be a candy thief, but he still has his uses on occasion. I'd hate to replace him."

Even for a virya, Isolde's balance was unprecedented. Even unnerving, at times. The flutter of wings descended from above as Fane came to rest on Isolde's shoulder.

"I'll do my best," Blyana said, running a finger down the hawk's chest. A soft chirp lifted from his beak at the touch. After a moment of silence, Blyana turned her gaze back out to the capital. To the streets that were starting to wake up. "Do you think it will work?"

Isolde shrugged with a sigh. "It has to. We don't have another plan. As long as Phontine and Frey come through on their end, we shouldn't have a problem."

The sound of her breath catching drew Isolde's attention. Such hope had filled Blyana's heart when she first laid eyes on her sister the day they arrived. A joy she wasn't capable of putting into words. Perhaps because there simply weren't any. But the look in Phontine's eyes, the sheer hatred that dwelt within them, destroyed her hope in one fell swoop.

"Bly…"

"If she doesn't," Blyana said, tucking her knees beneath her chin, "it will be my fault. She still blames me for what happened. I'm the cause of her pain, Isolde. Her fear…her anger."

"She has no right to blame you." Isolde's words were filled with such defiance, such passion Blyana nearly smiled at the comfort it brought. "If anyone is to blame, it's me. I should have realized what Vara would do. I should have taken them in the day I got you out."

"You couldn't have possibly known what Vara would've done, Isolde," Blyana said, wiping a tear away. "Do not burden yourself with guilt that is not yours to bear."

"One could say the same for you."

Blyana's eyes cut to her, their sharp gray gaze narrowing. "Pot and kettle."

"Yet again," Isolde said, a hint of a smile playing on her lips. Blyana's forefinger began rubbing at the tattoo on her finger. It was a comfort, or perhaps a self-imposed punishment she placed on herself. She scrubbed harder, willing the thing away. The pain was a blessing, a distraction. But still, the ink remained. It would always remain.

"I do have something for you," Isolde said, hopping up from her perch, jarring Fane on her shoulder. She strode to one of the small dressers and pulled a small bag from the top drawer. "I had planned on giving you this before one of those atrocious balls we will undoubtedly be forced to attend. But you know how my patience is."

"What patience?"

Isolde rolled her eyes and regained her seat. The faintest hint of rose and the forest filled the air around her. But as Isolde's deft fingers disappeared into the fine black silk bag, a hint of ember drifted through the air. "I hope it fits."

Blyana stared at the ring pinched between Isolde's fingers. Silver, pure as starlight, held a sapphire. Facets of its oval shape caught the light of early dawn. It was long and angular, large enough to cover...

Blyana opened her mouth to speak but not a single word came forward. A lump formed in her throat, and the familiar sting of tears filled her eyes. "Your past is nothing to be ashamed of, Blyana."

Isolde's other hand came forward and in her palm sat a bracelet. Its band was a delicate array of threaded silver matching the ring perfectly. They held a bundle of sapphires, each one ranging in size and shape, like stars scattered through a pale night sky.

Blyana had always loved the stars. When she was in the House of Pleasures, gazing up at the night sky was a luxury, one her attitude never afforded. The one thing Vara always forbid, apart from her freedom.

"Our past can lead us down many paths," Isolde said. "But we all have a choice in where we take our next step. That's what each stone represents. A path, a life of your own choosing. No one chooses it for you, Bly."

Blyana continued to stare, her eyes swimming with such emotion she could hardly see. Words wanted to spill from her lips, but the lump in her throat refused to let a single one pass.

Silence hung between them, and Isolde began to fidget. She licked her lips with the slightest shake of her head. "You don't have to wear it," she said, in a rush. "If it brings back too many memories or if you don't like them—"

"Of course, I like them," Blyana said, her voice the ghost of a whisper. The precious stones felt smooth beneath her touch. Her heart felt impossibly heavy, weighted down with the gravity of her unworthiness. "But these are far too nice for me, Isolde."

Isolde was quiet for a moment. Then the ring and bracelet disappeared as she gripped Blyana's arms, forcing to her look up. "I want you to hear me when I say this, Blyana," Isolde said, her emerald, silver eyes burning.

"There is nothing, and I mean *nothing*…too good for you. I want you to be comfortable and confident in who you are. And when you are ready, I want you to leave this ring and bracelet behind." Isolde's hands slid down her arms and she took Blyana's hands in her own. "You are not dirty, you are not broken, you are not unworthy. There isn't a single part of you that needs to be fixed."

A tear trickled down Blyana's flaming cheek, and a shaky breath left her lips. She nodded, unable to think of anything else to do in the moment. Isolde smiled and gently pushed the ring into place.

"And I swear Vara will pay for what she has done. By your hand, I vow it. She will pay."

The metal slid across her skin, finding a permanent home on her left thumb. The tattoo, the symbol of so much pain and agony disappeared beneath a bed of beauty and kindness. As did the pale scar encircling her wrist as Isolde helped her fasten the bracelet in place.

Part of her expected to hate the feeling of metal again. But only warmth and deep gratitude found its way to her. They were both a perfect fit. She wouldn't have expected anything less from her best friend, her sister in every way that mattered.

"Are these from your first trial?" Blyana asked, running her fingers over the beautiful stones.

"Taken from the top of Olos itself." Isolde nodded. "There were pearls as well." A sad, knowing smile crested on the edge of Isolde's lips. "But I wanted only silver and sapphires for you, Bly."

"I never was one for pearls anyway," Blyana said. "I don't know how to thank you, Isolde."

"Steal some of Cillian's candy for me," she said, a wicked smile pulling on her face. "I know he has a hidden stash somewhere."

A smile of her own pulled onto Blyana's face. "I think I can arrange that."

She threw her arms around Isolde's neck and squeezed, her embrace narrowly missing Fane who shot into the air. Gratitude flooded Blyana's heart, bringing on a fresh wave of tears. Warmth fell across her skin as Isolde wrapped her own arms around her, holding her close.

"Your past does not define you, Bly" Isolde said. "It never did."

A weight, one Blyana had been carrying for so long, lifted from her shoulders. "I love you, bossy bird brain."

Isolde's hold tightened. "I love you too, mangy fur ball."

CHAPTER 29

The House of Harrow Hall was nowhere in sight the following day. Isolde longed to see the emerald green of Milt's house as she rode through the streets of Elenarta. She missed the proud, golden stallion waving in the breeze, along with Milt's warm, infectious laugh. How desperately she wanted to see him stand in defiance of what Erebus had done to Gawen.

But as she turned the corner, deep in the heart of the capital, not a single Harrow Hall flag graced the sky. Versa walked beside Loria, her steps slow and measured. Alaric and Galaena led the company of Thornwood. A sea of maroon and gold filled the sidewalks as they moved.

"Of course, Erebus would order this," Isolde said, adjusting herself in the saddle. The back of her dress tugged uncomfortably as her legs draped over the side. "Parading us through the streets like this."

Malaki grunted from where he rode on her right. "He always did love a good show."

Flags from different houses snapped in the wind above the heads of those who lined the sidewalks. "How many do you think are here by choice?" she asked, mindful of her voice. Children stood along the edge of the street, their little faces filled with wonder.

"Hard to say," Malaki said. "I can't imagine standing outside cheering for a bunch of rich pricks who might one day rule over them is an enjoyable event for most of them." A flicker of joy filled Isolde's chest at the sight of him riding. Not an ounce of pain lingered on his face, nor did a twinge of discomfort make itself known. Secrettaker was tucked to his side, a dark, deadly reminder of who and what he was.

"I can imagine not," Isolde said, threading her fingers through the reins. A rich scent of baking bread and sugar filled the air, bringing Isolde up short. Through the throng of bodies, she spotted a familiar sight. It was adorned in flowers and vines, making it stand out from the stone buildings surrounding it.

"Malaki!" Isolde said, an excited smile breaking across her face.

Malaki followed her gaze, and a deep chuckle fell from his lips. "Rafe's," he said, an air of fondness filling his words. "It's still here."

"After all this time."

Isolde's mouth watered at the memory of the pastries and cakes she had enjoyed there as a child. Of the raspberry gauche chocolates they had made just for her. It had been a tradition, one her parents never let them miss. Every Sunday afternoon, when her parents were free of their duties for just a little while, they would all make their way to this small, beloved bakery for a treat.

Commotion filled the air, drawing Isolde's attention forward and away from the past. Up ahead, Buer had descended from his horse and was making his way through the crowd. He stopped before a group gathered outside a local tavern. Several men huddled around the entrance, each one thrusting a mug out to Briarhole's champion, spilling the contents onto the street.

"Seems the champion of Briarhole wishes to stop the parade," Malaki said.

"Perfect timing." Isolde slid from Versa's saddle. The heels of her shoes struck the cobblestones with a snap.

"Isolde!" Malaki said, but his voice was cut off, lost in the rush of the crowd. She tossed Versa's reins to a nearby soldier and made her way through the throng of people.

"Lady Isolde! Lady Isolde!" Her name came from every direction. She smiled as she passed and nodded to those who dipped their head in her direction.

Nostalgia swelled in her chest as she stood before the beautiful ornate door covered with intricate carvings of breads and sweets. Smiling, she reached forward with a shaky hand and tugged the door open. Stinging tears prickled at Isolde's eyes as the familiar sound of the greeting bell filled the small space.

"I'll be with you in a moment!" a voice called from the back.

"No rush at all," Isolde answered, fighting against the lump in her throat. Her gaze was already fixed on the gorgeous display before her. Golden, flaky crusts covered the surfaces of the counters. The scent of dough and chocolate filled the air. The small display case to the left was reserved for the chocolates she knew were handmade.

"How might I help—" The voice stopped mid-sentence, and Isolde looked up to see a ghost lingering across the counter.

"Hello," Isolde said.

The man stared at her as if in shock. His youthful, round face, one that was only made possible by his power, which she remembered lay with the earth, looked at her in awe. He was just as she remembered him. "La-Lady Isolde Cotheran…in my bakery!"

"Well, how could I resist," she said. "I could smell your cinnamon rolls from the road, Rafe."

A blush spread across his face, hints of flour dusted his round cheekbones. "And you know my name?"

Tears pricked at the corner of her eyes. "You come highly recommended."

After a moment, Rafe shook his head as if remembering himself and rushed forward to pluck a cinnamon roll from the display case. "Allow me," he said, folding a piece of parchment around the golden dough and handing it to her. "Careful, they just a came out of the oven."

"Thank you," she said, before sinking her teeth in the pastry. Icing and warm dough coated her tongue, forcing a moan of pure ecstasy from her throat. "Incomparable."

A smile of undiluted joy filled Rafe's face. "Thank you very much, Lady Isolde," he said. "My store is open to you. Anything at all, just ask and it's yours."

"Oh please, let me pay you," she said, guilt settling into her stomach.

Rafe held up a hand, his other pressed into the flour-covered apron at his chest. "Absolutely not! My champion doesn't pay here," he said. "You're the one I'm rooting for. The least I can do is ensure you're well fed."

Isolde smiled. "Thank you, Rafe." A faint tapping caught Isolde's attention, drawing her eyes to the window. Faces, small and dirty, were pressed to the clean glass running along the alleyway to the right of the shop. Their gazes were fixed on her and the treats filling the cases.

"Who are they?" Isolde asked, before taking another bite.

"The local orphans," Rafe explained, his warm eyes dimming. "Virya, all of them. Which is why they haven't been put into the mines. Not yet, anyway. Most are children of fallen soldiers."

"On with you!" a gruff voice said. A soldier stepped into the window frame, his armor dull in the shadow of the buildings. His boot slammed into the ribcage of one of the smallest children, sending him crashing to the ground.

Rafe's voice came from behind as Isolde strode to the door, but she ignored it. The half-eaten pastry fell to the floor in her wake. Careful to not damage the door, Isolde gently pulled the handle and stepped out into the alley.

"You know you're meant to be on the sidewalk!" the soldier said, his hand already moving to the whip at his side. "Maybe a few lashes will help you remember your place."

Isolde lunged forward, her hand twisting around the handle of the whip. She jerked it free from the holster and let it uncoil at her feet. A look of bewilderment fell across the soldier's face when he recognized who stood before him. Flicking her wrist, Isolde sent the whip around his neck. The fine leather bit into his skin and tightened.

"How a man treats those weaker than he is, says a lot about him," Isolde said, tossing the belly of the whip around a hook jutting from the brick wall. Fear bled into the man's eyes as she pulled the handle tight, lifting him off the ground. The soldier's feet kicked beneath him, fighting for any purchase. His gloved fingers gouged into his neck, trying and failing to free himself from her grasp.

He deserves it.

A hint of darkness, of deadly desire, brushed against Isolde's mind at the thought. But a small cry drew her back from the shadows to the small group of children lingering together behind her. Their eyes were glowing and wide, stilling Isolde's hand. They weren't staring at the soldier. They were staring at her, in fear.

"You're lucky," Isolde said, stepping closer, not wanting the children to hear. "I don't want to scar them with the memory of me cutting you into tiny, bloody pieces." His fingers fumbled against the whip's unforgiving hold. "Lay a finger on these children again, or any others for that matter, and I'll make sure nothing is left of you for anyone to find. Am I understood?"

A gargled sound pushed through his throat in response. A shade of purple, much like the one that had once covered Volkran's face, spread across the planes of his skin. Isolde let him hang for a moment longer before loosening her grip and letting him tumble to the ground.

"And don't forget," she said, watching him crawl away, his mouth gapping. "I might be your Left Hand in the not-so-distant future." A look of terror filled the soldier's eyes before he rose to his feet and disappeared into the crowd.

Isolde turned back to the children still hiding in the shadows. Tears cascaded down the face of the small boy clutching his side. "Are you alright?" Isolde asked, bending down, her hand outstretched. He flinched away from her. "It's alright," she said. "I won't hurt you, I promise."

His vibrant green eyes flickered from her to the hand she offered before him. "My side hurts," he cried, his little hand cupping his ribcage that was far too prominent. She looked up to the others, to the various wounds most of them possessed. Sadness, blended with the cold fury stirring in her chest.

"I have a friend who can help with that," Isolde said. "Wait right here." She turned and made her way back to where Malaki lingered in the stalled parade. "Your assistance is needed."

A slight glow filled his hazel eyes, and he slid from Loria's saddle without question. "What have you gotten yourself into now?" he asked, inching his way through the crowd. The sheer size of him made the task that much more difficult. Eyes stared after him and Isolde could see the blush forming on his cheeks from the attention.

"I haven't done anything," Isolde said, her words ringing with false innocence. "Well, nothing that wasn't deserved anyway."

The sound of Malaki's familiar sigh ghosted behind her as they made their way into the alley. The children had helped the boy up onto a small wooden crate. His head rested against the cool stone wall. The rest of the children backed away at their approach, their gaze focused on the massive virya at her side.

"Don't be afraid," Isolde said, with a crooked smile. "He looks big and scary but really he's soft and sweet as a cinnamon roll."

A growl, only loud enough for her to hear, leaked through Malaki's teeth. "I'll show you soft the next time we train."

"He's going to help heal you," Isolde said, ignoring him. "Would that be okay?" They hesitated. Uncertainty and distrust filled their shallow faces. "What if, you get a treat afterwards?" Their eyes lit up at the promise of sweets and a series of nods answered back. "Excellent," Isolde said with a smile. "Malaki, I think this gentleman needs your help first." She nodded to the boy on the wall. "I'll go see what Rafe has ready."

"Hello there," Malaki said gently, dropping down to one knee beside the boy. "Can you show me where it hurts?"

Isolde strolled back into the bakery. "What do they normally get?" Isolde asked, leaning against to the counter.

"I couldn't say," Rafe said, his eyes filled with regret. "They've never been in here before. I don't even know if they've ever had something like this. Unless their parents gave it to them before they died, but I doubt it. The life of a soldier isn't worth much to the current crown—living or dead."

Isolde glanced out the window to where Malaki was working. The children surrounded him, their eyes fixed on the tattoos covering his forearms and peeking out from the collar of his tunic. A chorus of laughter filled the air at something he said.

"Well," Isolde said, "we can't have that, now can we?" She pulled her purse from a hidden pocket in the lining of her dress. "I think they deserve to know what it all tastes like."

Turning the bag upside down, she dumped out the coins she had taken from the bodies of Helurtu's raiders. They clattered against the finely polished counter between them.

"This is far too much, Lady Isolde!" Rafe said, his head shaking slightly at the sight. "I couldn't possibly accept—"

"Please," Isolde said, cutting him off. "Use it to feed them for however long it stretches." Isolde licked her lips. The hint of cinnamon and icing still remained and pushed the pile to him. "Worrying about where to find their next meal, isn't a burden a child should have to carry."

Rafe pressed his lips together as he rested his hand over her leather-clad knuckles. "No," he said. "No, they shouldn't. I'll make sure they don't go hungry."

Isolde stood at the mouth of the alley and watched Rafe pass out treats of various kinds to the children who had completed Malaki's treatment. She smiled at the sight, even more so at the lack of exhaustion on Malaki's face. Not a hint of sweat or tiredness touched his brow. Only a smile that made her heart light.

"You've had a busy morning."

Isolde jumped at the sound of Ferden's voice. He stood beside her, dressed impeccably as ever.

A spark of annoyance ignited in her chest. How had she not heard him? "It might come as a surprise but some of us are capable of more than just sitting on a horse and parading around like a bunch of pampered peacocks."

"I certainly hope so," Ferden said, the hint of a smile tugging on his face. "We can't have our Left Hand with talents so shallow and useless. Not that you fall into such a category. You've done very well, Lady Isolde. So well, in fact, the local bookies have cast you as a top contender."

"Oh, how wonderful to know I'm leading the pack for a position I despise," Isolde said, bitterness filling her voice. "Still, it's something they should have done from the beginning."

Isolde froze as a pair of arms wrapped around her waist. The boy Malaki had first healed, was beaming up at her. "Thank you, Lady Isolde!" he said through lips covered in powdered sugar. A new light dwelt in his eyes, one Isolde hoped would stay.

"There is nothing to thank me for," she said, returning his hug, not giving a single thought to the smudges of dirt and powdered sugar now covering her dress. "Look after yourself."

"Yes, My Lady," he said, before releasing her and running back to the others.

Isolde heard a small chuckle, and she turned to the lord at her side. Ferden's eyes, pewter grey and depthless as the sea, seemed to glow with an emotion just as foreign and mysterious as the soft, half-hidden smile lingering on his handsome, perfect face.

"Care to share what you find so amusing, Lord Ferden?"

"I'm just now understanding what I overheard in a tavern the other day," he said. "The people were talking of the tournament and of you."

Isolde felt her cheeks flame. "I can only imagine what they had to say."

"They were claiming you as one of their own, one of the people." His sharp eyes turned to her. "They called you their Champion of Sorrows."

"Champion of Sorrows?" Isolde asked, her head shaking slightly. "It has a rather nice ring to it but it's hardly a title I'm worthy of. I haven't won anything yet."

"I beg to disagree," Ferden said, his eyes moving to the group before them. "Their sorrow is your own. You share in their grief, in their pain. You fight for those who are believed to be less by a world that values only power because they have none. I don't know what qualifies you to be their champion more than that."

"It's just a name."

"Yes, it is a name. A name the people feel in the very depths of who they are. It speaks to the struggles they endure day after day. Like it or not, you have become a beacon for those who chant your name every time you set foot into the arena. Both in those walls and outside of them."

"A beacon?" Isolde asked, her head shaking. "A beacon for what?"

Ferden smiled softly. "Hope."

Isolde felt awkward, her fingers twisting together before she forced them by her side once more. He always did that. Even as the Hood, Ferden made her feel uneasy. Like he could see right through her. Always speaking in riddles. "I'm no different in their eyes than the bastard who put me here."

"Not only do you fight for them, Lady Isolde. You fight *with* them. And that is why you now possess something many leaders strive to achieve but rarely obtain."

"Which is?"

"Their hearts, Champion of Sorrows," Ferden said. "You have seized the hearts of your people wholly and completely." The title settled on her like a weight she didn't want, one she felt so undeserving of.

"I am many amazing, wonderful things," Isolde said, forcing her shoulders back. "But bearing the hearts of the people is something I am not qualified for. Nor is it something I want. I would have thought someone such as yourself could see that."

"Someone like myself?" Ferden asked, sliding his hands into the pockets of his cream-colored britches. "And what, may I ask, do you think of me?"

"I think you love your people as much as I love mine. But you choose to don a mask of indifference. Even with the man who came with you, Sohan. He spoke of how much your people love you. Enough to volunteer for this tournament so you wouldn't be burdened with having to choose. Yet, you haven't been to any of the trials—"

"I have many affairs to attend to while I'm in Elenarta, Lady Isolde," Ferden said, creases of irritation forming on the corners of his eyes, adding years to his otherwise flawless face. "Besides, I don't wish to watch someone I care about die needlessly. Distance is necessary."

"Face it, Lord Ferden," Isolde said. "Despite your best intentions, you care for your people. Love them even and yet you still hold an air of indifference."

"Forgive me if I don't agree that I am worthy of such devotion," Ferden snapped. "I do love my people. But to love them is to put them at risk. To make them a weakness, a pressure point for those who wish to control me. You never had a choice either. And yet here you stand. Ready to fight for those who cannot fight on their own."

"Stop trying to make me into something I'm not," Isolde said.

"And just what am I attempting to turn you into?"

"Someone worthy of remembrance, someone worth following. I am none of those things, nor do I have the strength for such lofty, heavy titles."

A smile, one Isolde couldn't quite place, ghosted at the edges of Ferden's mouth. "Strength is only given to those brave enough to endure the journey to achieve it. It is earned, never given." Ferden's calculated gaze fell to her. "And I have a feeling, Lady Isolde, you are exactly the kind of person who would look down that path and smile."

Isolde forced her gaze forward. Unease settled into her chest, causing her to shift from one foot to the other. "Perhaps it is a strength I do not want."

"Doesn't sound like something a person who willingly joined the tournament would say."

"Who says I joined willingly?" Isolde asked, brushing bits of dirt and powdered sugar from her gown.

Ferden shrugged. "Oh, I'm sure it wasn't your first choice in how to spend your time in Elenarta. But I can imagine the alternative would have been most unpleasant for you and many others you care about."

"That's my business," Isolde said, her voice like grated steel. "And no concern of yours. I don't care what the people think of me, Lord Ferden. I care for their safety, for their happiness and well-being. And if being in this damned tournament is what it takes, if it's what Arnoria needs…what the people need… It's a sacrifice I'm more than willing to bear." And she would. A hundred times over, Isolde could endure it.

Ferden stood silent, his eyes unfocused as a muscle feathered in his jaw. "Not every sacrifice takes you all at once. Some take you piece by piece. Slowly…painfully." Every word was filled with a haunted memory, as if he was speaking from his own personal hell. "But I'm sure you know that already."

"More than you know," Isolde said. Another peal of laughter echoed down the alley. Isolde turned to see Malaki playfully attempt to snatch a cookie from one of children's hands. They danced away from his reach, a crumble-covered smile spreading across their face. "How did you heal him?"

"Not the thanks I was expecting but—"

"How did you heal him?" Isolde repeated, her eyes cutting to him.

"You're no stranger to secrets, Lady Isolde," he said. "This one is mine. I am a master of a great many things—including miracles." Isolde huffed a sigh and yanked a bag from her pocket. "It will last if that is your concern," Ferden said. "There's no fear of the wound reopening."

She released a silent sigh of relief, her worry easing. "Thank you."

"Of course," Ferden said with a bow. "We can't leave Thornwood's champion without a proper healer. That simply wouldn't be fair."

Isolde smiled as she brought a chocolate to her mouth, needing something to do with her hands. Rafe had been kind enough to gift her with a massive bag of her favorites. One she had every intention of hiding from Cillian.

"Where did you get that?" Ferden's words fell in raspy demand, making her jump. His gaze was locked onto her right hand holding the bag of sweets and the ring glistening in the afternoon sun.

Protectively, Isolde brought her hand to her chest, her fingers closing into a fist. Ferden's eyes followed, his teeth grinding. "It was my mother's," Isolde said. "I know it's beautiful Lord Ferden but it really doesn't fall in line with your tastes—"

"Who gave it to you?" Ferden asked, his eyes blazing with power. His words fell in a snarl that made her own power surface. "Who let you wear it?"

"None of your damn business," Isolde said, taking a step back. "That's who."

A coldness crept into his gaze. One that told Isolde the Lord of Dolinmere, wasn't one who was normally spoken to in such a manner. Not that she cared in the slightest. "It is my business, actually," Ferden said, an air of coolness filling his words.

"Really?" she said, her brow cocking. "And just how did you come to that conclusion?"

"Because it makes you a very dangerous threat," Ferden said. "To all of us."

"I hardly think—"

"Do you remember the tapestry?" Ferden asked, cutting her off. "The one in Briarhole?"

Isolde paused. The memory of the beautiful tapestry that portrayed their worlds and the gods who cursed it, filled her head. "What of it?"

"Do you remember the rings of the gods?"

"Yes, but—"

"That," Ferden spat, his finger pointing, "is Vae's ring—the Goddess of Wind."

A wave of warmth brushed against Isolde's skin, as if a breath of power cascaded from the winged, golden band. "You can't be serious." Yet even as the words left her lips, Isolde felt nothing but truth in Ferden's claim. In the warmth, the power trickling over her skin like a stream of water across a bed of river rocks.

"Do I look anything but serious at the moment, Lady Isolde?" Ferden asked, his eyes locked on her hand.

"You look like a man on the verge of having a fit."

"Damn it!" he growled, teeth bared. "You have no idea what kind of power you possess. It can end you!" Shock and something else radiated from Ferden's eyes as his hand cupped his mouth. "It will heighten your power, make you lethal. But it will also turn you into something else entirely. Make you more susceptible to the darkness residing within us all…and the darkness that does not. Do you remember the shadows you pointed out on the tapestry?"

"The power you said came from other realms?" Isolde asked. "The power you said should never have come into our world?"

"Yes. That is what you are opening yourself up to when you use this ring. It will try to turn your will more like Vae's. Savage and cruel."

"I've worn this for years and not turned into a monster yet."

"And why do I get the feeling that isn't entirely true?" Ferden asked, his brow rising in challenge. Isolde bit the inside of her cheek, refusing to admit, especially to him, that her power was growing increasingly more difficult to keep on a leash.

"Do not let it control you, Isolde," Ferden said, his hands fisting at his sides. It was the first time he had said her name without an ounce of formality. And it filled her with dread. "You hold the power of a god on your finger—Vae's power. You might have been its bearer for years," he said. "But from what I know of the gods, they never stay silent for long."

He wasn't wrong. Even now, she could feel power lurking around the edges of her mind, pressing into her skin. Ever since the disastrous night at Briarhole, the night she almost died, that power had never slept.

"This is insane," Isolde said, gazing down at the diamond clutched in the wings' gilded embrace. "It's impossible." Galaena would have told her if she knew…

"I have lived for a *very* long time," Ferden sighed. "My eyes have seen what no others have had the misfortune to witness. That ring's power, much like the ones flowing in our veins, was not meant for us to have. It too is a curse. The best thing you can do is toss it into the Adriam River and never look back."

Isolde brushed the pad of her finger over her mother's ring. A tickle of power answered back, and its touch was infinite and all-consuming. A shudder of apprehension rippled down Isolde's back. But she ignored it. This was a piece of her mother, the only thing she had left of her. There was no force, living or dead, that could make her give it up. Not even Ferden.

"Vae's ring or not," Isolde said, her fingers curling into a fist, "it is mine, and I will decide what to do with it." She met his gaze, and something passed between them. A promise she knew he understood. Death would be the reward of anyone who tried to take it from her.

"If that is your wish, Lady Isolde," Ferden said, his head dipping into a bow, "then so be it." He made his way back to the parade but halted before disappearing into the maze of bodies lining the streets.

"Your mind is your own, Isolde," Ferden said, his lips turning down into a sad, knowing smile. "Don't let the gods have one damn piece of it."

CHAPTER 30

Isolde hovered nearby as Nan removed another unsoiled bandage from Malaki's hip with a delicate, caring touch. It had been overkill, but an indulgence he'd allowed to ease her mind. A scar, nearly identical to the one marring Isolde's skin, blazed a trail down and across his right thigh, severing the names of the dead who had once resided there. Some were strangers to Isolde. Others…not so much.

Nan sat back with a satisfied look on her withered face. "Is it healed?" Isolde asked, her teeth chewing the edge of her nail that was already far too short.

"As far as I can tell." Nan said, smacking Isolde's hand away before turning her narrowed eyes on Malaki. "Whatever Lord Ferden did worked. But you should still rest, just in case."

"Good luck with making him rest, Nan," Isolde said, stuffing another cookie into her mouth. While she was grateful to Ferden for helping Malaki, there was an edge of distrust remaining in her mind, one refusing to go away. Never had such magic existed…or at least none that recent memory could dredge up.

The pad of Isolde's thumb traced along the edge of the gilded feather band on her finger. *That is Vae's ring.* Ferden's words buzzed in her head like a hive of bees.

She hadn't told the others.

Especially Galaena.

What if it was true? What if she really held the power of a goddess on her hand? The thought only sickened her. Isolde hated her own power and the thought of carrying something containing the might of a god in it on her hand, turned her stomach. The memory of her mother warmed the deepest parts of her heart and chased away the darkness within. She shoved the ring further onto her finger and clung to that nostalgic warmth.

"You've got about as much luck with me to sharing food as you do with getting him to rest." Isolde reached for the last of the raspberry shortbread cookies from Rafe's bakery, her stomach growling. But as her fingers brushed the delicacy, Malaki snagged it from beneath her fingers and shoved it into his mouth.

Isolde's eyes widened in disbelief. "Did you just…?" she asked, dumbfounded, her icing-coated fingers still hovering in the air.

Malaki merely smiled, and he licked his fingers clean. "Delicious."

Isolde narrowed her gaze and pushed to her feet. "You're lucky you're still on bed rest," she growled. "Otherwise, I'd have to put you in your place."

"You haven't been able to put me in my place your entire life," Malaki said, a playful, challenging smile breaking across face. "But it's adorable you think you can. And I feel fine."

Isolde opened her mouth to retort but was brought up short as a knock sounded from the door. "Saved," she said, pulling the door open.

Liam stood before her. His dark eyes took in the fitted tunic and britches. Isolde felt her core tighten as a knowing smirk played on the edges of his lips. The lips she wished desperately to have all over her in that moment.

"Good morning," he said with small bow of his head. "How do I find the fair maiden of Thornwood today?"

"That remains to be seen," she said stepping aside to let him in. The tips of his fingers grazed her hip as he passed.

"Liam!" cried Nan, painfully rising to her feet. Her withered hands cupped his face. "It's so good to see you." A light blush followed behind the kisses she left planted on his cheeks.

"Hello Nan," he said, wrapping his arms around her in return. "How do we find you today?"

"Well, all things considered."

"That's wonderful to hear," said Liam. His eyes traveled to Malaki and the newly formed scar. His brow lifted in surprise. "Gods, Malaki!" A smile, one of genuine happiness, broke out onto Liam's face. "How did this happen?"

"That's none of your concern," Malaki said, yanking a blanket up to conceal the scar. *"Captain."*

The smile and light faded from Liam's face, only to give way to a cold look of indifference. Isolde shot Malaki a furious look.

"Are you here to escort Isolde?" Nan asked, trying to dispel the tension.

"Indeed, I am," Liam said, his eyes dropping slightly. "I was told this event wouldn't take long or shouldn't anyway. The king has ordered another ball in a few days' time. I guess he wants the champions well enough to attend."

Malaki grunted as he sat up on the lounger. "And I'm sure you're devastated by that, aren't you?"

"I'm not one for social events," Liam said, hardly sparing Malaki a glance.

"Could have fooled me," growled Malaki.

"Shut it," Isolde barked, taking Liam's hand, and tugging him to the door. "I'll see you after the trial. Try to not injure yourself or pull a muscle climbing into the bleachers, Malaki." She pulled Liam through the door as Malaki's growl ripped through the air. Liam kept pace, his mouth pulled into a tight line.

"What is it?"

Liam shook his head, causing a mass of ebony curls to fall across his forehead. "I had hoped agreeing to help would change things. That I had proven myself, at least a little."

"Give it time," Isolde said, giving his hand a squeeze. "He'll come around. They all will."

A smile, one filled with boyish hope, pulled at Liam's lips. Even here, in the heart of the capital, she could see the boy from Thornwood. But as they rounded a corner, a battalion of guards turned their sights on them, and Liam quickly detached himself from Isolde's grip.

"We can't," he said, his voice low and filled with remorse. "If anyone were to see and report it to Gage..." His jaw ticked. "He's not one who takes others playing with what he believes belongs to him lightly. If he saw, if he heard...he would only hurt you."

"I understand," Isolde said, steeling her heart, forcing the bitterness away. "So, what wonderful trial does the Right Hand have planned for us today?"

"I'm not sure. Gage is keeping them very close to the chest. I'm not even sure he's informed of them until the day of. Erebus and Lenox discuss each trial beforehand to map out every detail." Isolde felt a block of ice fall into her stomach at the thought.

They walked in silence until reaching the outskirts of the arena. Isolde's heart pounded in her chest, making every breath harder and harder to gain. Something felt different about today. Like the calm before a horrible storm.

"Be careful," Liam said when they reached the holding area. His fingers wove their way between her own and squeezed. "And come back to me."

"Always, I do." She planted a quick kiss on his blushing cheek before slipping through the door.

Demir stood near one of the lavishly filled tables lining the wall; his thin lips were pressed to the rim of a fine, porcelain mug. Steam rolled around the edges as his cold, serious eyes landed on her. Isolde couldn't tell why, but a part of her knew to be wary of Demir. He was powerful, that much was for certain. But there was a craftiness about him, a slyness that had her on guard, her teeth on edge.

"Lady Isolde," he said, in greeting over the rim of his cup before taking a sip.

"Demir." Without missing a beat, Isolde strolled to the table and plucked a cup from the silver-lined tray. The scent of coffee filled her nose as she tilted the teapot forward. "How is the champion of the mighty Foxclove today?"

Demir shifted in her direction, his lean shoulder pressing against the smooth stone wall. He kept his gaze forward, the edge of his brow raised. "Very well. How do I find the former heir of Thornwood?"

"Simply divine," Isolde said, with an overly sweet smile and added heaping spoonfuls of sugar into her coffee. Demir watched with disdain, his lip curling. Isolde shoved a breakfast roll into her mouth with less than perfect manners, doing her best to pepper the fine velvet tablecloth with as many crumbs as possible. Chocolate and butter coated her tongue while bits of flaky, golden crust dusted her tunic.

"How very ladylike," Demir grumbled. It wasn't lost on Isolde that Demir held himself with a certain air of entitlement. A sense of decorum she despised. One that most pricks who looked down on others from their ivory towers harbored.

"I aim to please," she said. "Tell me, how did you get roped into being the champion of Foxclove?"

"His Lordship asked it of me," he said, still not deigning to look her way.

Isolde hardly believed Gage would simply ask. "What were you before?"

"I was the overseer of Lord Dagan's properties. His right-hand man of sorts, you could say."

Isolde arched an eyebrow. "That's very interesting," she said. "I don't recall hearing your name being mentioned. At any point in time as a matter of fact."

It wasn't a lie. Isolde couldn't remember Demir being named a single time during her visits to Foxclove or anywhere else. Nor was there any sign of him the night she slaughtered Dagan in his bedroom. Or the night she left Gage naked and humiliated after stealing thousands of pieces of gold from right under his nose.

"You wouldn't," Demir said, his voice flat. "I wasn't exactly known for carrying out deeds the public needed to be aware of."

Isolde felt her muscles tense, her guard rising. She wasn't just looking at Dagan's former second-in-command...she was looking at his mercenary—his executioner.

"Rumor has it," Isolde said, her voice dropping into a whisper as she leaned in close, "the Hood strung up your former master. Bled him dry like a stuck pig and left him hanging from the front door of Foxclove."

Demir leveled her with a glare, a muscle in his jaw ticking. "I also heard the Hood left the Right Hand in a very compromising position after stealing away a massive fortune."

Hatred brewed in Demir's eyes. Isolde ran the tip of her finger around the rim of her cup, her shoulder shrugging. "But you know the nature of rumors. I'm sure there isn't any validity to them. Especially if you were the one responsible for keeping the little lordlings safe." A sarcastic, malicious chuckle filled Isolde's cup as she took another sip. "What an embarrassing failure that would be."

Light shone from Demir's eyes, his lip curling into a snarl. As he opened his mouth, a shadow filled the doorway.

"This looks interesting," Kyros said, a mischievous smile tugging onto his handsome face as his eyes bounced back and forth between them. "Am I interrupting anything."

"Not at all," Isolde said overly cheerfully. She plucked another roll from the polished silver tray. "Demir and I were just discussing failure and the devastating consequences it can bring."

Demir set his cup down, the porcelain clinking against the wooden table. "Be very careful, Lady Isolde," he said, his voice smooth and dark as the coffee he left in his cup. "You never know how this tournament will end."

"I already know how it will end, Demir," Isolde purred. "With me as the winner. Any other outcome is just wishful thinking."

His dark, hard eyes brimmed with annoyance as he sauntered off to take a seat on one of the couches near the fireplace.

"You're awfully confident this morning," Kyros said, stepping up to pluck a cup of his own from the tray. "For someone who's done nothing but scrape by so far."

"Says the man who is here by charity," Isolde muttered before taking a sip. "Not only from the king, but your sweet Lady Circe, as well. Last time I saw you, a piece of wood was buried in your gut."

Kyros shot Demir a dark look, one promising retribution. "He got lucky."

"Lucky?" Isolde asked, picking at the roll. "Or were you just having an off day?"

Sohan and Buer eventually graced them with their presence.

"Doesn't seem nearly as crowded in here today," Buer said, his eyes gleaming. "Now that the weak trash has been dealt with." A growl flowed through Isolde teeth. Buer's smile grew. "Although, I see a little still remains." Before Isolde could say a word, the door to the chambers opened and Lenox stepped forward.

"Good morning champions," Lenox said, his eyes sweeping the room. Isolde felt their touch land on her and a small bead of light echoed in their depths. "His Majesty has rearranged today's event to be a rather short one in order to accommodate a ball that will be held in a three days' time. He wants you all well for the event."

The same feeling of unease swept through Isolde as she watched the smile on the bastard's face grow. Whatever Erebus had planned, she had no doubt it wouldn't be easy. No matter how short it was.

"If you will come with me."

"What of our lovely bracelets?" Kyros asked. "I wore this outfit just for the occasion." He pinched the corner of his evergreen tunic that had been expertly tailored to fit his form. Isolde had to admit, the bracelet, horrible as it was, would have completed the ensemble nicely.

Lenox looked over his shoulder, his grin stretching even further at the edge of his mouth. "You won't be needing them today."

Isolde cast a glance at Kyros, who returned hers with a dark look of his own. They filed in behind Sohan and followed Lenox out into the arena. Already the crowd was cheering. Their voices echoed off the cold, stonewalls. The uneasy feeling in Isolde's chest only grew as they ascended the tunnel and the massive grate rose before them.

The people of the capital roared at the sight of them. Isolde looked over to where she knew the others would be. In a sea of gold and maroon, she spotted Malaki. Not that her second-in-command was hard to find. The wide span of his shoulders easily took up two seats. He sat next to Alaric and Galaena on the top row, a small canopy nearly concealing them in shadow.

Malaki's hazel eyes were locked on her as she made her way to the center of the arena. To her left, a tall curtain had been strung up. The ends of five large wooden pillars, each one bearing the flag of a remaining territory peeked over the top. Thornwood's was positioned in the very center. The golden lion, rippled through the air as a gust of wind tore through the sky. Its mouth was open and fangs sharp, ready to devour all who stood in its path.

She nearly bumped into Sohan as he came to a halt and turned to the dais. Forcing herself to look away from the curtain, Isolde turned and met the eyes of the man she hated more than anything else. The scars on Gage's face were drawn tight around a charming, false smile pulling at the edge of his full, red lips.

"Hello, pet." A single torch was held in his gloved hand. Its flame caught Isolde's eye, and she fought to hide the fear that was undoubtedly shining in her eyes. "I hope you're ready for today." Her gaze lifted to where Erebus stood at the edge of the dais, his obsidian crown glistening in the early morning sun.

"Champions!" he said, his arms outstretched before him. "You have proven yourselves to be worthy opponents in this tournament thus far. But my Left Hand, one I will trust with not only my life but the lives of every citizen in our great kingdom, cannot just be clever, fast, or strong. There is one thing they must possess; a piece, far more important than anything else." His cold eyes fell to where she stood, and Isolde felt the weight of that stare. "Loyalty."

Erebus gestured behind them, and Isolde turned. Dust erupted from the gravel where the velvet curtain fell. Through the haze, Isolde picked out five bodies. Bodies that were up right but not moving. At last the plume of debris settled, and Isolde's blood turned cold.

"No!" The word fell from her lips in a cry as whips of sorrow lashed through her heart.

Tanor's arms were pulled painfully tight around his back, bending to the curve of the pillar. His wide, terror-filled eyes met hers. A river of tears cascaded down his cheeks. "Lady Isolde?"

"My Left Hand," Erebus continued, his voice cutting her deeper than any knife ever could, "must follow my orders without question and without pause."

Isolde's head pounded. The rush of blood, anger, and panic filled her ears like a storm. It did little to block out Erebus's voice. Did little to soften the blow she was sure would destroy her.

"These are criminals who have been tried and found guilty of crimes against the crown and they will be punished for it." Four soldiers stepped forward, each one bearing a torch in their hands. They stood beside a champion and held the torch out to them. Isolde felt Gage step up behind her, his mouth at her ear.

"Prove your loyalty to the king, Isolde." She flinched away from the heat of the flame as Gage held it out before her.

"What crime could a boy possibly commit to warrant this?" she asked, seething. Panic swelled in her chest, her mind racing, desperate to find a solution, a way out of this.

"I wouldn't say it's as much his crime as it is yours," Gage said, the leather of his jacket crunching with the shrug of his shoulders. "You are the one who taught him how to read after all, aren't you?"

"I'll marry you," she said. "Right now, I'll marry you if you stop this."

She could endure it— lifetime of being at Gage's side, of sharing his bed. All of it was a small price to pay for sparing Tanor, a boy she loved like her own, from such a fate.

"I already have your hand, Isolde," Gage whispered, the hint of smug victory hanging in his words. "There is nothing you can offer me I don't already possess or can't simply take if I wish. Even after you kill him, you will still marry me."

Isolde felt her heart shatter into so many pieces she knew it could never be fixed, could never be made whole again. "Then punish me," she pleaded through gritted teeth. "I am the one responsible…Punish me!"

A deep, wicked chuckle filled what little space there was between them. "I am punishing you."

Isolde's eyes swept the arena, desperate for any path leading away from the one she was staring down. But not a single glimpse of hope found its way to her. There were more soldiers present than there had been before. They lined the perimeter of the arena, each armed to the teeth with elithrium-laced weapons. A battalion was stationed at every territory.

Thornwood was surrounded. Four soldiers had a hold of Malaki's shoulders, his eyes blazing with fury. Two others had restrained Galaena and one detained Alaric, whose lips were pulled back into a snarl. Blades were pressed to Cillian and Blyana's throats, holding them in place.

"Erebus wasn't lying," Gage murmured, stepping closer, the heat of the flames kissing her cheek, "when he said you would know exactly what he requested of you in this trial." He shoved the flame in front of her face, forcing her to flinch away yet again. "This is the price for your defiance."

Isolde's gaze dropped to the pyre that had been constructed at Tanor's feet. Dried, dead branches jabbed into his small legs, breaking the skin. She felt the cold glee shining from Erebus's gaze. Not even her power came forward as shock reverberated through every part of her body…her mind…her soul.

"Burn him."

CHAPTER 31

"Take the torch, Isolde," Gage growled when she didn't move. *"Take it."*

Numbly, Isolde wound her fingers around the warm, wooden handle. The heat, that normally would send her into a panic, barely brushed the corners of her mind.

As if in a dream, Isolde stepped forward until she was directly in front of Tanor. In front of the boy she had sworn to save, the boy she had sworn to bring home. Her eyes brimmed with tears. Tears of heartache, regret, and anger.

"I can't, Tanor." The words slid from Isolde's tongue like acid.

"You don't have a choice," Tanor said, the warm eyes she'd loved since he was child were rimmed in silver. "You must."

"I won't kill you!" she growled, the words riding on a single wave of air Isolde pushed towards him. Tears threatened to break across her face as she stepped closer. She scanned the arena, searching desperately for a way, anyway, to get him out of this.

"If you don't," Tanor said, as remnants of the beautiful golden locks she used to tease him about fell into his face as he jerked against the bonds. "Then everyone we love will die. My life is not worth you ending yours or theirs for. Neither was Mary's." His throat bobbed. "They would kill me in the end anyway, along with you and all of Thornwood."

A single tear broke free and trickled down Isolde's cheek. A puff of wind sent a cloud of smoke into her face, hiding the traitorous tear. "I promised your father," said Isolde, the words cleaving her in two. "I gave him my word I would bring you home. That I would save you!"

"I am not asking you to save me," Tanor said, the corners of his lips softening. Isolde could see resolve settle into his face. An air of acceptance, of courage now shone from his battered face. "I'm asking you to live." Terror, heartache, and rage burned through Isolde as Tanor's words leapt from his lips. "I have one request."

"Anything!" The word came like a plea, a desperate hope against the horrible reality the gods had placed her in.

"Tell my father, I love him." Tanor's lips trembled as the words broke free. "Tell him, that I am so proud, of the man he is. That I am so proud to be his son."

"Tanor," Isolde's lips quivered. She did not care if anyone saw. "Tanor…please."

"I've never known you to beg for anything, Lady Isolde," he said. "Do not start now on my account." Tanor's face hardened once more into hatred. He yanked against the bonds holding him in place. "Death to Erebus Tenebriath and all who stand with him!"

A cry of anger exploded from the crowd. Their words formed into a single chant. One Isolde knew would haunt her for the rest of her life.

"Burn him! Burn him!"

Off to the side, Gage shifted his feet from side to side, his observant, cold eyes narrowing in suspicion. Realization blossomed in

Isolde's mind. A harsh reality she could not change, one she could not alter.

There was no escape…not this time.

A flicker of heat kissed her skin as the torch slid down her hand. The brief touch of pain sent a wave of panic cascading though her frame. Memories of a past burned into ash and shadow. A whip of flame cutting into her back and a laugh of pure angelic, malice piercing the cold, night sky. But it was Tanor's voice that drew her back.

"If this is my fate, then death is the kindest gift you can offer me." His eyes shone with a love Isolde knew she would never deserve. It felt as if a hand had reached inside her chest and squeezed. "Please," he begged. "I can't take another day in there. I can't endure another night in those chambers. If you love me, you will kill me."

Isolde's fingers constricted around the torch, the wood groaning in protest. Anguish ravaged her chest as she took a step forward…then another…and another. Until she stood but a foot from the pyre. Bruises decorated Tanor's skin beneath the dirty tunic clinging to his emaciated form.

Isolde refused to look away. Refused to tear her gaze from the child who she had helped raise. The one who's mind was so bright and filled with hope for a future he would never see. The boy who had started to take a step onto the path of manhood, down a path he would never tread.

With a shuddering breath, the torch fell from Isolde's hand. It bounced and jostled amongst the dry, dead branches at Tanor's bare, bruised feet. The merciless flames took hold and grew.

Tanor's eyes locked on hers. The beautiful pools of honey brown shone with so many emotions. Regret…Sorrow…Agony…But most of all love. Isolde couldn't accept the last one. That gaze of adoration was one she did not deserve. The fingers of the fire danced in his eyes but never grew. Not a single flame came close to touching his skin as Isolde pulled the air away.

"I'm sorry, Tanor," she whispered, hardly allowing her lips to move at all as the words fell from her tongue like ash. "So, so sorry."

"Don't be, Isolde," he said. The sound of her name, without her formal title nearly broke what small resolve remained. Only at the end would he listen to her. "You have given me and so many others a life worth fighting for, worth dying for. All or nothing."

Isolde fought to hide the shock, her lips parting. It was a saying only those in her cadre used. How did he know?

"My father knew," Tanor said. "And he wanted to make sure there would always be someone there to help. That is the legacy he left me."

Every day Tanor dared to learn, dared to open a book despite the law and the consequences it would bring. All were acts of defiance, of fearless rebellion. Virya or not, Tanor was a member of her cadre—now and always.

Tanor's gaze softened, his eyes brimming with tears. "I will see you again."

Isolde extended a hand forward, wanting everyone to see. She willed the tears swimming in her eyes to not fall as a small ribbon of air caressed Tanor's neck. Allowing her power to come forth, Isolde seized control of the air feeding the flames and starved them until only embers remained.

"I'll meet you in the air."

The small thread of air wound around Tanor's neck tightened and jerked. Death, Isolde's most dependable and hated friend, found him instantly. The sound of his bones breaking branded into Isolde's memory, staining her soul beyond redemption. Her hold on her power evaporated and the flames erupted from the bed of embers at the base of the pyre.

Protective numbness coated Isolde's mind. A numbness that had no chance of withstanding the endless guilt waiting in the shadows.

But it would keep the emotional assault at bay until she could escape the eyes burrowing into her like arrows.

Isolde couldn't take her eyes from Tanor's lifeless face. Never had she wanted to die so badly. Never had the thought of death been so appealing. Her foot inched closer to the blaze, as if she longed to be consumed by the inferno. Despite the horrors of her past, Isolde found herself desperate to follow Tanor into the abyss.

But a hand gripped her elbow and pulled her back.

"I believe your king told you to burn him," said Gage, his fingers keeping her from the flames.

"And I did," Isolde said, her voice flat. "He never said he had to be alive when I did it."

"Clever girl," Gage drawled. "Details do matter, I suppose. Still, I can't say I expected you to go through with it. I bet on you to lose this one, as a matter of fact."

"You bid on your fiancée to fail?" Isolde said, her voice lifeless and cold with the numbness. "How very un-husbandly of you."

"It could have been far worse," he said, with a shrug. "I wanted the king to pick your crippled uncle."

"You better thank the gods he didn't agree with you," Isolde said, her eyes turning to meet his. "Galaena would have taken her time in ensuring you felt every ounce of pain possible before you died, and I would have watched with a smile."

"Your bitch of an aunt would have died along with your useless, weak uncle." He took a step closer, his lips grazing the shell of her ear. "I hope you finally understand the situation, Isolde. You belong to him…and to me. It's a shame it took you killing a child to grasp that concept."

Despair racked through Isolde's heart as the cries of the others rose over the cracking flames consuming Tanor's body. Kyros was staring at a girl bound to her own pyre. Her face was wet with tears. Sobs, broken and desperate, spilled across her lips. "Please, please spare me! I have children!" The soldier held the torch out to him, and pain ripped through Kyros's eyes as his hand slowly closed around the shaft.

Buer snatched the offered torch from the soldier without pause and stalked to the pillar that held a man bound to its frame. He had the same look as Buer, but his features were far softer, kinder.

"Buer," he said, tugging against the bonds holding him in place. "Buer, please! I'm your brother!"

Without a word, the champion of Briarhole plunged the torch into the belly of the pyre and turned his back. The man screamed for him, begged for him to show mercy. But Buer kept walking until he reached his previous spot and looked up at the king, his face set in stone.

The flag of Dolinmere snapped in the wind as the old man tied to the pyre whispered something to Sohan. The champion's head bowed, and he dropped the torch at the man's feet. Sohan stayed by the man's side until his final cries of pain were carried away with the wind.

Demir's pyre had already been lit. Its victim reduced to nothing but ash.

Isolde wrenched her arm free of Gage's grip and turned her back to the dais. Without waiting for a response, without waiting to be dismissed, she made for the mouth of the tunnel. Panic filled her chest. It lodged in her windpipe, refusing to let her breathe.

Liam waited in the shadows of the tunnel. His lips were pulled into a tight line, and sadness shone in his eyes. "Isolde—"

"I need get out of here," she said. The beast inside her head raked its claws down what little remained of her self-control. "Now, Liam!"

"You can't leave," Liam murmured, looking back over his shoulder to the dais, to the king who was staring back at her, his eyes filled with fury. "Not until Erebus—"

"I don't give a damn about, Erebus!" Isolde snarled, her veins humming with power. "It's either I leave, or I kill everyone in sight."

She had just minutes before she wouldn't be herself anymore. Mere minutes before she would become the very thing she feared the most.

Liam seemed to finally grasp what she was saying and pointed down the corridor. "Take the first right, then—"

"I know where to go!" she growled, before taking off into a sprint. The walls sped past her in a blur. Anger poured through her veins like molten lead, pushing her harder, faster. Before long, she burst from the confines of the arena and sprinted through the deserted streets until she reached the path leading up to the mountainside. But as she ran, her will gave way and the monster within seized control.

A cry of pain transformed into the screech of a falcon as Isolde took flight. Her powerful wings beat against the harsh mountain wind as she climbed. The Oronilma Mountains, bathed in the bright morning sun, lay beneath her. Never had the will to escape, to run from everything hit her as hard as it did in that moment. To escape the horror of what she had just done. She could still smell the smoke, could still feel the heat of the flames against her skin.

Isolde came to rest on one of the peaks along the Gap of Duron. Bits of snow and rock fell over the edge and into the abyss below as her talons clung to the cliff side. Sadness and guilt swept through her heart and not even her mindless, blood thirsty power could stop it.

Tanor's face, twisted in pain, shone in her mind. A cry ripped through her beak and carried across the mountain range. Despair burned through her heart. It spread like a poison, leaching its way into every part of her being.

After a while, fragments of who she was slowly fell back into place. Her power retreated, as if it too couldn't take the agony of her reality. For once, it seemed to understand, appearing to be on her side of the fight, and relented control. The pain continued on as her cry morphed into a scream as she slowly changed back into herself. Her knees sank into the snow, saturating her pant legs and chilling her to the bone.

"I'm sorry!" Isolde cried, her face falling into hands, tears coating her palms. "I'm sorry...I'm sorry!" It felt as if her heart was crumbling into chard, blackened pieces she knew could never be repaired again.

Isolde looked towards the horizon, to the endless peaks that seemed to stretch to the end of the world. The tips of her knees kissed the crest of a cliff leading down into a ravine of darkness below. A darkness that seemed to whisper the promise of absolution, of reprieve from her pain. The thought was so inviting, so incredibly tempting, Isolde leaned forward even more.

You are the cause of this. You are the reason Tarvo will never see his son again. Death is the only thing you bring. It is all you deserve.

The familiar voice echoed through her head. Their words haunting her, infecting her like a disease.

Your fault...your fault...your fault!

Isolde wanted nothing more than to tilt forward just a little more. To fall into the nothingness and end her pain.

"Isolde."

She paused at the sound of his voice. The voice that had drawn her back from darkness so many times before. With a heavy sigh, Isolde turned to see Malaki standing a few feet away. Sweat soaked his clothes, and his chest heaved with exhaustion. He held a handout to her, beckoning her to him.

"Move away from the edge, Isolde."

She looked back to the ravine, to the sweet relief it promised. Her fingers brushed the edge, disturbing the perfect mounds of snow. Malaki slowly lowered himself to the ground beside her. Bits of snow tumbled over the edges and into the fathoms below. The voice grew louder in Isolde's mind as she watched them fall.

All you cause is pain to everyone you love. You're a burden, a mistake, a disease. They would be much happier, safer without you here. Just a little more...

The thought festered and grew into something truly terrifying—a desire. Isolde felt herself move closer, her gaze locked on the bits of snow growing smaller and smaller. The tips of her fingers gripped the edge, her knuckles blanching.

"Isolde," Malaki said, his deep voice laced with warning. She felt his warm, callused fingers rest on the crook of her arm. Still, she leaned forward.

"Why not, Malaki?" She asked. Her voice sounded so small, so broken even to her. "I have failed everyone I have ever loved."

Malaki's grip tightened and he pulled her to his chest, away from death's outstretched hand. A sense of relief and also anger filled her chest. His warm scent, sandalwood and rainstorm, instantly consumed her. A hint of smoke lingered as well. He smelled like the past. Of a time when hope existed, and she didn't want to die.

"No, you haven't," Malaki said. His fingers dug into her skin and thread through her hair, as if he was afraid to let go. "This is not your fault, Isolde."

"How is it not my fault?" she asked as all the reasons played out in her head for why it was.

"This is Erebus's doing. He made the trial, not you." Hatred laced through the words as they fell from Malaki's tongue. "Do you know what would have happened if you refused? Or if you had fought back? They would have slaughtered us all and burned Thornwood to the ground. And you would more than likely be married to Gage by now. Or at least given to him to do with as he pleased."

Isolde shook her head. "I should never have taught Tanor to read. I should never have started story hour."

"There are many regrets we have in life, Isolde. But bringing joy to someone else's should not be one of them. You helped those children understand that not all virya are evil, that there are people in this world who care about them. You gave them hope."

"I gave them death, Malaki!" Tears cascaded down Isolde's cheeks, and her arms wrapped around her middle as if holding herself together. "Let me die," Isolde cried, her fingers digging in her skin. "Please, just let me die, Malaki!"

Strong hands gripped her face, forcing her to look up. "Don't ever ask that of me!" he rasped, his eyes wide with panicked anger. "Don't you ever put me in a position of living in a world without you, Isolde. This is not your fault!"

"I killed him," she cried, her voice cracking as it carried over the mountain peaks. "I killed him... I killed him!"

"Erebus killed Tanor," Malaki said, his grip tightening as she tried to pull her face away. "Look at me! Lenox killed Tanor. Gage killed Tanor. Not you. *Not you!*"

Her tears fell across Malaki's hands, coating the names of the dead residing there in fresh, hot sorrow. She couldn't help but wonder, if the boy she couldn't save would find his way onto Malaki's skin as well.

Isolde squeezed her eyes shut, unable to look into Malaki's kind, loving eyes a moment longer. He tucked her head underneath his chin. "It's not your fault," he said. "It's not your fault."

"I promised Tarvo," she cried. Her fingers twisted into his tunic. "I promised I would bring his son home, Malaki. I promised!" Anguish and fear for what was to come lashed through Isolde's heart. She would undoubtedly see Tanor again. His face, along with all the others she had failed, would return to haunt her, to curse her.

"Tanor would not want this, Isolde," Malaki said. "He would not have wanted to see you lose who you are."

"I don't even know who that is anymore."

Malaki unfolded his arms so he could look her in the eye. Gently, his warm palm cupped her chin and tilted her face up. "You are Isolde Cotheran of Thornwood," he said, steel weaving its way into his voice. "The Hood of Arnoria, the Thief of Sorrows, and you do not bow to fear." Kamden's words fell on her heart like a balm. "Who does it bow to?" Malaki asked.

The words felt like a vow, a pledge as they left her tongue. "To me," she said. "It bows...to me."

Isolde's pain gave way to anger as something new and terrifying rose from the ashy remains of her heart. The same cold fire that had always been there was reborn. It rose, strong and powerful, like a phoenix remade. It hardened her heart to stone and sealed away the very essence of who she was behind an impenetrable wall of steel and fury.

Malaki peered into her eyes, and a look of resolution filled his own.

"You know who you are," he said. "You are not capable of being broken."

CHAPTER 32

Days passed in a blur, and still the hollowness remained. When not forced into the public eye, Isolde and the rest of the cadre, stole away deep into the mountains. In a snow-covered meadow, nestled between two peaks, Isolde unleashed her fury and agony.

She wielded every weapon Malaki brought, including his axe. They each took turns fighting her. Blyana, Cillian, Malaki, and even Galaena stood in the path of her wrath with open arms.

She felt as if there was nothing left of the woman she once was. That she had burned away with Tanor in the arena. Every strike of the blade released a fraction of the tension, chipping away at the anguish suffocating her.

Not a drop of water or a crumble of food passed her lips. Guilt and anger filled her heart, turning her soul into something she didn't recognize. A darkness crept along the edges of her mind. A shadow of fury and savagery she couldn't suppress, even if she wanted to.

"My rose," Nan said, taking a seat at the edge of the bed the day of the accursed ball. "You must eat." Isolde refused anything she had to offer. "Please."

It was the sound of Nan's voice that drew her out of the abyss. The worry and heartache that forced Isolde back into reality. A roll, smothered in melted butter and honey, rested in Nan's palm. "Just a small bite, my rose. Tanor—" she said.

"Don't," Isolde said, flinching. Her voice was a rasp, a hollow sound. "Don't say his name, Nan."

"He would not want this for you."

Isolde looked to the lounger, to the spot Malaki had slept for the past three nights. His eyes were closed, and his chest rose in steady, even breaths. Even in sleep, worry lined his face.

"Fine." Reluctantly, she nibbled at the roll. It was a treat that once would have made her moan with delight. Instead, it tasted plain and dry in her mouth.

"The ball is tonight," Nan said, pouring a cup of tea. Steam rose in light pillows of peppermint-scented clouds. "We haven't got much time to get ready."

"For once, Nan," Isolde said, swallowing around the lump of agony and bread, "I truly don't care what I look like."

Little did Isolde know that choice had been taken from her as well.

The sound of the heels Erebus had sent her to wear echoed off the stone walls. Fine layers of ebony silk and lace, brushed against her skin as she walked down the deserted corridor. She was surprised the garment had come from Erebus instead of Gage. Her fingers grazed the fine fabric, hating to admit how much she preferred his taste to Gage's.

Isolde felt the weight of Tanor's death like a stone around her neck. A pressure, a vice constantly trying to choke the life out of her. But Kamden's words said with Malaki's voice echoed in her head, easing that pain.

I do not bow to fear, it bows to me.

They filled her to the brim, turning the suffocating guilt into something else entirely. A malice, a hatred that burned so hot it felt cold within her chest.

Golden light of the chandeliers spilled across her shoulders and down the black, lacy train trailing the floor behind her. Isolde held her head high and met the eye of all who dared look her way. Some averted their gaze, their eyes shining with a look she knew very well.

Fear.

Others turned from her with a sneer, and a few held a look of open hostility. Her family stirred behind her as a female, covered in an absurd number of jewels, muttered, "Monster," as she strolled past. Malaki's warm, assuring hand pressed into the small of her back, urging her to keep moving. Liam stood at her left, his callused, familiar fingers grazing her exposed elbow.

Isolde knew exactly what she looked like to everyone present—a brutal and merciless killer. A villain stained in blood, harboring not an ounce of regret for what she had done. One willing to burn a child alive and not shed a tear over it.

Let them think that, Isolde thought as she plucked a goblet from a serving tray. *Let them fear me or hate me. It makes little difference.*

"May I present the champion from Thornwood and company, Lady Isolde Cotheran." Zego stood at the foot of the newly redecorated dais. Isolde fought to hide the look of disgust. Black obsidian stone fractured by rivers of gold, covered the stairs and platform. Their gilded branches bled from the gilded throne Erebus perched upon.

Isolde slid into a bow, her skin prickling at the touch of Erebus's gaze. "Your Grace," she said, her voice neutral. While she could hide the hatred from showing too much in her voice, Isolde knew it was impossible to hide it in her eyes. An amused smile pulled at Erebus's flawless face.

"What a lovely dress, Lady Isolde." The tips of his fingers grazed the plum-colored fabric running along the underside of Phontine's breast. A sensual smile tugged on her perfectly painted lips. But her eyes were cold and guarded. Erebus took in Isolde from head to toe with a critical, observant eye.

"I'm sure you're aware of who supplied it," she said with a nod. "He has…interesting taste."

Interesting was putting it mildly. Clearly, the King of Arnoria preferred the women in his presence to be wearing far more elaborate designs than his Right Hand. Isolde felt the cool mountain air drifting in from the open windows to the right brush against the exposed skin of her thighs.

"On the contrary, I would say he has impeccable taste," Erebus said, his gaze falling to Isolde's plunging neckline. "That dress suits you perfectly."

Isolde merely smiled. Her teeth grated as she forced herself into another bow before turning away from the dais. She had spotted a table at the back of the room, one she would be completely content with occupying for the allotted time her presence was required.

"Don't run off," Erebus said. Isolde turned to see Phontine rise from his lap and take her seat at the back of the dais. "I require a partner for the opening dance." His jacket, so fine and perfectly tailored, fit the contours of his body like he was born with it on. "Would you do me the honors?"

He held a hand out to her. Knowing it wasn't a request, Isolde lightly placed her fingers in his palm, and allowed him to pull her to the dance floor. Onlookers scurried off to the side. The sound of the orchestra filled the air, and Erebus spun her once before cradling her body against him.

"You left before being dismissed at the trial," Erebus whispered, his lips far too close to her ear for her liking.

"I do apologize, Your Majesty," Isolde said, leaning away as best she could. "But I was just forced to kill a child."

"A child who broke the law," Erebus retorted. "And it was what I commanded. You should have been pleased to have done your job."

"Killing children doesn't bring me pleasure," she growled, her tone laced with hatred. "That's what the monstrous pet you keep at your side is for. He has just the right amount of depravity for the job." A chill ripped through her hand as Erebus spun her away only to yank her back into his arms.

"When will it sink into that very stubborn, very pretty head of yours every lash of your tongue you strike me with is a lash across the backs of those you love?" Isolde felt numb in his arms, despite the warm breeze drifting through the archways. "And you might want to be cautious of who you're calling a pet, my dear. I can't imagine your future husband would take too kindly to being called such a thing. For that is exactly what you will be when you win the tournament. A shiny…new…pet."

Isolde stiffened in his arms, a look of disgust coating her face.

Erebus leaned in close, his nose blazing an icy trail along her cheek. "There are far worse fates, Isolde. Your friend Zibiah is learning that particular lesson as we speak."

A bolt of terror speared through Isolde's heart. "What the hell do you mean?"

"Just what I said," Erebus answered. He pulled her into one final turn and let her fall. Isolde gripped Erebus's arm as he held her suspended above the ground with ease. Muscles coiled beneath her palm. "There are far worse things that could happen to you. Be grateful."

"You expect me to be grateful you forced me to murder an innocent child?" she asked. "I will never be grateful for what you have done. Even when this is over, I will never—"

"Do you think your family is safe?" Erebus asked, tugging her upright. "That even if you win the right to be my Left Hand, they will be free? There is nothing stopping me from killing your traitorous aunt and uncle. Or making your dear Malaki endure so much pain, death would be a welcomed blessing." Isolde felt blood drain from her face, her skin going deathly pale. Erebus voice dropped, his words feeling more like a lover's caress.

"I can send your companion, Blyana, back to Vara if I wish. I'm sure my cousin would love to have her back under her roof and in her beds." Vara had always flaunted her relationship to the king. Yet, Isolde had a feeling he was ignorant to her lack of cooperation, where taxes were concerned anyway.

"And her mate, Cillian...Well, I'm sure a man of his talents would be best served in the mines. Do not delude yourself into believing you have power here, Isolde Cotheran. You never did. Anything else is but an illusion, a fantasy. One I would advise you to remedy, not only for your sake. But for the sake of those you claim to love. The absolution of my word, of my rule, is beyond contestation. Is that in anyway unclear to you?"

A shuddering breath rattled through Isolde's chest. "No."

"No, what?"

Isolde ground her teeth, and the words crawled up her throat. "No, Your Majesty."

"I do believe it is customary to bow when addressing your king."

Isolde hardened her heart and froze the raging storm inside as she forced her knee to bend and her head to tilt forward until all she saw before her was the glossy marble floor.

"Very good," Erebus said, his voice breathless. An icy finger pressed against her chin, forcing her to rise. His touch sent a shiver down her spine. It felt as if winter itself had touched her.

"You'll learn in time," he said. "I can be reasonable. I'm not the monster you cast me as in that beautiful, savage mind of yours."

"Threatening my family, torturing children, killing innocent people. Your actions speak otherwise," Isolde said. Hatred churned in her eyes, filling her to the brim. Erebus's jaw clenched.

"My actions," he said, "are necessary. I will make them again if you push my hand." He leaned forward, a faint light shining in the depths of his gaze. It was cold but held something in it as well. A longing, a desperation she didn't dare linger upon. "Do not make me prove it to you, Isolde. This childish disrespect ends now. Never turn your back on me again. My patience grows thin."

Erebus's lips brushed her cheek before he finally released her, a breath of winter kissing a flame. An expectant look crossed his face, forcing Isolde into yet another curtsy. She remained that way until his footsteps died away. A dull ache, one caused by the brutal training sessions, lingered in her legs as she rose. Isolde searched the ballroom, panic rising in her blood.

Couples began moving to the dancefloor. A few of them stepped in her path, feigning for a dance with the savage champion from Thornwood. But she ignored them and pushed her way to the edge of the crowd to where Malaki waited. To her relief, her hideous fiancé was nowhere to be found.

"We need to go," Isolde muttered under her breath. "Now!"

"Why?" he asked, gently tugging her to the side. "What's happened?"

"It's Zib. We can't wait any longer, she needs us!"

Malaki's eyes darted around them, his face set with grim understanding. "Gage isn't here. Neither is Volkran or Lauram."

"They have to be with her right now, in the room with the red door." Across the dance floor, she locked eyes with Blyana who immediately perked up. Isolde knew she could tell by just the look on her face that something was horribly wrong. "Come on."

Isolde made her way around the dance floor, dragging Malaki

behind her. The bystanders parted easily enough, not wanting to be near a child killer who could very well be the future Left Hand of the king. Cillian and Blyana met them halfway.

"It's Zib," Isolde said, her breath hardly a whisper. "She needs us."

"It was getting boring in here anyway," Cillian said, tossing back the last of his drink. "What's our plan?"

"The key," Isolde said. "I hid a copy in the book on my nightstand. I can get it on the way—"

"You need to stay here, Isolde," Malaki said. "In case Erebus or Gage seek you out. There can't be any reason for them to suspect you."

"I'm not letting you go off on your own, Malaki!" Isolde growled. "Not when it comes to Zib."

"He has a point," said Blyana. "If something happens tonight and you aren't around when they come looking that puts too much attention on you." Blyana surprised her by taking both of her hands in her own. The ring and bracelet she had given her twinkled against her bare, porcelain skin. "We trust you with everything, Isolde. Trust us with this."

Fear laced with frustration saturated Isolde's blood. Her fingers twisted around Blyana's. She knew they were right.

"Fine!" Isolde snarled, causing a couple beside them to jump and scurry away. "But if there's any trouble," she said, her eyes darting to Malaki, "and I mean any at all, I want you out of there. Understood?"

Cillian slipped into a mocking bow. A single strand of hair broke loose from the ebony mess that had been slicked back at the top of his head as he rose. "Anything for the fair maiden of Thornwood."

"Shut up," Isolde said, punching his shoulder. "Just be safe."

"We always are." Malaki's hand gently squeezed the back of her arm before he disappeared into the crowd with Blyana and Cillian at his heels. Worry tore through Isolde like a storm watching them leave without her. Normally, it was them telling her to be safe, to not do anything stupid. Yet as they vanished through the door, their pace measured but hurried, Isolde felt a pang of dread shoot through her chest.

A short while later, Blyana tugged the corners of the cloak into submission around her shoulders. The mask kept the frigid drifts of the cold, night air at bay at least. Every so often, as they made their way through the Gap of Duron, a blast of the cold's touch would make its way through the mask and tighten in Blyana's chest. "Remind me why we came this way," she asked.

"We have our entryway," Malaki replied. "We need to make sure our exit strategy is still open." He took the lead, leaving behind gaping footprints in the snow. Blyana hopped from one hole to the other, having grown tired of trudging through the knee-high snow.

"It's cold," Cillian said, his teeth chattering as they turned the final corner leading to the grate in the side of the mountain.

"I believe we heard you the first seven times, Cill," Malaki said.

"Yes, well, I know how one's hearing seems to disappear at an advanced age," Cillian retorted. "I had to make sure yours was still intact."

A growl rumbled from the confines of Malaki's mask. "How kind of you."

They took the final turn and Blyana saw Malaki's shoulders instantly relax. The hole he had created yawned before them like a mouth set with jagged teeth. Plucking Secrettaker from his belt, Malaki wedged his way through the opening and dropped down inside.

Blyana slipped in behind him. Her knives rested eagerly in her hands. Cillian was on her heels, his sharp eyes wide and searching. A sound stirred in the dark on the right and Blyana didn't hesitate.

The dagger in her left hand flew through the air, barely missing the bridge of Malaki's nose. A wet, stunned gasp filled the dark a moment later, followed by the unmistakable sound of a body hitting the ground. A stream of blood ran across the stone floor, its ruby red hue shining in the moonlight.

Malaki shot her a look, the tip of his gloved finger brushing the spot on his nose her dagger had nearly hit. "You did that on purpose."

"I would never do such a thing," Blyana said, yanking her dagger free to wipe on the guard's pant leg.

"You're a vicious, little monster," Malaki grumbled under his breath. "Try not to kill too many people tonight. The fewer bodies we leave behind, the better. We don't want them upping their numbers right now."

Blyana rolled her eyes and gingerly hopped over the pool of blood. "Is that just for me or for Cillian as well?"

"I'm the cool-headed one in this group, love," Cillian said, jumping over the pool of blood. "I believe that comment was for you."

"It was for both of you," Malaki said over his shoulder already starting to make his way to the door. He turned back to them and held up a single finger, his eyes narrowing. "No killing unless it's necessary."

"You're no fun," Blyana muttered.

Malaki rolled his eyes and gently pulled the door open. Light from the surrounding levels of the prison spilled out across their booted feet. Echoes of pain and cries for mercy filled the air as they filed onto the balcony.

They moved quickly, giving those poor souls inside not nearly enough time to guess at what had just slipped by in the dark. She tapped Malaki on the shoulder as they approached the one she recognized.

"The children," she whispered.

Malaki paused by the door, and his empty hand stretched out to grasp the lock hanging from the bars. Blyana gripped his wrist before his fingers could brush the metal.

"It nearly killed Nyla to be left behind the last time," Blyana said, her head shaking. "It will destroy her if we do it again."

Pain filled Malaki's gaze, and his hand balled into a fist, just inches from the cell door. A shaky sigh, deadened by his mask, vibrated through his chest. With one final glance, Malaki turned away and kept moving.

"We need a distraction," he said, peering around the corner when they reached the bottom floor. Four guards stood at post along the walls. "We'll never make it to the door like this."

"Or a wardrobe change."

Without waiting, Cillian turned back to the stairwell and began banging the hilt of his dagger on one of the metal handrails. The heads of the soldiers stationed on the bottom floor snapped in their direction, and they took off into a sprint. Blyana and Malaki had just enough time to slip into the stairwell before the first soldier appeared.

Malaki slammed the side of his head against the wall. Bone gave way, and the man fell to the ground at his feet. Cillian's dagger disappeared into the eye of the next guard. Two more fell to the blows Blyana delivered with brutal, merciless efficiency.

Quietly as possible, they each stripped a guard and donned their attire. The one covering Blyana reeked of body odor and piss. She gagged into her mask. "I'm taking the longest bubble bath after this," she grumbled.

"That's a lot coming from you," Malaki said, tugging on the guard's tunic. It was far too small for him, but it would have to do. "Considering how much you hate water."

"I can make an exception," she said, pulling on the helmet with a scowl.

After stuffing the bodies into a vacant cell, Blyana plucked the key from her pocket and slid it into the lock on the red door. It gave way without a sound, and they slipped into the dark unknown. Another tunnel greeted them on the other side, one leading deeper into the belly of the mountain.

"Charming," Cillian said, his voice strained. Blyana searched for his hand in the dark, needing his anchoring presence. His fingers wove their way between hers and a beat of calm reassurance echoed down the bond.

Their footsteps were soundless on the slanted floor. Before long, a light, faint but true shone in the distance. Malaki kept Secrettaker at his side, the razor-sharp blade winking in his grasp. Blyana felt Cillian's fingers tighten when the sound of cries filled the air.

The tunnel gave way to a colossal, cavernous room. It was easily ten times the size of their hideout in Blackford Forest. Gigantic sharp rocks hung overhead like fangs. Papers decorated the surface of the tables stationed across the floor.

Crates filled with vials of powders and liquids in various shades of green, were stacked along the walls. But as Blyana's eyes travelled down one of the tables, something else caught her eye. Small knives meant for precise cutting, shone in the light of the torches hanging along the walls. Axes and saws were there as well, their sharp, jagged teeth were stained with blood.

Not a single soldier was at post, giving them the freedom to check every cell at the back of the cavern. Each one was different, yet not a single one was left unoccupied. Through a small window, Blyana spotted what she could only assume used to be a virya. Their body was bent and broken in ways she never thought possible.

"What are they doing here?" she asked, unable to tear her eyes away from the creature writhing on the floor.

Malaki paused at the last door. His body shook, and the light in his eyes grew in the depths of his hood. A growl seeped through his lips.

Even muffled, it sent a shrill of fear down Blyana's spine.

"Malaki?"

His gaze turned to her, and a look of anguish met her stare. He held out his hand, and she gently placed the key in his awaiting palm. The lock gave way without complaint, and he pulled the door open. A small cry echoed through the air from within. It was a sound she had no idea a person could make. So, broken, so incredibly terrified.

She stepped around Malaki and Blyana's mouth fell open in a sob. "Zibiah!"

Gone were the braids Blyana used to envy so much. Scabs, both new and old, covered her shorn head. Bones protruded from every part of her body. Cuffs of iron bound her wrists and ankles to the cold stone slab sitting in the center of the room. Sores had begun to form where they chaffed her skin.

"Zib?" Blyana reached out a hand to touch Zibiah's shoulder but froze. Cuts and bruises, all in different stages of healing, decorated her skin from head to toe. Tugging down her mask, Blyana blew a gentle breath across Zibiah's face. Her eyes fluttered open and her body jolted in terror at the sight of someone else in the oversized cell. Her body shook uncontrollably, and she fought against the chains holding her in place.

"It's alright, it's us!" Blyana said, ripping the hood and mask off, allowing strands of her pale golden hair to frame her face. "It's us, Zib!"

Zibiah's golden eyes winced in the light of the torch clutched in Cillian's hand. She looked from Blyana to the two who stood behind her. She heard their masks and hoods fall away. A sob broke through Zibiah's lips as tears cascaded down her face.

"Bly," Zibiah said, her hand stretching out to her as much as the chain would allow. "Blyana!"

"I'm here," Blyana said, grasping onto Zibiah's hand. She was so weak, so incredibly frail Blyana couldn't hide her own tears. "We're here."

"Where is she?" Zibiah asked, her eyes darting around the room. "Where's Isolde?"

"In the palace," Malaki said, taking a knee on the other side. His fingers gently wrapped around Zibiah's hand. "She wanted to come, demanded to in fact," his tone laced with loving annoyance. "But—"

"Gage?" Zibiah said, her voice heavy with hatred.

Malaki nodded. "And Erebus."

Anger filled Zibiah's gaze. "I've heard what they are making her do. What they have made her do."

"How?" Cillian asked.

"They come here," Zibiah said, her lips trembling. Her eyes burning with anger. "Every day they come."

Zibiah's fingers gripped Blyana's hand. "Zib—"

"No," she said. A new stream of tears, hot and full, fell down her face. "Please, not now." Her eyes squeezed shut, and a deep breath filled her chest. "Have you found the children?"

"Yes," Blyana said. "They're here in the dungeons. We can get you out."

"You can't take me now," Zibiah said, looking to Malaki. "Not unless they come too."

Malaki's voice was a ragged whisper, his jaw set. "We can't leave you, Zib. We *won't* leave you here!"

"You have to," she said, clinging to his hand. "Erebus and Gage will know I'm not the Hood. If you take me now, those children will die. All or nothing, remember?"

Malaki ran a hand over his face. Blyana knew Zibiah was right, but that didn't make it any easier to accept. "You know Isolde's going to kill us, right?" Malaki said.

"She'll understand," said Zibiah, her hand squeezing his. "In time."

Cillian stirred at Blyana's side, and she looked to where his attention had landed. Slowly, Cillian turned his gaze to Zibiah, his obsidian gaze filled with torment. "Zib, these aren't elithrium chains."

A shaky breath lifted from Zibiah's lips. "No," she said as more tears fell from her golden, lightless eyes. "They aren't, Cill."

Malaki stilled. "Why aren't they elithrium, Zib?"

"They aren't necessary for me anymore."

"What do you mean?" Blyana breathed. There was only explanation, one reason why they wouldn't keep Zibiah, the most powerful water wielder she knew, in elithrium chains.

"Their experiments work," Zibiah said, her lips trembling. "My power is gone."

Suddenly, Blyana understood why Zibiah's grip felt so light, so weak. Tears swelled in Blyana's wide, horror-filled eyes.

"They made you human."

CHAPTER 33

The last of the wine filled with hints of grape and blackberry slid over Isolde's tongue. If she weren't filled with worry, she might have enjoyed it. But hours had passed since Malaki, Cillian, and Blyana had disappeared.

Scenario after scenario tumbled through her head. Images of them locked behind bars, or far worse, plagued Isolde every second they were gone. She itched to chew at her thumbnail, to give into that nervous tick.

Her gaze landed on the table just next to her own and froze. Milt, the Lord of Harrow Hall, sat slumped in his chair. His eyes were glassy and streaked with red. A near empty bottle of amber liquid sat on the table before him. With a heavy heart, Isolde rose from her seat and sauntered over to his nearly empty table.

"If you continue to sit like that," Isolde said, sliding into the seat in front of him, "your posture will suffer greatly for it."

Recognition slowly unfolded in Milt's unfocused gaze. A lazy, crooked smile pulled at the corners of his mouth. "Well, at least I wouldn't suffer alone. Not when Gage has you wearing that…*dress.*" His lip curled at the sight of it. "Or was it the king?"

"This was a gift from the latter," Isolde said. "Not exactly what I would have picked out, but it is far better than what Gage would have selected, I can assure you. He has the taste of a brothel owner; no imagination. Besides, I look stunning in anything."

"That is a gift you possess, Lady Isolde," Milt said with a smile that didn't come close to reaching his eyes. It wasn't hard to guess where his mind had wandered. Her eyes flickered to the empty chair at his side—to Gawen's seat.

"While this is a rather glorious affair," Isolde said, waving a dismissive hand through the air, "I'm in much need of some fresh air. Would you mind escorting me, Lord Milt?"

His warm brown eyes twinkled as he drained the rest of his glass and slammed it down on the table. "What kind of a gentleman would I be for letting the future Left Hand of the king walk around the capital without an escort?"

"Not a very chivalrous one," Isolde said, tugging him onto his feet. Milt swayed to the right and bumped into her shoulder. "I'm not carrying your giant ass all the way there," she grunted, pushing him upright.

Milt laughed and worked Isolde's arm through his own and made for the doorway. "I am a gentleman who can hold his liquor, my lady. Never fear!"

Isolde had to catch him two times before they made it to the stables. It was the only place she could think to bring him. Milt's deep, throaty laugh filled the air that held hints of hay and horseflesh. The sound of stomping hooves echoed through the stables as the Master of Horses stumbled to the far end. Isolde felt his power wash over her like the rays of an afternoon sun. Calm and warming. A radiant, crooked smile slowly formed across his face. Versa's hooves struck the stone floor, and her neck stretched out over the stall door, desperate to reach him.

"There you are," he said, his forehead falling to hers. Milt's warm, broad hand stroked her neck, and Versa's eyes fluttered shut.

Isolde leaned against the stall of Alaric's chestnut stallion. He nibbled on her shoulder, demanding attention. "She's always so calm when you're around," she said, her fingers grazing his soft, velvety snout.

"She's special," Milt said. "My favorite girl."

A twinge of guilt strummed through Isolde's heart. "Then why did you gift her to me?"

A sad but knowing smile broke through the drunken fog clouding Milt's eyes. "Because she's yours," he said, as if the explanation was truly that simple. "It's…a feeling, an intuition, I suppose. It's how I knew that big bastard belonged to your uncle," he said, pointing to the chestnut stallion. "And how I knew Loria was a perfect fit for Malaki. They match each other. And so do you and Versa. The same spirit. Both made of light and darkness." The stallion nickered and nibbled at her shoulder once more. Isolde smiled as her fingers grazed his face. Slowly, his eyes fluttered shut and he leaned into her touch.

"You always had a way with horses," said Milt, his brow quirking. "Any animal really. Even as a little girl, they're calmed by you. As if…they're listening. Like someone else I know. Or did know, I should say."

The same sadness bled back into Milt's face. A sadness that apparently his love of horses could not deter from.

"I'm sorry about Gawen." Isolde wanted to say more. But there was nothing she could say or do that would bring back what Milt had lost. No words that would ease his pain.

Milt's hand stilled on Versa's cheek. A muscle ticked in his jaw. "I saw what you did," he said with a deep breath, his thumb gently moving beneath Versa's lashes. "You tried to wound him just enough to be taken out. You tried to stop Buer." Milt's throat bobbed and his eyes dropped to the hay covered floor. "There aren't words to express how grateful I am for that."

Isolde bit her lip. She was unsure of what to do with his gratitude. "Who was he to you?" she asked. "He must have been someone very important."

"He was." The words sounded strained, as if they were choking him. "He was my god son." Milt licked his lips and collapsed into a pile of hay at the foot of Versa's stall door. "His parents had worked in my house for years. As did their parents before them. One night I was gone on business when Helurtu attacked Harrow Hall."

Isolde's mouth went dry.

"They tried to stop them but…" A piece of straw twirled between his fingertips. "Gawen was their only son. He saw the whole thing." Milt's thumb ran along the creases of his palm. "I took him in as my own that day. But seeing his parents murdered made Gawen a fearful child—timid and unsure. Still, it didn't stop him from doing what he thought was right and entered into the lottery for the tournament."

Isolde's heart broke for him. For the loss he was enduring. "He was a brave man, Milt."

"They asked me to look after their son," said Milt, his eyes shining with regret. "And I failed them."

Isolde slid down beside him and placed a hand on his knee. "I'm sure a lot of people have said this you and it might not be what you want to hear, but you did everything you could for Gawen. His blood isn't on your hands."

Milt nodded. His hand landed on her knee and squeezed. "I'm very sorry about Tanor." The walls Isolde had formed around her heart shook. Little fissures worked their way up, splintering what little defenses they offered to begin with.

Isolde nodded, teeth digging into her cheek. "Thank you."

"I suppose we're both sorrowful messes, aren't we?" he asked, dropping his hand to his side. A huff pushed through his lips, and Milt's head fell back against Versa's stall door with a bang. In no time at all, the sound of soft snores rumbled from his chest. A soft smile pulled at Isolde's face as she stared at the Lord of Harrow Hall. In sleep, gone was his worry and pain. What remained was one of the most genuine men she had ever met and one of the kindest.

Isolde looked around and found a horse blanket hanging next to Versa's stall. She got to her feet, mindful of Milt's impossibly long legs and tugged the heavy blanket down.

"A mess is putting it lightly," Isolde said, draping the blanket over Milt's legs and chest. Versa stomped on the floor, her head shaking. "It's not like you'll be needing it," Isolde said. She planted a kiss on her snout and stole a sugar cube from the stash Milt hid in the lining of his pocket. "I'll see you soon." Versa snickered as Isolde pressed the cube to her lips.

Drifts of music carried through the corridors, leading her back to the ballroom. As she drew near, a flickering of gold caught her eye. Phontine's silhouette turned the corner to one of the side passageways, leading away from the royal apartments. Away from where she should be going.

Isolde knew exactly where she was headed and decided to follow. She kept a healthy distance, having already been to the servants' quarters once before. At the final corner, Isolde peeked around to see the faintest hint of Phontine's gown disappearing through a familiar door.

She leaned against the cold stone wall and knitted her arms across her chest as she prepared to wait as long as it took. The look on Blyana's face, the pain that lashed through her eyes every time they fell on her sister, filled Isolde's mind, stoking that protective fury into an inferno.

After a while, the door to the small room creaked open, and tendrils of golden hair shone in the light of the torches lining the hallways.

"Interesting company you keep, Phontine," Isolde said, from where she lounged in the shadows. Phontine jumped at the sound of her voice, and the door closed with a bang. Isolde held in a chuckle as a familiar mask fell across Phontine's face. The one she herself had worn many, many times. A mask that hid the real fear lurking beneath a layer of furious indifference.

"For the favored whore of the king?" Phontine asked.

"Your words, not mine," Isolde said. "I wasn't aware Erebus was the kind of man who shared what was his."

"He isn't," Phontine snapped, her arms knitting across her chest, tone flat and dark. "But you'll find that out soon enough." Her eyes were cold and weary. A slight sneer pulled at the edge of her mouth. "If you're here on behalf of my sister, you can leave."

"I'm not here because of Bly," Isolde said, holding up her hand before her, giving her nails a glance. "I haven't seen you on His Majesty's lap nearly as often as one would expect. Have you been leaving his bed cold?"

A low growl rumbled through Phontine's chest, a subtle warning leaking into her gaze. Isolde wasn't sure what power Blyana's youngest sister possessed, but she knew to be cautious. With a sigh, she rested the back of her head on the wall.

"But I have a feeling the king's bed is not the one you care about though, is it?" Isolde's brow quirked as she nodded to the door. "He's human, is he not?"

"That is no concern of yours," Phontine hissed.

"Oh, but it is." A smirk that did not reach her eyes tugged the corners of Isolde's lips. "It is very much my concern."

"If you dare touch him," Phontine snarled, taking a step towards Isolde, "I will end you."

"I don't doubt you would," Isolde said, still inspecting her nails. "Or try to at least."

"You must love to hear yourself talk."

"I do, in fact," said Isolde with a grin. "My voice is quite lovely, don't you think?"

Irritation ignited across Phontine's face. "What do you want?"

Isolde finally turned her full gaze to Phontine, and the mask of civility fell away. "The answer to a question." She pushed away from the wall and came to stand before Phontine. "Are you happy?"

Shock rippled through Phontine's features, jarring the mask of anger she hid behind. For a moment, Isolde saw the little girl beneath. The one who had been robbed of everything and was still paying the price for a good deed committed so many years ago.

"Are you happy?" Isolde asked again, her voice soft and low.

A shadow fell over Phontine's face, sharpening her beauty into a weapon deadlier than any blade could ever hope to be. "And why would the person who left me in the House of Pleasures to be battered and traded, have any interest in my happiness?"

"Because I have a debt to pay. One I had no idea I even owed. And because we have a means of getting you"—she nodded her head to the door—"and him out of here."

Phontine chuckled darkly and shook her head. "Oddly enough, you aren't the first person to make such a promise to me. You really think it's that simple?" she asked. "That Erebus will simply let us go? Let you go? Your daftness is really quite impressive."

"You're the daft one if you truly believe he'll keep you around as his plaything forever," Isolde said, a shard of hardness creeping into her voice. "That he won't get bored of you and look for the next shiny new toy. You are on borrowed time, Phontine."

"I keep him happy," she said, with the lift of her chin. "Just as Vara taught me."

"For now, you do," said Isolde. "But how long until he finds out about your secret? What will he do then? He must mean a great deal for you to risk not only your life but his as well." Phontine refused to look anywhere but at the corridor behind Isolde. "He will find out, and when he does, death will be the kindest punishment you can hope for. That you *both* can hope for."

Phontine's eyes fluttered closed, and she took a deep breath. "What are you proposing?"

"If you had the chance to be free, would you take it?"

Phontine's left hand curled into a ball at her side. Isolde watched as her long, perfectly manicured nails dug into the skin of her thumb. The hint of a tattoo lingered in the shadows of the torches.

"And what would someone with my particular skill set do with freedom?" she demanded, her head shaking. "Who would give someone like me a chance to do anything other than what Vara trained me to do?"

"Vara will pay for what she did to you and your sister," Isolde said, her voice ringing with the familiar black fury. "I vow it here and now, just as I did with Blyana. As much as it pains me to say it, Vara does have your past, Phontine, a piece of it anyway. But don't let her win by stealing away your hope for a future. You are worth so much more than being used as a toy for that bastard to play with."

A shaky breath lifted from Phontine's lips. "I need time," she said, her jaw clenching. "Time to… to think."

"Time's not something we have very much of, but I understand. You know where to find me when you decide if the chance of freedom is worth the risk." Isolde gave her a final nod before turning back. But the sound of Phontine's voice drew her up short.

"If you're doing this because of my sister," Phontine said, her voice filled with hatred. "There is nothing that will make me forgive her for leaving me there. Or you for that matter. Nothing will change that. *Nothing.*"

Blyana had told her a fraction of what she had endured at Vara's hands. But as she looked back at Phontine, Isolde realized how little she truly understood.

"I want you listen to me, Phontine," Isolde said, turning around to face her. "When I paid the debt for Blyana, I had no idea what chain of events that would set in motion. Neither of us knew what had happened before it was too late. We were told you all had died that night." Phontine's full lips pulled into a tight line as she began to shake her head. But Isolde pressed on. "We went back to your house the second news reached Thornwood. But all that was left of your home, of your family, was ash. How could we have known she had taken you?"

Silence hung between them like a blade. It pierced Isolde's heart, forcing the words from her mouth. "But if we had known," she continued, "if we'd discovered Vara had you. There is nothing in this world, not even the gods themselves, could have kept us from you. There is no line we wouldn't have crossed to reach you."

Tears swelled in Phontine's impossibly beautiful eyes as she met Isolde's gaze. A bead of blood trickled down her tattooed thumb and landed on the floor at her feet.

"Even now, we won't hesitate to cross them. Not even the ones you're drawing yourself, can stop us." Isolde took a step forward. She needed Phontine to hear, to understand every word she said and know she meant them. "We will not leave you again." Isolde swallowed against the lump in her throat. "But if you are so desperate for someone to blame," Isolde said. "Then I will be the villain of your story. Lay the blame on me, not Blyana. She went through the same horrors you did. She's just as innocent as you are and is hurting just as much."

Shock flittered across Phontine's face. The glow of power shuddered before disappearing completely. Silence filled the corridor, save for the crackling of the flames contained within the torches on the walls. Tendrils of anxiety crept up Isolde's spine at the sound.

"I hope you make the right choice," Isolde said. "For your own sake." She turned and left Phontine in the dark.

The echo of her heels clicking against the marble bridges tumbled down into the abyss. It was the only sound penetrating the cool night air. Not even the soldiers who stood at post along the main corridors stirred as she passed. Silent as stars and still as statues, they watched.

The halls of Elenarta held more beauty than Isolde remembered. Drifts of memory lingered in every corridor she passed. Like little embers, they kept her past alive. A past she wished to forget. Isolde kept her eyes forward, refusing to look around at the place she had spent so much time as a child. But as she passed the library, her steps faltered.

It was deserted. Not even a soldier stood at the massive doors that held intricate carvings of Arnoria's sigil. Beams of moonlight filtered in through the open windows lining the ceiling and northern most wall.

"Hello again," Isolde said, her fingers caressing the spines of the books nestled on the shelves. Breathing in deep, she felt the scent of old parchment and leather fill her lungs with sweet despair. Towering, spiral bookshelves shot up into the air in every direction, each one covered in books. So many lives, so many wonderful, beautiful lives filled the space she loved so much.

She ventured further in, each step echoing over the marble surface. Fireplaces, cold and lifeless, covered the eastern wall. Empty chairs sat before them. Isolde smiled as a memory filled her heart. She had sat by Kamden's side as Nan read to them dark stories of the Wilds of the North. Of the brutal, savages who lived there, of Erebus's people—ice wielders.

The sound of voices, ones she recognized, broke the haze. "The experiments are working," Gage said, his voice icy and hard as steel. "That is all you need to know." Acting quickly, Isolde pulled her heels free and slipped behind one of the bookshelves on her left.

Volkran's deep baritone voice infected the air. "What of the children being produced by these successful experiments?" he demanded. "Do they inherit their parents' gifts?"

"That is not your concern," Gage retorted. His voice echoed through the room like a clap of thunder.

Isolde steadied her breathing and carefully peeked around the corner of a shelf, doing well to stay within the confines of the shadows. Gage was standing by one of the smaller bookcases, his arm draped casually over the back.

"The king will inform you of the results as he sees fit," he said. "And until then, be thankful for the gifts you've been granted."

"I'm not ungrateful," said Volkran, his pudgy face reddening. "I'm merely thinking of Briarhole and the responsibilities I have there."

"Oh yes," said Gage, his tone mocking. "Because you care so much about it. If you cared as much about running that place as you do about squashing the rumors of there being another Viributhian still drawing breath, I wouldn't have to worry about it."

Isolde's mouth went dry. *Another Viributhian?*

"I made sure every member of that wretched family was destroyed," Volkran growled, his eyes glowing. The hand gripping the sword at his side, Airendia, tightened. "But when rumors surface of another one being found, hiding in the Forgotten Lands like a rat, it's something I must deal with."

"And why is that?" Gage asked.

"Because if it is true, then that means I failed. And I will not rest until every drop of their blood has been spilled just so I can piss in it. Because they're a threat. Not only to me and to you, but to the king as well."

Isolde's heart raced. *Another Viributhian…in the Forgotten Lands?*

"You seemed rather confident," Gage said, his steps echoing as he took a few steps around the shelf. "So certain you had eliminated their entire line, you bragged after the fact. Watched their bodies burn, one by one. Isn't that what you said?"

"I did," said Volkran, panic flashing in his eyes.

Isolde felt someone stir behind her, as if a gust of wind had brushed her skin. Before she could take a breath, a hand clamped over her mouth and pressed her into the bookshelf.

"No need for that," whispered Kyros, snatching her wrist and pinning it beside her head as she reached for the dagger at her thigh. "Be quiet now. Let's hear what the Lords have to say."

Kyros kept his hand firmly placed over her mouth as they listened. Hints of mint and pine filled Isolde's nose. She had half a mind to sink her teeth into his flesh but thought better of it as Gage continued.

"I suggest you get these rumors under control, Volkran, before the matter is brought before the king. The last thing he needs is a rebellion brewing over rumors of a lost Viributhian rat."

"One's already brewing," Volkran said. "My men have brought word from the eastern boarders of Endurmure."

Silence descended, covering them all like a suffocating blanket. "Why have you just now said something?" Gage asked, his voice low and filled with such calm Isolde knew he was anything but.

"I needed to confirm the information," Volkran answered, words spilling over his lips in a rush. "And now I have. A large force musters in the west. A force that could pose a threat to Elenarta. They say there is one among them unlike any other. A warrior from the north, vicious and powerful as the warriors of old—a savage."

Isolde's blood ran cold. Kyros's body went rigid, his grip tightening. The people of the north, Erebus's kingdom, had laid siege to the palace decades ago, coating Arnoria in shadow and blood.

"Warrior of the north?" Gage scoffed. "A barbarian at best."

"They say his blood is filled with ice and death. That he cannot be killed." Volkran's words slid across Isolde's skin like ice water. "They say he is something more— a monster. Scarred and deformed. He's the leader of the rebellion, or a general at the very least."

"I wasn't aware you cower at the whisper of a rumor, Volkran," Gage scoffed. "That bedtime stories leave you trembling where you stand."

"Some would think me wise to know what I might be facing," said Volkran, his tone filled with malice. "That I wasn't bringing false concern to His Majesty's doorstep. If this savage is from the Wilds of the North...If he holds the power the king does...and there are more of them, what does that say for us?"

"The Tenebriaths and the other inhabitants of that frozen shit hole might have the power of ice at their beck and call," Gage said, his voice laced with contempt. "But they are savages—untrained and unchallenged. The might of this kingdom will pommel them into the ground, along with this savage from the north, if they dare come here. Leave whatever information you have before you depart, Volkran. I would advise you not return empty-handed. The king is not a very forgiving man, as you have seen before. I am even less so."

The threat echoed across the library. It held a promise of pain, of death at failure.

"As you wish, Lord Gage."

The sound of Volkran's retreating steps disappeared through the library doors. A breath of relief brushed across Isolde's lips as Kyros lowered his hand from her mouth.

"What are you doing here?"

"Well, I was looking for a bit of light reading but found something far more interesting to lay my eyes on," he said, with a wolfish grin.

"Pig," she said, yanking at her wrist still pressed to the shelf. "Mind letting me go now?"

"Mind asking nicely?"

Isolde's eyes narrowed, and she pulled against his grasp. The force propelled her forward and the heel of her shoe slipped through her fingers. Panic swelled in Isolde's chest as it struck the floor, sending a deafening echo through the silent library.

Kyros's gaze shot over her shoulder. His jaw ticked, and a flicker of light ignited in his eyes. "You don't make a very good spy, Lady Isolde," he said.

"You don't make a very good gentleman," she snapped back in a whisper. "This is your fault!"

"Agree to disagree."

A heavy silence filled the air only to be broken by the sound of steel being pulled free from its sheath and Gage's cautious steps as he began walking in their direction.

Kyros dropped his hand from her wrist and slid his fingers into the hair along the nape of her neck. "What are you doing?" Isolde asked, pulling against his grip.

"Don't stab me for this," he murmured, pressing his body into hers, a devilish grin playing on his lips. His mouth collided with hers without warning. The tips of his fingers tugged at her hair, forcing her head back, allowing him better access.

Isolde felt his sense of urgency, his lips pushing, encouraging her to play along. Biting down a bit of annoyance, Isolde met each kiss with the same sense of need. She ran her free hand up his chest, feeling the muscle beneath. A moan, deep and thrilling, spilled from his mouth and into hers.

Suddenly, Kyros's lips were ripped away and Isolde was left standing alone. He crashed into the far wall and tumbled to the floor. Gage stood before her, his eyes glowing as he locked a hand around her throat.

"Would you care to explain yourself, pet?" Gage asked, the tips of his fingers squeezing as he pressed the heel of his hand into her windpipe.

"The fault is mine, Lord Gage," Kyros said, struggling to stand. Bits of crumbled marble fell about him, peppering his midnight-black coat with debris. "I wasn't aware she was spoken for."

"I find that difficult to believe, Kyros," Gage said, through clenched teeth. "But yes, she is spoken for. A fact, Lady Isolde is very much aware of." He pressed his hand further. Isolde's fingers pried at Gage's hand, her chest burning. Dark spots danced across Gage's face.

"She had a lot to drink, My Lord," Kyros said, dusting himself off. He held the perfect mask of civility. "I'm sure she was just confused."

"Yes," Gage mused. "Just…confused." He looked her up and down, a sadistic smile pulling at the edge of his lips, deforming the scars even further. "I'll make sure she understands. Thank you, Kyros."

Kyros looked to Isolde over Gage's shoulder, his eyes hard with concern. "You should get some rest," Gage said, loosening his grip on her throat. Isolde choked as air slowly, painfully filled her chest. "The next trial is sure to be an interesting one."

"I should make sure Lady Isolde is delivered to—"

"As her fiancé," Gage growled, sliding the sword back into its sheath, "I will make sure Lady Isolde is delivered safely back to her chambers once we're finished. But thank you for your concern, Kyros."

Kyros cast one final look of concern before bowing to Gage's demands. He disappeared through the library doors, his face etched in apologetic worry. Dread filled Isolde as the sound of his retreating steps died away, at the silence they left behind. Just as air filled her lungs once again, Gage struck.

His fist slammed into her midsection, sending spasms of pain and nausea rolling through her like a storm. Isolde dropped to a knee, her arms cradling her abdomen. Her muscles clenched and Gage's knee collided with her ribcage, sending her flying across the unforgiving marble floor.

She felt the kiss of the night air on her thighs as her dress bunched up around her. Gage stood over her, his eyes filled with a cold, cruel light.

"I know we aren't married yet," he said brushing a piece of hair from her face. Isolde cringed away from his touch. "But consider this an early lesson." He brought his foot back yet again.

The tip of his boot slammed into her side, jarring the bones within. A muffled cry escaped Isolde's lips, her body screaming as she rolled across the floor. Again, her arms wrapped around her, as if holding herself together.

"You really like to make me angry, don't you?" Gage growled, drawing his leg back. "We'll see if you let another man touch you after this." His leg swung through the air and met Isolde's palm. She jerked her grip to the side and swung him off balance.

Forcing herself onto her feet, Isolde pulled the dagger from its sheath and turned to face him. "Oh, I have every intention of letting another man touch me," Isolde said. "Just not you."

"You certainly are full of surprises, pet," Gage said, his eyes raking over her in anticipation. Isolde didn't hesitate. She launched forward, swinging the blade to the right and left, cutting through the air. Strips of fabric, once residing on Gage's tunic, fell to the floor in ribbons. Her muscles ached with pain at each step, making her slower than normal.

Malice burned in his gaze as he caught her wrist before the dagger could find a home in his chest. "That's enough now," Gage said, bending her wrist back until the dagger slipped through her fingers and clattered to the floor. His knee rose and slammed into her bruised stomach. Bile spilled over Isolde's lips as the pain forced her to bend over, her arm draping around her midsection.

"I do love a good fight, Isolde," Gage said, digging his fingers into the roots of her hair, forcing her to stand up straight. Her eyes stung with tears she refused to let fall. "Making me work for it."

Before she could utter another word, Gage drove his knee into her side again. Blinding pain exploded along the scar Gage had left behind as she fell to the floor. "I can't deal with you as I wish right now," he said circling around to face her. "But all in good time." He drew his foot again and Isolde braced for the blow that would undoubtedly shatter her ribcage.

"Enough!"

The sound of Alaric's voice, the sound of a lord, boomed through the library. Pain swam in Isolde's eyes as he, Galaena, and Liam strode forward. Their eyes were glowing and filled with furious power.

"I do not take commands from cripples!" Gage said, his lips curling in disgust.

"It is still against the rules for another Lord to lay a hand on a champion that is not from their territory, is it not?" Galaena snarled, her sharpened teeth flashing. "Perhaps, we should take this to the king and see what he thinks of you beating our champion to the point that she can hardly stand!"

Gage stood between Isolde and the others. He seemed to pause, his gaze flicking back to where she lay on the floor. Isolde had no doubt Erebus's warning was running through his mind. Spasms of pain shot through her stomach as she slowly, carefully rose to her feet.

"No need to bother, His Majesty, Lady Galaena," Gage said, his voice far too cheerful. "You're quite right. There will be plenty of time for me to…*correct* your niece after she wins the tournament, and we are married. Liam, see to it my sweet, Isolde makes it back to her chambers in one piece."

Liam's eyes burned with hatred, his body shaking in fury. A muscle ticked in his jaw. "Yes, sir."

"Good boy." Gage turned back to Isolde, his blue eyes piercing and narrowed. "I'll see you tomorrow. Sleep well." A shuddered breath ghosted past Isolde's lips as Gage's footsteps finally died away, her legs crumbling beneath her.

Liam's arms instantly wrapped around her, lifting her up off her feet. "Let's get you back to your room."

The metal handle bounced off the wall as Liam shoved the door open. Nan, who had been sitting on the couch reading jumped at the sound. Her warm, blue eyes instantly hardened when she saw Isolde in his arms.

"On the bed," she said, pointing to Isolde's chambers. Every breath was agony made anew as Liam carefully placed her on top of the silk duvet.

"We need Malaki," Alaric said.

"He isn't back yet," Nan said, her expert fingers pushing the fabric out of the way. They probed her ribs, causing the occasional wince of pain. "I don't feel a break," Nan said, her face doubtful. "But that doesn't mean there isn't one."

"What happened?" Alaric asked. "If Kyros hadn't told us where you were…" His words trailed off into a growl that died behind his teeth.

She made quick work of explaining how she came to the library, Kyros kissing her, and all that followed.

"So, its Kyros's fault then," said Liam, his dark eyes glowing. "Arrogant prick!"

"He actually saved us both," Isolde said. Gently, Nan pressed a cloth to Isolde's side. Its soft surface was laced with herbs and cold as ice. "But that's not what's important. I overheard Gage tell Volkran that the experiments in the dungeons are working."

Galaena stilled, her grey eyes widening. "You're certain he said that?"

Isolde nodded. "I'm sure. But Volkran wanted to know if their children were still virya, despite them not having powers anymore. Is that possible?" The horror of it didn't make sense. "Could they really be taking powers away from virya only to then breed more?"

Alaric sighed. "It was an idea from a long time ago——"

His words were cut off as the door to the chambers opened with a bang and her cadre stumbled through the doorway. Malaki's frantic gaze landed on her, his eyes roving the scar at her side. "What happened?" he demanded, his accusatory gaze shooting to Liam.

"I didn't do this if that's what you are implying," Liam said, his eyes cutting.

"You normally are the cause of her pain so why would this be any different?" Malaki shot back, his fingers already probing her bruised ribs.

"Would both of you just shut—" But a bolt of pain shot through her side, keeping her pinned to the bed. "Gage might have broken something."

"Can you heal her?" Nan asked, pulling the icy cloth away.

"Of course, I can," he said, ripping his mask and hood off. "Move!" he growled at Liam, who reluctantly retreated to the other side of the room. Pain ignited in her side as Malaki poured his power into her. She gritted her teeth as muscle and bone shifted beneath her battered skin.

"Did you find Zib?" Isolde asked through clenched teeth, desperate for a distraction.

Blyana pulled her mask free. Her normally sparkling grey eyes were dull and streaked with red. "She's alive, and we know where they're keeping her."

But there was no relief to be found in her eyes. Nor was there any in Cillian's. He slid down the wall to the floor and let his head fall into his hands.

"What is it?" Isolde asked, pushing up on to her elbows. Malaki pressed a hand to her shoulder willing her to lie down. But Isolde gripped his hand, forcing him to be still. "Tell me…now!"

Malaki looked back to the others, his chest heaving with a sigh. "We found her, Isolde. But Zib, she's…she's not the same."

Isolde's eyes widened and the familiar touch of dread sank in. "What do you mean, she's not the same?"

CHAPTER 34

"They took her powers, Isolde," Blyana said. A line of vengeful sorrow rimmed her eyes. "They made her human."

Isolde blinked. Blyana's words didn't make any sense at all. She looked to Cillian whose hands were balled into fists. "It's true," he said. "Their experiments work."

Malaki pressed his fingers along her side, continuing to push his power into her skin. But any pain that might have come from his probing, Isolde didn't feel it. All she could think about, all that mattered, was Zibiah.

"I'm not leaving her in there," she said, trying to sit up "I'm not leaving her in there one more damn day, Malaki!"

"We'll get her," Malaki said, pushing her back down. "I promise we will. But if we take her and leave the children behind, there's no telling what Gage and Erebus will do." Isolde ground her teeth as her anger fought against the sense in his words.

"I suppose now we know why Erebus paid dearly for the virya, humans, and half-bloods from the territories," Alaric murmured, his jaw flexing. "He was purchasing test subjects and slaves to work the mines." Galaena stood frozen at his side, her eyes fixed on the floor. A look of memory and pain filled her gaze.

Nan wiped the side of her face and offered a steaming cup of tea. "Do you have something a little stronger?" She asked. Nan offered her a nod before heading to the cabinet.

"What were you doing in the library with Kyros anyway?" Liam asked, his arms folding over his chest as he leaned against the door.

"She doesn't owe you an explanation," Blyana growled, her eyes glowing. "She isn't yours."

"I wasn't claiming—"

"Yes, you were," said Malaki, his eyes blazing.

"I was walking back from stables," Isolde said, taking the cup of wine Nan offered with a grateful smile. She could see why Liam was jealous. If anyone had been caught in the library with her, especially in that position, it should have been him.

"Milt needed some fresh air before he said or did something he'd regret later. I was on my way back when I happened to pass by the library. Kyros was already there. I just didn't know it." She looked down at the ruby-red liquid. Her emerald and silver eyes stared back as if they were looking at a stranger. "That's when Gage and Volkran showed up. But what I heard is far more interesting than why I was there." Isolde told them what she had overheard about the rebellion brewing in the west. That apparently Erebus had not been made aware of just how great the threat had become. "Could be an interesting piece of blackmail to hangover Gage's head," Isolde said.

"Or a guaranteed way to ensure he kills you," Liam said. He had taken a seat by the fireplace, as far from Malaki as possible. "He won't hesitate, Isolde. He might want you, but not as badly as he wants the power of the position he holds."

"Do you think it's really true, Alaric?" Isolde asked.

"It's possible," he said, running a hand over his jaw. "There have been rumors of colonies forming in the west. That's where all the people you've saved over the years have been taken, as far as I know. But it seems that Erebus didn't deem it a worthy enough venture to sink money into sending people out to investigate. Not that I am privy to such information, given my previous affiliations."

"Does it really matter if a rebellion is forming if we can't get the people here out first?" Cillian asked. He tossed back the rest of his drink and poured himself another. Isolde didn't miss the subtle frown hanging at the corners of his eyes. The slight tension that seemed to roll through his shoulders as he poured. "That would appear to be step one."

"He's right," Galaena said. "We can't leave them in Erebus's hands once our plan is in motion." Her gaze shifted to Isolde. "What's your play, Hood?"

A smile tugged at the corners of Isolde's mouth, drawing a groan from deep within Malaki's chest. "Chaos," Isolde said. "Glorious, bloody chaos."

"So, no different than any other day then," he said.

"With the prisoners loose, at least we'll have better cover when we make our move," Blyana said. She picked at the bones of a roasted chicken resting on the serving table.

"Murderers, thieves, and gods know what else," Alaric said, from his spot on the lounger.

"Exactly our kind of people," muttered Isolde. Hunger rumbled through her stomach in annoying, demanding waves. "The night of the last event, Phontine will give the copies of the keys to Frey to distribute to the prisoners. While the guards are busy trying to round everyone up, we'll sneak in, get everyone out we need to, and go through the opening in the mountainside."

She took another sip of wine and shoved the last piece of a cherry tart into her mouth. "From there," Isolde said, cupping her hand around her mouth to keep the crumbles in places, "we make for the Gap of Duron and head west."

Alaric's eyes widened in disbelief. "Are you insane, Isolde?" he asked. "You do realize it's incredibly difficult for a virya to make it through, let alone a human."

"We'll help them," Blyana offered. "Our exit runs along that path. It'd be foolish to backtrack."

"It's also the only path Erebus and Gage won't believe we've taken," Isolde said. "It's also one they'd be less willing to follow even if they figured out that's how we escaped." Her fingers grazed over the edge of a knife, her eyes sweeping to Nan, who rested on the lounger near the fire. A twinge of guilt spiked in her heart. The Gap of Duron would be a hard one for them and a cold one. But that wasn't the problem at hand. Right now, they needed evidence a rebellion even existed.

"Gage instructed for Volkran to leave the information he has in his quarters before he left with Lauram," Isolde said, her gaze sliding to Liam, who rolled his eyes. "And I know just the man to get me into those chambers."

"Now I know you need more healing," Malaki said. "Because only someone who isn't in their right mind would even think about sneaking into Gage's chambers."

"They might be able to help us," Isolde said, pushing herself up. "Once our plan starts, we will need a place to go. It's not like we have a lot of options."

"Isolde," Liam said, rising to his feet. "This is insanity."

She ignored him and turned her gaze to Cillian. "Do you mind if Liam borrows your spare hood and cloaks?"

Cillian ran his gaze up and down Liam's form, a smirk pulling on the corners of his lips. "Not at all. Although, it might be a tight fit."

Liam looked between him and Isolde, his mouth open and eyes wide. "This is insane!"

"I agree," Malaki said, his voice dripping with disdain for having found some commonality with Liam.

"And are you aware of where Gage's chambers are?" Isolde asked, her eyebrow cocked in challenge.

Malaki shuffled from one foot to the other. "They can't be that hard to find," he mumbled, his teeth grinding.

"I know you have a fear of missing out on all the fun, Papa Bear," Isolde said, making her way to the bedchamber. "But this is one party you are not invited to."

"I'm not letting you go alone with *him*," Malaki said, throwing the words at Liam like an accusation.

Isolde crossed her arms over her chest, and a sigh pushed through Galaena's lips as she took a seat by Alaric. "And I wasn't asking for your permission to do so. I don't need it, Malaki. Besides, this isn't this first time we've done something like this."

His eyes grew wide and shot to Liam, who seemed to have shrunk into himself. "What do you mean not the first time?"

"We might have…killed a small battalion of soldiers the other night."

"An entire battalion?" Malaki repeated, his face reddening. "When was this?"

"After the opera."

Malaki opened his mouth to argue, but the sound of Alaric's voice silenced him. "It's her choice, Malaki." With a heavy sigh, Alaric rose from his seat, the wood of his cane groaning.

Her uncle's sharp, assessing eyes ran over Liam. Distrust still lingered, but something else sparked in their gaze. Something Isolde had longed to see. Acceptance.

"I know it's a lot to ask. Impossible knowing her," Alaric said, his mouth set in annoyance, "but don't let her get herself caught…or killed."

A rumble echoed through Malaki's chest. "I know you want to protect her old friend," Alaric said, turning to his best friend, to his brother. "But we need this. It's our only hope after we get out of here."

A look passed between them. Over time, they had created their own language, one not so different from the one she and Malaki shared. And after a moment, Malaki's gaze, heavy with worry, slid to Isolde. He nodded his head and allowed a small amount of tension to fall from his stance.

"It won't take long," Isolde promised, giving his shoulder a squeeze as she strolled into her bedchamber. She heard Liam follow behind. "Close the door and turn around," she said, her fingers already pulling at the strings of her dress. "I'm sure they're more than aware you've seen me naked, or at least partially, but let's not do it in front of them."

Red blossomed over Liam's cheeks, and he turned to shut the door. Isolde hid the grin playing on her lips as the door closed before Malaki, Liam's eyes pointedly looking down.

"Isolde—"

"If there is a rebellion forming," she said, tugging the black leather britches over the swell of her back side and tucking the tunic into place, "even the chance of it, we need to know. And besides, you seemed to enjoy our last little outing."

"It's not the same thing," Liam said, turning around to face her. "That was…very, very different."

"How so?" she asked, coming to grip his hands in her own. "How is this any different? After the other night, Liam, you are one of us."

Liam's lips parted as if he couldn't believe the words she had spoken. His eyes met hers, and a look she couldn't quite understand passed in their dark depths. But she could still see a hint of hesitance as well.

"The choice is simple," she said, her fingers squeezing. "Either you are with us…or you are with the people who forced me to kill a child. There's no in between." She dropped Liam's hands and took a step back. "Make your choice."

His hands were held aloft, as if waiting for her to return to him. But Isolde turned and began strapping weapon after weapon along her belt. When everything was in place, she reached for her bow, but found it gone.

Her eyes darted around the room, desperate fear climbing up her throat. But a wave of calm irritation soothed her growing panic a moment later. The handle looked oddly small in Liam's hands. His fingers trailed along the bow string, his eyes taking in every detail. "This was his, wasn't it?" Liam said, his gaze meeting hers at last. "Kamden's?"

His face flashed in her mind, and the crevasse within cracked open once more. "He gave it to me a week before he died. An early birthday present." The familiar pain and eternal fury burned through her chest.

Liam nodded, his eyes falling to the bow once more. "It's beautiful."

Isolde's throat bobbed. "He worked hard on it."

Liam cradled the precious weapon in his hands, the last piece of Kamden she possessed. "Can there be room for me in your heart, when he still dwells there?"

A smile pulled up at the corners of Isolde's lips, and she rested her hands over Liam's fingers still wrapped around the bow. "Kamden will always be a part of me, Liam," she said. "But that doesn't mean there is any less room for you." Her fingers grazed the harsh line of his stubble-covered jaw. "It's not a competition between the two of you. It never was."

"Can you please stop killing people, Isolde?" Liam snapped, as he shoved another dead guard into a storage closet. "I'd rather you not kill the entire guard staff."

"Agree to disagree on that point," Isolde said, yanking the arrow free from the man's skull before Liam could shove the door closed. "One less pawn for Erebus is a good thing in my book."

They crept down the hallway, their footsteps soundless in the dead of night. "They're not all bad men."

"There are no good men in these walls," Isolde said and the truth of that pierced her like a blade. "Only monsters live here now." Torches lined the hallway Liam led her down. A dagger was held snug in his gloved grip, the elithrium hue shining off the black leather of his tunic.

Liam halted at the end of the corridor and pressed Isolde's body flush against it. He peered around the corner and jerked back. "His chambers are just around this corner," Liam whispered, his voice muffled by Cillian's mask. "But there's two guards at post." A dark chuckle was Isolde's only reply as she pulled a pair of arrows from the quiver and notched them into place. "Isolde, don't!"

But it was too late. She stepped around the corner and let the arrows fly. Their tips buried in the necks of the guards who stood on either side of Gage's door. Gloved hands clawed helplessly at the shafts protruding from their flesh as their desperate cries went unanswered.

"You didn't have to do that," Liam said, his gaze raking over the men whose eyes had faded into nothingness.

"Yes, I did," Isolde said, already working at the lock on Gage's door.

"This isn't you," Liam said, squatting down beside them.

Isolde continued to work, her attention on the task at hand. Liam didn't need to see just how far gone she was at this point. That a part of the Isolde he knew, the one he loved, was gone, burned away with Tanor in the arena.

The lock gave way, and Isolde pushed the door inward. After slipping the lock picks into the pocket of her britches, she grabbed one of the guards from under the armpits and began dragging him inside.

"What are you doing?"

"Hiding the bodies," Isolde said, with a shrug. "Care to help?"

Liam's eyes bulged. "In Gage's room?"

"Why not?" she asked, letting the man drop to the floor. "It's not like he's not going to notice someone was here."

An irritated growl filtered through Liam's mask as he helped Isolde deposit the bodies in one of the closets positioned near the door. Extravagance and waste covered every inch of Gage's chambers. Gossamer curtains swayed from the patio doors that had been left open. A hint of the Oronilma Mountains shimmered beyond the beautifully arched windows.

A blood-red silk duvet covered the obnoxiously massive four-poster bed. Repulsion filled her stomach as Isolde moved past. It unnerved her being anywhere near the place Gage laid his head at night.

She made her way around the room to the desk residing near the open windows. Parchment lined the desk in perfect, orderly stacks. "At least he keeps things tidy," Isolde muttered, flipping through pile after pile of reports.

"He is thorough," Liam said at her side, his tone bleak. "What are you looking for exactly?"

Isolde tossed the stack away, spilling the contents onto the floor. "Volkran's reports," she said, purposefully knocking over a well of ink. Its glossy black contents ran across the desk's polished surface, leaving behind a permanent shadowy stain.

"Can you not make a mess?" Liam demanded, his hands already busy trying to blot up the ink.

"I just painted the hallways with the blood of Erebus's soldiers." She plucked a red leather pouch from one of the drawers. "And broke the lock to Gage's door. I doubt a little spilled ink is going to make that much of a difference. Besides, keeping Gage's things clean isn't high on my list of priorities."

"This wasn't part of the plan," Liam said, smearing black ink across Cillian's dark cloak.

"Yes, it was," she said, filing through a new stack of parchment. "I just didn't tell you the full plan."

"You're unbelievable," Liam said, his hands bracing on his hips.

"I am quite extraordinary, yes," Isolde mused. Her gaze snagged on the word sprawled across the page and her eyes widened. "Liam…"

A sigh of frustration filtered through Liam's mask as he came to stand at her side. But after a moment, she saw the same shock begin to grow on his face. "Is that what I think it is?"

A tally of populations, or a guess based on the source of the information, ran down the length of the page, assumptions pertaining to how many humans, half-bloods, and virya resided in the far west. Liam sighed. "I believe you just found proof of a rebellion in the Forgotten Lands."

Isolde flipped the page over, and a map stared back at them. The western coast of Arnoria, the Forgotten Lands, had been painted by someone with incredible skill. The Vailoron Mountains served as an impressive, deadly obstacle for those who dared venture further.

"So," Liam said, his gloved fingers running over the map. "They think the rebels are in the heart of Endurmure, in the Anar Desert, and along the Enyaloria River."

"Quite a few of them, it would seem." Isolde read the rest of the page and her heart fell with uncertainty. "But I'm not sure how accurate that is. This report is nearly twenty years old."

"Twenty years?" Liam said, snagging the page from her grip. "That's all Volkran has?"

"It would explain why Gage was so adamant about him bringing back fresh information," Isolde said, running her eyes over the map again. "If something is gathering in the west, I have a feeling Erebus would be most interested to learn it, don't you?"

She looked down to the desk, to another stack of documents spread along the table, and her brow furrowed. "What the hell is this?" She turned the page, and a lump formed in Isolde's throat. Her hands shook as her power hummed to life.

"Isolde?" He looked to the paper in her hand, and every muscle froze. The light from the dying fire danced across the receiver's name, as if the gods wanted her to know exactly who Gage had planned on contacting. "Oh gods."

Dear Tarvo,

Your son, Tanor, was found guilty of being in possession of forbidden materials for someone of his station. Lady Isolde Cotheran of Thornwood proved her loyalty to King Tenebriath by carrying out the execution of your son. Tanor has paid the price for his treasonous actions-

The paper crumbled beneath Isolde's unforgiving fingers. She threw it into the fire and yanked a blade free from its scabbard at her side.

"What are you doing?" Liam asked. But she wasn't listening. Moving without thought or reason, she ripped the doors from the hinges of one of the nearby armoires and began slicing through every article of clothing Gage possessed. She didn't stop until every piece lay in ribbons at her feet.

When the armoire had been thoroughly assassinated, she turned the desk on its end, sending the contents spilling onto the floor. Blotches of black ink, glass, and parchment covered the finely polished marble. The guilty anguish charring Isolde's heart brought a sob to her lips. She braced her back against the wall, her chest heaving. Air refused to move, refused to answer her call as panic and despair clogged her throat.

"I'm sorry," Liam said, as his warm, familiar touch broke through the fog of shame and guilt threatening to consume her. It felt as if his arms were the only things holding her together. "I'm so sorry, Isolde."

She clung to him, desperate for anything other than reality. Her gaze found its way to Gage's pristine, untouched bed. Murderous anger, cold and unforgiving, filled her heart. How she wanted him to suffer, to feel the sorrow burning through her in that moment. To cause him pain, anguish, and fury. To take something he could never get back.

An idea struck her, and a smile slowly spread across her face. Pulling away, Isolde tugged the mask free from her face and allowed the lip of her hood to fall back. Tendrils of hair that had escaped from the braid fell about her face, tickling her cheeks.

Liam held still, allowing her to do the same to his. The other hand found its way to his thigh. The muscles bunched beneath her light touch and a breath caught in his throat.

"Isolde." Liam's eyes, wide and glowing, flickered to the door. "We need to get back to—"

"The guard shift won't change for a while," she said. "We have the place to ourselves."

Liam's eyes shot to the bed behind her. Desire burned in his gaze as the power beneath Liam's skin roared to life.

She began to retreat, pulling him along with her. When the back of her knees hit the edge of the bed, she pressed her lips to his. Anger melted with need, making every nerve ending come alive in a savage, demanding plea.

The tip of her tongue ran across the smooth surface of Liam's bottom lip. "Do you know how jealous Gage gets when I talk about you?" she asked, her fingers tugging the hem of his tunic free. "Every time I mention your name, his eyes fill with rage." Isolde let the tips of her fingers travel downward to the bulge that was straining against the lining of Liam's britches.

A growl seeped through Liam's clenched teeth. "How wonderful would it be to know that every time I'm forced to be on his arm, you can look at me and remember, you had me in his bed?"

Liam's jaw ticked, and his gaze fell to her mouth, her breasts. A cocky grin tugged at the corner of Isolde's mouth as her eager fingers worked his belt loose and disappeared. His hard flesh twitched in her grasp as her fingers circled him. She made quick work of turning him around and shoving him down onto Gage's bed, her hand never straying, never stopping.

"Gods, Isolde!" he grasped, his fingers digging into her hips.

"Tell me what you want," she said, working to bring her knees up to straddle him, keeping her hand working a slow, torturous pace.

"You," he said, his hands snapping forward to haul her against him. "There's only ever been you."

She leaned forward, her lips hovering over his. Her teeth nipped at his bottom lip, drawing a moan of need from his throat. "Good," she said, working her hand faster.

His fingers gripped her hips and slid her pants down. A flicker of irritation flared as she stood to push the troublesome garment down. The cool night air kissed her bare back side as Liam gripped behind her knees and brought her back to sit on his lap. Her knees slid across the silken sheets on either side of him.

Liam's mouth caught her sigh of ecstasy as his punishing hands brought her down in one fluid thrust. Pain and pleasure blended together as she adjusted to the fullness of him and began to move. She started slow, wanting him to feel as much pleasure as possible. But soon, she unleashed herself and began moving at a punishing pace.

"Fuck, Isolde!" Liam growled, his grip tightening as he met her thrust for thrust. Her nails dug into the fabric of his tunic, desperate to hang on. A cry lifted from her lips as one of his hands moved down, his thumb circling that overly stimulated part of her. The other moved up, disappearing beneath her cloak and tunic to cup her breast.

A sigh, one caught yet again by Liam's mouth, sang from her throat as he teased every sensitive part of her. His tongue pushed into her mouth in long, sensual strokes that only spurred her forward. Her paced picked up, becoming more demanding.

She rode him until a wave of sheer pleasure ripped through her core and down her spine. She had not wanted him to be gentle, far from it. Every thrust, every touch was enough to drive away the pain raging through Isolde's heart. Isolde needed Liam to use her in Gage's bed. Needed him to take something she would never willingly give to that bastard.

"Harder," she gasped, her voice a straggled cry of pleasure. "Harder, Liam!"

He didn't stop, didn't utter a single word as he continued to drive up mercilessly with each thrust. A few moments later, a growl filled Liam's chest as he followed behind her. His chest heaved beneath her palms, his eyes glowing. Isolde felt her racing heart slow as Liam's lips grazed her jaw, his hands held her in place, refusing to let her get up.

"Did I hurt you?"

Isolde smiled. "Not at all."

"Gods, Isolde," he sighed, a faint sheen of sweat glistening for his brow. "I can have you a hundred times—a thousand. And it will still never be enough."

Her lips brushed his in a tender, gentle kiss. The fine points of his stubble tickled her palms as she cupped his face. "Savor it," she breathed. "I don't know when we'll be alone like this again. Don't forget tonight."

"How could I?" he asked. "Forgetting this would be like forgetting the sun or the stars themselves—simply impossible."

It wasn't the revenge she wanted. No, only Gage's blood could satisfy that need. But taking Liam in Gage's bed, letting him have her body in a place that was entirely her enemy's and in a way Gage never would, was a revenge she could live with.

For now.

CHAPTER 35

"I can't imagine it was a cheap dress, Nan," Isolde said, from where she lay buried beneath her silk duvet, voice heavy with sleep.

"I'm sure there's more where it came from," Nan said, shoving the intricate layers of the dress she has worn the previous night into the glowing embers with the poker. A note of heaviness hung in her voice. A tired sound that filled Isolde with worry.

"How are you, Nan?" Isolde asked, pulling the covers up to her chin. "With being back here?"

Nan fell silent, and her withered hand shook around the brass handle of the fire poker. "It's hard, my rose," she said, her voice hardly a whisper. "So many years, so many memories." Her lips quivered, and the light in her deep blue eyes glistened.

Isolde tossed the sheets away and hopped out of bed, the cool morning air caressing her bare skin. She wrapped Nan in her arms and held her as tightly as she dared. Isolde felt Nan's arms constrict around her waist and hold firm. A shiver ran through her body and into

Isolde's.

"I thought I could handle coming back," Nan murmured. The tips of her fingers gently pressed into the ridges of ruined flesh running down the planes of Isolde's back. Tears swelled in her eyes as Nan's voice broke. "But I see them everywhere. I hear their screams echo down every corridor. I want to go home, Isolde. I want it to be over!"

"I know, Nan," Isolde said, planting a kiss on the top of her grey hair. "It'll be over soon."

"I'm so proud of you, my rose." Nan said. She pulled back to cup her hands around Isolde's face. Streams of glistening tears ran down Nan's cheeks that had pulled into a loving smile. "Of the woman, of the symbol you have become for so many people. He would be proud too."

Isolde's heart broke beneath Nan's loving words. "Kamden wouldn't even know me, Nan." Her voice shook as she rested her forehead to Nan's and allowed her chest to fill with her scent—lilac and rain. "I'm not the girl I once was."

"No," Nan said. "You're so much more."

"Are you alright?" Liam asked, from where he walked at her side.

"Couldn't be better," Isolde said, her voice forcefully cheerful. "Just another day in the capital fighting to the death."

"You know what I mean," he said, shooting her a reproachful look. "Did Malaki heal you enough? Are ready for the trial today? Because if you're not, Erebus needs to know what Gage did—"

"It won't matter, Liam," she said, cutting him off. "You know damn well Gage will lie. That his word will be taken over ours. No matter how many witnesses were there. And I'm not putting you or anyone else in that kind of position."

However, Isolde knew that wasn't entirely true. Erebus's anger at the bruises left behind by Gage still confused her. He might be the one putting her life in danger, but he certainly didn't like anyone else laying a hand on her. At least, not in that way.

"But to answer your question, yes. I'm fine. Malaki made sure before I left."

A muscle in Liam's jaw ticked.

"You seem particularly ill-tempered today," Isolde said. "Why?"

"It's nothing." His tone said otherwise.

Isolde licked her lips, understanding settling into her stomach like ice. "Gage talked about it, didn't he? About what happened in the library."

Darkness fell across Liam's face, his lip curling. "Among other things."

Silence hung between them until they reached the door of the holding area.

"Two more," he said, taking her hands in his. The leather felt warm against her skin, soft and worn.

"Two more," she echoed, clearing her throat. "Then we can go." Liam hadn't said if he would go with them when the time came. And while, a part of Isolde truly thought he would, another part had its doubts.

"Then we can go," he said, the corner of his mouth tilting up into a half smile. The pounding of drums echoed through the corridor, and Liam sighed. "Be safe." Giving her hands one last squeeze, he headed down the hallway, and disappeared around the corner.

Isolde took a deep breath, willing her heart to still. When a sense of calm at last returned, she pushed the door open and slid inside. Demir and Sohan lounged at the refreshment table, its surface covered with its usual unnecessary piles of food, all of which was left untouched.

Buer hovered near the fire.

"Nice of you to join us, Lady Isolde."

She turned to see Kyros resting against the wall, one foot braced behind him. His lean arms, covered in a deep, evergreen tunic, were crossed over his chest. "So glad to see you this morning…and in one piece."

"No thanks to you," she said under her breath, her hand dropping to her abdomen as the phantom pain returned. Soreness still lingered in her side, not that she would have told Malaki. Especially with what was to come.

Pushing off the wall, the champion of Marsh Hall stepped into the light. A gasp stuck in Isolde's throat as she took in the dark bruises lining Kyros's face. One of his eyes was nearly swollen shut and the other was so bloodshot Isolde wondered how he could see properly. But his attention had fallen to where her hand pressed against her side.

A shadow, dark and teeming with violence, fell across his maimed face. "Looks like I wasn't the only one who was *taught a lesson* last night."

"Oh no," Isolde said, her voice gaining an ounce of softness. "I was thoroughly educated."

Kyros rolled his eyes or attempted to anyway. "All because of a kiss." A humorless laugh pushed through his swollen, split lip. "What a fragile ego your fiancé must have."

"As an eggshell," Isolde said, with a smile reaching her eyes. "Men like him who have little to offer in…other areas tend to have incredibly fragile egos."

A knowing smile pulled at the corners of Kyros's lips. "Well, good thing mine is rock hard. Indestructible, one might say."

"Is that so?" Isolde asked, blood rushing to her cheeks. She swept her eyes over him, giving his ego the tiniest stroke.

He leaned in, his lips brushing the shell of her ear. "You're more than welcome to find out for yourself."

A laugh, light and sensual leapt from her mouth. "Tempting, but I'll have to take your word for it."

Kyros shrugged but kept the same incriminating smile in place. "Your loss."

Isolde kept her lips sealed as the door opened and Lenox entered. Isolde fought to hide the look of disdain playing on her face.

"Good afternoon, champions," he said. "Today is an individual event. One champion will compete at a time. When it is your turn, you will be escorted to the arena to face your trial." Isolde noticed he didn't carry the box containing their bracelets today. A conflicting wave of relief and fear crashed through her chest at its absence.

"The first up is the champion of Marsh Hall. If you would please follow me."

"Oh, how lucky I am getting to go first," Kyros whispered, brushing past Isolde, his fingers grazing along her lower back. "Can't imagine who would have arranged that."

The door shut with a bang, and Isolde made her way to the refreshment table. Every type of meat and pastry imaginable was present. After piling her plate full of croissants and cinnamon rolls, she took a seat at the back of the room, furthest away from the fire.

"Is eating a nervous tick for you, Lady Isolde?" Buer asked. "I'd be careful if I were you. I hear your fiancé likes a smaller woman."

A humorless chuckle rumbled through her chest. "Oh, I'm sure he does. But a woman also prefers a fiancé who has the right equipment to satisfy her. And Lord Gage falls short in that department, embarrassingly so. If the rumors can be believed of course. I'd say that makes us even."

"Gage said you were a fighter," Buer said, his eyes darkening with challenge. "But you'll wind up on your back in the end." Isolde stuffed an entire cinnamon roll into her mouth, not breaking eye contact with him.

"You're welcome to come find out," she said around a mouthful of sugary cinnamon dough. "Or do you want a repeat of the last time you got in my way?"

Sohan cupped a hand to his mouth as if to keep the laugh at bay, his shoulders shaking. Buer opened his mouth, red spilling out onto his cheeks. But he was cut short by a piercing growl erupting from the arena above.

Isolde froze mid-chew. It came again. This time, whatever creature lurking on the surface above, sounded wounded and very angry. Isolde's appetite vanished, and she turned to Sohan, whose eyes were glued to the ceiling. "Remind me," she said. "Does Kyros have the ability to transform?"

"Yes," he said. His voice was a deep whisper, like a soft wind in the dead of night. "But not into anything capable of making that sound."

Kyros did not return.

And soon the roar of the crowd pierced the small holding room. Isolde glanced at the rest of the champions. Demir stood near the door, his eyes occasionally flickering to the ceiling above. Buer stayed by the fire, his eyes glazed and wide as if he was lost in thought. Isolde had the feeling that happened more often than not. Although, she could not imagine how. His mind couldn't have held any level of complexity beyond, fighting, sex, and eating.

Sohan lingered off to the side. His colossal arms were crossed over his chest, completely at ease. Isolde found herself unable to sit still. She paced back and forth from one edge of the room to the other. Her teeth dug at her nails, needing something to do besides think about what awaited her on the arena floor. Before long the door opened once again, and Lenox called for Buer. He didn't look Isolde's way as he crossed under the doorway.

They waited what felt like an eternity before the cries of the audience rained down on them. A moment later, Isolde's blood ran cold. A terrible growl filled the air, one Isolde knew certainly didn't come from Buer.

Lenox returned far sooner than Isolde would have thought possible, his robes painted with fresh blood. "Foxclove." Demir's face, while stoically calm, drained of color as he took a deep breath and headed for the door.

"Do try to stay alive, Demir," Sohan said, his face breaking out into a wide grin. "I'd hate for you to die before the final challenge."

"Not a fan of yours?" Isolde asked, as Demir disappeared through the door. She leaned back into one of the overstuffed chairs and threw her feet on top of the table.

"You could say that," Sohan muttered with an air of dismissal and turned his gaze back to the fire.

"What's the story?" Isolde pressed, ignoring his attempts at dodging a conversation.

Sohan shrugged his massive shoulders. "There isn't one. I just don't like him."

"Seems pretty harsh to say for someone you simply don't like."

"His reputation precedes him in certain circles." Sohan turned his eyes on her, a light igniting in their depths. "Don't tell me you've never wanted to kill someone for the simple fact of not enjoying their company, Lady Isolde."

She nodded in defeat. "You have me there." A smirk tugged at his mouth as Sohan turned back to the fire, but she wasn't letting him off that easily. "Why did you join the tournament? You mentioned Ferden does it on a volunteer basis. What made you choose to come?"

"You ask an annoying amount of questions," Sohan said, his beautiful, soulful eyes narrowing at her over his shoulder.

"I'm a curious girl," she said, her voice light and filled with an air of innocence.

A deep chuckle rumbled from his chest. "Yes," he said. "And I'm sure you're aware of what curiosity leads to."

"Answered questions?"

"Trouble."

Isolde rose an expectant eyebrow as she sunk further into the chair, waiting. After a moment, Sohan sighed and allowed his arms to unfurl. "Killing goes hand in hand with breathing for men like, Demir. Mercy is not something he is well aquatinted with. As the former heir of Thornwood, I'm sure you're no stranger to the rumors involving Foxclove, of the nightmares that once lived within their walls before Dagan's sudden demise."

Isolde shrugged. "I might have heard a tale or two." An image of Dagan's dead body flashed in her mind, and it took all of her will power to keep a smile at bay. "It was the Hood who killed the little lording, wasn't it?"

"That's the story," Sohan said. "Which is what led Demir to Elenarta. He has a personal vendetta against the Hood now."

A humorless laugh tumbled from Isolde's lips. "I'm sure he's one of many."

"He was blamed for Dagan's death and the deaths of all the men the Hood killed that night. The only reason Gage let him live was because of his power and skill with a blade. But there was a price for his freedom."

"Which was?"

Sohan's hand swept the room in a casual wave. "Be his champion— or one of them, I should say. Demir and Gage share a hatred for the Hood. He has sworn to rid Arnoria of the memory, the very idea of the masked vigilante. To make an example of anyone who dares take up their mantle. I have known men like Demir my entire life. He is a murderer, a monster among men."

"If he's anything like Gage," Isolde said. "He's worse than a monster." She thought back to her time at Foxclove. Never had

Demir's name graced its halls, even during the time Theort still lived. Although, she couldn't imagine Dagan's father allowing such a man to exist in his territory. A sad fondness filled her heart. Theort had been a kind lord, one his people loved dearly.

"Your turn, Champion of Sorrows," Sohan said, jerking her from the past. "Why did you join?"

Isolde opened her mouth, but a piercing scream rang out above, silencing the words on her tongue. It wasn't animal but wholly man. Demir's scream, or what Isolde believed to be his, was followed by a hiss Isolde couldn't place. She looked to Sohan who ground his teeth.

"Well," she said leaning back into the cushions of the chair, doing her best to hide the fear pounding in her heart. "At least we know today will be interesting."

They didn't speak again until the sounds of the crowd died away. Its absence left a hollowness in the world, a silence that was far too heavy. Before long Lenox returned yet again. He looked between Isolde and Sohan as he stepped back into the room.

"Thornwood, if you please."

It felt as if Isolde's stomach had dropped to the bottom of her feet. She rose gracefully from the chair, her head held high and followed the Master of Games down the hallway. At the end of the tunnel, her toes brushed the edge of the sun, its rays cutting a line across the gravel at her feet. Lenox came to stand beside her, his breath foul and reeking of mead.

"Your trial is simple, Lady Isolde. Either you leave the arena alive, or it does. There is no in between." His lips stretched across a set of horribly stained rotten teeth. "Is *that* in anyway unclear?"

"No," Isolde said, facing forward. "What's unclear is how you got this job with teeth like that."

The growl seeping through Lenox's lips was drowned out by the steady rhythm of the drums. Just as Isolde took her first step, Lenox gripped her arm, holding her in place. "I hope she eats you alive!" He rasped.

Isolde yanked free from his grip and marched into the arena. The roar of the crowd was deafening. But what gave Isolde pause were the colossal sheets of chain mail that had been placed around the walls. They ran along the rim of the lowest level of the arena and soared into the sky. A wide length stretched overhead, sealing her in. The ground was littered with numerous, gleaming weapons, placed in various corners or half buried beneath a mound of sand and gravel. She spotted the bow and quiver where they rested on the far side, next to one of the unopened gates.

She looked to the mass of gold and maroon. Malaki sat at the very bottom of the stands his hands braced on the railing, along with Blyana and Cillian. Alaric and Galaena stood at the top and a look of terror filled their faces.

"Lady Isolde of Thornwood!" The sound of Erebus's voice drew her eyes to the dais. An extra sheet of elithrium-laced mail was draped over the opening, ensuring no one and nothing could penetrate its boundaries.

"You have proven to be witty, skilled, and loyal." Erebus's voice rang loud and clear on that last word and Isolde's lip curled. "A champion fit to stand at my side. But there is one question left unanswered. How brave are you?" He smiled down at her, his eyes gleaming. "Let's find out."

Erebus waved a hand in the air, gesturing to the tunnel at her back. Isolde slowly turned, and the grate at the opposite end rose. The crowd shot to their feet, their fists pounding against the one thing keeping them safe. From the shadows of the tunnel, a sound Isolde didn't think would ever touch her ears again cried from deep within. It was impossible to forget. The screech haunting her nightmares filled the air. Her eyes widened and panic filled Isolde's chest, forcing her to take an involuntary step back.

"Oh, my gods!"

A pair of familiar, glowing brown eyes ignited from within the depths of the tunnel and the voice of a black vulture pierced her mind like a blade.

"Hello, thief!"

CHAPTER 36

"Y*ou look surprised, Isolde?"* Yvaine laughed, her words bouncing off the inside of Isolde's head like arrows upon stone. *"You thought I died that night, didn't you?"*

Terror seized Isolde where she stood. It snaked chains of iron around her feet and welded them to the ground, refusing to let her move. Every breath left her chest in a gasp as the hideous creature stepped into the light.

"How is this possible?" Isolde said, her hand cupping the side of her head. "How can I hear you?" The unknown filled her with horror as rays of the afternoon sun glistened off Yvaine's inky, black feathers.

"It matters not," Yvaine answered, her beak coming together in a snap. *"You're going to die today."*

"How did you know it was me?" Isolde asked, the question shooting through the air before she could stop it. "Why haven't you told them?"

"I saw you on the shore that night at Blackwater," Yvaine said, her talons digging into the gravel with every step she took. *"I saw you pulling that*

mangy beast from the water. The one who will die right after you do." Her cold eyes shot to the stands. Isolde turned to see Blyana's face pale, her eyes wide in disbelief and terror. *"And as for not telling the king, it wasn't for lack of trying. No one can understand me. Except for you."*

Isolde swallowed against the swell of fear bubbling inside her chest. Every beat of her heart slammed against her ribcage as Yvaine took another step forward.

"My own guards captured me. Chained me like an animal and brought me to Elenarta in a cage. But no matter how hard I tried, I could never change back into what I once was…because of you."

"I hardly think I had anything to do with that," Isolde said, resolve and courage finding their way back into her bones. "It isn't my fault you can't control yourself."

"You bear many faults, Isolde Cotheran," Yvaine said, her eyes narrowing. *"Faults, I have every intention of making you and your merry band of thieves pay deeply for."* A dark chuckle drummed through the corners of Isolde mind, stirring her power even further. *"But first, I believe you and I have some unfinished business to attend to."*

Isolde looked past Yvaine's razor-sharp talons to the bow and quiver. She shifted her stance, preparing to sprint for the one weapon she knew she could kill Yvaine with.

"Well, I do hate to leave a job undone," Isolde said, resolve settling over her shoulders like a shield. The sound of the drums died, and Isolde sprinted across the arena.

Allowing just a fraction of her power through, Isolde shot a plume of air directly into Yvaine's bony chest. The blast sent the vulture crashing to the ground at the mouth of the tunnel she'd crawled out of. Isolde's smile faded as Yvaine straightened and launched herself into the air.

Climbing higher, Yvaine hid in the rays of the sun. The light stung Isolde's eyes, forcing her to look away. Acid filled her muscles as Isolde took off, her feet digging into the gravel. Triumphant hope swelled in her chest as she reached for the handle of the bow. But a black wing cut into her path, her fingers barely grazing the fine polished wood.

Yvaine's shoulder slammed into Isolde's chest, knocking every bit of air from her lungs. She landed several feet away in a heap of limbs and dirt. A stinging pain trailed up the side of her arm and shoulder as gravel tore through the skin. Isolde slowly rose to her feet and forced a steady stream of air to fill her lungs. Every gulp of air felt like the lick of a flame in her chest.

"We have a long way to go, Isolde," Yvaine rasped, pinching the bow between her beak and clamping down. It crumbled into pieces on the ground, along with Isolde's hopes of making it out of the arena alive. *"By the time I'm done with you, no one will recognize you."*

Yvaine took flight again, her wings stirring the dust around them. Cough after cough punched through Isolde's chest, forcing her to draw up the corners of her tunic to cover her mouth and nose. Dirt stung her eyes as she looked into the sky. A great shadow sailed through the air on her right, then disappeared a moment later.

She rolled just in time to escape Yvaine's talons slashing through the wall of dust like a set of blades. The gravel ate at her back, tearing the scar tissue free. Her hands dug into the gravel, and the tips of her fingers grazed something long and sharp.

Rising, Isolde beheld a beautiful longsword. Even in the light of the dimmed sun, she could see it was laced with elithrium. Rays of sunlight broke through the clouds of dust around her, granting her a view of Yvaine just twenty yards away.

Her beady eyes turned, and a shriek erupted from her beak. Isolde's fingers wove their way around the pommel and her body moved as it had done for decades. Her hand swept through the air, sending a gust of wind into the ground.

Gravel and dust filled Yvaine's eyes, blinding her to where Isolde lurked to the left. The edge of a wing came into view and Isolde drove the blade through the fine membrane, coating the sword in blood. Yvaine shrieked and snapped out with her beak, catching Isolde's shoulder. Her fingers tightened around the sword as she was hurled back across the arena, refusing to let go of the one weapon she had managed to snag. The ground rose to meet her, drawing a cry of pain she couldn't contain from her mouth.

"You've been through worse," she said, riding out the tide of agony that ebbed and flowed. "Far, far worse." The monster within beat against the chains of confinement, its teeth sinking into the corners of her mind. But she couldn't risk it, couldn't risk unleashing herself. Not here. Grunting, she plunged the tip of the sword into the ground and forced herself to stand. The dust-filled breeze ran along the slashes in her tunic, setting the wounds now decorating her body on fire.

Yvaine's frame hovered like a terrifying darkness standing at least twenty-five feet tall. *"That's the only blood you draw from me today, you little bitch!"*

Isolde's mind rattled with Yvaine's voice. But a savageness now echoed through every word hammering inside Isolde's skull. As if her anger was breaking through, allowing the animalistic side to take more control.

Confusion still pommeled Isolde's mind at what she was hearing. *How can she even think logically at all?* Yvaine didn't give Isolde time to ponder. She launched into the sky. Her right wing trembled, showering the arena in blood.

The crowd cheered as Isolde sprinted for a spear protruding from the ground on her left. Her feet pounded against the uneven gravel, her chest heaving. As her hand wrapped around the spear's shaft, sunlight gave way to darkness. Isolde turned her eyes up to see Yvaine diving through the air.

The ring on her hand ignited, opening up a well of endless, deadly power. Isolde didn't question it as she threw her hand up, sending a colossal wave of wind up into the sky. It hit Yvaine square in the chest and threw her to the side. The chain mail cage shook under the weight of Yvaine's body. Cries of terror filled the arena as the tips of her black feathers brushed the heads of the spectators. But the chains held firm, keeping them safe from the horrors trapped inside the arena.

The spear's shaft was far too thick, making it nearly impossible to hold. Isolde's fingers tightened around the longsword still in her right hand. She could feel the threads of her will clinging to sanity slowly dissipate, her control waning. Even with the help of her mother's ring, Isolde knew it wouldn't last long. The restraints she had placed on the monster, on that terrible power, couldn't withstand this forever.

Blood and sweat covered Isolde's palms, coating the sword and spear she desperately clung to. Her eyes stung with dirt and her ears rang with the vulture's ear-piercing screech. Isolde tried sending another wave of air up into the sky, but Yvaine was ready. She dodged the first gust, her feathers ruffling with the outskirts of Isolde's strike.

The ring hummed, demanding she give more, do more. But already Isolde could feel the shift in her bones, that drive to give in hovering at the edge of her mind. The broad side of the bird's talon slammed into Isolde's side, sending her flying once again across the arena's unforgiving ground. Isolde twisted just in time to not impale herself on the longsword's sharp, deadly blade.

Gravel dug into the knuckles of the hand gripping the handle, her flesh tearing anew. Dirt coated her tongue and filled her chest, causing another coughing fit. But Yvaine gave her no reprieve. As Isolde tried to stand, Yvaine's talon sunk into her thigh, drawing a scream from Isolde's lips. She was lifted off the ground, and drops of her blood fell through the air like discarded rubies.

"I never did find out," Yvaine said, her voice filled with madness that hadn't been there before. *"Do thieves break?"* The merciless talon dug

into her thigh, tearing muscle from bone as Isolde hung upside down. The blades fell from her hands and disappeared into the dust cloud below.

"I can't be sure," said Isolde, stars shining before her eyes, the pain growing. "Doesn't seem like a good day to find out though."

"Don't be silly, Isolde," Yvaine growled. *"It's the perfect day for you to die."* A dark chuckle rattled through her mind, and Yvaine swung her foot forward, releasing Isolde from her grip. The sensation of falling gripped Isolde's stomach in a vice. Acting on every instinct she possessed, Isolde threw her hands out, shooting blasts of air in any direction, hoping to find the ground.

It rose to meet her in one mighty blow. A blast of power helped to soften the impact, but not by much. Her head collided with something hard and unyielding. Stars exploded before her eyes and something warm and thick ran down the side of her face.

Pain. It was all Isolde could think about. It was everywhere, leaving no part of her untouched. Rolling onto her back, she looked to the sky. A small figure flew just outside the confines of the cage. A figure she would know anywhere.

"Fane."

The ends of his talons dug into the cage keeping him from her. His sharp eyes were wide with fury as he turned to the right, drawing Isolde's attention. Yvaine was moving to the stands, the part of the arena covered in maroon and gold.

"Mangy beast," Yvaine said, her voice wholly devoid of logical thought. *"I'm going to enjoy tearing you into pieces."* Blyana's shaking hands moved to the blades at her sides. Cillian stepped forward, his eyes glowing with malice. A growl rumbled through the air as Malaki stood at Cillian's side, his teeth bared.

"The mate and the Bastard Prince." Yvaine chuckled. *"You were there too. Good. I want Isolde to see those she loves die before she takes her final breath."*

A high-pitched ringing filled Isolde's ears. She forced her uninjured leg beneath her and stood. The crowd was pleasantly muted. Even the shriek of victory Yvaine let loose from her beak hardly made a sound. Light danced off the blades littering the arena floor, but Isolde knew they would be of no help to her.

Anger, cold and unstoppable, burned in her blood. It seared away any doubt of what had to be done. Of what she would have to do now that Yvaine had turned her sights on her cadre. There was but one way out of this arena.

Only one.

Power echoed through every part of her. Pain and fury sang their familiar duet as they wove through her body, forming a single horrible melody. One of darkness and one of power. Isolde felt every bone begin to shift, to bend, to break as her will fell away. Her blood hummed with a hatred she knew all too well. And as Yvaine reached the arena's edge, Isolde let go of her control with a vicious smile.

Malaki thought he was an expert on pain, on terror. But nothing had prepared him for this. For the horror of watching that bitch's talon sink into Isolde's leg and hoist her into the air. His power, his vow, his very being demanded he help her.

But Malaki knew, just as well as Blyana and Cillian, if they made a move now, if they tried to intervene in any way, it would cost Isolde her life. So, he gripped the railing at his waist and willed himself to be still. A cry of fury broke through his clenched teeth as Yvaine slung Isolde to the ground. Her cry of pain shot across the arena and his teeth ground.

Panic seized him when she didn't immediately rise. Red glistened from the side of her face, clotted with dust. Malaki's gaze rose to the dais. To where Erebus looked down on where Isolde lay. His eyes were focused and unmoving. In a way that had Malaki believing, for just a moment, he actually cared. Gage was at his side. The long, hideous scars Isolde had gifted him were pulled back into a smug grin.

"Get up!" He heard Blyana cry, her tiny fists beating on the railing. "Isolde, get up!"

"You have to move," Cillian roared, his hands cupping his mouth. Gusts of wind created by his power, carried his words through the air. "Move your ass, now!"

As if she could hear them, Isolde slowly rose to her feet. Blood covered her right leg and the left side of her face. She was nothing but a rag doll to the mindless virya—a torn, ratty plaything.

Yvaine turned her murderous gaze on Blyana. Her beak snapped through the air as she started their way.

"I fucking dare you, bird bitch," Cillian seethed, stepping in front of Blyana. Malaki took up the other side and a growl rumbled through his chest as his hand wrapped around Secrettaker. Then he stilled.

A change fell over Isolde as she looked to the sky. Her eyes…

A piping hot, metal ball of terror dropped into the pit of Malaki's stomach. Her eyes began to glow. They hummed with a power she alone was capable of.

"Oh gods," he said with a sharp breath.

Malaki had seen her transform before, countless times. But this was different. Never had she faced another virya in true open combat in her transformed state. Bone after bone bent and broke as her skin split apart, making way for the plume of gorgeous, white feathers beneath. A battle cry, one ringing with the promise of blood and vengeance, exploded from her golden beak. She was massive, nearly as tall as Yvaine.

They stood in stark contrast. Day versus night, light versus darkness.

Blinding rays of light danced off Isolde's white feathers as she shot into the air. Yvaine followed, but she was no match for Isolde. While she was slightly bigger, the vulture wasn't nearly as fast. The tips of Isolde's talons ripped into the side of Yvaine's wing, painting the arena floor with black feathers and blood.

Cry after cry of anguish and malice filled the arena. The sound joined the calls for blood coming from the people who cheered them on. Yvaine drove her beak into Isolde's left side and ripped away a clump of feathers.

Her answering shriek was like a bolt to Malaki's heart. Already he could feel his own power lingering at the edges of his sanity. Looking back up into the crowd, he saw Alaric and Galaena were on their feet, hands clenched at their sides. Worry and fury filled Gal's gaze. But Alaric's face had already begun to shift. Sharp teeth filled his mouth, and the first hint of the crocodile's scales dusted his cheekbones.

Malaki knew without a shadow of a doubt, if Isolde died in this arena, they would all be joining her.

He turned back to the fight just in time to see the virya collide midair. Their talons interlocked in a knot of sharpened bone. The tip of Isolde's beak drove into Yvaine's shoulder as they fell through the sky in a spiral. At the last second, they broke apart, narrowly missing the hard, unforgiving ground. Yvaine flew for higher ground, leaving Isolde to hover below.

"Get up there, Isolde," Malaki growled. Her emerald and silver eyes rose to the sky and a cry burst from her beak. Her mighty wings pushed up, sending a cloud of dust into the dais. Malaki smirked as those who loitered on the platform glowered after her.

She hunted for Yvaine, her sharp eyes darting from left to right. But the bitch had learned where to hide in the sun. Without warning, Yvaine broke through the veil of sunlight and Malaki's heart stopped.

Isolde looked back with just enough time to turn on her back and meet Yvaine's talons with her own. Her sharp beak pecked at Isolde's wings and chest. A screech filled the air as a patch of her beautiful white feathers turned red.

"Fly!" Cillian yelled, his hands cupping around his mouth. "Damn you, Isolde, fly!"

But they continued to fall, neither virya letting go. "Fly!" Blyana cried. "Isolde, fly now!"

They neared the ground and Isolde threw her head back, dragging Yvaine along with her, refusing to let go. The vulture screeched and tried to rip herself away from Isolde's grip. But Isolde's talons dug into Yvaine's legs, refusing to let go.

"Isolde!" Malaki roared. Half a century of love and panic filled her name that carried over the arena as they hit the ground. The impact jarred the arena and rattled the elithrium cage. Feathers, black and white, danced in the breeze, their tips stained in blood. Disbelief kept Malaki firmly planted in place. His hands shook with the power rushing forward.

"She's not dead," he said to himself. "Not dead…not dead."

After the dust settled, a mound of black and white feathers emerged in the heart of the arena. Their tips swayed in the light breeze ghosting through the air. Neither of them stirred.

"Isolde!" A growl pierced the air, drawing Malaki's gaze to Blyana. Her eyes were glowing, her teeth sharpening as her eyes flew to the dais. Cillian's gaze was fixed there as well, and his body hummed with a well of power Malaki didn't believe him capable of. He turned back to the arena and felt the chains of his control slipping. Failure and heartache pummeled his mind. As he took a step forward, his eyes shifting to Erebus, a flicker of movement caught his eye.

White feathers rustled as Isolde's wing flexed to the sky. Slowly, she rose from the crater they had made, her body trembling. A faint, hollow cry slipped from her beak. Relief, so potent to the point of pain, shot through Malaki's heart. He swallowed around the lump in his throat and forced the chains of control back around his power.

A steady stream of blood trickled from the wound left by Yvaine's talons as she cradled her right leg beneath her. Isolde turned her heated, unforgiving gaze to the dais. Erebus met her stare, his eyes were glowing with wonder. The corner of his mouth tugged up into a smile that put Malaki on edge. The sound of feathers scraping against the ground drew Isolde's attention back to where Yvaine lay.

"How is that bitch still alive?" Blyana asked.

Malaki didn't answer. All he could do was stare. Isolde, hopping on one leg, moved to Yvaine's side and clamped her beak around the vulture's neck. Yvaine thrashed in Isolde's hold, her desperate shrieks filling the hot afternoon air. But it was no use. There was no escaping for her, not this time.

Isolde's head snapped to the left and right in quick, merciless jerks. The sound of shattered bones, bones that could never be repaired, echoed through the arena. Yvaine's body dropped to the ground at Isolde's feet in a mound of bones and feathers. Her golden eyes, once shining with malice and anger, faded into darkness.

The crowd stilled. Their mouths were gaping and eyes wide as if they couldn't believe what they had just witnessed. Lenox strode forward, causing Malaki's lip to curl.

"We have our winner!" Lenox announced, his hand waving to the bloody falcon at his back. "Isolde Cotheran of Thornwood!"

Isolde's furious gaze snapped to the Master of Games. Every ounce of that viryian anger poured from her eyes. Her beak snapped in his direction and Lenox froze, his mouth gaping in disbelief and terror. Isolde shrieked, drawing a pathetic cry from Lenox's pale lips. He took off back towards the tunnel, his robes billowing around him. But a wall of white feathers stopped him dead in his tracks.

"Get your soldiers down there now!" Erebus roared, turning his blazing eyes to Gage. The Right Hand disappeared behind the dais, his hand gripping the pommel of his sword. Malaki shoved past a row of people and sprinted for the access door leading into the arena. A soldier stood in his path, a boy not much older than he had been when he got his first assignment.

"Move!" Malaki ordered, his lips pulled back into a snarl.

"I can't permit you to enter—" the boy said, his shoulders flinching at the sound of Isolde's cry.

"You either move or I kill you where you stand, boy!" Malaki growled. He must have seen something in Malaki's eyes to know he meant it. Stepping aside, he allowed him to pass through without another word of protest. Malaki raced across arena at the same time as a battalion of soldiers led by Gage.

"Isolde!" Malaki cried, his hands cupping his mouth. She turned at the sound of her name. She had Lenox pinned to the stone wall, her talon's locking him in place. A look of recognition flickered in her eyes.

"Look at me," Malaki said, taking a cautious step. "Only at me."

Isolde's wings eased down to her side, and her eyes blinked.

The sound of clinking armor and footsteps filled the air as Gage and his men took up formation around the arena floor. "Spread out!" He ordered. "Chain mail only, no blades! By order of the king!"

Her eyes glowed as decades of hate poured into a shriek that stabbed into Malaki's ears. She dropped Lenox and left him to curl into a ball on the ground. A dark stain spread across the robes at his crotch. Isolde turned her sights on Gage; to the man responsible for so much of her pain.

Malaki almost let her have him. How badly he wanted to give that bastard's pathetic life to her. But the only path Gage's death would lead down was one of death for them all.

"Isolde!"

The sound of his voice halted her steps, and she turned back to him, her chest heaving. Malaki stepped forward and held his hand out. "You know what will happen. Don't do it." A war raged in her glowing eyes. She looked between him and the man who had taken everything from her. "Don't let it control you," Malaki said. "Fight it."

Isolde's eyes squeezed shut, and a cry erupted from the depths of her chest. Her pain and anguish filled the air as she forced the monster within back into its cage. It was a pain Malaki knew well and his heart ached for her. "Breathe, Isolde," he said, daring to stand at her side. "Breathe!"

Isolde stumbled, and a familiar cry filled the air as she dropped her injured leg down to the ground. She fell at his feet in a mess of feathers and blood.

"Easy," Malaki said. "Easy now." Slowly, the feathers began to recede, and Isolde's body began to shrink. "You're doing well, Isolde. Nice and steady."

Gage was on her left, his eyes locked on something at her side. Malaki followed his gaze and his heart stopped.

As Isolde slowly changed back, the scar left behind by Gage's blade at Briarhole began to take shape. It lay bare within the gaping hole left in her tunic. Malaki darted to her side, blocking Gage's view. He drew up the edges of her ruined tunic and cupped a hand to her ribcage, hiding the scar as best he could.

"Isolde?" Malaki whispered, his fingers brushing across her face. Blood from a gash running down the curve of her cheek soaked into the strands of her hair. Without thinking, Malaki shoved his magic beneath her skin. He pulled what he could from the creatures lurking beneath the arena, the virya who were doomed to live as monsters. He felt their well of power beneath his feet and yanked it all to himself. A few soldiers fell as well, their bodies crumbling beside the beasts they were charged with guarding.

The wound on Isolde's head healed instantly, leaving nothing behind but flawless, bloody skin. Slowly, the gaping hole in her leg knitted together. When the last of the feathers drifted back beneath the layers of her skin, Isolde's eyes fluttered open.

"Did I win?"

"Barely," Malaki said, through a sigh of relief as he willed more of his power into the remaining wounds.

"Stop, Malaki," Isolde said, her eyes flashing as they searched his face. "You need your strength too."

"I'm not the one who just took on a virya single-handedly," he retorted. He felt the bones of her arm mend and the torn flesh made anew.

"And I did it spectacularly well," Isolde said, letting him pull her to her feet. A wince lashed across her face as she tried to stand on her own.

"I can't argue with that," he said, keeping a secure hold on her arm. "Well done, pet."

Malaki did his best to keep Isolde out of Gage's line of sight. But when Malaki turned back, all he could focus on was the grin plastered onto the bastard's face. A hint of malice that hadn't been there before, hung in Gage's voice. "Quite a show you put on. The king is quite pleased."

"Oh, I'm thrilled," said Isolde, her usual smartass mouth turning up with a smirk. "We wouldn't want to disappoint him, now would we?"

Gage's smile grew. "No, we certainly wouldn't. Go and get yourself cleaned up. I'll see you tonight. It will be an evening worth remembering."

Gage turned and strutted out of the arena, his company of soldiers following behind. Malaki felt Isolde's hand on his shoulder. "I may need help," she muttered, under her breath.

Without hesitation, Malaki placed himself on her left and wrapped an arm around her waist. Slowly, they headed across the arena to the opposite tunnel Gage had disappeared down. And as the shadows swallowed them whole, Malaki couldn't shake the feeling that everything had just changed.

CHAPTER 37

"If you keep frowning like that, Malaki, your face will stay that way," Isolde said, stuffing a cookie into her mouth. Her body felt light and completely free of pain after Malaki's relentless healing.

"She's not wrong," Cillian said, where he lounged next to Blyana.

Malaki shot her an annoyed looked and cupped his hands to his mouth. Still he didn't relax. Something was bothering him, but Isolde couldn't for the life of her think of what. "I'm fine!" she said, plucking another cookie from the tray. "Healed up and everything."

"You nearly weren't though," he said at last, his shoulders rising as a sigh pushed through his lips. He stared at the newly healed scar on her leg. The faint, white line stood starkly against her tanned skin, a perfect match to the one Yvaine had left on her shoulder at Blackwater.

Isolde jumped at the sound of the door busting open, her power flaring to life. But her irritation froze at the sight of Liam standing in the doorway.

"Liam?"

"Things have changed," he gasped, chest heaving as if he had sprinted there. "I overheard Gage giving an order to the soldiers. The prisoners from Briarhole, Foxclove, and Thornwood are to be executed at dawn. He's pulling half of those on duty tonight to help with arranging the arena. They're to be executed before the final trial tomorrow. It seems Erebus is growing tired of the crowd and wants the tournament over with quickly."

Malaki's fingers laced into his hair. "And what better way to end this *momentous* tournament than to publicly execute the Hood?"

It felt as if the floor was crumbling beneath Isolde's feet. "The keys should be ready by now," she said, her eyes still locked on Liam. "It's the last piece we need."

"I'll retrieve them," Blyana said, already on her feet. "If they aren't, we'll take what Hayes left us."

"I'll go with you," Cillian said, his fingers toying with the handles of the blades at his side. "We'll meet you back here when we have them."

After tugging on his cloak and mask, Cillian clasped Isolde's shoulder, his fingers squeezing. "See you in a bit."

Isolde nodded and gave his hand a firm squeeze. "In one piece, Cill."

He grinned. "The same goes for you."

Blyana wrapped her arms around Isolde's shoulders. "Be careful, and don't do anything reckless without me."

"No promises," Isolde said, hugging her back. "All or nothing."

Blyana grinned. "All or nothing." She retrieved her mask and hood then disappeared through the curtains leading out onto the balcony with Cillian at her side.

"Isolde," Liam said, taking a step towards her. "It's too soon...What if—"

"We don't have time for what ifs, Liam," Isolde said. Shadows fell across the room as the sun began to make its final bow across the mountain peaks. "If we don't do this tonight, they all die." War and indecision raged in the depths of his eyes. "Now is the time to decide."

"Decide?" he asked, confusion etching into his face.

"After tonight, we'll be fugitives, outlaws—official enemies to the crowns." Isolde stood before him, and the depth of his shadow engulfed her easily. "You have to choose if you're coming with us or not. There is no in between, not in this."

Liam swallowed thickly and his gaze shifted to those left in the room. Questioning, expectant eyes met his stare—even Malaki. Acceptance fell into Liam's gaze as he turned to looked at her once more. "I'm with you, Isolde," he said, steel lacing his words "Always."

A smile peeked on the edges of Isolde's lips. "You look good in a mask."

"We'll get things ready here," Galaena said, as she and Alaric rose. "We'll make sure the horses are prepared and meet you outside the prison. Help us with these would you, Liam?" Galaena asked, tossing him one of the packs she had fished from the beneath the couch. "We've also placed packs along the path, just in case we had to make a run for it."

"Where's Nan?" Isolde asked, her eyes sweeping the chambers.

Alaric shouldered one of the packs and adjusted the grip on his cane. "I'm not sure, but we'll find her. I can't imagine she ventured far."

"Good," Isolde said, making her way into her bedchamber. Malaki followed, his brow slick with sweat. While he was fully healed, it had taken a lot out of him to patch her up again.

"I need you with Gal and Alaric," Isolde said. "Waiting for the prisoners in the Gap."

Malaki's teeth ground as he stared at her. He knew she was right, but still she hated seeing him this way. "We've been separated on missions plenty of times before, Malaki."

"And how well did that turn out for us the last time?"

Isolde shot him an annoyed look but continued tossing blades onto the bed. "We don't have a choice. Please trust me."

"I do trust you," he said, engulfing her hands in his, forcing her to look at him. "But I want your word you'll wait here, until Cill and Bly return."

Isolde stilled in his hands.

"Someone has to stay in case one of Erebus or Gage's men comes looking. We need all the pieces together before we act. Promise me you'll wait." Isolde's jaw clamped down, refusing to say the words. Malaki's grip tightened, drawing her attention back. "Promise me, Isolde!"

"I promise," she said, unable to meet his gaze. The words were strangled and thin as they left her lips. "But if they aren't here in one hour, I'm leaving."

"I suppose I can live with that."

He pulled her into his chest and Isolde felt a shudder roll through him as her arms wound around his back. Hope filled her chest as Malaki squeezed her to him one final time.

"Please, be safe," he said, pressing a kiss to the top of her head.

A smile tugged at the corner of her lips. "Only if you are."

Malaki, along with Galaena, Alaric, and Liam, stole from the room, their hoods and masks tucked safely in the lining of their cloaks. Without her family there, Isolde felt the room begin to close in. Every worst-case scenario played out in her mind like endless torture.

Zibiah and Nyla hanging from the rafters alongside Mary, her family tied to the pyres, destined for the same fate she had been forced to deal out to Tanor. She wasted no time in yanking the hood and cloak from their place under the bed. The blades, having been fixed by Tarvo, slid into place at her back. The quiver fit easily between them, its stash of arrows, freshly cleaned and sharpened. Her beloved bow sat perfectly in the palm of her gloved hand.

Reaching beneath the bed once more, Isolde pulled a small bag from behind a stack of books she had shoved against the wall. Metal keys, copies of the one Cillian had lifted from Phontine, jingled from within. She had retrieved them the same night she had retrieved Blyana's gift.

"I worked hard to finish your order," Hayes had said. "But its only half of what you asked for."

"That's plenty," Isolde had said, shoving a bag of coins into his hand. "Especially for what I have in mind."

She had made her decision the first night they had snuck into the prisons. The night she had seen what would become of her family if they were caught. It had never been Isolde's intention for the others to join her. Never for them to risk their lives emptying out the prisons. This was her task and her task alone.

It would take them a while to reach the remnants of the jeweler's shop. She had arranged for Hayes to hide something for her in a small safe, buried beneath a mound of burned wood and metal. Blyana and Cillian knew where to look. But instead of a handful of keys, they would find a note.

Phontine and Frey will meet you in the Gap.

As will I

Forgive me.

All or nothing.

They would be beyond furious with her for going into the prison alone, for lying to them. Especially, Malaki. But their fury was something she could endure. It was a burden she was more than willing to bear if it meant they would be safe. Their deaths were not. They were her cadre…her friends…her family—her everything. And there was no line she wouldn't cross to keep them safe.

Taking a deep breath, Isolde closed her eyes and shoved the keys into her pocket. "I'm so sorry, Malaki." Her promise hung in the air like a guillotine. "Please forgive me." After taking one last look around the chamber, Isolde pulled the hood into place and blended into the growing shadows lurking outside her door.

Only a handful of servants crossed her path as she made her way to the secret passage located in Frey's room. She shoved the door open and was met with gasps of shock. Phontine and Frey lay in a tangle of limbs and sheets on the bed, their bodies shimmering with sweat.

"What the hell?" Phontine cried, covering herself. Recognition filled her eyes as she took in the mask and hood. "What are you doing here?"

"There isn't much time," Isolde said, as she moved to the wall. "The plan started much sooner than we thought."

"What plan?" Frey asked as he looked between them. "Do you know this person, Phontine?"

"Not really," she said, her teeth grinding. "We're more like forced acquaintances."

Disbelief filled his face. "I don't understand what's—"

"Nor do you have time to," Isolde said, her fingers grazing over the wall, searching for the lining of the door. "The plan starts now, Phontine. You have a choice to make."

Phontine stilled at Frey's side, and she pushed a hand through her golden, disheveled hair. Even in this state, she was radiant. "I don't…I don't know—"

"You've had your time," Isolde snapped. "Plenty of it! You either take your chances with us, or you stay in Erebus bed until he either gets tired of you or…" Her gaze shot to Frey and his cheeks drained of color. "It's your choice but make it now. Don't worry about distributing the keys. I'll take care of that. We meet in the Gap of Duron, West of Olos. Take the long way. Your sister will be waiting for you."

"Quite a lot of trust you're demanding," Phontine spat as she shoved up from the bed. She held the sheet securely around her chest. "Especially when you give none in return."

The ridges of the door passed beneath Isolde's fingertips, and she pushed. A gust of cold, wet air kissed the exposed part of her face as she turned back to Phontine. "I've given you the location of everyone I love. Seems like a pretty big leap of faith to me. But if you must know," Isolde said, her voice softening. "I am the villain of your story."

Phontine's eyes grew wide as they looked the Hood up and down, her gaze lingering on her eyes. Eyes Isolde knew she recognized. Phontine's hand came to cover her mouth as Isolde slipped through the door and disappeared into the dark. The sound of rocks scraping against each other echoed down the darkened hallway as the door closed behind her. She kept an arrow loaded, its tip glowing eerily in the light given off by the torches she passed.

As she breached the closet door, Isolde let the first arrow fly. It disappeared into the neck of a guard standing post who crumbled into a lifeless heap of metal and leather. The soles of her boots skittered across the pool of fresh blood spreading across the floor as she yanked the arrow free and continued on.

When she reached the cell where Nyla slept, Isolde thrust the key in the lock and slipped inside. Being as quiet as possible, she picked her way through the sea of children and gently placed a hand on Nyla's shoulder.

"Nyla." Her name carried like a phantom through the dark. She stirred in her sleep, her brow furrowing. "Nyla, wake up!"

Slowly, Nyla's eyes peeled open one by one and turned to Isolde. "Am I dreaming?" She asked, her eyes heavy with sleep and uncertainty.

"Not today," Isolde said with a wink.

When the heavy daze of sleep finally cleared, Nyla threw her arms around Isolde's neck. Her grip was suffocating, but Isolde smiled all the more. "Is it really you?" Nyla cried, her voice heavy and loaded with disbelief.

"The one and only," Isolde said, pushing her back. "I told you I'd come back for you."

The wounds on Nyla's face had begun to heal, allowing the swelling in her eye to recede just enough for it to open. "I'm ready to go."

"Good, because I have a very important job for you." After passing a key to one of the older children and instructing them to release the others, Isolde led Nyla to the doorway. "You see that ledge?" she asked, pointing to the overlook at the top of the prison. "There's a tunnel that leads to a hole in the mountainside. My friends are waiting for you there. I need you to lead the others there. Can you do that for me?"

Nyla's brow bunched as she looked from the overlook and back to the Hood. "But I want to stay with you."

"I won't be far behind you," Isolde promised, her hands landing on Nyla's thin shoulders. "I have to get Lady Zibiah out, but I can't do that unless I know you and the others are safe."

Nyla's wide, fearful eyes drifted to the red door residing at the bottom of the prison. Isolde felt a tremor roll through her small frame at the sight. Nyla stared at Isolde for a moment and a look of determination settled into her gaze as she nodded.

"Brave girl," Isolde said, gently cupping her face. "Follow the stairs but keep quiet. Don't take any shortcuts, just go straight there. Do you understand?"

"I can do it," Nyla said, with a nod.

"Good," Isolde said, her eyes crinkling. "And as you go, toss a key into the cells you pass. Don't stop to open the doors, and don't deviate from the path. Just the cells you pass."

Nyla nodded as she took the bag of keys and clutched it to her chest.

"Alright, I'll see you up there."

Isolde watched as the little girl who had seen and endured far too much helped each of the children through the door and up the stairwell. Once they were out of sight and on their way to freedom, Isolde turned and made her way down.

She didn't waste arrows on the final two guards guarding the red door. The air from their lungs sat in the palm of her hand as she watched them suffocate. Her power hummed beneath her skin as the monster inside grinned. When the last shred of light faded from their eyes, Isolde released her grip and they tumbled to the floor.

Taking a deep breath, Isolde shoved the key into the lock and pulled. The door swung open without a sound, its crimson surface glistening in the light of the torches within. She made her way down the sloping tunnel. Shadows, black as ink, painted the walls. Isolde felt every ounce of warmth disappear. Nothing and no one stirred as she stepped into a wide, cavernous room.

A table sat in the middle of the floor, its surface covered in powdered elithrium. Along with flasks of all shapes and sizes, small dishes and sharp tools were scattered throughout. Tiny devices, the size of a sewing needle, were attached to a small cylinder, filled with what appeared to be liquid elithrium.

Without thinking, Isolde gripped the table's edge and flipped it on its end. Shards of glass, raw elithrium, and parchment scattered across the floor. Whispers and moans bled from the darkened doors surrounding her. Isolde made her way past the cell doors, looking into each one until she found who she was looking for.

Nothing could have prepared her for what lay within. After slipping the key into the lock, Isolde yanked the door open and stepped inside. Zibiah stirred as the hinges groaned, the sound echoing off the wide cell walls. Her friend, her ally, was sprawled across a slab of rock. Each hand and foot was secured with a cuff far too small for her wrists and ankles.

"Zib?" Isolde's voice carried like a muffled cry. Horrified and furious, tears of wrath blurred Isolde's vision. She took in the bruises on Zibiah's paled skin. Some in the shape of fists, others in the shape of handprints, decorated her upper legs and torso.

Blood oozed from within the mangled folds of her right eyelid, so much blood Isolde didn't know if an eye remained beneath it. Deep wells resided beneath Zibiah's eyes and along her cheekbones. Bony prominences covered her body like hideous mountain peaks.

Leaning forward, Isolde sent a gentle breeze across Zibiah's face. "Zib?" Isolde said, her voice shaking with rage. "Zib, please wake up!"

A sigh of relief pushed through Isolde's lips as Zibiah's undamaged eye fluttered open. But her relief was short-lived. The light once living inside her friend's eyes, the fire, the power, was gone.

"No," Isolde said, in a horrified gasp. She clasped Zib's hand. "No...no....no Zib!

"Isolde," Zibiah cried, her voice strained and not her own. "You shouldn't have come." A single tear fell down her cheek, her lips trembling. "You can't be here!"

But before Isolde could ask what she meant, chaos erupted from the world above. Shouts of soldiers and cries of prisoners carried down the corridor and bounced off the walls. Terror pumped through Isolde's veins as she shoved the key into one of the locks at Zib's wrist.

It didn't open.

She tried harder, pushing the key until the metal began to bend. But every turn was met with resistance.

"He changed them," Zib said, her golden eye wide and filled with shadows of despair. "Gage changed earlier today." Isolde's breath lodged in the back of her throat. "The cuffs…the locks…the chains …they're all elithrium, Isolde. He knew you were coming."

The key fell from Isolde's fingers and bounced across the floor. Tears trickled down Zibiah's face as the one thing Isolde thought she'd never see filled her friend's eyes.

Hopelessness.

Gripping the chains, Isolde yanked against the metal ring holding them in place. A furious growl ripped through her teeth as she pulled. The elithrium-laced iron refused to move, refused to bend. Echoes of footsteps sounded from the ground above, but Isolde didn't care.

"Isolde," said Zibiah, her voice heavy with panic. "Isolde, they're coming!"

"I don't give a damn," Isolde said, through clenched teeth. The leather of her gloves split, and still the chains refused to budge.

"Leave me!" Zibiah cried, trying to pull the chains from Isolde's grasp. Her heart shattered at how easy it was to fight her off. At how fragile Zibiah had become, how thoroughly and completely they had broken her.

"I'm not leaving you, Zibiah!" Isolde cried. She braced a foot against the stone slab's edge and wrapped her hands around the chain. "Not again." Isolde felt the muscles in her arms stretch and fray but still the chains refused to break. Her teeth clenched, and pain erupted up her arms. A roar of anger and frustration built in the back of her throat.

Another sound, one that drew Isolde away from the chains, came from the shadows clinging to the doorway. Her bow was in her hand and an arrow locked in place in the span of a heartbeat. The rush of blood pounded in Isolde's ears. Each beat of her heart was like a hammer in her chest. The smallest movement had the bowstring rolling across her fingertips. But a split second before she let the arrow fly, realization took hold and Isolde understood what she was seeing with a horrified reality.

"Nyla!" Isolde cried, her hands shaking. "What the hell are you doing here?" She released the tension on the bowstring and let out a shaky breath. She had come close, so very close to...to... The thought sent bile crawling up her throat.

"I wasn't going to leave you," Nyla said.

"I told you to go with the others!" said Isolde, her voice rising.

"Well, I did…and then I came back," said Nyla, her arms crossing over her chest.

Isolde couldn't believe what she was hearing. She ran a hand down her face and bit the lining of her glove to hide the growl wanting desperately to rip through her teeth.

"Sound familiar?" Zibiah sniffled, as she took Nyla's hand.

"Remind me to apologize to Malaki," Isolde said, reaching for the chains yet again. "We are *not* done discussing this," she said, pointing to Nyla across Zibiah's chest. Nyla had the good sense to look sheepish, but Isolde didn't miss the subtle squeeze Zibiah gave her hand.

Shouts and cries sounded from the hallway and Isolde turned to the door, her hands freezing on the chains. Countless footsteps thundered down the tunnel, each step bringing them closer and closer.

"Take her and go before it's too late!" Zibiah said, her teeth bared and eyes pleading. "Go!"

But Isolde knew it was already too late. She could hear where they were and how many had come. With a heavy, regretful heart, Isolde looked at Nyla. Her little hands were curled around the chains holding Zibiah's left arm as if to help pull her free.

"It's far too late for that, Zib," Isolde said. "They're already in the tunnel." Guilt wrapped its clawed hand around her heart as one undeniable fact became clear. There was no escaping, not this time.

Swallowing the lump lodged in her throat, Isolde notched an arrow onto the bowstring. She looked down at Zibiah who reached up as far as the chain would allow and Isolde met her in the air.

"I love you, my sister," Zibiah said, as a stream of fresh tears rolled down her sunken cheeks.

"And I you," Isolde said, her voice steady and sure as she leaned forward and pressed her forehead to Zibiah's. "Thank you for all you and your family have done for me. All or nothing."

Zibiah's voice rang with the spirit Isolde remembered and loved. "All or nothing."

As the sound of the first soldier charging through the main chamber echoed through the cell, Isolde turned a sly smile to Nyla, whose eyes shone with the fear.

"Come stand behind Lady Zibiah, little one," she said, her eyes crinkling at the corners. Nyla did as she was asked but her eyes remained locked on the darkened doorway. Reaching down, Isolde pressed a hand to her cheek. "Time to be brave, little warrior."

Nyla's wide eyes stared up at her and Isolde truly saw her for what she was. Just a scared little girl who had been brave for so long. Her eyes shifted to the doorway, to the sound of soldiers thundering down the passage. She shook beneath Isolde's palm and a stream of tears spilled over her cheeks.

"Sing to me, Nyla," Isolde said. "Sing me the song your father taught you. The one I heard in the stables at Briarhole." If these were to be Nyla's last moments, then there would be at least a shred of sunlight in them.

Nyla's eyes grew wide, and her mouth parted in disbelief. "Lady Isolde?"

Isolde smiled as the first notes lifted from Zibiah's lips and carried through the cell.

A moment later, Nyla's beautiful voice joined her, and the sound of music and memory filled Isolde's ears. It was the song of a father's love for his daughter. Her father and his love for Isolde. They were his words, his music he had created only for her so long ago. Words that had found their way into the heart of a little girl from Briarhole—transcending time and fate. It was the sound of a past that was stolen, a past that had been burned to ash.

With her father's music filling her heart, Isolde drew back on the bowstring, its familiar bite caressing her fingertips.

"I love you both."

The arrow shot forward and disappeared into the darkness.

CHAPTER 38

"Keep moving!" Cillian's muffled voice lifted over the countless bodies streaming down the tunnel. The tips of his daggers drove into every soldier crossing his path. Their eyes, once glistening with power, faded into dark nothingness.

Mayhem filled the tunnel leading to the only escape route their cadre could provide—the only path to freedom. He fought to keep the soldiers back. His teeth gritted as the unforgiving edge of a blade slammed down into the daggers secured in his hands. Pain reverberated through his arms and into his torso. He shoved back, sending the guard into the awaiting tip of Blyana's elithrium dagger. She yanked the blade free, drawing a moan of pain from the dying man's lips, and kicked him to the ground.

"Damn Isolde," Blyana said, her eyes ignited. "Damn her! She promised to wait. She promised, Cill!"

"I don't like it any more than you do, love," Cillian said, waving the crowd forward. "But you know why she did it. She didn't want us getting hurt."

Despite his words, Cillian couldn't ignore the small ember of anger, the tiniest part of himself that burned with fury and betrayal. They were a team, a cadre…a family. And Isolde had lied to them all.

"That doesn't mean I can't still be mad," Blyana growled in return, her tone softening. "I wouldn't want to be her when she sees Malaki again."

A shudder trickled down Cillian's back at the thought. "Neither would I."

Malaki had been the angriest, the most hurt by Isolde's deception. She had never broken a promise to him. Had never gone back on her word and the look in his eyes told Cillian that something was broken between them.

It had been a shock to see the children waiting in the Gap, freezing and huddled together in the snow drifts. Malaki had immediately understood what Isolde had done. Cillian grimaced at the look on his face. The anger and betrayal burning in his eyes.

"She promised me," Malaki had said. The words fell from his lips in ragged breathes as he fought to control his power. "She promised!" It was then that more bodies came forward, along with the sound of the guards. Malaki's gaze shifted to the new threat, his hand reaching for the battle axe strapped to his back.

"We need you out here," Cillian had said, gripping Malaki's arm. "In case there are injured. It's what Isolde would want—"

"I don't give a damn what Isolde wants!" He roared. "She clearly doesn't care about what anyone else wants, Cillian!"

"You know that's not true," Cillian said, seething. "You know damn well that's a lie. She did this for us because she does care, Malaki. She cares a great fucking deal!"

"Nonetheless, you know you are needed here," Blyana said. "She had her reasons…I'm sure of it."

A war had raged in Malaki's eyes as the first group of prisoners made their way through the small opening on the mountainside, each harboring a wound or injury in need of his attention. A growl of frustration pierced the night as Malaki stepped forward to help. He ushered them to the side, his touch and voice gentle.

Malaki had been angry at Isolde before, plenty of times. But Cillian had never seen that look of betrayal before.

"Where are they?" Blyana asked, her eyes searching the tunnel.

"I'm sure they're on their way," he said, doing his best to ignore the tendrils of doubt.

Cillian and Blyana plunged back into the fray. Every few steps he had to push and shove a poor emaciated body out of the way of another blade. Sweat and blood poured down his face, stinging his eyes and saturating his mask.

"Keep moving," Cillian said, pushing a man forward who had halted at the sound of a guard's barking order. "Don't look back! Keep moving!"

Each death left a mark on him in one form or another. Whether it was a scar upon his flesh or one imprinted upon his soul, he remembered them all. Just as Isolde did. It was one of the first things that drew him to her. Death was as much a friend and enemy to Isolde as it was to him. She understood it, and she accepted it.

Blood coated his gloves, making the polished handles of his dagger that much more difficult to grasp. Dropping a blade in battle had never been acceptable, had never been tolerated as a child. It was a fear, along with heights, that came from his father and brothers.

His gaze swept down the tunnel, searching for the hooded figure bringing up the pack. Men, women, and children, all nothing but bags of broken bones, shuffled past him, their eyes filled with fear.

"That's it," Cillian said, doing his best to keep them calm. "Just through there, keep moving." A break in the masses allowed a small ray of light to dance across Blyana's face. Even concealed from the world, surrounded by so much darkness, she was still the most beautiful creature he had ever seen.

Another cry filled the cold, stagnant air and Cillian turned to see the head of a spear pierce a man's back, the elithrium glittering around the frayed skin of his chest. His hands moved before he knew what was happening. The sharp blade resting in his hand sailed through the air and buried itself in the soldier's neck. It was moments like these he wished he possessed Isolde's abilities. To tie a noose of air around his enemies' throats and squeeze. Or to rob them of every breath residing in their body.

He yanked the blade free from the dead man's flesh and wiped it across their unsoiled pant leg. Then again, he knew what that power did to her. None of the others seemed to realize one glaring reality he thought was devastatingly obvious.

Isolde's power was a curse.

While she could do nearly anything with her abilities, it made life unbearable, constantly throwing her into a battle with herself for control. Never resting, always on guard from what lay within. While he possessed certain facets of an air wielder, Isolde undoubtedly held most, if not all of them.

"Cillian!"

Blyana's cry cut through his thoughts, and he turned just in time to see a flash of metal. A warm, aching pain kissed Cillian's skin as he caught a longsword between the palms of his hands. With a grunt of frustration, he yanked it free from a soldier's grasp before flipping it on its end.

The handle, while foreign, still felt comfortable in his grasp—as did every blade. Giving the soldier no chance to fight back, Cillian slammed the heel of his boot into his chest. Bone shattered beneath the blow and a guttural cry lingered in the air as he fell to the floor and did not move again.

"Bastard," Cillian grumbled, his face grimacing with pain. The fresh wound on his hand throbbed through his leather gloves. The skin was still intact, but a nasty bruise would form by morning. He froze mid-step as a subtle shift of the air slithered over his body, his power stirring. It was the only warning he was granted before Blyana's feral cry filled the tunnel.

A lone soldier, one who had hidden in the horde of prisoners, pressed a blade to her perfect, pale throat. Cillian felt a fear he never knew possible. He burned with a rage he never dreamed he was capable of. It touched every part of who he was, scorching every fiber of his soul.

"Drop your weapons!" the man roared, yanking Blyana back against his chest. A muffled cry leaked through her mask, her eyes wide with terror.

Cillian felt his mate's fear down the bond, caressing his mind like the cold touch of death. Memories of Blackwater, of the night he almost lost her, slammed into Cillian without mercy. His power tore through him like a hurricane. Fingers created by the air itself, gripped the handles of the blades at his sides, the ones hidden within the compartments of his cloak, and those lying scattered along the tunnel floor.

"Turn that beautiful face to the left, love," Cillian murmured, his voice cold and hard as steel. Blyana did as he asked, and Cillian's power exploded.

The blades seemed to have a mind of their own as they flew through the air on gusts of wind. One embedded itself just to the right of Blyana's face, a breath away from her cheek. The others found their own piece of flesh, their own blood to spill. Surprise shone in the soldier's eyes, blending with the malice already residing there. As he fell into death's awaiting arms, the man pressed the dagger to Blyana's throat and dragged its blade across her skin.

"Bly!"

Cillian's guttural cry filled the night as blood spilled across Blyana's neck. He moved through the tunnel like the air itself and caught her in his arms. His boot slammed into the man's face shattering every bone present. His fingers, already slick with blood, pressed into the wound. A faint greenish shine glistened from its edges.

"Just a scratch, love," Cillian said, his words felt like bits of broken glass in his mouth. "You'll be fine. You'll…You'll be fine."

Blyana stared up at him, her eyes shining and wide with fear. She nodded, her hand grasping at his fingers that were pressed into the wound, sending more blood spilling down her throat.

He cradled her to his chest and made his way down the tunnel. Guard after guard met them head-on. But all fell beneath the might of Cillian's power that rose and fell in a wave of pure air, hard as iron. It slammed into the chest of all who stood in his path. Body after body fell in his wake. Each with an indentation of a fist left in their breast plate.

"Malaki!" Cillian roared, stepping into the freezing, night air. "Malaki, I need the antidote now!"

His best friend stalked forward, his hazel eyes glowing as he took in Blyana.

"Cillian…" Malaki said, his voice filled with a horror that nearly turned Cillian mad.

"Help her!" he cried. Reality hacked away at the love in his heart, at the hope he still clung to as more of Blyana's blood spilled between his fingertips.

"Cill." His name slipped past Blyana's pale lips. It was so weak and frail it pained him to heart it.

"I love it when you say my name, love," Cillian said, his heart twisting into a vice. "But for right now, be quiet."

"Lay her down," Malaki ordered. His tone, while absent of any blame still filled Cillian to the brim. The only thing keeping him tied to his sanity, was the bond. It stirred in his chest, weaker than normal but still there.

"It was a lone soldier," Cillian said, murderous anger burning through him. "One who had snuck past with the prisoners." Cillian could feel Blyana's blood begin to cool on his skin. Her cheeks were so pale, nearly matching the hair framing her face. "Can't you go any faster?" Cillian growled, a fraction of his power breaking through.

"I'm going as fast as I can, Cill," Malaki said, sparing him a glance. "My power won't help her much without the antidote."

"How do you know?" Cillian pressed, his teeth gritting.

"Because of what happened with Isolde at Briarhole," said Malaki, applying the pink paste. "My power stayed her death for a time but without the antidote—"

"She's lost so much blood," Cillian said, his voice filled with panic.

Malaki didn't lift his gaze from Blyana. His focus was solely on the task before him. "Trust me, Cill."

Blood continued to flow, painting the snow beneath her red. Blyana's eyes had fluttered shut. The one who carried Cillian's very soul stilled beneath his hands.

"No, no," he said at her side. "If I don't get to sleep, then neither do you, Bly."

She didn't answer.

Malaki gently pried one of Cillian's fingers up one at a time and smoothed a heaping of the paste beneath. "Keep pressure," he ordered, already dipping into his pouch for more. "Until, I say so, don't move."

And as the pink mess filled the wound, Cillian waited for the screams of pain. For the bellows of agony he remembered from Malaki. But only silence and stillness followed.

"Bly," Malaki said, his teeth gritting as he pressed his own fingers into the wound that refused to stop flowing. "Blyana!"

"It's not working!" Cillian screamed. Panic, true panic took root and he felt the edges of his sanity begin to fray. "Do something, Malaki! Do it now!" The bond trembled, its hold on him growing weaker and weaker. It felt as if his heart were being torn in two, leaving behind a shredded, gaping wound he could never survive.

So much agony had befallen Blyana. So much had been done to the one who held his heart in her hands. But Cillian wasn't a healer. This wasn't something he couldn't save her from. In this he was truly powerless.

"Don't you dare leave me, Blyana!" Tears spilled across his cheeks as he yanked his mask away. "Do you want to know when I first fell in love with you?" he asked. "It was the time you bested Isolde in the Pit. You were so beautifully fearless. Nothing stood in your way."

Tears continued to cascade down Cillian's cheeks as he turned her face to him, forcing her to hear only his voice. Malaki's power brushed his skin as he drove his healing power into the wound, willing it to close. "It also was the day I knew you were my mate. The happiest day of my life, Bly."

Still Blyana didn't answer. Even the rise and fall of her chest was shallow and far too fast. As if she knew she only had so many breaths left to take. Cillian's heart shattered as he pressed his hand further into her neck, refusing to allow another drop of blood to fall.

"BLYANA!" Cillian wailed, as the final thread holding their bond together shuddered. "Wake up, Bly, please! I'll do anything!"

"Careful now, such statements have gotten you into trouble before."

Cillian froze at the sound of that voice. It had been decades since it had last graced his ears. It held so many memories, so many fears. Slowly, he turned and took in a lone figure standing at the edge of their escape route.

He was just as terrifying as Cillian remembered. A towering man, one who always played a role in the nightmares tormenting him day and night. Or at least a near exact copy of the one who did. His childhood memories, cold and cruel, filled his mind as the man stepped into the moonlight.

Dark brown skin, kissed by the sun that shone on the deserts of Endurmure, glistened against the fine, jet-black beard covering his strong jaw. Obsidian eyes, his eyes, that held so much power shone through the dark. They were bright...and filled with mocking amusement.

"Eryx?"

His name fell from Cillian's mouth like a curse. His free hand moved to the blade at his side. Rage saturated his heart, and a smile broke out on Eryx's face.

"Good to see you too," Eryx said, his posture relaxed and at ease. "Little brother."

Only the cool, mountain breeze dared make a sound.

"Brother?" Malaki's confuse voice cut through the stunned silence. Cillian felt him still at his side. He could feel his friend's gaze on him like a brand.

"I'm not your brother," Cillian growled, "not anymore." His power sped forward, pummeling against his restraint.

"Not happy to see me, it seems," Eryx said, his smile widening to show a row of perfect, white teeth. "How unfortunate."

"What are you doing here?" Cillian said, his voice anything but friendly.

Eryx shrugged with the same smugness Cillian loathed as a child. Turned out, he still hated it. "I'm doing the job you were instructed to. The one you failed to complete, it seems. Father will be...most disappointed."

A shudder cascaded down Cillian's back. The scars covering his body stung with the sound of those words. He remembered all too well what it meant to disappoint their father. He felt it in every scar decorating his skin.

"Cill," Malaki's voice broke through the fog in his mind, and the web of memory and anguish that caught him in its vices once more. "What is he talking about?"

Cillian felt his mouth go dry with panic. His eyes shot to Malaki, to his best friend, his true brother. Reproach and confusion was all he found. An edge of uncertainty lingered there as well. A look that cut Cillian deep.

Eryx's dark chuckle broke through the air. "Still keeping secrets, are we, Cillian?"

Cillian couldn't bring himself to look at Malaki. Could not bear to see the look of betrayal that would soon fill them. Instead, he turned back to Eryx, his eyes narrowed, and teeth bared. Blyana's blood pooled under his fingers, forcing him to press hard.

"What do you want, Eryx?"

"I told you," he said. "I'm here to complete the job you could not." His dark eyes looked past Cillian's head and his smile faded. "Where are they?" he asked, his eyes sweeping the small area and out to the Gap.

"Who?" asked Malaki. One of his hands, slick with Blyana's blood and stained with the antidote, gripped Secrettaker's handle at his side. He kept feeding his power into her with the other, never breaking contact with Blyana's throat.

"Where is Lady Zibiah?" Eryx demanded, his white teeth glistening as his face turned into a fierce snarl. His eyes locked on Cillian, and he felt like a child again, caught under their father's harsh, unforgiving gaze. "Where is Isolde Cotheran?"

Shouts cleaved through the cold, night air, freezing them in place. They all turned to the black, gaping hole in the side of the mountain. Cheers of triumph hammered against Cillian's skull, filling his heart with dread.

"The Hood!" a voice shouted from deep under the mountain. "The Hood is here!"

CHAPTER 39

With another arrow notched and ready, the Hood pulled back on the bowstring, her target already in sight. Before the string left her fingers, a wave of air shot through the room and collided with her chest. She slammed into the wall on the other side of the cell, her back barking in pain.

Debris rained down on her hood, covering her in mildew and dust. A growl of fury ripped through her teeth as the soldiers climbed over their fallen comrades barricading the door.

"That's my move," Isolde said, firing the final two arrows left in the quiver. One found its mark in the eye of the closest soldier. The second severed the artery of another, allowing blood to spray across their fine metal armor. Isolde pulled the bow across her shoulder and yanked the blades free from the scabbards at her back, the elithrium metal shrieking.

The newly forged weapon, laced with more elithrium than before, clicked into place as Isolde brought the handles together. Twirling the blade in front of her, a vicious smile that reached her eyes, the eyes of a monster, formed behind the mask.

"Let's see if Erebus's men are any better trained than the ones at Briarhole."

The two soldiers who had managed to crawl their way through the field of dead, drew their longswords. Their edges glistened in the light of the torches. Isolde drove the end of her double long blade forward, giving the soldier no other choice but to retreat. The other came at her from the left. She kicked out and her boot collided with his chin, forcing his teeth to clamp down on his tongue, severing it in half.

A strangled cry rang through the chamber as he came for her again, his eyes glowing and blood pouring from his mouth. His sword was standard issue, but his skill was anything but. Isolde met his blow, and his comrade came at her again. They drove her back, forcing her closer to Zibiah and Nyla. Sparks erupted along the edge of her blades as they collided. They were strong and skilled, nothing at all like the brutes she had faced at Foxclove or even Briarhole.

Isolde's wrath surged forward, bringing with it a well of power, that surprised even her. She shoved against their blades, sending them stumbling back to the dead littering the doorway. But Isolde didn't stop. She came at them again, her swords gleaming in the firelight. She thrust the tip through the chin of the man on the right. His eyes bulged and the sword in his hand clattered to the ground.

A rope of air, fed by Isolde's power, wrapped around the remaining soldier's throat. His sword fell to the ground and his fingers dug uselessly at the invisible bond tightening around his neck. Her power hummed with glee and a savage, murderous grin filled her mind.

Without warning, a shot of white-hot pain exploded in her right leg. Her hand dropped to her side, grasping the pommel of a dagger that had embedded itself in her upper thigh. A soldier stood in the doorway, his hand aimed at her heart. Isolde didn't hesitate as she shoved off the ground and threw her connected blades through the air like a javelin.

It landed in the center of the guard's forehead, pinning his body to the wall behind him.

The man's feet twitched uselessly from where they hovered above the ground. Fury and pain spiked in Isolde's blood as she gripped the handle and yanked upward, severing the guard's head up the middle.

Bracing for the pain, she jerked the dagger from her leg and a steady stream of blood saturated her pant leg. Through ragged breaths, she turned to see Nyla still pulling at the chains. Zibiah's eyes widened in fear as she looked passed Isolde, her mouth opened in warning. Isolde turned just in time to raise her blade to stop the mace from splitting her in two.

"I was hoping to get a shot at you," Buer said, his black eyes gleaming. He brought the weight of the mace down again, its impact driving Isolde to her knees.

"Always looking for opportunities to fail," Isolde ground, her arms and back quaking under the pressure. "Why is that, I wonder?"

Shifting back enough to throw Buer off balance, Isolde swept her leg out, colliding with the side of his knee. A sickening pop echoed through the cell, and he fell to the ground with a howl of rage rumbling through his teeth. Rolling back, Isolde brought her feet behind her head and launched forward. The balls of her feet connected with the ground, sending a bolt of pain through her thigh.

Fury spewed from Buer's face as he rose. "I'm going to enjoy killing you," he snarled. The wood groaned as his grip tightened on the mace's handle.

Isolde chuckled, the sound dark with a promise of violence. "Well, I do hope you enjoy disappointment."

Buer's hand curled into a fist and the air shook with power as the earth beneath Isolde's feet trembled. It was her only warning before a pillar of solid rock shot towards her. Instinct took over, taking Isolde's power with it. A wall of air collided with the living rock, jarring her hold.

Isolde felt the call of Vae's ring and the dark chasm of power dwelling within. Pillar after pillar of earth raced forward as Buer made his way across the cell. Each one was met with a wave of her own power, turning them into nothing but piles of shattered rock.

Isolde retreated a step, her chest heaving. Beads of sweat raced down her temple. At last, Buer paused his assault, and brought the mace overhead. Light filled his eyes, his face slack with exhaustion.

Isolde struck, forcing ribbons of air to form in her palm. They shot out, striking Buer in the face, forcing him to retreat. She continued to move him back. Either by blade or power, she kept him on the defense. Towers of sharpened rock sprung up around her, poised to strike. But for everyone Buer created, Isolde's power met it head-on with an impenetrable shield of her own, shattering them on impact.

"Is this really all you have to offer, Buer?" Isolde asked, sweat and blood saturating her leathers. "I expected far more from you."

A growl ripped through his teeth and his mace swung wildly from side to side. While Buer certainly had strength on his side, Isolde knew he was no match for her agile footwork. Ducking a blow, Isolde brought the edge of her sword up the broad side of his back, laying his flesh open. Blood soaked through the lining of his tunic and into the waistline of his britches as a roar of pained fury shook the cell.

"That was for Gawen," Isolde growled, her eyes burning with hatred.

Exhaustion coated her skin and its fingers dug into her very bones, refusing to let go. Still, the ring warmed with need, demanding more. Isolde felt a smile pull onto her face as a stream of air wove its way through her fingers. Distantly, she heard Zibiah calling her name, her voice urgent and filled with fear. But Isolde didn't care, nor did the beast lurking beneath her skin.

"Tell me, Champion of Briarhole," Isolde said, stepping up to Buer, her foot slamming into his wrist. Bones shattered as the mace was sent flying across the cell. A growl of anger filled the air and he clutched his hand to his chest. "How would you like to meet death?"

Even to Isolde, she didn't sound like herself. The darkness linked with the power her mother's ring provided, seeped into her voice. It fueled the stream of air she created, urging it forward. The cool, invisible band constricted around Buer's neck and tightened. His eyes popped with panicked terror.

"Would you rather suffocate…or have me cut you into tiny little pieces?" she asked as a wicked smile formed on her lips. "Or should I just take your head?"

Isolde felt something at her back, the air shifting ever so slightly. But as she turned, her eyes leaving Buer for only a moment, a pillar of rock shot up from the ground. It cracked against her jaw, sending her flying to the other side of the cell. Pain echoed through her face and the familiar taste of blood coated her tongue.

The cold, unforgiving floor bit into her shoulders and back, driving her to roll onto her stomach. Dazed, the hold on her power slipped, and the noose around Buer's neck vanished. He rose to his feet and kicked her precious weapon from her grasp. It clattered to the ground, well out of reach as the weight of an elithrium chain mail wrapped around her, forcing her to the ground.

Its eerie glow filled Isolde's vision. Zibiah and Nyla's cries died as the roar in her ears grew deafening. The monster within retreated. Every ounce of power was sapped way, leaving her weak and defenseless.

No…no…no!

She waited for the death blow, for the crushing pain of Buer's mace. But only a malicious laugh filled the dark, blood-soaked cell.

"Now, Zibiah. what did I say about having guests in your cell without permission?" Isolde heard the rattle of Zibiah's chains go quiet as a strangled breath echoed through the air.

Flames of light danced off the strands of Gage's auburn hair as he stepped forward. The gruesome scars she had left behind seemed deeper in this light. Isolde tried to shove the impossibly heavy blanket off, but all she could manage was a slight raise of her head.

"I do believe our guest is uncomfortable," Gage said, his toes brushing the crown of her head. "Let's fix that."

The weight lifted off her back, and Isolde struck out with as much speed as she could muster. But hands instantly seized her shoulders and arms, holding her in place. Elithrium shackles were slipped onto her wrists and tightened with a painful bite. A foot collided with the backs of her legs, driving her knees to the ground with a sickening crack.

Nyla's angry cry forced Isolde to turn. Her tiny fists beat into the backs of the soldiers holding Isolde in place. "Stop it!" she cried, her teeth bared. "Get off—"

"Come here you, little shit," Buer growled as he tore Nyla away and gripped her by the throat.

"I'll kill you if you hurt her!" Isolde warned, fighting the hands holding her. Buer brought the edge of a dagger to Nyla's throat, filling Isolde's veins with pure rage.

"And what if I kill her, Hood?" he asked. "What will you do then?" Nyla whimpered as a small cut blossomed on her skin, sending a trickle of blood down her neck.

A savage cry of fury filled the chamber as a bloodlust filled Isolde's gaze. She thrashed from side to side as merciless fingers dug into her arms and shoulders. A fist collided with her stomach, knocking the air from her lungs, bringing her struggles to a halt. She gasped, trying to fold in on herself, to find some relief. But the unforgiving hands of the guards kept her painfully upright.

"I don't believe you're in a position to make threats, Hood," said Gage. Triumph filled his piercing blue eyes. "I was going to wait for the king and your husband, Zibiah, but I think I've earned this."

The moment Isolde had been dreading for nearly thirty years came all too quickly. A hurricane of emotions swept through her chest as Gage reached forward. His fingers, the ones stained with the blood of so many, gripped the leather of Isolde's hood and pulled. Bits of her hair went with it, bringing a small cry to the edges of her teeth. Cool air kissed her sweat-coated skin, making her feel more naked than she ever had before. A gasp rang through the battalion who held either the point of an arrow or a spear at her heart. Prideful anger burned through Isolde's veins as she held her chin high.

Gage's eyes darkened with fury, his teeth flashing. Her mask, one Nan had worked so hard to make, groaned in his hands. "I knew it was you," he said, malice filling his voice. "The moment I saw that scar in the arena." His eyes fell to her side. "I knew."

"Congratulations," Isolde said, her lips turned up in a sneer. "I would give you a treat but—" Gage's fist shot out, striking the scar he left behind. She lurched forward as waves of nausea and pain rolled through her side in unrelenting waves. "Fine," she ground. "No treat, then."

Gage squatted down before her, his eyes searching. "All this time, all these years...it was you."

A sarcastic smile pulled at Isolde's lips.

"The only question that remains is who else was involved?"

Isolde's face was blank, her eyes cold and unfeeling. "You really think I would share the spotlight?"

Gage rolled a piece of her hair between his thumb and forefinger. "I know you love the attention, no matter what mask you wear. But I have a hard time believing you acted alone."

"There's hardly anyone I would deem worthy enough to join me."

"Not even Liam?"

A breath caught in Isolde's throat, her teeth grinding.

"I should've known," Gage sneered, his sharp eyes missing nothing. "Zibiah's involvement is understandable. She's a human sympathizer just like you. But I thought I beat the weakness out of Liam years ago." Isolde yanked against the hands of those who held her still. A growl rolled through her bare teeth and a satisfied smile pulled onto Gage's face.

"He always was weak, lower in every way that matters. A gutter rat pulled from the halls of your pathetic little territory. It's a shame you couldn't see that I am by far the bigger, better man."

"Oh, I beg to disagree," Isolde said, a ruthless chuckle falling on her lips. "You really should be careful when comparing yourself to other men and claiming to be the bigger one, Gage. Take my word for it." Her pointed gaze dropped to Gage's crotch and a knowing smile formed on her lips. "Liam is by far the bigger, better man in all the ways that matter. I can attest to this since I fucked him in your bed."

Gage's fingers gripped her face as power ignited in his eyes. Pressure built until Isolde felt the already bruised bones in her jaw groan in protest. Red burned across his maimed cheeks, his eyes sweeping the chamber filled with soldiers.

"You do realize he's going to kill all of you, right?" Isolde asked, forcing the words around Gage's grip. "Just like he did the men who found him tied to a chair at Foxclove. He can't let his *itty…bitty…tiny* little secret out. I'll bet I'm the only woman who's ever found pleasure in your bed, Gage. And it wasn't even your cock—"

Gage brought his fist down on the open wound at her thigh and a cry of pain ripped through Isolde's teeth, leaving her throat raw.

"I am going to truly enjoy making you pay, Isolde," Gage said, forcing her to look up at him. Heavy pants broke through her lips as she rode out the waves of agony. "The death of so many, at your hands. Lords...ladies...men loyal to the crown. Erebus is going to be so disappointed. He had such plans for you."

"Oh yes," Isolde said through painful pants. "Being a plaything for you two assholes for the rest of my existence sounded like quite the life."

"There are far worse fates." Trailing a finger along her lower lip, Gage's perfect, white teeth raked across his own. "I'll be sure to keep your head. Who knows, I might find some use for this mouth after all."

"I doubt that," Isolde said. "From what I remember, you don't have anything that would reach past my teeth—"

Fire ignited along her cheekbone as Gage's knuckles cracked against her face. She landed in a heap on the floor and the taste of blood coated her parched tongue.

The sickening crunch of shattered bone echoed throughout the dungeons as Gage's foot crashed down on her side. Despite her best efforts, a cry of pain broke through Isolde's lips. Pain...so much pain radiated through her side and face. Another blow landed in her midsection, forcing all the air from her lungs. She gasped for breath as she curled in on herself as much as the hands biding her would allow.

Nyla and Zibiah's cries and shouts reached Isolde's ears. Gage gripped her hair by the roots and pulled her back to her knees. Even as blood poured from the wound at her thigh, she would not budge, she would not yield—especially, not to him.

"You love this human filth so much, don't you?" Gage said, his gaze shifting to where Buer held Nyla. A soft caress coated his voice, and the scars pulled tight into a horrible smile. "So very, *very* much."

Isolde pursed her lips and spit a mouthful of blood and spit into Gage's face. His eyes fluttered shut as a muscle ticked in his jaw. A drop of blood-tinged saliva dripped off the end of his nose.

"Good."

Without warning, Gage's closed fist, the one gripping her mask and hood, collided with Isolde's face once more, and her world went black.

CHAPTER 40

Isolde didn't register the cold metal beneath her. Nor the biting chill of the air kissing her sweaty, blood-encrusted face. Agony found her first. Brutal waves of unrelenting pain made themselves known as consciousness slowly returned.

Isolde bit down on her swollen lip and rolled over onto her back. A shooting pain ignited in her leg, forcing a gasp from her dry throat. The tips of her gloved fingers brushed the gaping hole in her britches. The frayed edges were hard and crusted with blood but only a raised scar met her touch.

Relief mixed with an unrelenting wave of nausea, flooded her stomach. They had healed her. But only enough to keep her alive. Isolde swallowed down the fear of what that meant. Of what they had planned for the true Hood of Arnoria.

"Isolde?"

Her name echoed from the right, and Isolde willed herself to look. There, sitting on the other side of the cell, her hands gripping the bars, was Nyla. A thin ribbon of dried blood fell her from neck. It wound its way down her clavicle and disappeared beneath her shift.

"Nyla!" Her voice was hoarse and tongue bone dry. "Are you alright?"

Nyla nodded, and tears swelled in her eyes. She opened her mouth, but another's voice cut in before she could utter a single word.

"She is for now."

Isolde's lip curled at the sound of Erebus's voice. The calm, smooth tone grated against her control. Gone were the elithrium shackles, but still her power made no move to come forward. Isolde clasped onto the bars with her bare hands in an attempt to pull herself up. Every ounce of her strength disappeared instantly, and she dropped back down to the floor. Her face struck the floor with a sickening crack. Looking around, Isolde took in the elithrium-plated cage surrounding her.

"Yes," he said with an amused grin. "I thought it necessary to keep you in a place where you can't cause any more trouble."

"Oh yes," Isolde said, forcing her knees beneath her. "Because you haven't caused enough damage to this kingdom already."

"I am perfecting this kingdom," Erebus snapped, his eyes glowing with a malice Isolde remembered well. "You had the opportunity to be at my side, to reap the benefits of that perfection as my Left Hand. To bask in the glory to come!"

"I have enough glory of my own," said Isolde with a dismissive wave. "You can keep yours. Besides, being your whore and mercenary isn't exactly the kind of glory I'm in the market for."

"Once again, you believe the desires for yourself are actually worth something." Erebus smiled. "But your petty self-righteousness isn't why I'm here. I wanted to be the one to tell you I'm giving everything —your territory, your people, and your home—to Gage."

Isolde kept her face neutral, sealing away the panic and sorrow raging inside her behind a mask of indifference. "Well, do tell him the front door sticks and there's a terrible draft in the downstairs bathroom—"

"Alaric and Galaena," said Erebus, his tone laced with irritation, "will be hunted down along with that Bastard Prince and any others who aided you. I'll take great pleasure in killing every single one of them, Isolde. Or perhaps, they can become like Zibiah."

Erebus's eyes wandered to Nyla, who recoiled from his gaze. A breath lodged in Isolde's throat. "Yes, I rather like that idea. When they are found, and rest assured they will be, I will turn them into the pathetic creatures they claim to love so much."

They escaped. Isolde clung to that hope, that small mercy. *They had escaped.* If the others had gotten away, that was a win for her. They could go on. They could live. And that was a fate she could live with.

As Erebus reached the door, he turned back. "Your execution is scheduled at the final trial tomorrow. One last time in the spotlight, for the Hood of Arnoria. Sleep well."

The door closed with a bang making Isolde jump. She had never been afraid to die, far from it in fact. But the look on Erebus's face promised her death wouldn't be a quick or painless one.

"Isolde?' Nyla whispered.

"I'm here," Isolde said. "Just give me a moment." Inch by inch, she crawled across the floor and propped herself up as best she could, careful to not let her bare skin touch the metal. "Are you alright?"

Nyla nodded, her eyes lined with silver as she looked to the door. "I didn't know if you were going to wake up. He hit you so many times."

"If he wanted me dead, I would be," she said, through gritted teeth. "Where is Zib?"

"I don't know. They brought me here the same time as you. He said I was going to die tomorrow, the one with the scars," Nyla said, her voice trembling. "He…he said I was going to be a lesson for you.

Your final lesson."

Isolde reached through the bars, uncaring of the elithrium's effect—it didn't matter now. Her hand closed over Nyla's, and she tugged her forward. A sharp pain pierced Isolde's ribs as Nyla wound her arms around her waist as much as the bars would allow. Sobs broke through the air, and Isolde felt Nyla's shoulders begin to shake.

"I'm scared." Her voice was so small, so incredibly innocent and terrified. "I don't want to die, Isolde!"

The unjustness of it all crashed down like the mountain looming above her head. Tears formed at the corner of Isolde's eyes and the weight of her reality crushed her soul. As she stroked the unkempt strands of Nyla's hair, Isolde felt her heart begin to break.

A cry of pain echoed through the small window of the door to their cell. It was distant but not one Isolde had the good fortune to not recognize. Her eyes squeezed shut to the sound of Zibiah's screams, sending a tear trickling down her cheek. Nyla's small, emaciated body began to shake uncontrollably, and her own sobs joined the ones filling the air.

Swallowing the lump in her throat, Isolde turned to the one thing she knew would bring Nyla comfort.

Music.

The sound of her father's voice echoed in Isolde's mind and the song he sang to her as a child came forward, flooding her very soul with memory. Music swelled in Isolde's heart and wove its way through the cracks and shadows the years of darkness had left behind. As the first note lifted from her tongue, Isolde felt herself give way to the memories that had haunted her for so long, allowing the levee she had formed around them, to crack and crumble.

Pushing up onto her knees, Isolde worked her arms through the bars, and held Nyla as close as she could manage. She leaned into the wall, allowing it to keep her up right. The little girl held her tighter, the pain in her ribs and side screaming. But Isolde paid it no mind. Her pain didn't matter now.

For the first time since Kamden died, Isolde let music fall from her lips. The words her father had created, the ones he had ingrained in her heart, filled the cell. It opened up every part of who and what she was. Her voice carried over the cries of agony ghosting down the hallway. Every note, every word was a piece of her—a piece of her past and heart. Isolde cupped the back of Nyla's head and a well of sorrow cleaved her chest in two.

After a while, the sound of muffled cries faded, and Nyla fell silent. The little girl fell asleep pressed against the bars of the prisons of Elenarta and in the arms of the thief who had led her to her death.

The sound of grinding metal jarred Isolde from a restless sleep. Her eyes shot open as strong hands gripped her by the shoulders and yanked her to her feet. A groan slipped through her lips, her body singing in pain.

"Good morning, pet," Gage said in greeting. He was dressed in a new black leather jacket that stretched over his broad chest, not a single scuff mark in place. A beautiful sword was strapped to his belt.

"I hope you didn't get all dolled up just for me," Isolde said. She tried to put weight on her mostly healed leg and a bolt of pain shot through her hip and thigh. But it at least held her weight.

"It's your special day," said Gage, his smile widening. "Of course, I'm going to dress my best."

"This is your best?" Isolde asked, her eyes taking in his attire.

A dark chuckle lifted from his mouth and cruel smile pulled at his lips. His gloved hand gripped her chin, forcing her to look into his eyes. "That mouth of yours is going to get you into trouble someday."

"Part of my charm," she said, fighting his grip. Old bruises from the day before barked in pain as he began to squeeze.

"Well, we mustn't keep the public waiting. We still have a final trial to contend with before you die." He shoved Isolde's face to the side and she caught sight of the empty cell next to hers.

"Where is she," Isolde asked, fighting the guards' grip, desperately hoping Nyla was curled up in the corner fast asleep. Panic rose in her chest when only an empty cell met her eyes. "Where's Nyla?"

"Oh, is that what its name is?" Gage asked, pulling the door open. "Don't worry, she's waiting for you."

Terror stilled in Isolde's chest, freezing her in place. A rough kick to her lower back sent her stumbling forward and out into the corridor. Pain echoed in every part of her body as they pulled and pushed her through the layers of the prison and out into the light of the afternoon sun.

Sunlight, bright and blinding, burned her eyes as they stepped into the open air. She tripped over the uneven street and her elbows crashed against the cobblestones. Blood blended into the black of her tunic as the guards yanked her to her feet once more.

"I don't think shackles will be necessary," Gage said from where he trailed behind her. They led her through the streets of the capital. Eyes found their way to her face and shocked gasps followed in their wake.

"Feast your eyes!" Gage called out to the crowd lining the walkway to the arena. "The famous Hood of Arnoria, your Champion of Sorrows!" His tone was mocking but Isolde saw the look in the people's eyes. Regret and shock ran through the crowd. Some took one look and ran back inside. Others gave her a subtle nod as she passed. A muted thanks she could carry with her into death.

"Lady Isolde?"

Her head snapped up to find Rafe rushing down the street, his flour-speckled apron billowing around him.

"Friend of yours?" Gage whispered into the shell of her ear.

"No," Isolde said, averting her gaze. "I have no idea who that man is."

Rafe stood behind a line of soldiers stretching down the streets, his face red with anger. "Lady Isolde! Where are you taking her?"

"Come to the arena," Gage called back over his shoulder. "I guarantee it's a show you don't want to miss."

It felt like an eternity before they reached the tunnels of the arena. And there to greet them at the gate was Lenox. An evil smile bordering on maniacal was spread across his podgy face. "Isolde Cotheran, you are indeed the trash I first pegged you out to be."

"So, glad to have met your expectations," Isolde said with as sweet of a smile as she could muster. "I'd hate to be the cause of your disappointment."

The Master of Games sneered before his hand flew through the air. It collided with the side of Isolde's face in a loud slap, sending a wave of stinging pain across her cheek.

"I'm going to enjoy this," Lenox said, turning back to the gate. The guards shoved her forward, sending a shock of agony through her leg. She bit down on her lip, refusing to let even an ounce of a whimper loose. Already she could hear the roar of the crowd, their call for blood ringing in the air.

"Hear that?" Gage asked, his breath tickling her ear. "They're expecting you."

Isolde refused to feel, refused to acknowledge the dread running its cold fingers down her spine. She had known it might end this way. It was a fate she had accepted and was willing to face head-on. But as they made their way up the final slope, Isolde couldn't help but feel a twinge of fear. They jerked her to a halt just below the tunnel's end. Over the edge of the gravel, Isolde could make out the top of three poles. No flag flew from their tops, only a perfect blue sky accompanied them.

within the very foundations of who she was.

"How many lashes do you think it'll take before they die?" Gage asked, running a finger across the whip at his side in slow, thoughtful strokes. "I'm guessing Zibiah will hold out the longest. The other two are a toss-up. Perhaps we should start with the oldest. Age before beauty and all that."

"Please," Isolde whispered as the horror of what was about to happen sank in. "Please don't."

Gage paused and lowered himself back down before her. "What was that?"

Isolde licked her cracked lips, her eyes swimming with unshed tears. She stared straight ahead, never taking her eyes off Nan. "Don't do this," she said. "Please, don't do this."

A smile blossomed onto Gage's face and a sigh of satisfaction pushed from his chest. "I love the sound of you begging, Isolde." His fingers gently cupped her chin, forcing her to look at him. "Do it again."

Tears of hatred and fear broke free and cascaded down Isolde's burning cheeks. "Please, don't do this, Gage. Take me. Punish me instead."

A groan lifted from Gage's lips as he ran a thumb along her bottom lip. He leaned in close, his eyes boring into hers. "That's exactly what I'm doing, Isolde." His voice was low and soft as if speaking to a lover. "I'm punishing *you*." And with that, Gage rose and flicked a thumb along the lining of his belt, releasing the whip from its holder.

"Don't," Isolde rasped, and Gage took a step back. She crawled on her hands and knees after him, her cloak dragging behind her. She pushed against the gravel as that fire, cold as ice and just as unforgiving, began to burn brighter.

"My rose."

Nan's voice was so full of fear when it reached Isolde's ears. Gage cracked the whip, and Nan flinched at the sound, causing her shoulders to shake. Rivers of blood made by the ropes binding her wrists ran down her forearms.

"Gage, please!" Isolde cried. She pushed herself faster, the pain in her leg roaring to life. The monster inside woke, and the flame grew brighter, burned colder. She felt every bone begin to bend, to take a new form. One she hadn't felt in decades.

A satisfied grin spread across Gage's face. He cracked the whip again, and Nyla wailed in fright. Zibiah turned her head, her golden eyes swimming in dread. Nan continued to shake, her voice quivering.

"Isolde…"

Her name, filled with terror on Nan's tongue, consumed Isolde with wrath. It ignited a sense of desperation she couldn't take. Despair gave way to anger. It burned through Isolde like wildfire, scorching away any doubt, any fear remaining. All that was left, all she was now…was pure rage.

Gage cast Isolde one final smirk before he turned back to the woman who had helped raise her. To the mother of the man Gage had murdered so many years ago. Her only connection to Kamden. A mother, a friend, a confidant…He brought the whip back, his chest filling with a deep breath. Gage's grip tightened and every muscled coiled for the strike.

"Isolde!" A single tear glistened from Nan's withered cheek as her voice broke.

"NO!"

Every thought left Isolde as her body was torn apart. The creature she had been hiding for so many years broke free and sprinted forward. The beast that haunted her nightmares launched into the air and ripped the whip from Gage's grasp. He turned to face her, and the look of anger melted into fear.

A wolf, monstrous, with fur streaked in pure silver, filled the reflection of his eyes. Isolde's mind hardly recognized herself as a cold flame burned away any part of her remaining. Before she could take a step forward, a burning pain ripped through her flank. A bloodied spear fell to the ground, and she turned, a snarl ripping through her sharp teeth.

She looked past the poles to Buer who was already reaching for another by the time Isolde turned and attacked. His cries died away as she sank her teeth and claws into his flesh. She didn't stop until only pieces of him remained. The taste of his blood coated her tongue, fueling that bloodlust further. Dropping a chunk of his arm, Isolde moved on to the next soldier…then the next… and the next.

Cries of terror echoed around Isolde, but the beast that had consumed her didn't care. A film of red draped over her mind, consuming every thought and desire. And as the torn leg of a soldier fell from her snout, Isolde turned her sight back to the front of the arena. Gage, the focus point of her fury, was standing with a battalion of archers, arrows drawn and ready.

She stalked forward, her lip pulled back to bare her fangs as a vicious growl, that clapped like thunder, cleaved through the air.

"My rose."

Nan's voice echoed through the air, bringing her to a halt. A flicker of her true self returned, and Isolde fought to clasp onto it. The monster's teeth were borne in anger as it tried to tear control away. It wanted Gage's blood; it demanded it. For decades, it had stayed caged behind the bars she had created. For years it had been made a prisoner in her mind, hidden from the light of day.

"Come back to me, my rose," Nan said. Isolde's steps faltered. Her paws racked through the gravel and a growl ripped from her teeth.

Image after image ran through her mind. Each one she shoved at the creature, evidence of what was at stake if it continued down this path. Every person she loved was a reason, a reminder for her to stop.

To fight against her most basic, savage self.

Pain erupted throughout Isolde's body as she slowly, painstakingly shoved the creature back into its cage. Every time it tried to push back, she threw the face of someone she loved in its path.

Nan.

Malaki.

Blyana.

Cillian.

Galaena.

Alaric.

Her mother.

Her father.

Her brothers.

They all flocked to her in one great wave, shoving the monstrosity back until only Isolde remained.

Her skin prickled at the feeling of gravel and sand beneath it. The scar tissue of her back and side screamed in protest, demanding she move. But she couldn't even if she wanted to. Every ounce of her power had been spent; nothing else remained. Her eyes slowly open and the pale blue sky was there to greet her.

The sound of approaching footsteps fell on her ears and Isolde's gaze lifted.

"Well, well." Erebus's sultry, sensual voice found its way to her a moment before his face came into view, blocking out the sun. A brilliant sword, one she recognized from long ago, dangled in his grasp.

Erebus crouched down beside her, and the point of her mother's beloved sword, Melevor, dug into the gravel beside her face. The blade made of purest silver, welded by the mightiest of earth wielders from ages long since passed, shimmered in the light of the sun. Old viryian ran up the center in flowing, beautiful script. It ended at the hilt that was adorned with sapphires encased in silver. Her house colors. A wolf's head rested at the end of the pommel, its mouth open and fangs bared.

A look, both wondrous and terrifying, formed on Erebus's face. A name fell from his lips. A name someone else had died with so many years ago. It had been carried away with the ashes of those she loved most. The ones who bore the same name.

"Odette Histavilar Viributhian."

Her true name fell from Erebus's lips like a blade sinking into her heart. Decades of grief came roaring back to life like a storm on the plains of her beloved Arnoria. It filled Isolde with a dread that had haunted her every waking moment.

A cold, victorious smile filled Erebus's flawless face. A face she remembered as a child in the halls of Elenarta, the halls of her home.

"The Songbird of Arnoria," Erebus said, trailing his fingertips across her cheek…her throat... her collarbone. "I've found you at last."

The darkness of the past was lifted, and Isolde Cotheran felt herself burn in its light. Dark exhaustion took her in its sweet, infinite embrace. And as her eyes closed to a world she knew would never be the same, Isolde's mind was filled with Erebus's voice. His words echoed with dark, victorious glee.

"Seize her."

The journey continues…

Stay up to date on everything in the Thief of Sorrows universe.

www.kristenmlong.com

Be sure to sign up for the newsletter to get early access to new and exciting announcements from Kristen M. Long

Tiktok: @kristen.m.long
Instagram: @kristen.m.long

ACKNOWLEDGMENTS

There are so many who have helped make Champion of Sorrows into a reality. However, I know with absolute certainty, that this book would not exist without God. None of this would be possible without Him. All the glory is His.

To my incredible, loving, selfless parents. Thank you for always supporting and believing in my dream of becoming an author. I hope you know how much I love and appreciate everything you do for me. Having you in my life, is one of the greatest blessings I have ever been given and I am so very, very proud to be your daughter.

To my wonderful Emergency Room coworkers. Heather, Carolyn, Emalee, Dale, Miranda, Tammy, Gail, Kevin, Lance, Mary, Jeff, Barbara, Hannah, Kristy P., Esther, Kristy H., Nicole, Eva, Pam, Kenzie, Lynn, Debbie, Daniel, Anna, Parker, Sego, Cunningham, and Melissa. Your support and encouragement means the world to me. Thank you for putting up with my weird, bookish, nerdy self. I love you all.

To my dynamite Beta Readers: You guys read Champion of Sorrows when it was just a baby and have helped it grow into what it is now. Thank you so much for your incredible feedback and patience.

I can't tell you how much I appreciate your help and support. I couldn't have done it without you.

To Ashley, my sweet ray of sunshine. Thank you for always being such a positive person and for helping me see the light in any situation. You are such a blessing to me, and I am so very thankful to have you in my life and to call you my friend. Also, you make the best book merch! Check out her amazing collection at Valor and Lore!

To my awesome book friends. Thank you for your amazing support and encouragement. I love you, you bunch of nerds.

To my lovely cover artist, Alice Marie Power. I couldn't imagine anyone else designing the covers for the Thief of Sorrows series. You have captured this world in a way no one else can. Thank you for bringing it to life in such a beautiful, unforgettable way.

To Beck, no one has more patience than you. Thank you for creating an amazing book that I am so proud to have on my shelf. It truly is a pleasure working with you.

To my editor, Katie. Your encouragement and guidance have been invaluable. Thank you for helping me become the writer I always wanted to be.

To my outstanding narrator, Laura Horowitz, thank you for having so much love and excitement for my story. You have captured these characters in a way no one else ever could. Thank you for breathing life into my story.

To Marisa at AcryliPics Bookish Nook. Thank you for taking a chance on my story. I'm so happy you love it and am beyond thrilled to be working with someone as passionate about books as I am. Thank you for making the most stunning special editions of my books. I can't wait to see the whole series up on my shelf and everyone else's.

To Trevor Barrett of Barrett Knives. Thank you for continuing to create beautiful pieces of art that make me want to write the most epic fight scenes.

To Halestorm, Breaking Benjamin, The Bad Omens, Hans Zimmer, Howard Shore, Lee Pace, Florence Pugh, Amy Manford, Andrew Loyd Webber, Samuel Kim, Kelsey Woods, Adele, Hauser, thank you for being my sources of inspiration for not only this book, but the whole series.

And to my beautiful readers.

This book was incredibly difficult for me to write at times. My mental health wasn't the greatest for the majority of writing this book. Imposter syndrome had me by the throat more often than not. Quiet is not always the result of anger. At times, dark hopelessness lies within the words that aren't spoken. Thank you to the ones who did reach out, who did ask. It means more than you will ever know. I cannot begin to tell you how much your kind words have helped me. Your messages and comments kept me going.

Being an ER nurse takes its toll on a person. A very heavy toll. While writing CoS, events in my professional life changed me in ways I never knew I could be changed. A lot of that was shown in this installment of the series. While there are some heavy moments in this book, a lot of them are very real emotions. Ones that I didn't know how express except with a blank sheet of paper. So, thank you for coming on this journey with me, Isolde, and the cadre. I'm so excited for you to see what happens next.

About the Author

Kristen (Kris) Long is the author of the Thief of Sorrows series. She is a graduate of Tennessee Tech University with a degree in Biology and Nursing. When Covid hit, Kris left her home to become an Emergency Room travel nurse. It is her dream to one day leave her stethoscope behind and become a full-time author. She is happiest sitting on the front porch reading and looking up at the mountains in her home town of Whitwell, TN. Her favorite books include: A Court of Mist and Fury by Sarah J. Maas, Dracula by Bram Stoker, Jane Eyre by Charlotte Bronte, and The Book Thief by Markus Zusak.